Pacific Dash

From Asia Vagabond to Casino King

A Novel

Chet Nairene

AUTHOR'S NOTE:

This is a work of fiction. The story's characters and names, businesses, events and incidents are wholly the product of the author's imagination. Any resemblance to actual persons, living or dead, or actual incidents is purely coincidental. Time, space and historic events have at times been adjusted to enhance the story flow of the plot.

www.bananaleafbooks.org

Second Edition April 2024
Copyright © 2021, 2024 Chet Nairene
Copyright © 2021, 2024 Banana Leaf Books
All rights reserved.

ISBN 9798745977275

For Fay, always.

CONTENTS

Book One:
    Dash to the Far East
    Hong Kong, 1968 5

Book Two:
    A Literary Rocket Ride
    New England, 1972 68

Book Three:
    Backpacker in Bali
    Indonesia, 1979 107

Book Four:
    The Floating Diamond
    Straits of Malacca, 1980 188

Book Five:
    Celestial Winnings
    Macau, HK, Taiwan, 1988 277

Book Six:
    The General's Mistress
    SE Asia (in transit), 1995 349

Book One

Dash to the Far East
Hong Kong, 1968

CHAPTER ONE
A Chinese Manhattan on Malibu

On final approach, Kai Tak Airport
British Crown Colony of Hong Kong, 1968

After puddle-jumping across the Pacific for thirty-six hours, our Trans Oriental Airways flight arrived in Asia . . . just in time, apparently, to crash. When the jetliner rolled and dropped into a sudden nosebleed plunge all the other passengers roared out, but I was too shocked to utter even a peep. I just silently tingled and locked my armrests in a death grip while the hair on my arms and neck stood straight out like porcupine needles.

It all seemed totally surreal, almost impossible. I mean there I was, just a kid on my first plane flight ever . . . and now only seconds from fiery death? Some kinda crazy bullshit.

Yeah, *crazy bullshit*. We kids had been using that expression all summer long for anything weird or amazing. It was handy and multi-purpose (could be serious or ironic) and it just felt cool to say.

For example, take that evening a month ago when Dad came home from the tractor company and announced, just like that, that we were moving to God-knows-where in Asia. *Hong Kong?* Yeah, that b.s. was *seriously* crazy.

Or like last week at my combination happy birthday and farewell party. With the stereo cranked up high, all the kids were dancing to Van Morrison belting out *Brown-Eyed Girl.* That's when Becky Miller came over, grabbed my hand and led me off behind the garage for a totally unexpected and personal good-bye. My first kiss and a little more.

Talk about crazy bullshit: before that, I didn't even know she liked me, at least not *that* way. Seemed like an all-timer, never to be topped on the CBS meter. But boy, was I wrong.

Because compared to one's impending death in a bloody aviation disaster, everything else shrinks to the importance of about a fly turd, you know?

It seemed we'd been flying just about forever on our family relocation flight to Hong Kong when the aircraft abruptly began to fall. It bounced with a thud off the bottom of an air pocket, shuddered and then continued to fall. During this steep descent I peered out the window and saw the billowing cloud cover open up, revealing glimpses of a great green hillside wall, rising up and barreling straight toward us.

I felt Mom grab my hand and I squeezed back.

A bell chimed through the cabin hiss as the plane began banking hard right and increasing its dive.

I fought nausea and disbelief as I stared out the tiny Plexiglas portal and saw hulking gray cement apartment buildings whiz past our wing tips, looking close enough to touch. Thousands of bamboo poles stuck out from those balcony windows with laundry flapping like flags, making the sad buildings resemble monstrous pin cushions.

I braced for the inevitable crash, just moments away, and even the infants on board all knew something was wrong. They wailed their complaints in a high-pitched chorus while their stern-faced mothers tightened their seat belts. Some said prayers.

Fighting to keep control and stave off panic, I found myself focusing on how surreal this all was. I'd hardly started out in life yet and was about to perish in a bloody plane crash.

I could picture the banner news headline in the Bluffs Daily Gazette, back home in rural Illinois: *Asian Air Disaster Claims Local Family!*

You know all that stuff about life flashing before your eyes? Seems to be a lie. Or else maybe I was just too young: not yet enough footage in the can for a quality instant mental documentary.

Whatever.

Seconds later came the impact. I was holding my breath when the jetliner's wheels slammed into the tarmac with an actual sound like *blam!* and the captain jammed on the brakes. He reversed engine thrust and passengers lurched this way and that.

The aircraft bounced and skittered down the runway, seeming barely under control. Random overhead bins and poorly-secured storage cabinets began to pop free and send briefcases, make-up bags and kids' toys clattering down the center aisle. Bathroom doors rattled and flew open.

And for that final special touch, an overpowering stench began to fill the cabin as we taxied to the far end of the runway.

Unable to breathe, I peered out the window for my first look at Kowloon. That's the part of Hong Kong that hangs off mainland Asia. It looked unfriendly, like a cold cement fortress, alien and intimidating.

And now we're supposed to live here?

Flight attendants jumped up and scurried about, doing whatever it was they did after landing. A relieved murmur washed through the cabin and me, I just looked across the aisle at Dad, who just sat there looking amused.

"So, son, welcome to the Mysterious East."

That was just like him, always being outrageous and facetious. But his humor didn't really help much, just now.

He smiled and folded his newspaper. "Pretty cool, huh? Maybe I forgot to mention about that hairy Kai Tak Airport landing. Must've been a fun surprise for you. It's like that every time! Tight fit here, squeezing an airport into this cramped harbor on a peninsula. So, the landings between the hills are always dramatic. But big fun, no?"

"I guess, Dad. But what the heck's with that smell?"

He chuckled.

"Well, son, you got a million Cantonese flushing their toilets into the Hong Kong harbor every day. Think it's gonna smell like roses? Just be glad you're not a fish in there." Then he looked down and unfolded his *South China Morning Post*. Discussion time over.

So I tried my mother. "You know, Mom, this place feels kinda weird. You sure we're gonna be okay?" She stroked my hand as I leaned a little closer, big tough teenager playing grade schooler for a little sympathy. She twisted a handkerchief and dabbed at her forehead.

Why was she sweating? It was freezing in there.

She patted my hand. "Just trust in God, dear. He has a plan."

Maybe so, but I didn't much care for how it was shaping up so far.

"By and by, everything will be fine, dear. By and by."

But her face denied those words and telegraphed worries perhaps even greater than mine. Was she freaking out too? Oh boy. Wonderful.

The plane taxied toward the terminal and my father's voice boomed across the aisle. "Okay, look at you two! Nervous Nellies. Where's your sense of adventure? Enough with all your worry and melodrama." He huffed and shook his head. "Think of it! Here we are at the British Crown Colony of Hong Kong. Gateway to Asia! Start of a great Bonaventure Family adventure. Thank your lucky stars. You don't know how blessed you are."

Easy for *him* to say. After all, the entire family was being transplanted to the far side of the planet for *his* benefit, to accommodate *his* career, *his* promotion at the tractor company. Lucky break for Dad, sure, but what about me and Mom? All I knew was that instead of starting high school in Moderate Bluffs, Illinois, I'd been uprooted and slingshot across the Pacific into a mysterious void. Everything familiar and comforting in my young life had disappeared.

And upon landing at Kai Tak back in 1968 there was no way for me to know how this move to Hong Kong would change the rest of my life and trigger all that was to come.

The Kai Tak terminal was a buzzing mass of humanity. People milled all about, yelling, burping and jostling. Great inexplicable gobs of phlegm lay on the ground. Pretty gross. And every so often I heard people hacking up new ones, too.

Over at the baggage claim a short, fat perspiring man in a dark suit and black glasses bowed and smiled as he greeted Dad. Then he turned to me and Mom and clicked his heels, I think, and barked out something in a growling low voice. It sounded like "*Joe Sun blah blah blah rahkeetam, ha!*" His grin was fierce and unsettling. Sweat stuck strands from his bowl haircut to his forehead.

Dad grinned. "Family, this here's my right-hand man. Stallion's first hire in Hong Kong."

"Pop, I heard him say his name is Mr. Joe Sun. Right?"

My father waved off the comment like a pesky fly. "No, boy," he chuckled, "*Joh-sun* is how the Cantonese say *good morning*. This fella here's Rocky Tam, a very handy local—you name it, he gets it done. We been real busy last couple months, all my visits here while you two were luxuriating back home in Illinois." Dad patted Tam on the shoulder and the plump man looked grateful and laughed a bit too hard.

Then he abruptly sprang into action, perhaps to demonstrate his industriousness. He barked out something in Cantonese, an alien-sounding language with harsh tones that sounded like anger to my young Western ears. He waved at a skycap and the man in a blue uniform sprinted over and loaded our bags onto a large wooden cart, inside a cage of fat green pipes.

We followed the squeaking cart down a wide black rubber ramp to the curb out front.

Dad narrated as we walked through the sea of people, crowds held back by only thin yellow plastic ropes on either side. "Last couple months," Dad yelled over the din, "Tam and I been setting everything up. Signed a lease for the new Stallion-Asia office and found us a great house, dear, in Stanley Village. And Dash, Tam pulled strings and got you admitted into the new international school. Not an easy matter." Tam nodded, so happy. "By the way, you start next week."

Next week? I'd barely just landed. I was hot and dizzy and could hardly concentrate, tired from the long trip with all those layovers and connecting flights: Chicago to LA, then Alaska, over the pole to Japan, to Taiwan and finally Hong Kong. And now the August humidity in Hong Kong was thick enough to stir with a spoon and killing me already. If I leaned back, I was sure it would hold me up. So, Dad dropping that *school next week* stuff really caught me by surprise.

Two sleek limousines idled at the curb, their air conditioners running full blast. When we approached out jumped both chauffeurs, in caps and militaristic uniforms complete with epaulets. One rushed to open the passenger doors while the other popped the trunks.

We needed two cars to handle all our luggage. We brought six large suitcases, two for each, crammed mainly with clothing plus any essentials we'd need. Everything else we owned—furniture, my bicycle and baseball card collection, Mom's kitchen stuff, the lawn mower, our car, everything!—had been put into storage, back in Illinois.

"The Stallion Equipment Co. can't just piss money away," Dad lectured, "by shipping entire households around the globe. No need, especially not for a short three-year posting like ours. Understand? Plenty of furniture and anything else we need can be bought here." He smiled at Mom. "And Honey, just wait till you see the hand-carved rosewood furniture they sell here in Hong Kong. Silk curtains, too."

The limos were Rolls Royces, one a creamy yellow and the other black, both with windows tinted black as midnight. Even as a kid, I was impressed. "Hey, Dad, nice going. Classy rides." He shrugged but I could tell he liked my saying that.

We rode in one car and filled the other up with luggage. Mom and I sat in back while Dad and Tam squeezed in front with the driver. Riding in cool comfort and sinking deep into luxurious brown leather seats, we cruised out of the airport through Kowloon and headed toward the tunnel under the harbor, over to Hong Kong Island.

Just beyond the limo glass I saw the streets of Kowloon teeming with shoppers, workers and tourists. Expensive cars jammed the roads. Garish commercial signs in squiggly Chinese script stacked up and crowded each other, all fighting for attention.

This vibrancy and activity softened what at first had looked to me as only gray, concrete and frightening. Everywhere I now saw color. There were brilliant neon signs, bright red or blue double-decker buses, the azure harbor, green hills behind us and on Hong Kong Island across the harbor.

Green-and-white Star Ferry shuttles cut criss-cross paths over the narrow channel, all the while chattering *putt-putt-putt-putt*. The vista of Hong Kong Island thrilled me with a world-class vision of towers that clustered and crowded right to the shoreline, with stunning Victoria Peak imperiously hovering overhead and topping the island with green grandeur.

We disappeared into the cross-harbor tunnel and when we emerged the Rolls veered onto an elevated ramp. The road headed inland and began a climb toward the green hills at the center of Hong Kong Island.

"Quick," Dad said, "look now, before we get too far inland!" He pointed over to the right, down the island shore at a teeming metropolis. "That amazing city over there is Central District, as glorious as a Manhattan in Asia. Famous for the world's best hotels and restaurants. Prime business and banking center. That's where Tam and I set up our office. It's basically New York City but without the crime. Plus everybody's Chinese 'cept the bloody Brits, of course. The Cantonese let the Poms *think* they run this place."

Central looked as dense and urban as Kowloon, but somehow a bit classier. More of the people flooding the sidewalks on this side wore dark business suits like Mr. Tam.

Tam nudged Dad and pointed off to the left with his chin. They both chuckled.

"Rocky wants me to show you something. See down there? That's Happy Valley. Many a Cantonese fortune made or lost there." What we passed just looked like an old horse race track to me, nothing special. But when Dad explained the enormous betting pools generated there by gambling-crazed Hong Kongers, even I was impressed.

"Why do you keep calling them *Cantonese*, Dad??"

"Them's the locals, Dash. *Hongkies*." Both men chuckled again. "This part of South China was originally called *Canton*."

The engine groaned when the driver downshifted and we began a steeper climb. Hey, nobody told me there'd be any mountains in Hong Kong. Ascending the ramped highway, we passed a cramped Chinese cemetery that was all angles and concrete tiers, running up the hillside like stairs.

The road was an asphalt ribbon that wound and rose up through a lush, forested landscape. Mansions flashed by, just off the road, precariously perched and part-hidden by foliage. Occasional vistas of deep blue ocean, far away, burst through gaps in the trees below.

We were quite high now and just when I feared the car might overheat, a roadside board announced *Wong Nai Chung*. "It's all downhill from here," joked Dad.

Tam knitted his eyebrows in deep concentration and then spoke carefully, in English, in his deep and guttural voice. "*Wong*

Nai Chung—Chinese word mean 'gorge where yellow mud gushing out'."

Huh? "Okay, great, Mr. Tam. Thanks for telling me that." Actually, Tam seemed like a real nice guy. Trying hard. Dad just shot me a wry smile and shrugged.

The descent started abruptly, with no warning. It was like suddenly going over the top of a roller coaster and taking the plunge.

Heading down toward the backside of the island, a parade of impossibly dramatic views staggered us. Even Mom, silent and wringing her hands up till now, erupted with a thrilled "Oh, my!" Vistas washed over us and spectacular scenes surrounded us. Deep green hills ran off in every direction, down toward the brilliant blue ocean below, dotted with boats and small islands with grand white estates. Our eyes drank it all in like a delightful hallucination that we didn't want to stop.

"So," Dad said, sweeping his arms across the grandeur, "it seems the Cantonese have invented time travel or the ability to teleport."

Mom made a *tut-tutting* sound and mumbled, "Now, Dashiell, be serious . . ." She always called Dad by his full name. And even though I was Dashiell Xavier Bonaventure II, there was never any of that *junior* stuff for me, just *Dash*. Dad liked to joke that he was Dash #1 and I was Dash #2.

"I *am* being serious, Honey." But he stage-winked at me. "This is Cantonese teleportation and time travel. Just now, we drove from New York City (that's Central District) and then up through the green Appalachian hills and are already now speeding down toward Malibu—and all in about a half-hour. Am I right or am I right?"

I laughed. "Good one, Dad."

Mom just shook her head.

Soon we were back at sea level and following a road that ringed a large semicircular beach beside a small village backed by undulating green hills. A signboard we passed announced *Repulse Bay*. Funny name, this place was the opposite of repulsive.

"So this is where you'll spend most of *your* time, Dash."

Wow, cool. "We gonna live here, Dad?"

He chuckled.

"No, you goof. Your school is here. Hong Kong International School. HKIS is brand new, just opened a year or so ago." But before I could see much of the set-up (mainly a multistory building and outdoor courtyard, above the far end of the beach) the road exited the Repulse Bay area and climbed back up into thick hillside woods.

We drove on, rising and descending through more forested hillsides of astonishing beauty, sprinkled with impressive homes. Finally we turned off at a small intersection and veered down onto a charming peninsula.

"Almost there now." Dad squeezed Mom's hand. "We've leased a fantastic house here at Stanley Village, honey. Just look at this setting! You're gonna love it here." Tam nodded vigorously.

Though dizzy and tired, I began to see his point.

We reached a cute village center at the tip of the peninsula near a beach and an outdoor market, plus cafes and shops popular with tourists. An ancient, primitive-looking blue truck blocked the road as it noisily backed up to make a delivery.

I stared idly out from the limo at "downtown" Stanley and spotted a stunning Chinese girl, chic and beautiful and about my age, with several feet of dark, silky hair hanging down and gently swaying. She cocked her head at an oh-so-cute angle as she studied an item on a table in front of a shop.

Her frock was simple but shimmering and cut above the knees. She looked to me like a Bond girl, in a stylish beret-style cap and oversized sunglasses. I couldn't help but stare, having never seen anything like this exotic goddess back in Illinois. She looked better than any model I'd ever seen in any magazine. And before this moment I never even realized I might find Asian girls attractive.

Then just like that, with her hair still glistening and swaying, she takes off her sunglasses and stares right back at me through the glass and flashes me a million-dollar smile. Our eyes lock and—*boom!*—my heart stops. A jolt of electricity raced through me, as powerful as if I'd stuck my finger into a light socket. Just fifteen, I'd been struck dumb in a sneak attack by a mysterious, exotic and overwhelming animal magnetism.

I sat back in the limo backseat, confused and perspiring, euphoric and covered in goose pimples.

The blue truck finally began to move so we could drive on and head for the house. And only then did I start to recover. Finally able to breathe again, I suspected that maybe—just maybe—this place was going to be okay.

CHAPTER TWO
Jackson, Chickie and The Max

We leased a showy white stucco house, spacious by Hong Kong standards, on gated grounds on a forested hillside overlooking the sea. *Casa Bonaventure*, Dad liked to joke. It would prove to be a dream for an adolescent male like me: I could sleep late, roll out of bed, hop in a taxi and be at HK International School before the first bell.

But my first day of classes (a momentous day that would change my life forever) Mom took me. The chauffeur drove us to Repulse Bay where she dropped me off at the vertical, eight-story school building that loomed at one end of the horseshoe beach.

The entire student body was jammed into the gymnasium for a half-day orientation session and boring welcoming speeches consumed the morning.

The principal told us about how HKIS had opened just a few years earlier with 600 students. It was an American school with twelve grades and all the familiar subjects but significant additions, too. After all, HK *was* a British colony inside China, so Chinese language classes were mandatory and history courses covered both Great Britain *and* its most famous ex-colony.

The teachers lounging against the back wall were an international mix of mostly Americans but also Brits, Canadians, Aussies and various Asian nationalities (predominantly from the Philippines).

"You will wear a simple uniform here," the principal told us. "A red or white polo shirt, navy blue shorts, white socks and sneakers. The logo on the shirt pocket combines the letters H-K-I-S into an Asian-looking typeface with a cross. That reflects our school's founding alliance between businessmen and Christian interests."

He read an unending list of rules that sent my mind and eyes both wandering.

It was then that I spotted a youth at the far edge of the bleachers, off by himself and ignoring it all. He looked intent, busy studying the contents of an expensive-looking burgundy leather binder and unaware when something fluttered from it to the ground beneath the bleachers.

I quietly went over and retrieved the item.

It was utterly cool: a black-and-white photo printed on thick cardboard that showed a famous NY Yankee, maybe in the locker room. The baseball player had an arm draped around the shoulders of a wee, smiling Asian child. There was an unreadable personal inscription wriggling across the bottom in thick blue ink and only the name, *Mickey Mantle*, was legible.

"Hello!" I called out with a smile, holding up his card. "Yours?" I was cautious and spoke slowly, not yet knowing how much English might be in play. "America . . . baseball . . . good!" I nodded and put my hand on my heart. "I love!"

The boy stared back, his eyes popping wide with confusion. Funny but up close I now noticed his fingernails looked perfectly groomed and even lacquered. They shone. Nothing like mine. A priest once scolded me (when I was an altar boy) for my dirty nails. "Bonaventure, they could plant a vineyard in there."

The boy glittered from a lot of gold on him. A ring. A watch. A necklace and wrist band.

I motioned downward below the seats and pantomimed a fluttering card. "You picture . . . fall . . . down." I handed it back to him. "Mickey Mantle!" I smiled wide. "Home run king!"

His puzzled look slowly morphed into a smile and then blossomed into a wide grin. Finally, he erupted in laughter. "Well thanks, old boy," he said with a nod. "So much appreciated, but your English really does rather need some work. You perhaps from Eastern Europe?" He smiled.

"No, America." I felt my face begin to tingle and warm.

"Ha! Really? You sound rather like the Frankenstein monster, you know? '*Smoke . . . good!*' and all that rot." His tone was clipped and efficient, a bit British but definitely not a native speaker. Western educated? I could tell I was fully blushing now.

"Gee, I didn't think—"

"Just kidding, Old Man. Don't take it so hard." He gave my shoulder a playful poke. "Fantastic to find a fellow baseball fan! I was rather worried, looking at some of these other chaps in the stands. All so bloody earnest-looking, no?"

The sparkle of gold chains on his neck and wrist distracted me. Then I noticed the red, blue and white gems that studded his leather binder and spelled the initials "TOH." Those wouldn't be real rubies and sapphires, right?

He passed a handful of cards to me and began to narrate. "This one's an utter beauty. *The Splendid Splinter.* A 1960s Ted Williams card. This was the last year he ever played, but at age forty-one he still hit .316!"

My mouth hung open with envy as we pored over scores of his compact autographed photos. So many superstars, mostly Hall of Famers now, the likes of Willie Mays, Ernie Banks and Sandy Koufax. The high-quality images reminded me of magnificent private-issue baseball cards. I'd never seen anything like them.

And each celebrity photo included that same Chinese kindergartener.

"Of course, the cute little chap in each photo is Little Jackson. Baby version of me." He winked and must have seen my eyes widen. "You see, my father often traveled to the States on business. New York, Las Vegas, and Los Angeles. He enjoyed taking me along. I quickly became quite enamored with American baseball. The big leagues, gods in uniform, the wonderful settings. We went to a lot of games and naturally he took me into clubhouses to meet all my heroes."

Naturally? I couldn't imagine how one arranged even a single meeting with such sport celebrities, yet he was pictured with hundreds, all across the USA. Just who *was* his father? Lots of pull. What kind of business could provide such access?

A bit numb and awed, I continued to thumb through the binder. Easily a few hundred cards with that same spoiled, lucky child being embraced by famous sports heroes.

"Okay, now wait a minute," I said. "This one's different. Is that—?"

"Ha, yes! Sinatra. And Dean Martin, too. Dad spotted them poolside once at the Sands Hotel in Las Vegas. They were really nice to us. We ate lunch together! The Rat Pack days were just starting."

The Rat Pack? Criminey sakes, just who was this kid?

"So, buddy, what's your name?"

He barked out harsh sounds in an Asian language. Seeing my distress he laughed and handed me a crisp white linen card embossed in gold leaf with a name in Chinese ideograms at the center.

He had his own business card?

It was 1968 and I'd never seen *any* kid give these out, anywhere. He smiled and said his name again. No better result.

"But perhaps this will help." He grabbed the corner of the card in my hands and flipped it over. The back was in English. "See, my name is Jackson Toh. From Macau. But just call me Jackson, like everybody does."

"What's Macau?"

"It's a Portuguese colony in China, just an hour from here, across the Pearl River Delta."

"And me, I'm Dashiell Xavier Bonaventure II, from the USA—that's just a few days across the Pacific from here." I spared him the Moderate Bluffs angle for now.

"Bonaventure, huh? Well *good luck* with that name!"

Funny guy. But I had to give him credit. First time I'd ever met a kid clever enough to make a smart-ass pun with my name.

"So, just to keep things easy, should I call you 'DXB'?"
"No, please, *Dash* will do just fine."

I looked up and realized the half-day orientation had already ended. The gym had nearly cleared out. Jackson tucked the binder under his arm and we began to climb down from the bleachers when a short chubby boy and his tall companion cut us off.

"Hey, amigos, wait a minute." The little guy furiously chewed his gum and seemed intense. All wired up. The taller boy, blond, just stood there with a goofy grin. "So how's it going, men? Looks like we all managed to live through that snooze-fest." He sighed theatrically, winked and laughed. "So anyway, nice to meet ya. I'm Chickie—Chickie Schmidt. And this here," he said, pointing a thumb, "is Max."

Jackson and I exchanged a quizzical glance but reached out to shake hands and introduce ourselves too.

Chickie moved past me and sidled up right beside Jackson. "So anyway, man," he said, eying Jackson's binder, "hope you don't mind my asking, but is that what I think it is? Was watching you guys all through assembly. Are those freakin' *baseball cards?*" Chickie snorted with delight. "Geez I'd literally *kill* for some of those! Been in this cockamamie Hong Kong for weeks already and still can't find a decent store that sells 'em. Believe that? Not in Central, Causeway Bay or Kowloon. *Nada*."

Jackson chuckled. "Actually, old boy, these are a bit of a yarn."

"Huh?" Chickie looked perplexed.

"I'll fully brief you, shortly," Jackson smiled.

We invited them to join us to explore Repulse Bay town for the rest of the afternoon and wound up down at the beach, wading through gentle waves and chatting the entire time.

Thus was formed my Hong Kong crew.

Chickie was an aggressive, wisecracking Jewish kid from Brooklyn. His father ran Asian operations for a Swiss bank. Born Herbert Schmidt, he was idiosyncratic, with exaggerated likes and dislikes. A real character!

He wore the same style of clothes every day: cuffed tan pants; a pressed, powder-blue dress shirt with a three-button neck opening; and burgundy penny loafers.

He insisted his parents paint his room black and white at their house in Stanley. So hanging out at Chickie's always felt like diving through the TV screen into an old black-and-white program. His razor-sharp mind was always quick to form unshakable opinions. Chomping on his gum and talking nonstop, the guy was quirky and funny. And fiercely loyal once he'd embraced you as a friend.

Every pack has its leaders and followers. Max was the latter. A tall athletic Australian, born Maxwell Rutherford Johnson, we nicknamed him *Maximum* or *The Max*. He seemed to lack common sense. Max's father ran the back office for the Australian Consulate, where his mother processed visas. By pooling two government housing allowances, the Johnsons leased a sumptuous flat in the Mid-Levels, a ritzy area below The Peak and above Victoria Harbor. To a boy from the prairie with a lot to learn, I just assumed the Johnsons were rich. Even their Aussie accent sounded kinda noble. What did I know?

Jackson, though, was amazingly humble and never volunteered much of his background. Over time I would piece together his incredible situation as the anointed princeling in one of Asia's wealthiest and most influential families. His father was mega-powerful and somehow involved in running a gambling empire over in seedy Macau. He didn't talk about this much.

Jackson spent several earlier years in his childhood at a British boarding school, which explained his odd, English-tinged accent. And once it was announced a prestigious new international school would open in Hong Kong, his parents never doubted Jackson should attend. To facilitate that his father purchased a sumptuous estate atop Victoria Peak where his son would live during the school week, helicoptering home to Macau on weekends, forty miles across the Delta.

They hired a retired Macanese Jesuit priest as a live-in guardian at The Peak. Most of the time the old minister stayed in his room, read books and prayed. That was fine with Jackson. Maids washed his clothes and cleaned the apartment and a star chef from one of the colony's finest restaurants, was hired and always on call. He had the easiest job in HK: Jackson was almost never home for meals.

A fearsome pair of burly bodyguards constantly hovered nearby. One doubled as Jackson's chauffeur, responsible for maintaining a cream-colored Rolls-Royce. The other was in charge of the boy's personal safety 24/7. The two usually parked just down the road from HKIS and sat in the Rolls, smoking and playing cards.

Despite all the fuss and pampering, Jackson turned out remarkably normal (though a real brainiac) and ambitious. Top scores in every class. He was genuinely brilliant and never had to work at easily absorbing complex information. With his stunning capability and impeccable family connections, he was clearly pointed towards an extraordinary future.

But to me, for now, he was just a kindred spirit, another confused international transplant lugging his jumbled background down the halls of HKIS.

After the first month, Jackson stopped helicoptering home to Macau on weekends and opted instead to sleep over at my house in Stanley.

We all treated each other with the friendly, joking disdain native to teenage boys. And despite our different backgrounds we still hit it right off, thanks to many mutual interests: Batman and Superman comics, Duncan yo-yo's (the 1960s comeback craze had crossed the Pacific), and old Universal horror movies. We whiled away hours debating pop music groups (Beatles versus Rolling

Stones) and agreed that the relatively lower-talent Ringo was the luckiest man on the planet.

We endlessly explored the perplexing mysteries of the opposite sex and offered each other unqualified advice. None of us were dating yet, so the prospect of girls both tantalized and unnerved us. Sexual relationships loomed, close but just out of reach.

We snuck occasional beers from my father's ice box. Dad either didn't miss them or didn't care. Good ol' Dad.

CHAPTER THREE
The Bonaventure Family Goes Expat

The Bonaventure family began to settle in as first-time expatriates and found that compared to life back home in western Illinois (the real world), HK couldn't have been more delightfully different. Especially for me.

Instead of weekend bike trips with friends through Midwestern prairies and seas of cornfields, we played here on the *real* sea, cheaply renting creaky wooden Chinese junks plus a captain for excursions to nearby islands. Sometimes we just anchored off the New Territories and swam in the South China Sea.

Or rather than rummage through vacant lots to hunt for empty pop bottles (to mine the deposits and buy comic books), in HK we prowled funky oriental markets for cheap weird stuff like crusty old opium pipes or snuff bottles.

Overall, life was free from security worries and kids could jump into a taxi, day or night, and cheaply buzz off to Kowloon or some night market. We found this freedom intoxicating and lovingly came to call the place *Honkers.*

English was spoken everywhere in this British colony though one bumped into a Cantonese language barrier the moment one veered beyond the boundaries of normal expat life. And as to my initial fears of a dearth of English language TV or newspapers with U.S. pro sports scores? Unfounded.

I settled in fast and to my delight became quite popular at school. Other than Jackson, Chickie and Max, I made many other friends: first with other American expat brats, the sons of diplomats and businessmen who shared a similar bizarre experience as an adolescent uprooted and transplanted to Asia. Then my circle widened across all national boundaries and soon I had new friends from everywhere. Australians, French, local Chinese and Brits.

Some even hailed from nearby Asian nations, the offspring of wealthy or politically-powerful parents, but seeking an American-style education.

The Hong Kong kids gave themselves quirky English nicknames (for fun, I guess, but more to be unique). So I mingled with the likes of Napoleon Lee, Oxygen Kwan and Riviera Wong.

Climbing stairs all day in HKIS's vertical school building, I bumped into young princelings from Asia's ruling class and though our origins could not have been more different, they all just seemed *normal* to me—the son of a Midwestern corporate bumpkin on overseas assignment and temporarily passing for a powerful man in Asia.

Pooling upper-class international adolescents like this brewed a unique new shared culture. We became open-minded globalists, juvenile elitists with a world view, whose lives incorporated a smorgasbord of interests from all ends of the earth. Take me, for example. Once an American who only knew baseball, I became an avid rugby player and dedicated fan of the New Zealand and South African super teams. Introduced by pals from South Asia, spicy foods invaded my diet and shouldered aside favorites like hamburgers and pizza.

Dad enjoyed entertaining at dinner with his war stories as a business pioneer in Greater China.

"Nearly every day, I am mostly making it all up as I go along," he would chuckle. "No business manual explains how to do this. Maybe someday, *I'll* write the manual."

He had leased the top floor of a building in Sheung Wan in Western District. Below the first Stallion-Asia office were several floors of a department store lined with rows of silvery woks, rice cookers and bicycles. And right across the street buzzed the busy Macau ferry terminal.

He thumbed through resumes every night, those first months in Hong Kong, spreading them out across the dinner table and sorting them into stacks of winners and losers for the upcoming hiring blitz. "Building a sales team, Dash, to knock on doors all across Asia—Taiwan, India, Korea and all them Southeast Asia *domino nations*."

The papers on the table reminded me of that day several months back in Moderate Bluffs, when he shocked us with the news we were heading overseas.

"What? I don't even know where the heck Hong Kong is, Dad. In Vietnam or something?" The war dominated each day's headlines and news shows.

That's when he harrumphed and unfolded a map. He flattened it out and pointed at an insignificant dot. "There!" he boomed. "That's H-K!"

I felt dizzy like all the blood had leaked out of my brain. Mom just stood there, quiet as a prayer, twisting a dish towel into rope.

"But why do we have to go there?" I demanded. "This is home. Here. We *like* Moderate Bluffs."

He snorted a demeaning chuckle in response and put a hand on my shoulder. "Listen, son, it's because Stallion Equipment Co. wants me to go there. That's why."

"I still don't get it."

"Dash, there's this entire continent starting to ride an economic boom. Right now! Billions of Asians are climbing out of poverty." His eyes grew bigger. "So they need new roads, new bridges, and new parking lots. And then of course comes the new sewer systems and railroads. The airports and shopping malls. So-oooo . . .?" He looked at me expectantly with his eyebrows raised.

"Huh?" I hated when he did that.

He huffed and thumped the dinner table with a fist. "So? Tractors, Dash, tractors! They're gonna need hundreds, thousands of Stallion tractors! And bulldozers, too. Earthmoving equipment."

It kinda scared me a little, how he'd turn a little red when he got all excited like that.

"Honey," Mom interjected helpfully, "Dad's company manufactures equipment like that. Remember?"

"Yeah, I guess so. But Hong Kong sure looks tiny on the map."

Dad was having a fit and his cheeks glowed scarlet. He shook his head, pitying my youthful ignorance. "Listen here, Dash. HK is the gateway to mainland China and a prime spot to serve all of Asia. Believe me, those Red Chinese commies are dying for Stallion equipment, something fierce. Problem is their money doesn't convert into dollars yet, so it's worthless to us. So for now, they can't pay. But some day," he said, thumping the table, "that'll all change and the door will swing open to that monster market. And when it does Stallion will be ready, thanks to me and the office I am now opening and the work we're doing. And THAT, my boy, is how you get to the top." He smiled, probably imagining his future as a bigwig back at Stallion world headquarters.

I was remembering that night as Dad now shuffled through resumes on our dinner table in Honkers. He would share little stories or discoveries he'd made, pleasant surprises to a new expatriate businessman.

"So I'm half a world away from the head office," he said. "And a wise Chinese proverb goes: *Life is happy when the sky is high and the emperor is far away.*"

"But we're not Chinese, Dad."

He muttered and shook his head. "Dash, that means those blustering idiot bosses and the board are far away, back in Moderate Bluffs."

"So?"

"So they're kinda forced to trust me, Dash. To faithfully execute their wise orders."

He explained that due to unreliable communications his reports sometimes arrived back in Illinois only weeks late or not at all. And incoming, huffy dictatorial memoranda from headquarters often disappeared en route. "Strange," he said, winking, "but when messages contain headquarter commands that are full of crap and just wrong, they are *especially* likely to go missing."

I think I got his meaning.

"Phone calls across the Pacific can be a real headache, too, with weak voices and a roaring background hiss. And you know, Dash, the lines often get chopped off in mid-sentence." But then he grinned. "Especially when we're tired of listening to those know-nothing yahoos back in Moderate Bluffs! Know what I mean?"

Untrustworthy phone security also meant they had to use clumsy spoken codes to protect business secrets. ("Yes, sir, the *governor's bird laid two purple eggs last night."*)

Dad started Cantonese lessons but gave up in frustration after just a week, unable to hear even the most basic tones.

"Speaking Cantonese is overrated anyway," he growled. "Plenty of English here in government and in business channels. British colony after all. And as for the rest, I hire bilingual staff."

Mom was fresh from the beauty shop early that evening and looked great in her shimmering new dress. "We'll be going out tonight, dear. Gaddi's at the Peninsula Hotel."

"I'd already guessed that, Mom."

"I've asked Ah Fong to fix your favorite dinner. And please give those jeans to the wash maid. They look *filthy*. Don't forget. Whatever were you doing in them?"

"Nothin', Ma, just hanging out with the guys."

Maybe life had changed most of all for Mom, as a first-time expat spouse in Asia. Gone were the red barns and wheat fields of central Illinois. Absent was the summer-long droning of locusts and grasshoppers and the nightly sink full of dishes. No longer did she spend mornings feeding laundry into a noisy machine or her afternoons cooking. Now she shopped for groceries only when *she* felt like it, otherwise handing off such tasks to a small army of domestic servants.

Released from chores that previously defined her life she was freed (no, required!) to pursue the intoxicating whirl of a rich new social life. As wife to the boss of a powerful American company, Mom was suddenly a whale in Hong Kong's social waters. She immersed herself in international women's groups and their charitable events and rose to unpaid positions of rank. She joined art council boards and museum foundations, grounding herself by studying Chinese and British colonial history. She regularly flew off with peers on week-long cultural tours.

From the start, she dove headfirst into Cantonese language lessons. With communication always potentially dicey with household staff, yet so critical, she took the advice given most Western expat wives and hired a conversational tutor her first week in the colony. She quickly mastered daily slang and in six months was sufficiently conversant to give the cook dinner menu instructions or to dress-down the driver for showing up late, hung-over or out of uniform.

Running the household demanded the focus of a CEO for a small but tricky business. Employees were maids and cooks, gardeners, guards and a driver, all of whom regularly seemed to misunderstand or simply not follow directions, with often grievous results. Occasionally one failed to turn up for work, sometimes permanently, triggering the major headache of a replacement search.

My parents dined out nearly every evening, hosting dinners in support of Stallion's budding Asian business. They entertained a vibrant network of international friends and associates (often married couples) representing British colonial government, American diplomats, friendly French neighbors, German competitors, Swiss hotel operators and senior Cantonese civil servants. Add to that a flood of customers, both current and potential.

And on nights when Mom stayed home, Dad still went out with clients and staff for stag affairs that featured a dozen courses of Chinese food interspersed with abundant shots of fiery local liquor.

And every few months a monster dinner party rocked our house in Stanley, complete with rented waiters in white tuxedos, a band, and tables overflowing across the back lawn with catered food . . . the works.

CHAPTER FOUR
Life Among the Princelings

Late one afternoon our crew sat up against a wall at a local mom/pop mini-market, exhausted from pick-up basketball and our clothes sweat-drenched from the colony's smothering humidity. I pressed a wad of newspaper against my knee to stanch the bleeding from a spill on the blacktop.

I chugged an icy cola but Jackson sipped steaming tea, claiming it was actually more cooling. Sure. Max, our best athlete, only allowed himself purified mineral water. But Chickie was always ready for the latest fad and drank a local vitamin-stoked soybean drink from a foil-lined paper box and made a big deal about the high-tech tetra-pak carton. Typical Chickie, he added off-color jokes while poking the tiny sharpened straw through the container's target hole.

He was a funny guy and generous, too, always demanding to pay for stuff even though we all knew Jackson's family owned half of Asia.

It had taken us weeks to solve the riddle of Wong's variety shop just down the road from school. Its large white signboard displayed three huge red Chinese ideograms with an entire storefront below that and hidden behind a wall of goods hung from wires. There were woven straw baskets, buckets and stools, hats, brooms, you-name it. The inside was damp and dirty and packed with weird stuff stacked right up to the ceiling.

So one day out of curiosity we finally took a shot and went in, just for the hell of it, never suspecting wrinkled old Mrs. Wong would lead us past cases of soy sauce and pungent dried fish to a buzzing, rusty refrigerator in back stocked with myriad cold drinks.

It became our habitual stop.

As we sat outside Wong's that afternoon, leaning against the wall and sipping drinks, we were still pumped up over our recent good fortune. A T8 typhoon flag had just been hoisted and the Hong Kong Observatory forecast a violent storm on track to graze the colony. It would shut down everything for a day or so: subtropical HK's version of a snow day. Families were already flocking to grocery stores and video shops, preparing to cocoon for the next twenty-four hours. The entire school exploded in raucous cheers when the principal announced this over the intercom just before lunch.

We sat and gazed diagonally across the street and watched people enter or leave the school, sharing clever comments on them all. Chickie furiously chewed his gum and put on the usual hilarious show. An occasional gaggle of lovely Chinese girls would walk by with their black silken hair swaying and he'd yell out, "Hel-looo, ladies! I think I'm in love!" Some giggled but most usually just looked down and walked faster.

So when he suddenly demanded our attention we just assumed it would be more of the same. "Hey, look at that, guys! Whadafock?"

I gazed over at a sleek black Bentley limo double-parked at the school entrance with its emergency lights flashing. Two beefy men jumped out.

"Bodyguards," said Jackson. He knew. His own were always nearby though we hardly ever saw them.

A short heavyset boy with a dark complexion slowly eased out of the vehicle, looking anxious. His close-cropped hair stood straight out like porcupine needles and he wore thick black spectacles large as aviator goggles. His rumpled puffy white shirt sprouted a large floppy collar and short sleeves. His brown pants were too short, emphasizing his white socks and brown/white saddle shoes. To finish off this awful look, he clutched an expensive-looking briefcase of tan belting-leather.

Poor kid looked kinda pathetic, like a 15-year-old playing lawyer.

"Now there's a kid that's gonna catch some hell," Chickie predicted, whistling low. "Somebody really ought to teach that guy how to dress. Soon."

We all nodded.

The child slowly shuffled along, his head down and face morose. He walked between his menacing bodyguards like a prisoner being delivered to the lock-up. The security men constantly scanned the area in front, behind and on all sides. One briefly paused and stared at us across the street but then waved at his partner like *it's nothing*. They entered HKIS.

"Jeez what a little creep," opined Chickie with a chuckle. Smart-assing as usual. "An absolute moron." Based on little more than a quick superficial appraisal, Chickie was already building a case against the strange child.

"I wonder, old boy," Jackson mumbled softly to me, "where the lad's from?"

"Me too. Funny his joining school so late like this, a month into the term."

One of the bodyguards returned to the Bentley. Jackson studied him. "Now that one looks Southeast Asian maybe, wot? Definitely not Korean or a Chinese mainlander."

Chickie shouldered in between us. "Boys, looks to me like we got a visitor from *Asshole-Land*." He elbowed us and laughed. "What a friggin' creep. A new pimple on the HKIS ass! And that kid seems to move as slow as, um, one of those, ah, whaddya call it. . ." The word eluded him and scratched his chin.

"A sloth, perhaps?" Jackson the genius to the rescue.

"Nope, but close. You know, one of them slimy worm-like things. "

The Max screwed up his face, thinking. "Wait, I think I know. Don't tell me, um . . ."

Chickie growled. "Thanks, Maxie but just shut up."

"Hey wait," I chirped. "Think I've got it."

Chickie looked up, expectantly. Maybe Jackson was the resident brainiac, but he knew I was always Mr. Vocabulary.

"Maybe you're thinking of . . . *a slug*?"

"Yeah that's it!" Chickie kicked his gum chomping into high gear. "*Ding-ding-ding!* Give that man a cee-gar!" He rubbed his palms like he was soaping up. "So from now on that's gonna be his name, okay? That fat kid is gonna be *The Slug*. Our own personal slimy, slow-motion crawly thing."

Oh shit. I had helped (unintentionally, of course) to coin an insulting nickname. I immediately tried to defuse it. "Well maybe he's actually a nice guy, after all—"

"What, you crazy?" Chickie snorted. "Just look at the jag-off."

"Yeah, Dash," Max huffed. "Wake up, man!"

I did little to promote the nickname but, to my considerable regret, it really took off and rapidly spread throughout HKIS. I guess it was just too appropriate. The boy indeed was slovenly and poorly-groomed, attending classes unbathed and giving off a faint stink. He seemed stand-offish and aloof, not going out of his way to make friends, which only made things worse. Maybe he was just shy, I didn't know, but his boorish manners still didn't help.

He also appeared to think he was special or privileged, cutting lines in the cafeteria or marching out of class before the dismissal bell.

But worst of all, by far, was the enormous, wretched nervous tic that would regularly collapse half his face. Nerves, I guess. It was abrupt and ugly and dramatic and impossible to not stare at in horror. An utter freak show that compounded his problems. That awful quivering grimace was enough, all by itself, to make him famous in the worst possible way throughout HKIS.

His bodyguards acted like they were protecting royalty and always hovered at arm's length except on school grounds, where such "helpers" were prohibited. On the first day, the two men had followed him right into the classroom before being reprimanded and escorted out.

Inevitably, the youth became a school-wide target for juvenile ridicule and mild hazing. The teasing was continuous and items were often stolen from his locker. He was jostled while standing in lines and insults were issued in calculated stage whispers, well within the child's earshot. (*Aiee-yah, what's that awful smell?*)

It was nasty and relentless and it soon became clear he wouldn't last long at school.

Because I'd inadvertently helped coined the nickname, my guilty conscience bothered me and spurred my occasional attempts to try and help. When the usual gossip boiled up, criticizing his hygiene or coordination, I tried gentle counter-arguments ("*Yeah, but on the other hand . . .*"). Didn't really work. But within limits, I was popular enough to get away with it.

After a month passed, oddly enough, Chickie stopped hanging out with us after school. Maybe it was for the best because his obsession against that poor kid was getting borderline weird and awfully irritating.

One day, out of curiosity, I checked with Max, who was closest to Chickie. "Hey, Maxie, what's going on with Chickie?"

"Why?"

"No big reason. Just wondering."

He shrugged. "Dunno. Think he's mainly just busy. Big project or something."

Wrong. There were no huge assignments. Chickie and I took the same classes—where he studiously froze me out and never made eye contact and left as soon as the bell rang, probably to avoid me.

So what *did* Max know? Something, for sure. He wasn't clever enough to lie convincingly.

Finally one afternoon, the two of them cornered me outside the cafeteria and Chickie started on his usual diatribe against The Slug, supported by Max. I pushed back, hard. I was angry and had had enough.

Chickie's face darkened. "Well, if you love him so much, you perv, why doncha just *marry* him?"

Max piled on. "Yeah, Dash, who made *you* his guardian angel?"

I felt my face warm and redden. "Hey, I—"

Chickie smirked and cut me off. "So when you and your smelly boyfriend *do it*, Dash, are you the pitcher . . . or the catcher?"

"You, Chickie . . . you're just an asshole. You don't even really know what that means!" I didn't, either, but could recognize a deep insult when I heard one.

I somehow fought off the urge to punch him and hurled harsh comments instead of fists, but instantly regretted it. After all, for all their flaws, those idiots were still among my closest friends. And I well knew their good side.

"I haven't seen Chickie or Max around here in a while," Mom said over dinner. "Everything okay, hon?"

"Everything's fine!" My words exploded out.

She just looked at me and shook her head. "Now, Dash, there's no need to use *that* tone."

Max and Chickie had been keeping their distance for weeks that now stretched into months as the extended February break approached for Chinese New Year.

Jackson remained cordial with all of us and played the go-between when needed, but was smart enough to steer clear as much as possible. But during the holidays Jackson went back to Macau with his family so I spent the entire break alone. Chickie and his henchman, Max, remained invisible.

Normally the New Year festival period transformed Hong Kong into heaven for teenage boys. No classes, abundant good food and plenty of Chinese firecrackers cheap and everywhere, making it every boy's sacred duty to detonate things, morning to night. Just like the 4th of July back home in Moderate Bluffs where we found it endlessly entertaining to perch an empty tin can atop a firecracker, light the fuse and watch the explosion propel it straight up into the air. We enjoyed blowing up trash cans, plastic model airplanes, sisters' dolls and their houses, and even small live animals, like frogs or hamsters. Cruel? Yeah. That's kids.

I lay in my bed a lot, alone and just thinking, feeling sad and nostalgic. Despite his flaws, Chickie had been a great friend: generous, always fun, larger than life, and he made me laugh.

I remembered the time when I lost my silver St. Christopher medal while swimming. The chain around my neck had broken. It was precious to me, a gift from my deceased grandmother. Everyone else already left but Chickie stayed there with me and searched (for hours, it seemed) in the waist-high water at Repulse Bay. I'd lost all hope and the sun was going down.

"Hey numb-nuts," he called out cheerfully, "I hurt my toe. Can you take a look and see if it's bleeding or something?"

"Aw come on, Chickie, it's almost dark"

He lifted his foot up out of the water and propped it up against my stomach.

"Oh for Christ's sake, man . . . hey, wait!" And there it was, my silver medal, the chain wrapped around his big toe. Just finding it wasn't enough. With Chickie everything was always a production.

Another time, I guess I was being overly-moody about some girl and he walked me home (nobody ever walked in HK), all the way home from school to Stanley, just chatting. And then he stayed a few more hours at my house to cheer me up, before walking home after dark.

And now that friendship seemed gone. It felt like death.

School resumed after my boring Lunar New Year and they continued to avoid me. Weeks sailed by until finally, about a month before summer break would scatter kids across the globe, Jackson approached me with news. He was breathless and his eyes wide.

"Hey, Chickie and Max want to be friends again. They want to talk with you but, well, they are too embarrassed."

Such wonderful news! I was overjoyed. Everything would soon be patched up. The warmth of affection coursed through me in waves and I could not stop grinning. *Those knuckleheads!* To be honest, at that moment The Slug and his problems meant nothing to me. My defense of him had just started one day, small and unplanned, and trapped me. But once underway, I felt committed but at a huge, unanticipated personal cost: the destruction of two close friendships.

Jackson arranged a brotherly get-together. That night we'd all make peace over fried noodles at our favorite wok stand in Causeway Bay.

We slurped noodles and chop-sticked little dumplings at our favorite greasy eatery in Causeway Bay and it felt like we'd never even quarreled. Speaking loud over the sizzle of woks, we talked about girls and sports. Chickie, Max and Jackson all razzed each other, affection disguised as insults. We excited one another with our plans for the upcoming summer break. Even Jackson (who was only heading home to Macau, a short chopper ride away) was keen to flee HK.

"But seriously: you guys are really such assholes," I said with a wink. They all smiled back. "I can't even remember what our argument was about . . ."

Jackson nodded. "Agreed. Friends shouldn't get so worked up over little things." As always, he was right.

"Well," Max said, "maybe *you* were the one who was wrong, Dash. Getting so pissed off at us like that. But seeing how you're such a little girl, it's hard for me and Chickie to stay mad at you."

What a friggin' bozo.

Max grinned like his words were hilarious, but they really cut. I flashed a wide grin but knew irritation must've shown in my eyes.

Chickie jumped in. "But you know he's right, Dash? This whole thing *was* your fault. Putting some weirdo stranger ahead of your brothers." He took the tone of an adult reproaching a child and shook his head in slow, dramatic disapproval. "We were shocked, to be honest! You must never, ever, do that again. Friendships like ours are sacred."

I couldn't let that stand. "Look, I'm just happy this is behind us. And I'm first to agree our friendship is more important than, um, The Slug." Probably should have stopped there. "But I'm also glad you're dropping this stuff. Just move on. No need to even think about that miserable kid, ever again."

Max shot a smirk at Chickie, whose face stayed neutral. What was that about? Then like flipping a switch, Chickie started laughing and flung noodles at us with his chopsticks, starting a free-for-all.

"Right," he said when it ended. "Looks like we're all back to normal."

Jackson along with his bodyguards gave Max a ride home to the Peak. Chickie and I shared a cab down to Stanley. But I felt an odd vibe as we sat together in the back seat. Something felt off. Chickie seemed a bit hyper and wired, even emotional. And knowing it was his nature to never forget *anything,* I decided to make sure. "So, Chickie, we're good, man. Right?"

He draped an arm around my shoulder and faked planting a theatrical kiss on my cheek.

"Hey, you idiot, damn it. Stop it!" I pushed him away as he giggled, almost mildly hysterical. I didn't recognize this guy. After a minute he settled down and punched me in the arm and, with a laugh, moved back into his favorite persona: the blasé tough guy.

"Yeah, *senor,* of course we're cool. You may be a bit of a fairy, Dash, but you'll always be *numero uno* with me." This new habit of his really annoyed me, forcing Spanish 101 into everyday conversations. Just that morning he exited the boy's toilet at school and announced to one and all about his *muy profundo* bowel movement. But I guess that was just Chickie.

By the time that goofball got out of the taxi, at his house, it seemed pretty clear our friendship had been fully restored.

Next morning at school, Jackson walked up.

"Hey," I smiled, "look, it's my second-favorite Jackson. Right behind Michael but just ahead of Reggie."

Jackson scowled. "No time for that. Cut it out." The intense, irritated look he wore was unfamiliar and rarely seen before. The closest was when he'd a botched test (*botched* for Jackson meant scoring only the *second-highest* grade in class) or when his favorite soccer team, Manchester United, lost a championship. "Dash, I've got something important to discuss with you, old boy."

"Shoot." I chuckled at his melodrama.

"Last night on the way home, Max finally told me what Chickie is up to."

"Yeah?"

"And made me swear to not tell."

"Nice job keeping your word."

Jackson shook his head. "This is serious, Dash. Listen, it seems he's kinda really gone off the deep end. Full Chickie-style, you know?"

What's was that all about? I shrugged. "Well, he's just being Chickie."

"The thing is this. Chickie hasn't *dropped* anything, Dash. He's plotting something serious against The Slug."

"Well, in that case, maybe we should just stay out of it. Stay far away." I only wanted to survive the final days of the school term with all my friendships intact. Over the long summer break, everything would settle down and relations heal.

"Chickie's saying some pretty nutty stuff."

"Normal nutty or *Chickie nutty?* That'd be worse." I flashed a conspiratorial smile. "Come on, Jackson, cool off, man."

He drew a deep breath, removed his glasses and rubbed his face. "Listen. Maybe it's just a load of bull, but Chickie's talking about hurting that kid."

"No way. Can't for a moment believe that."

"Max says he's going to give that Slug kid the full Chinese New Year treatment."

"Meaning what?"

Jackson shrugged. "Remember that firecracker-in-the-frog stuff?"

Blow up The Slug? That was crazy. "Nah, that can't be right."

"Wait, Dash, remember Chickie's stockpile of firecrackers?"

"Yeah, a closet full. Wish I had even half."

"Max thinks he's using them somehow."

This all sounded downright foolish, like juvenile daydream stuff. "Come on, Jackson, you're being like an old woman, getting all worked up over nothing. First off, Max is no mental giant so don't go putting any stock in his interpretation of *anything*. And second, while Chickie is funny, it's *haha*-funny, not *dangerous*-funny."

"Well, you'd better be right."

Jackson's concern was unmistakable and it nagged at me over the next few weeks. But every time I saw Chickie I realized anew that such a threat was impossible. Really: how could that knucklehead ever seriously injure another student? Had to be empty talk.

And one afternoon, as we were walking down a school corridor The Slug approached from the other direction.

"Hey man," Chickie called out to him. His voice was loud and friendly. "How's it going?" He smiled and raised his chin at the victimized child, who appeared altogether stunned by this unprecedented friendly gesture. All he could manage in return was a mumbled "Err, hello?" as we passed.

Stuff like that happened a few more times that week, Chickie sending out peace feelers, so I was comforted.

I was sure Max and Jackson had it all wrong.

CHAPTER FIVE
Dangerous Idea

On the last day of classes the students were almost levitating, they were buzzing with so much excitement. The total freedom of summer vacation hovered only hours away and lives would soon transform into a sweet summer nirvana. Every problem would vanish.

Many kids already wore their getaway clothes, ready to be whisked straight to Kai Tak airport after the final bell and depart for destinations in Europe, America or Asia.

I spotted Chickie during the break before the last period. He walked right up to The Slug in the school courtyard and warmly shook hands and placed his left hand on the kid's shoulder. The beleaguered youth appeared stunned and at first just stared back until a small smile crept across his face.

As the two briefly chatted and The Slug beamed.

Chickie pulled a beautiful package from his backpack and handed it over. Glistening with gold foil wrapping paper and tied with thick red ribbons, the gift box was lovely, about the size of a large box of chocolates. The Slug put it into his *junior lawyer* briefcase of tan belting leather.

It felt like I was hallucinating to see Chickie schmoozing the former target of his unrelenting humiliation. I was shocked but delighted and breathed a sigh of relief at this astonishing sight. We'd not discussed The Slug for quite some time because frankly, I was fed up with the entire matter and talking seemed pointless. I feared it would only create more friction with Chickie, a good friend. You know, that whole thing about sleeping dogs and stuff.

A sense of shame smoldered within me. I was totally wrong and had misjudged my friend's heart and basic good nature. I owed Chickie a huge apology and right away, before classes ended and we all scattered to the four winds. So I headed over but Max beat me there and chortling, pounded Chickie's back.

Chickie just stood there looking smug, his head nodding like a bobble-head doll. Proud of something.

"Guys," I laughed, "almost time for vacation! Only one more hour and we're free!"

But Max only shot me a look of disdain.

What was his problem?

"Sure, Dash-hole," he hectored, "but that's nothing. Bigger fish soon gonna fry." Chickie elbowed him.

"Hey, fellas, something up?" I was basking in a contact high from the entire student body abuzz with the gleeful countdown to summer vacation.

Chickie waved me closer and furtively (like a criminal in an old grade B gangster movie) looked side to side. "Trust you with a big secret, Dash?"

I chuckled. What a goofball. "Sir, yes, sir!"

"Okay, then. Time to finally brief you on *Operation Slug*."

What? My face remained frozen in a silly grin as I watched Chickie jiggling with excitement. "Huh?"

"Big stuff going down, Dash."

Good God—not again.

I was so sick of this shit and thought the whole sad little melodrama had already burned itself out. If we could just get to summer break all lingering traces would be forgotten and the problem would permanently resolve itself. Maybe the unfortunate child would just go away and never return, convince his parents to send him to some other international school like in Manila or Jakarta.

"Chickie, bro, no offense," I said, squeezing his hand in both of mine, "but don't tell me anymore. I'm finished hearing about that bullshit." And never had I been more truthful.

Chickie waggled his head subcontinental-style and shot me a self-satisfied grin. "But *senor*, you don't *really* want to miss out on this, do you?"

"Sure I do."

"Nah. You'd be missing a *real blast*."

Max burst out laughing right on cue. "Yeah, Dash: you'll get a *real bang* out of this." Max smirked as the two leaned against each other, breaking up in giggles.

It was all I could do, just to stand looking at those two idiots. But the bell for the last class was about to ring. No time to waste.

I tried to smile. Now, I don't really believe people have auras, but Chickie genuinely seemed to be glowing with malevolent anticipation. I regretted opening my mouth but had to ask: "So, Chickie, what's going on??

He grinned and drew in a deep breath, tossing an arm around my shoulder. He pulled me close.

"The hardest part," he said, keeping his voice low, "was getting all the gunpowder. Lots of work. Every night I sat in my bedroom at my desk with a razor blade opening up a shitload of firecrackers. It took me a whole freakin' month! And what a mess, too, all that black silvery powder on my fingers. Had to be careful. Didn't want to blow myself up, of course."

Max couldn't resist. "Geez, there'd be shit all over the walls of your room then, huh?"

Not a bad one, even for dumb old Max. But I had no time for childish jokes. I grabbed Chickie's arm. "Are you shitting me, Chickie? There's some kind of bomb?"

He broadcast an irritating smile. "Well, it's not *that* huge." His tone of false modesty seemed intended to signal the opposite. "But more'n enough to blow that stinkin' Slug to bits. Send him flying back to whatever shitty country he crawled outta."

And then finally I understood: The gift. If that package was filled with gunpowder, it would be more than enough when detonated to decapitate somebody.

"The trickiest part, *amigo*, was finding a way to set it off. A delayed trigger."

Good Lord. "Yeah, so?"

"Well, I found a battery timer in the back of a comic book. One of those science project ads. I mailed away and was worried it wouldn't get here in time. Fuckin' HK! But *caramba* it did, just last week! I practiced rigging it to ignite match-heads. And those would light the fuse. I experimented, setting off some ladyfingers . . . and damn if it didn't work!" He shook his head. "And to think that my mom says comic books are a waste of time."

Floating within his grin was the unmistakable, almost innocent pride of achievement. As evil as his scheme was, Chickie didn't appear to fully comprehend the horror of his actions. As if it was pretend, only playing.

"You know, Dash, this may be my greatest triumph." He sounded like a Hollywood mad scientist and grinned like a big, stupid adolescent clown. This was just crazy. Something was very wrong with my friend.

The alarm bell suddenly shrilled out and momentarily stunned us. Chickie started to pull away but I locked onto his arm.

"Hey, man, let go! I'll be late!" My fingers dug in hard enough to leave marks, squeezing the blood from his forearm. "Ow, stop it!" He yanked his arm away and rubbed it, acting mortally injured.

The bell stopped and students began to scatter, disappearing through the line-up of hallway doors. I blocked Chickie's retreat.

"Sorry, but when does that thing go off?" I was numb and fighting off shock, disgusted by even the remotest taint of my complicity in such a scheme. Somehow I had the presence of mind to keep on smiling. Didn't want to spook Chickie.

He clicked his tongue, sounding the ticking of a clock. "Classes are out at 3:00 and The Slug should be driving away in his limo by what, 3:10? The timer is set to go off at about 3:15 . . . *mas o menos* . . . and then *ka-blooey.* Minced Slug." He turned and started to jog off to class.

But halfway there he stopped and turned to face me. "So *amigo,"* he hollered, "see ya later, okay? Grab a couple pops before we all head off on home leave?" His innocent smile and naivety astounded me. Here he was, a potential murderer but acting like none of it really mattered. Like nothing was real.

Chickie waved and ducked into his classroom. My stomach clenched in revulsion and my head went light at a barrage of thoughts hammering at me while I sprinted to class.

What should I do?

Realistically, it all seemed rather too far-fetched to be real. Maybe it wasn't even worth the worry. Chickie's technical incompetence was sure to doom any device from working, right? Yes, that was it: a false alarm, albeit a scary one. Only a fantasy.

Yet how could I take that chance? I kept replaying his smiling invitation for colas after school, soft drinks with either a cold-blooded killer or a total nutcase.

One thing was certain: I'd be passing on that.

Mr. Stewart Stuart-Hall blathered on. There would be no early release from *Stew-Stu's* final period class, last day or not. Why did he need to expand his lecture to fill that entire period, right on the verge of summer freedom? I'll never know. Exams were over, grades were set and the clock was counting down.

But no one was listening, especially not me. Numbed by imagined scenes about Chickie's bomb going off, I struggled with a choice between moral responsibility and loyalty to a troubled friend. Betrayal would land my blood brother in enormous trouble. But if I didn't intervene and The Slug was injured, I'd somehow share in the guilt, too.

The biggest (and only) comfort was that it was only a remote chance that my goofy pal could succeed in constructing a functional, time-delayed bomb.

Totally preoccupied all through class, I stared up at the clock and hoped for a miracle. I willed its hands to freeze, forestalling both a decision and any detonation. So totally obsessed in thought, I didn't realize when Stew-Stu called on me.

"I say there," the teacher intoned, his voice raised as he thumped a fist on his desktop. "Earth to Bonaventure!" His plummy accent failed to hide growing irritation. The class tittered, grateful for this diversion to help kill off those last few, eternal minutes before vacation.

"*Master—Dashiell—Xavier—Bonaventure—the Second!*" The class erupted but immediately fell silent again upon seeing the teacher turn crimson. A small blood vessel throbbed over his left eye.

I rose at my desk, head bowed. "Sorry, sir. I was—"

"Mentally on leave already, eh? Unlike you, Bonnie." His pet name for me (I was his favorite) so his mood was already softening. "Come forward." With a small flourish he handed me a parchment certificate with an embossed HKIS gold seal glittering at the bottom. "In Recognition of Writing Excellence" it said. My essay "Truman and The Bomb" had won as the semester's best. I mumbled my thanks and trotted back to my seat, still immersed in a fog of surrealism, my body doing one thing and my mind totally somewhere else.

As 3 p.m. dismissal neared and potential disaster loomed just minutes away. I'd wasted my time and failed to come up with a plan, but soon had to act. Or not. Either be a hero and a traitor, or a coward and an accomplice to evil. I argued maybe it wouldn't even work or that Chickie was just bullshitting.

This most serious trial of my young life had emerged from nowhere and burst upon me in an instant, leaving me paralyzed by shock and unable to make a decision. My mind went mainly blank as I watched myself in a surreal performance.

If only Jackson were still there, he'd know what to do. But he'd left school early, off on a grand European vacation tour with his family. (No big deal for a brainiac like him to get out of school a week early)

The bell to end classes for the semester pierced the school with eardrum-shattering intensity and triggered an immediate, frantic roar of hundreds of joyous voices. Children scrambled in all directions in utter pandemonium as they ran for the doors, hurled books into the air and tore up school papers to toss around like confetti.

Quiet and resigned, Stew-Stu sat motionless at his desk and rested his chin on his fist. He'd seen this storm rage so many times in the past and knew it best to just shelter in place and wait for it to pass.

The school's inner courtyard overflowed with a roiling sea of children, all cranked up and moving in a riot of delight. The penitentiary doors had been thrown open, granting instant freedom to all. Friends came up to me and joked, teasing and slapping me on the back. Some held out yearbooks but my mind was elsewhere and I had no clever phrases to inscribe.

I scanned the crowd for The Slug. The clock overhead indicated I'd already wasted two minutes. Time was the enemy and seemed to be speeding up.

I spotted Chickie, off to the far side with Max, schmoozing with other kids. He grinned and waved at me. What's wrong with that guy?

Then I spotted The Slug slowly sauntering toward the front entrance. His bodyguards and limo would be waiting outside, ready to deliver him from his daily ordeal. For him freedom and a happier summer beckoned, an escape back to the family somewhere that loved him. But if I failed to act his only future might involve a bloody maiming . . . or worse.

I still couldn't think but before I knew it I was speeding off through the rabid crowd and bouncing off kids like a pinball, with no plan or clear idea. I was just on the move until I intercepted the pudgy victim near the front entrance. I reached out from behind and placed a firm hand on his shoulder. He immediately crouched, a learned defensive reflex, probably expecting the worst.

When he turned, there was that awful nervous tic again, right on cue, the one that made him a special target for derision. It collapsed half his face in a tormented grimace while his sour, nervous body odor filled the gap between us.

"Hey, buddy!" I sang out in as happy a voice as I could muster. I had no idea what came next.

He recognized me as someone who had never given him trouble. Maybe not a friend, but at least not an enemy. "Oh hi," he said. His ugly facial spasm subsided and a tiny smile began to cautiously emerge. "It's *Dash*, right?" His voice was high and soft and only now did I realize I'd only heard it once or twice before. And I still didn't even know his real name.

"Yeah. Bonaventure, Dashiell."

"Hope you have a nice break," he said. His smile bloomed even further. Actually, he seemed like a rather okay guy.

"You, too." I had nothing else to say and time was depleting fast. If Chickie's handiwork came even close to working as planned, the explosion was imminent. Maybe five, ten minutes?

In a sudden jolt of clarity, I knew what I needed to do. The Slug deserved sympathy and apologies from all of us, including me, for the merciless purgatory we'd all created. But for now, there was simply no time.

"Hey, Dasherino! *Que pasa,* buddy?"

That was the last voice I wanted to hear. I turned and saw Chickie, laughing and mugging, with Max in tow.

"Looks like you found a new buddy there, eh?" He looked at The Slug beside me.

"Yeah, looks like a fun guy," Max said, going in for style points. "A real *blast*."

Chickie's face darkened. "Hey, Dash. We gotta move fast, remember? As in *right now*. Gonna go get those cokes, remember?" He raised his eyebrows at the wall clock. "Need to hurry, okay?"

Exactly.

Pivoting from my heels, I launched a wide roundhouse punch. The impact with Chickie's facial bones made a dull plop and I felt hard bone structure giving way beneath my knuckles. Really clocked him a good one. He crumpled to the ground and convulsed for a few seconds. That really freaked me out but then it stopped. (I'd later learn I broke a knuckle but, at this point, I was so juiced up on nervous energy I felt nothing.)

The Max, despite being the largest and most athletic of us, was just a coward at heart. He instantly turned and ran, not wanting any part of this crazed angry version of Dash.

The Slug glanced down at Chickie, his primary nemesis crumpled on the ground, bleeding and unconscious. Then he gazed over at me with fear in his eyes. In one continuous motion I pushed him to the ground where he stayed and cowered, protecting his head with his hands and arms, anticipating another round of schoolyard bullying. Instead, I yanked away his tan leather old-man-style satchel he always carried to tote his lunch or whatever. But today, I knew it contained a ticking, foil-wrapped gift package.

I tucked his briefcase under my arm and sprinted off through the crowd amid laughter and random, innocuous cheers from other (misunderstanding) school kids.

I ran out the main entrance and right past The Slug's flashy black limo parked just up the street. His bodyguards were napping in the front seat. I flew past them and up the two-lane blacktop road that climbed up out of Repulse Bay and cut through the forested hillside, above and following the shoreline south toward Stanley Village.

My pounding heart threatened to thump right out of my chest. No athlete, I was already severely winded but kept running up the road, occasionally seeing the ocean through the wooded slope, glimmering down below. After a few minutes (I don't know how long but it felt like forever) a commotion began to stir from behind me, the whine of a car transmission laboring hard to climb uphill. Gears shifted and a horn blew and angry voices floated up at me.

The bodyguards were after me. Probably The Slug, too.

Only now did I realize the fatal flaw to this unplanned getaway. I couldn't leave the road. The woods on either side were too thick and nearly impassable. To the left was a rising dirt wall and to the right was a forested sheer drop-off down to the sea.

I was trapped. All I could do was wait for the car to reach me.

All three jumped out of the vehicle, their voices high and arms flailing. "My bag!" cried the child. His face was wet with tears and his cheeks as red as if rouged. "Give it back!"

The bodyguards smiled cruelly, knowing they had me as they hustled in my direction, their fists clenched and threats growled in an unfamiliar language.

That's when I did the only thing I could think of. Wind milling my arm for momentum and rotating my body, I hurled the satchel through an opening into the woods down the hillside toward the sea. The brown leather square cartwheeled along, end over end, and bounced off trees, madly caroming down the slope and toward the water below. The briefcase finally caught on a tree and came to rest just short of the shoreline.

One of the bodyguards cuffed me across the ear, muttering curses. The other also swore at me, spewing pungent, garlic-infused breath. The Slug just sat on the ground, abject and shaking his head, sobbing and snorting streams of clear mucus into tissues. "My bag," he whined, his voice high and English oddly-accented. "It's *just* my bag. Why did you . . . I, I thought you were different, not like the rest. I don't know why . . ."

The two bodyguards performed some Asian hand-based game to pick a loser, like *Rock-Paper-Scissors Goes to China*. Mr. Garlic Breath lost and with a groan climbed over the iron safety rail at the road's edge and began to pick his way on down, slowly descending the dangerous, near-vertical hillside. His partner held my arm tight, as if guarding his life savings. I was going nowhere. Garlic Breath worked steadily downhill, careful to always maintain a hold onto one tree and then the next. After several minutes he neared the satchel and reached out for it.

But then—with an abrupt, deafening and powerful concussion we could all feel, way back up top on the asphalt road—the briefcase detonated with a powerful thud and a bright flash visible even in the daylight. It was amazing: Chickie's bomb had actually worked.

His greatest triumph.

Most of the tree that held the satchel had disappeared. Trunks and limbs of surrounding trees were sheared off and some bushes and underbrush had burst into flame. Dirt and stone flew and a small rounded pit appeared beneath the explosion.

Up on the road we were all stunned. Especially me. We looked at each other, mute, as if waking from a dream. Even forewarned as I was, the detonation astonished me. My ears rang but another sound softly penetrated the dull buzzy ringing. I realized it was the screaming of Garlic Breath, who'd lost the hand he'd reached out. It was horrific and I thought I might puke. From down below, he pointed a stump up at us, spurting blood. Spewing invective, he wailed for help.

He was probably lucky to be alive.

In a blur the second bodyguard released my arm and jumped the guardrail to head on down the hillside to help his partner. My out cue. I took off and ran down the road back toward Repulse Bay.

"Hey!" I could just barely hear The Slug's high-pitched voice through the ringing in my ears. "Hey, wait!" he called out from behind me.

But I kept sprinting and fell several times. Soon he was out of earshot. I momentarily paused to catch my breath and looked back up the road. He was still up there and yelling something. I tried to read his lips. *Fuck you?* Wow, was he really hollering that?

As I got down near Repulse Bay village, I spotted an idling taxi and jumped in. "Get me to Central. Hurry." We sped away. I sat in the backseat with my eyes closed. The air con was set to maximum and I shivered. As my heartbeat finally slowed, the afternoon's bizarre events replayed in my mind.

In particular, the ending.

Fuck you?

Or had the kid possibly come to understand what I'd done for him. Was it actually *Thank you*?

Perhaps. But I wasn't about to hang around to find out.

CHAPTER SIX
Asian Endings

After driving around Central to make sure nobody had followed, I had the taxi take me home to Stanley. I tossed my book bag down and veered off toward my bedroom but Mom cut me off. "Goodness, dear, where have you been? You know we have to leave for Kai Tak in less than an hour, right?" Dash! What happened to your hand—it's bleeding!" She reached for it, all bloody, swollen and bluish.

"Yow!" I yanked it back. She'd gone straight for the knuckle broken on Chickie's cheekbone.

"Honey, whatever—"

"Mom! I'm okay, it's *nothing*. I just fell. Jeez."

"Watch that mouth, young man." She shook her head. Language always touched a nerve. "I just hope you're already packed."

Until we left for the airport, I kept expecting a uniformed contingent to arrive at any moment from the Royal Hong Kong Police. But that was way too melodramatic. A few hours later, our *Pan Pacific Airways* flight lifted toward our home leave in America. Dad was off in China and could only join us in the USA a few weeks later. He had some critical company function forcing him to stay back.

I pulled the itchy gray wool blanket up to my chin against the air cabin's chill and settled back, trying to ignore my throbbing hand. Nestled in white noise at 30,000 feet, I willed myself to dismiss the day's bizarre events. Continuing to replay them didn't help and changed nothing.

For now, the solution was to clear my teen-aged mind, as if nothing had ever happened, and hope time would sort everything out. I began to decompress and feel a sense of relief. It was all behind me and would soon be half a world away. With any luck, by the time I returned to school in HK in three months, all would be forgotten. Ancient history.

Our homeward journey consumed several days. There were refueling stops and connecting flights forced by aircraft range limitations. We puddle-jumped across the Pacific. I bought some Chinese candy in the Taipei airport and photo magazines at Tokyo. We flew up across the pole and over Alaska's snowy mountains to Fairbanks. We zipped down the west coast and even buzzed the famous Hollywood sign and landed in LA. Finally, after a brief stopover in Denver, we made it to Chicago. Landing at O'Hare, utterly exhausted, we cleared immigration and booked a three-hour motor coach ride to Moderate Bluffs.

The small doctor's office hid upstairs from a Rexall drug store in a yellow brick building in downtown Moderate Bluffs. Mom brought me there the next morning.

"Well, you're awfully lucky," chirped the young doctor as he slapped an x-ray negative onto the light box. "See? Only one knuckle. What we call a *boxer's fracture*."

"He got it at school," Mom said, "playing basketball. Not from fighting. Dash fell on asphalt."

Sounded like she definitely bought my story.

"Hard foul," I explained, holding up my puffy hand. It was now an angry purplish-black. "But why do you say *lucky,* doc?"

"A little break, no big deal. No surgery. Just a small cast and then a brace. Couple days' aspirin for pain. And in a couple months you can resume your NBA career."

Suddenly back in America after a year away, everything seemed so modern and easy. I didn't remember it being so wonderful here before. The spotless, enormous, super-provisioned grocery stores blew me away. Perhaps it was I that had changed, now evaluating it all through new, globally-refined eyes like a bemused visitor.

New yellow-and-red franchised hamburger outlets seemed to beckon everywhere, along with chilly bowling alleys and noisy go-kart tracks. Every evening, Top 40 pop radio stations from Chicago faded-in at dusk.

I caught up with old friends and shopped with Mom for our family home leave shipment. Once a year, expats shipped (at company expense) a big crate of goods back to their overseas post. I bought stacks of comics, magazines and paperbacks; record albums; a glove, bat and several boxes of Topps baseball cards. Mom laid in a year's supply of her favorite cosmetics, bed sheets and cases of our favorite soups and peanut butter. Dozens of boxes of pudding.

But my plan to just forget about The Slug incident fell apart nearly immediately. Every time I glanced down at my plaster cast, I remembered. And I awakened the middle of each night the first week, jet-lagged, with nothing to do but lay there and be haunted by questions with no answers: about the bodyguard, Chickie and The Slug. Would I get into trouble back in HK? Did everybody hate me now?

I calmed myself by constructing the benign outcome that the blast had slipped by unnoticed. I nearly convinced myself it *was* possible.

My thinking went like this: The bomb was small and went off in a remote, wooded area well outside Repulse Bay. There were no other witnesses. Other than explaining away the bodyguard's injury at a hospital (yes, a hefty "other than"), authorities might have never found out. What if The Slug didn't want to further complicate things or press charges? Maybe he just wanted to get away from Hong Kong and immediately go home? Sounded possible, almost reasonable.

But that soothing hypothesis only went so far in calming my jangled nerves. I needed to know more and came up with a plan.

"So you're going with a group of other boys?"

Mom didn't quite trust this idea but was wavering. I'd told her some friends were visiting Bradley University, the typical campus tour for high school students. A parent was driving.

"Sure, Mom, and we'll all be back by dinner. Don't worry. See?" I flexed a bicep. "I'm big now. A high school sophomore soon."

The next morning I left the house before she woke and biked to downtown Moderate Bluffs (now *there's* a contradiction) to catch a bus to Peoria. After an hour's ride I found the college library and its periodicals room.

Jackpot! In the international publications room, they stocked recent editions of the South China Morning Post with only a couple weeks' lag. There were papers from around the time of the incident. I gathered them up and went off to a small study carrel to pore over every inch of newsprint.

I found nothing relevant, other than a short item congratulating HKIS for the young school successfully completing another academic year. Certainly nothing about hands being blown off or punched students convulsing on the courtyard grounds.

I couldn't believe it. There *had* to be something. So I took another run through the papers and reread every last column inch, every single item no matter how innocuous.

At last I stumbled over something picayune that I'd overlooked, just a tiny blurb, a filler tucked into a section of vague news shorts cribbed from police blotters and hospital admittance ledgers.

"An overseas tourist was admitted Friday to Adventist Hospital after losing his right hand in a gardening accident in Repulse Bay. After being stabilized and treated, he was released to travel back to his home country for further medical care."

Overseas tourist? A gardening accident?
Right.

Though woefully short on details that sure sounded like ol' Garlic Breath. And that HKIS article made it sound like everything was fairly routine at the school, too. It was also a good thing to not see my mug shot anywhere.

I arrived back home in high spirits, just in time for dinner.

Trying to be thorough, I took one more stab and bought a blue international aerogramme at the post office and composed a friendly letter to Jackson, back in Macau. I kept it purposely vague and told him a little about my summer in Moderate Bluffs. I said I was buying baseball cards for him and then, at the very end, casually hinted Chickie and I were on the outs again. If Jackson had heard anything about the punch or knew *anything* about the explosion, he'd surely rise to that bait.

So that was it. I'd now done all I could from this side of the ocean. It was time to just relax and enjoy my summer.

Well after 2 a.m. one hot night in early July, the phone's harsh ring pierced the quiet of our Illinois ranch home and jarred me from the luxuriously deep slumber of a teenager. Disoriented and groggy, still half-asleep, I was already dropping off again when my mother's panicky voice jolted me fully awake.

"What did you say? Please, again?" She gulped air and choked out words between sobs. I stood at the door to her room, shocked to see her wailing into the cream white bedside phone.

"No, sir, I *don't* understand . . . how that can be? Again, what did you say?" Her mind seemed unable to process some illogical information. Something made no sense.

When she finally hung up the real drama began. In comparison, her earlier sobs were just murmurs. Now they rose and built in power, peaked and ebbed in cycles, each time reaching a higher emotional plateau like successive waves rolling further up a beach.

I wrapped my arms around her and made comforting *shushing* sounds. "It's okay, Mom. Please don't cry."

Her body trembled in my embrace. After an eternity and a half box of tissues, she composed herself enough to speak. "That was Hong Kong, Honey." She sniffled. "Long-distance from Mr. Tam."

I'd already guessed as much, considering the hour. But why was Dad's assistant phoning?

"It's your father." She reached for more tissues.

"Yes?"

"Well, he's gone." She slowly shook her head and began to softly moan again.

I gripped her shoulders and gently shook her—no time for her to start that up again.

"Whaddya mean *gone*, Mom? Gone where?" Dad disappeared? Oh shit, was he leaving us, divorcing Mom? Did some sexy young Cantonese chick get her hooks into him?

Wrong.

It turned out Dash #1, my indestructible father, had collapsed during a ten-course Chinese dinner after countless rounds of toasting fiery *baijiu*, the infamous and potent, sour-tasting liquor distilled from sorghum. It was a stroke and he died a few hours later while in a coma at a Hong Kong hospital. Over the next few hours the sad details all emerged as more trans-Pacific phone calls straggled in.

An enormous lump seemed to fill my stomach and I couldn't swallow. I felt numb.

Poor Dad!

I couldn't believe it. His presence had defined every aspect of our lives but now he was gone. Mom and I sat up the rest of the night crying together, drinking tea and phoning relatives. We tried to digest the mind-boggling new shape our world had taken, but it was impossible.

"I kept *warning* your father . . ." Mom constantly dabbed at leaky, reddened eyes and a dripping nose. "It's so unfair—he was still so young! Only 58." My father's new overseas executive lifestyle had begun to frighten her: all the chain-smoking and heavy drinking, those frequent cholesterol-clobbering, all-male, ten-course business dinners entertaining clients from the Mainland or Japan.

Starting around dawn, executives from Stallion in Illinois started to phone their condolences as word passed through the corporate grapevine.

I was sad and stunned but most of all, to be honest, scared. Without Dad, how did life even work? What would happen to Mom and me?

She flew back to HK to close down our life there. So poof, just like that, my brief but amazing expatriate adventure was over. Mom hired movers to pack up the house and canceled my enrollment at HKIS. After she visited the school I was dreading a furious middle-of-the-night phone call ("A *bomb*, Dash? And *why* did you punch Chickie?") But it never happened. Dunno why, but thank goodness.

While Mom was away, I also took some initiative and phoned the local high school to arrange my fall admission.

Mom had Dad's body cremated and two weeks later flew back to Illinois, carrying Dad's ashes in a lovely Chinese porcelain urn wedged into her suitcase between shimmering purple bathrobes and a lifetime supply of flowery silk pouches.

After Dad was gone she didn't seem too concerned about money so I didn't pry—maybe there were savings or a life insurance settlement. Only once did I share my concern.

"Don't worry, dear. Your father took good care of us all. The money is there for your college, even graduate school."

I began my sophomore year at Moderate Bluffs High, biking to school through the cornfields as the Hong Kong memories faded and even seemed at times like unreal dreams. I was now definitely stuck back in the boring, awful *real world* again, with Illinois prairie all around me.

But my eyes had already been opened to the rest of the world and I couldn't close them again. My greatest fear was that I might never live abroad again, maybe not even travel overseas. I became hypersensitive to the small-town mindset that surrounded me. *("You lived where, Dash, in Hong Kong? That's in Japan, right?)*

It felt like I was imprisoned, sentenced to a life at hard boredom.

"What's wrong, dear," pried Mom one day.
"Nothing."
"You seem a little sad or something. Everything okay?"
"I said stop it!" I turned my back on her. She could have figured out I was just pretty much dying from boredom there in Moderate Bluffs, after a scintillating year amid the international glamor of Hong Kong. That's all.

"Maybe you want to start going to church again, Honey? That might help. You were such a holy child, remember? It made you happy being an altar boy and in the choir."

"Mom!" I growled at her but knew she was only trying to help. True, I enjoyed those simpler days in the choir and as an altar boy. I liked the cassock and surplice, the smell of incense and burning candles, the feeling of total safety and security. I was a child.

But right then, what would make *me* happy was to escape from rural Illinois.

One day the Stallion headquarters phoned. They were holding a letter forwarded to me via their Hong Kong office. After school I pedaled over to the corporate center outside town and a secretary handed me a large brown business envelope displaying the Stallion Tractor Company logo.

Inside nestled a small, thin aerogramme on feather-light blue paper with delicate handwriting. Inscribed on the back was the sender's name: Jackson Toh.

I eagerly slit it open with my jackknife. The date was from months back, very slow in transit.

Dear Dash:

First off, old boy, I was very sorry to hear the sad news about your father. My sincere condolences, dear friend.

A lot of weird stuff has transpired here in Honkers and it now looks like I am the last man standing. Chickie never came back from his home leave in Brooklyn. No details, just a sudden family decision. And ditto for The Max, who's now back in Oz.

The day before fall classes began, I visited the Mid-Levels and found a Sikh watchman (turban and all) guarding Max's empty house for the landlord. Then I taxied down to Stanley and found YOUR house also rented out to another family. I hoped maybe you moved to The Peak or something. Chickie's house was vacant, too. Rather mysterious.

But I didn't see you the next morning at HKIS, so I checked with the school office. They told me about your father and that you were staying in Illinois. That hit me pretty hard, Laddie.

Your letter to me only arrived yesterday so I am immediately answering.

Anyway, remember that weird kid, The Slug? Well he's gone too! Never fit in, so probably not so a big shock he didn't return. Funny how we never even learned his real name or where he was from. Well whoever he was, he's back home, wherever that is.

One more thing. Some kids said you and Chickie scuffled—actual fisticuffs—on the last day, while I was in Europe. I can't believe it but . . . well?

Okay, don't forget your brother still here in the Colony. Write when you can and also feel free to ship boxes of baseball cards, comics or Playboy magazines from America.

Who knows? Maybe someday we can get back together. For now, I need to assemble a new after-school basketball and soccer crew! Sigh. Thanks greatly, Old Man.

    Your friend,
    Jackson

I shook my head and breathed a sigh of relief. As horrible and potentially deadly as that blast had been, it seemed to have vanished from history's ledger. The record appeared clean—no further consequences.

Despite our best intentions, Jackson and I only exchanged a few letters before our communication lapsed. Adolescent males can be poor correspondents.

At home, Mom, in just her late forties, grew increasingly glum and lonely. Not only had Dad been taken away but her active Hong Kong social whirl also vanished, replaced by afternoon TV soap operas. Dad had been an enormous presence in our lives so his departure left a huge void.

So I was happy when Mom began seeing someone, one of Dad's old business associates, a recently-divorced lawyer. She met Ernest Butcher at a Stallion holiday party and things developed fast. I sometimes wondered what Dad would have thought about Ernie barging in like that, but after a while got more comfortable with Mom becoming romantically involved. Good thing I did—they married in less than a year.

As for me, I began to worry a lot more.

You know, about life and stuff. I wondered if, at just sixteen, I had already peaked and my life was already on the downside after that incredible HK adventure had been so rudely terminated.

I decided to really concentrate hard on my studies and hoped a stellar performance could open the door to an elite university and a new life. That seemed a good plan because, Lord knows, it was all I had. I'd sorely outgrown rural Illinois and needed a way out.

Middle of my senior year, a thick envelope dropped through the mail slot. It was decorated with the fusty coat of arms for Olde Albion University, a notoriously elite private liberal arts college, top-ranked in the nation. Olde Albion accepted only 200 candidates each year from a pool of ten thousand applicants. The waitlist for Olde Albion was always packed with applicants already accepted at Harvard or Stanford, hoping to upgrade.

I tore the brown parcel open and out spilled several brochures, a course catalog, sheets of housing information and a business letter printed on crisp linen paper.

"Congratulations, Mr. Bonaventure," it intoned. "We are pleased to welcome you to our freshman class this fall in New Hampshire . . ."

I stopped reading and let out a whoop. Mom ran in, worried. Then she saw the open envelope and letter and my shit-eating grin and immediately knew. She hugged me, her eyes glistening. "I'm so proud of you, dear."

"Well, I don't know," grumbled Ernest Butcher, my new stepfather, who followed her into the room and seemed intent on crushing the happy vibe. "You'll be like a poor coal miner's son there, among all those fancy rich people."

"Nah, Ernie, I'll show em." Since he married Mom, right from the start I never felt comfortable calling him dad or stepdad so early on, we settled on first names.

"Seems like a real lot of money to blow, too. A big waste." He shrugged his shoulders with a grunt and wandered out of the room.

My grades and test scores *were* flashy but to gain Olde Albion admission I'd leveraged my credentials as an international student, powerful currency back then, able to transform a simple farmlands boy into something unique and exotic, a global asset for schools to tussle over. High school in Hong Kong? Bravo! Colleges lusted to enhance their student populations, so virtually all my college applications triggered acceptances.

Regarding scholarship money, the schools were all equally generous. But I didn't worry much about that anyway, thanks to my late father's life insurance policy and savings.

But any talk about finances always seemed to steam up Ernie, who would turn a deep shade of pink while his breathing sped up. Not sure why it mattered so much to him. His salary as

Stallion's VP-Legal must have been hefty, for defending the company against farmer lawsuits when tractor brakes failed and cows got crushed. Stuff like that.

    Who cares? I didn't.

    All I knew was that I'd won my ticket out.

Book Two

A Literary Rocket Ride
New England, 1972

CHAPTER SEVEN
University Days

Olde Albion College
In the leafy hills of New Hampshire - 1972

I settled right in at Albion's charming campus, a fantasy-land of colonnaded red brick buildings with arches and domes sprawling across a green, semi-wooded area. The elite school was regarded as the nation's top literary incubator, a glamorous hotbed that regularly churned out brilliant new writers. And that perfectly aligned with my dreams, having already discovered my budding talent as a writer.

Most important to me was that my idol, Demetrio Luminoso, the century's unchallenged maestro in all things literary, taught there.

During my first semester I couldn't get into any of his classes but did start writing an opinion column in the student newspaper. Behind a shield of anonymity my columns gained some notoriety on campus as I teased and challenged readers with my offbeat, hopefully witty observations. I stirred controversy with outrageous humor as I pronounced on politics and culture. I often heard ideas originated in my articles being repeated in dorm room debates and over mugs of beer at the student tavern.

I was a mini campus celebrity, but whenever I was tempted to reveal my identity and bask in acclaim, I realized my harsher columns had already made that a bad idea.

So I stayed anonymous and uninhibited and transgressed the bounds of good taste whenever that made for good reading.

Professor Demetrio Luminoso was an historic talent, having twice won the Nobel Prize for Literature by his early thirties. He then parked himself in New Hampshire as Olde Albion's writer-in-residence, coaching a new generation of writers. Some commented he was taking things down a few notches in the face of the unrelenting pressure of trying to surpass his own achievements.

The family name *Luminoso* was remarkably appropriate for he did shine like a star, turning out a lifelong torrent of masterpieces in fiction and poetry that piled up awards and honors. His adoring students dubbed him *Professor Demy* and he was a familiar sight on campus, often seen walking backwards while lecturing and leading worshipful students across the cozy, tree-lined quad, his arms flailing and voice booming.

Demy's classes were the hottest ticket on campus. Other than a few graduate seminars, he taught only two undergrad courses: *A Luminous Survey of Modern Fiction* and *Creative Writing with Demy*. Both were always jammed and wait-listed. Rumor had it some kids used family (large donor) connections to jump the queue. But that of course wouldn't help me, the coal miner's son, as Ernie put it.

Second semester of freshman year, I learned just a half-hour after registration had opened both Demy's classes were again already hopelessly oversubscribed, five times over.

I was beyond frustrated. The main reason I'd chosen Olde Albion was to study under this modern master but for the second straight semester, I couldn't get in. I had to do something. So with nothing to lose I decided to ambush him at his office.

The late afternoon was already deep-winter dark and his door was closed. Office hours were already over but a yellow light glowed through the green frosted glass so I knocked.

The heavy wooden door swung open to reveal that same famous face that appeared on covers of national news magazines and network TV. I felt a visceral buzz and (totally star-struck) laughed, unable to contain my reaction. He surprised me by laughing right back and waving me into his ramshackle office.

Books were stacked everywhere in dusty piles amid heaps of yellowing newspapers and journals.

Youthful middle-aged and vaguely Mediterranean in appearance, Demy was handsome with flowing shoulder-length locks of wavy, swept-back silver hair and a salt-and-pepper beard trimmed to a neat Van Dyke. Muscular though not tall, he gave off the aura of a giant with a force field that dominated any room.

His smile was spectacular and voice powerful and bassy: mellifluous and rounded by decades of pipe-smoking. He wore custom jeans, a silver gray tweed blazer and black European-style glasses.

He seemed warm and friendly. I immediately liked him, in person.

So I pleaded my case and would've pulled out my hair and rent my shirt, if I thought that might help. He was a good listener, smiling and making consoling sounds *("Mmm, yes, I see . . .")*.

But I soon learned that had been a well-rehearsed performance.

"Anyway I'm sorry but you see, my hands are tied. Perhaps you'll be luckier next semester." The professor shrugged and smiled sympathetically.

"But I—"

"Sorry, that's final."

Rather than surrender just like that, I took a last desperate shot and dropped a bomb. "Perhaps I shouldn't mention this but—"

"Yes, probably not. So please don't. Okay?" He probably anticipated I was going to recite family connections, like privileged past supplicants.

He turned away, placed his pipe in an ashtray and began sorting papers to signal our discussion was over. Aromatic threads of sweet cherry blended smoke curled from his pipe, twisting up past his shoulder and gathering at the ceiling.

"Professor," I drew in a deep breath to calm myself, "would it matter if I told you I am actually the campus writer, *Lucian*?"

He didn't turn around but tilted his head a moment. "You mean the journalist?"

"Yes." I grinned. Trump card having been played, I awaited his inevitable praise.

"Hmm." He grunted. "Hope you don't mean that snotty fellow in the student paper. Horrible, such a malicious wit. Seems such a boor. Surely not him, eh?"

My mouth went dry.

"That Lucian is highly skilled, no doubt. But unencumbered by style or good taste and wasting a lot of his talent, I fear."

That was enough already. "Well you, sir, may not be a fan but many *do* enjoy my work—"

He chuckled and smiled. "Ah, Mr. Bonaventure! I see you're not very used to criticism, eh?" He glanced at my rejected course application. "Your name is Dashiell, correct?

"Dash is fine, Professor."

"Good. And why don't you just call me *Demy*, as well." He nodded. "Dash, believe me it's a danger to grow addicted to praise. I know." I said nothing and just listened, thrilled by his sudden intimacy and the familiar tone. "Good thing you've remained hidden behind that *nom de plume*. Apt choice, too. *Lucianos* was a very talented Greek satirist during the classical era."

First time anyone had *ever* commented on my pen name's genesis. I thought I had been clever and obscure.

"Nasty piece of work, though. Lucianos particularly loved to lampoon what you kids these days call *phonies*."

Demy suddenly bounded around the desk and placed a meaty hand on my shoulder. My heart raced. This was not a man, this was a writing deity, so his next words stunned me.

"All right, then. It is done. You are accepted into both my classes, this semester."

"Just like that?"

"Exactly like that."

He peered deep into my eyes, as if he could explore my very soul and know all my secrets or understand my every fear.

"You have vast talent, Dash, anyone can see that. Remarkable in some ways. So, if things go well, perhaps you can work with me the next few years. We'll file down the rough edges, remove the weaknesses and polish your skills. Define a path forward."

I absolutely floated back to my dorm. Did all that really just happen? Had literature's golden god actually tantalized me with the concept I could become his protégé?

My mind overflowed with daydreams. I savored a future as an internationally successful novelist, penning award-winning bestsellers that were naturally all made into blockbuster films. Fame, glamour and money . . . and of course there would be women. Lots of 'em.

I aced his undergrad courses and then, by special exemption, joined his graduate seminars. Thanks to Demy's personal intervention doors swung open and I also was able to enroll in other grad seminars conducted by academic *glitterati*.

My Lucian column, once a source of such pride, fell by the wayside as I was propelled toward my calling in *literature*, not in grinding out sarcastic pap.

Demy became my trusted patron and wherever he led, I followed. My prospects looked quite brilliant and yes, I began taking them (and myself) rather seriously. Drawing ever-closer to my mentor, our relationship became increasingly visible on campus.

When Demy named me his student assistant, while I was still a mere undergrad, my academic adoption became official and the university recognized my special stature, as well. I was accorded a tuition half-waiver along with a small stipend to help offset room and board. Compensated positions like that were normally reserved for grad students, so this was a unique honor.

My status rose in the university community and by proximity to a superstar I began to twinkle too, like a Demy Jr.

By junior year, my life trajectory appeared fixed and glorious. Sky-high with optimism, I was blinded to any other possibility.

"Mr. Bonaventure?" The voice on the phone was curt and officious. "This is the Moderate Bluffs PD"

Huh?

Late night phone calls, especially from the police, usually weren't good news.

"Sir, sorry to advise but your mother was involved in an automobile accident."

"What?" My heart began to pound. "A collision? Is she okay?"

"No other car was involved, sir. She just lost control on an icy road and . . . well, we're informing next of kin."

Next of kin?

I knew what that meant and didn't want to hear any more. An overwhelming but familiar feeling began to suffocate me, the same way I felt the night I learned about Dad. Oh, Mom! I loved her so much: the closest, most loving person in my entire existence. I missed her already and knew, if there was a heaven, she was already there. A saint.

I teared up and my grief sobbed out. My entire body shook. I'd just turned twenty and realized I had no real family anymore. I was all alone in the world, like an orphan. After the initial shock, I mustered some control and vowed to not allow myself to wallow.

It was time to grow up and be an adult. Incredibly, that seemed to help at least a little. And I already understood from experience that with each passing day, things would get a little better.

I flew back to Illinois for the funeral and it soon became clear my relationship with my stepfather had also died on that country road. In the two years since Ernest Butcher had married Mom, we'd never really warmed to each other. But now, his demeanor was even frostier than the January winds blustering across the prairie. Acting formal and standoffish, he rebuffed all overtures at familial empathy.

I understood.

Okay, Ernie, fine—go ahead and be an asshole.

At first it really disturbed me that the police, not my stepfather, had informed me of Mom's passing. After all, Ernie was family, at least officially. And though we'd never built much rapport, now more than ever we needed to remain civil, what with the funeral and other matters (legal and financial) to settle.

I reconstructed the horror of that winter night from the police and coroner's reports.

The story in the *Moderate Bluffs Bugle* was colorful and upsetting, with a large photo of the car overturned in a corn field. Mom had just dropped off a home-cooked meal at Ernie's office. He was working late, probably counter-suing some poor farmer who'd knocked over a wheat silo when his Stallion tractor brakes failed or something.

Mom hit a patch of black ice and her compact car skidded out of control—no seat belts on that older model. Metal scraped against pavement and sparks flew as the vehicle tumbled across the blacktop, flipping and bouncing off the elevated county road and then down into a frozen cornfield. Her body had been violently thrown about and, according to the coroner, she was probably dead before the vehicle settled into a snowbank.

We never interacted very well so it was no surprise that while sharing a limo in the funeral procession, after sharing warm memories of Mom, Ernie and I soon ran out of things to say.

Finally, I broke the uncomfortable silence by gently raising a question about family assets. I was flying back to school the next morning and thought this was the adult thing to do, to take advantage of our proximity to handle some necessary financial details. Estate talk probably wasn't such a smooth move (bad timing, at best) but I felt it had to be done, and fairly soon. *Big* mistake.

"Assets?" Ernie huffed and pounded the seat upholstery. "Listen, kid, I just buried my wife. Your mother. And at a time like this all you can think about is money?"

"Oh no, no. It's not like that at all . . ."

He just stared out the window and scowled in silence. Fields of dried severed corn stalks flashed by, sticking up from snow-covered ground.

Ernie exhaled heavily and fogged the window. He finally spoke. "I'm just shocked. Shocked and disappointed in you, Dashiell. Besides I thought you were now already fixed up money-wise at that fancy-pants school of yours. Some kind of scholarship."

"It's a work stipend, yes, but what about later? Grad school or maybe some gap year travel or . . ."

"You kids! I don't believe you." He shook his head in disgust and then spoke in a tone syrup-thick with derision. "Why not just one step at a time, pal? Like first maybe finish your undergrad degree? Then go get a job and save a little money. And maybe only *after all that,* start thinking about grad school or foolish travel ideas, like your permanent vacation."

All that sudden, unexpected disdain seemed to come from nowhere and shocked me. Granted, maybe we didn't get along well before but, jeez, what was that all about.

My heart raced and for a while I just stopped listening or processing his words. *Another* mistake. Because when I finally came around, I realized he seemed to be wrapping up an argument.

". . . and so, besides, what makes you think there's any money remaining for you, anyway?"

Huh? Well, for one thing, there were Mom's clear assurances, Ernie. I thought that but stayed quiet.

I figured Dad's estate must've been pretty fat. Life insurance, savings and so forth. Surely Mom and this clown hadn't already spent all of it. But things were running too hot for further productive conversation. "Sorry, Ernie, never mind. I don't know."

No hurry, I decided. Give this some time for the raw feelings to scar over and I could raise the issue at a later date, closer to when I might actually need some cash. We could have a calmer discussion then.

The next day I flew back East to school, blind to what was already transpiring.

That shyster (earnest butcher, indeed) moved quickly to lock down his full possession of the Bonaventure family estate and my anticipated inheritance simply vanished, snuffed out right along with my mother's life. I couldn't sleep the entire night after receiving the law firm's letter that essentially announced I was a pauper.

Nothing was left for me in Illinois beyond the paltry sum in my childhood savings at the S&L, from my paper route. So I severed all contact and made a total break with my past.

I stopped traveling back to Illinois and the beautiful campus at Olde Albion became my only home.

Still envisioning my future as a world-famous writer and a comfortable, part-time academic like Demy, I applied to grad schools during senior year, supported by a sparkling undergraduate record and insistent recommendation letters from Demy and his trailing cadre of august professors.

Olde Albion offered the most generous package: full tuition, room, board and a stipend so generous, I'd have trouble spending it all. And it would be all mine, while I fulfilled my dream (something I would have done for free), serving as top graduate assistant to (whom else?) Professor Demetrio Luminoso.

I was a minor satellite fully swept up into his orbit. Living in Demy's incandescent literary world, I inhaled deeply of the fumes given off by his celebrity and became addicted to the media interviews, cocktail receptions and presentations to academia. Envious peers tossed occasional barbs at me which I learned to snag from midair. Rather than trouble me, they only confirmed my rising stature.

Demy lectured undergrads on Mondays and then turned them over to me for study group sessions.

"But how will Prof. Demy determine our grades?" The bespectacled freshman in a patched khaki military jacket was so cute in all his concern. "Is he going to mark on a curve?"

I shook my head. "Marks are just a triviality, man! Don't worry. Focus, instead, on writing well. Find your own authentic voice."

"Far out, man," replied the youth. But I knew he'd ignore me—after all, that was me just a few years ago.

The rest of my job was whatever Demy said. I was essentially his personal academic slave.

My girlfriend at the time didn't care much for that. "What can you possibly be doing for him, night after night, that takes until 3 a.m.?" Her eyes were darting, a sure sign of fury.

"Everything, babe." I didn't even try to tell her all of it. She'd never believe me. "I draft correspondence and write first drafts of speeches. I grade papers." So those naive freshman cherubs *didn't* need to worry after all, about Demy's grading standards. "I prepare notes for upcoming appearances. I help plan trips."

She grumbled. "You also do his grocery shopping, run clothes to the laundry?"

"No, but some other grad assistants do." I didn't say it but if so asked, I would have happily complied.

She shrugged. "Sounds awful."

"No, actually it's intoxicating to be so close to genius. I love it. But my most critical duty is *research*."

She laughed. "What's to research? He writes *fiction*. He makes things up. How can facts matter?"

If she only knew. Demy might casually say, "Dash, be a good fellow and go look up X for me." And his simple request would lead me to spend days crawling through the stacks at the university library, rooting around for factual meat to support some vague notion he had for a short story.

Once he asked: "What were the norms, in the early 1900s that controlled interracial sex? Get me facts, statistics, and stories. The words *and* the music." I'd search days for data about bonking between the races, thumbing through dusty books and running down leads from bibliographies, poring through old journals preserved on microfiche machines, scribbling notes on index cards.

But I was thrilled to be involved in any way and supporting his transcendent brilliance. Most of all, Demy relied upon me to steer him clear of literary ground already well-trodden. The footprints of other writers nearly always extinguished his interest. One time in a hundred, he might go ahead and write on a well-covered theme or topic but, when he did, he would so completely overshadow his antecedents as to make them disappear.

As his name proclaimed, he was a luminary, an artist with unmatched creative ability. So for him, the harshest possible criticism was too unoriginal or derivative in any way. "Never forget," he told me the very first day, a hand laid upon my shoulder, "the only unforgivable sin in our world is the theft of ideas. Plagiarism." He actually shuddered. For Demy, there was nothing lower and it was my job to protect him.

CHAPTER EIGHT
Fateful Dinner

One Saturday evening Demy hosted an intimate, laughter-filled, wine-soaked dinner. The gathering felt like family as Demy and his wife, Evangelina hosted me and my new girlfriend, Marielle. We'd only been dating a few weeks and I'd hoped dinner at home with an international literary superstar might impress her.

When the door to the Luminoso cottage swung open, a moist, warm and meaty aroma came flooding out and wrapped us in its succulent embrace. It pulled us inside, helpless to resist. A fire was roaring and flickered off the whitewashed walls crisscrossed by heavy brown beams.

And everywhere I looked were Evangelina's own, extraordinary paintings. I didn't know art, at all, but found the images bold and powerful. Neither simple nor overly complex, they hypnotized me with splashes of orange, red and yellow and blobs of green.

Evangelina's family hailed from sunny Aegean shores, her bloodlines mixed, both Italian and Greek.

"She worked days to concoct this Mediterranean feast," Demy said as he gave her a peck. "And here's her specialty." He hoisted a cooking platter and carried the slow-cooked shank to the table, still sizzling and glistening with crackle and drippings. The meat, already brined and well-spiced for a leisurely time, was instant transport to carnivore nirvana. Juicy, succulent helpings fell from the bone at the merest touch of a fork.

Platters of flavorful side dishes overflowed the table, vegetables swimming in savory sauces and baskets of home-baked bread. We washed it all down with goblets of a robust red wine. "This vintage hails from a petite Italian vineyard," Demy said, "operated by a former grade school mate, back in the village where my family still resides."

And lastly we nibbled on flaky, honey-drenched pastries and sipped a potent dessert cordial.

Leaning back, sated and euphoric, we opined on current events and university gossip. But I knew what would come next. At such meals, the chatter inevitably drifted toward Demy's forte and the master would hold court, an indescribable treat as modern literature's living deity shared with us his world of controversies and flaming issues, stars and cads.

His opening gambit was always a tease. "Now, I probably shouldn't say this . . ." We listeners would smile and encourage him by our silence.

"Awards, especially literary awards, are such foolish trifles," he started as he refilled his glass. "Unnecessary to validate one's art. Yet, how so many thirst (and suffer!) for such acclaim. Disgraceful."

Such disdain was easy for him *now*, I mused: he already possessed a mountain of awards. Every high school student knew the Luminoso story. And upon winning a second Nobel Prize by his early thirties he was proclaimed the artistic miracle of the century. His work suggested the intricacy of Joyce, the power of Hemingway, the multi-layered beauty of Marquez. His language was pristine and moving. Compared to all other living authors, he was playing 3-D chess to their tic-tac-toe.

So the world of letters held its collective breath and awaited his next act. How would he further elevate the universe of fiction and poetry, surpassing the soaring heights he'd already attained? Unfair though it was, anything less would be failure.

Fifteen years had passed since that second Nobel so the whispers had begun among the literary elect. Why the delay? Had the debonair young maestro lost it, failing to turn a third miracle? Articles in prissy journals had begun to tease with titles like *Luminosity Lost*. Unflattering and irreverent analogies were drawn between Luminoso and Christ, both having finished their life's work by age thirty-three.

"Well, no more awards for me. I don't care." Demy topped up our wine glasses. "Who needs it?"

"Meaningless trinkets." I sympathized.

"But I am resolute. Staying patient in my hunt for that single topic worthy of being the culminating work of my career."

Patience was one thing, sure, but fifteen years? I was empathetic but also frustrated by my mentor's seeming paralysis.

"My next work must be world-changing in its power and impact. A story that will create art of the highest order. Therefore, the topic must be an impeccable exploration of humankind's very essence. Existence itself. Why do we love and, just as important, why do we stop loving? Why does Evil exist? Or Death?" He waved his hands as if stirring the air to clear away a foul odor. "All those foolish awards will of course parade right in, the inevitable and natural consequence of such a work, even were I to refuse them in advance."

He usually kept it quite hidden but that night, it was plain to see from up close that artistic dormancy was weighing on his spirits.

Then something miraculous occurred.

Blame it on the evening's bewitching atmosphere—the wine, the dizzying load of meat in our guts, the surfeit of warmth in the room from the fire and still-heated oven, the safety of our familial embrace — whatever. But that night, Demy swung a door wide open and set inner secrets free to run. It was like a troublesome little devil danced about the room, taunting the frustrated genius.

In essence, Demy opened his very soul to us as an after-dinner discussion topic and laid his existential problem right there in front of us. His humanity fully exposed, the superstar artist had placed himself entirely at our mercy, in the hands of those who loved him.

I had never before seen him quite like this.

Evangelina was strong. They had been lovers forever, since long before all his success, and she uncorked another bottle and took charge, steering the conversation while Demy sat back, slumped and silent.

"So, dear," she said, "a story that is 'important' enough? Life, death, love and evil in the world?" She shrugged. "Doesn't sound much like you, darling, almost religious—"

"Religion?" His voice boomed and he thumped the table. "That would be a typical cop-out. The usual third-rate treatment." His sudden eruption of energy surprised me.

But Evangelina just smiled. "Those are tired old themes that have been tried many times before."

Demy raked his silver locks with a hand and grumbled. "But never done once, even half-well."

Evangelina nodded. "Your gravest danger would be getting lured into something trite."

It then astonished me that my girlfriend, Marielle, chose that moment to speak up. First time all evening. She'd been smiling and quiet for hours, intimidated by Demy's stature.

"Those situations and emotions, love and what-not, may be totally common," she said, "but what about when they are taking place under the *most inhuman* of circumstances? The resulting story might be quite amazing. Certainly not trite."

"What?" Demy made a sour face and wrinkled his brow.

Marielle sounded almost apologetic. "Love and betrayal are at the center of so many stories we see every day. But what about love and betrayal within captivity, inside a prison or something?" Her words hung in the air and she looked down, shy.

Demy looked befuddled and just stared at his plate.

"Yeesh," I muttered. "Mari, who in their right mind would want to read depressing drivel like that? No offense, but who gives a damn about love between prisoners? By definition they are unsympathetic. They did something bad and went to jail to be punished. So, of course they are unhappy! In jail they are *supposed* to be. Nobody cares."

"Yes, but . . ." Mari's eyes flared. I'd probably hear a lot about this, later.

Demy rocked his head back, squinting as if emerging from deeper thought but still pondering. He looked off, eyes unfocused, and his face began to subtly come alive. "Why yes, of course . . ." His voice was a whisper.

What was he thinking?

"Prisoners but *not* criminals," he mumbled. "Hmm."

I hated to discourage him but that idea sucked. "Whoa, Demy, hope you're not going for that. Lovers in jail but somehow not criminals? What, both framed? Sounds like pretty lame stuff."

But Evangelina recognized something in his odd expression. "What is it, Dem?" She stroked his hand.

As the maestro stared at us around the table and a beatific grin began to spread across his face. Charismatic heat flowed from him and spread over us like lava. When his energy and aura peaked like this, the man looked fifteen years younger, once again the marvel who had scaled literature's highest summits.

"Darling, please. Share with us! What've you got?" Evangelina held his hand, tight.

His eyes shone bright with inspiration, absent all fear. "Thank God," he whispered, "the wait is finally over." That was all.

We drained the last of two bottles of fortified cordials and honeyed pastries, trying all the while to reengage Demy on his topic but the barriers had already gone up. He was no longer soliciting input. He didn't shush us or silence our ideas, but he had obviously exited the sharing mode.

Internal artistic construction for a masterpiece for the ages was already underway and he alone would struggle to form his ideas about plot and themes, characters and conflict.

Overjoyed and energized, Demy had finally begun to work on his life's most significant creation. His fifteen-year stretch of creative hibernation was over.

Just a few days after the dinner party, an avalanche of work started to spill down upon me.

"Dash," Demy said in the most casual tone, "can you do me a favor?" I smiled. "I'd like you to look up background about internment camps down through history. Be comprehensive. I need everything from layouts and construction to capacities and administration. How they were run? Practices and procedures that governed daily life in those hellish places. I want everything you can find. No information is too insignificant."

Huh? "Sure, boss, no worries." I was scribbling fast. "Anything else?"

"Well, yes, actually. Also start creating a thorough, detailed overview for me to capsulize all the political histories you can find—also economic and philosophical treatises, I suppose—in relation to the rise of the Nazi death camps—"

Nazis? "Sorry? Dem—"

"—and get me precise maps of camp locations, detailed architectural plans for the camps themselves. Also we'll need histories of individuals, their families, real people who were sent to the extermination camps. As much detail as possible, the richer the better, whatever you can track down."

My hand was cramping, I was writing so fast.

"Okay. Camps, plans, locations, stories of real people and their families—"

"And don't overlook the camp *employees*." Demy gently poked my sternum in emphasis. "That's critical. What about administrators and especially guards? They were human beings but who were they and how did anyone wind up with such horrific jobs? I need stories about real people."

This abrupt information demand fell upon me and felt about as broad as the galaxy. And that was just the beginning.

Over the next two years it never ended. My life was consumed in assisting Demy's creative genius. I still taught a few classes but spent most free waking moments tracking down additional grisly information as the star author charged ahead toward his epic new novel, confident and focused, knowing failure was impossible.

I captured everything and condensed the results into pithy summaries and maintaining a master bibliography. This exercise soon outgrew what U.S. libraries could provide so the two of us began traveling to Austria and West Germany, to seek primary data: visiting former campsites, tracking down survivors and interviewing relatives. These trips profoundly affected us both and each time we returned from Europe, an immense sadness and a haunted look settled over Demy that took weeks to dissipate.

"Dash, as a Nobel double-laureate," he said one day with an odd smile, "there are certain strings I can pull. And it was time, so I did." He dropped a pair of air tickets on the desk. "We are going behind the Iron Curtain, to see camp sites in Poland, East Germany and Hungary."

But with suspicious government hosts always hovering close by, those visits were less productive. Once back we would pay grad students at the European Languages Department by-the-page to translate the German and Polish source documents we'd acquired.

At the same time as he digested the historical research, Demy was formulating his storyline and building momentum behind character arcs and plot lines.

Finally came the point when he felt compelled to start, knowing that for a *magnum opus* like his, on a topic as overwhelming as this, the research might never end.

"There will *always* be more, Dash." But he could no longer justify stalling. He started to write.

The story burst free from some hidden place, deep within his genius. Thoughts and ideas began to pour out as he hammered away, six or more hours each day in his office at his clunky vanilla-colored Royal typewriter. A beautiful and romantic, but highly disturbing story streamed out in a fast-growing pile of double-spaced onionskin. Twelve months later, while my never-ending research continued apace, he finished his first draft. Pulled along by the work's own momentum, he then upped his daily schedule to twelve hours of editing and rewriting.

This creation of great art looked, to me, like a brutal master. None of it seemed easy at all. The process owned the author and inhabited his very soul, driving him ever onward. Demy lost weight, didn't sleep well and fell into ill health. Yet, he said he'd never felt happier or more complete. He completely rewrote the work, again and then again, three more complete draft revisions.

He would pass sections to me for feedback as his beta reader, relying upon me to spot shortcomings, inconsistencies or conflicts with historical fact. "Is that character believable?" he might ask, or "What about that plot twist? As a reader, did you believe it? Be brutal, Dash."

I came to know the novel as intimately as the author and was proud of my minor role in its creation.

Finally, one day in the early spring, Demy announced the novel was complete. He continued to tinker and polish the manuscript for a few weeks, but that was just nervous energy. His masterpiece was ready.

After lunch we met back at Demy's office. The manuscript as a foot-high stack sat in the middle of his desk. Demy rummaged in his desk drawer and found a crumpled piece of paper. Smiling, he dialed the number written in pencil.

He covered the mouthpiece and chuckled. "My literary agent, Dash. It's been years. Watch this."

He waited a moment for the connection.

"Yes, yes. Mr. Blackthorn, please. Oh indeed he'll want to speak to me. Just tell him . . . it's *Luminoso*." He paused and scowled. "No, that's Luminoso. Lu-mi-NO-so!" His face darkened. "He what? Oh, no, I didn't . . . I . . . Sorry. Never mind, then."

He hung up, his face flushed. First time trying to contact his agent in more than a decade of professional hibernation, and he learns the man died several years earlier.

"Wow, Demy, what a bummer. Sorry." I patted his shoulder.

He shrugged. "Eh. It's okay. Barely knew the man, actually."

"So now what?" I knew nothing about publishing and just assumed after one wrote a scintillating novel, it somehow just got itself printed and millions of books were sold.

"Here's my Amex card, Dash. Book us two flights tomorrow to LaGuardia."

"From Manchester?"

"I don't know!" he snapped, laughing. "That's your job, no?"

We landed just after noon and jumped into a dirty taxi at the New York airport. A smudged and chipped Plexiglas divider protected the driver from us. Demy took a business envelope from his pocket and loudly read off the return address, through the glass. The driver nodded and drove off.

"Fifteen years, Dash," Demy said, tapping the envelope from his publishing house, "and they still send me checks twice a year. Fat ones, too." We glided through New York's glass canyons and arrived at a building on Lexington where his publisher occupied three floors. Demy scanned the reception directory but recognized no names. Pensive, he stopped and lit his pipe, took a few puffs and marched up to the front desk.

"I," he intoned, "am *Luminoso*."

The red-haired receptionist gave him a cock-eyed look. "Well, whatever, buster. But first you're going to have to put that thing out. And then go sit down over there and wait." She waved toward a bank of chairs already populated by literary peasantry.

Surprising even myself, I exploded. "Good lord, madam, you can't treat him like that! Don't you people even recognize the world's greatest living writer?" I slammed a hand atop her desk. Heads perked up all around, including building security in the corner. "Why, Demetrio Luminoso *made* this crappy publishing house! He—he—"

She sat upright and pushed her chair backward, away from Dash, the crazy man.

Demy raised his palms and smiled at her, then grabbed my elbow. He quietly shuffled me over to the reception display case, the publishing house's greatest hits. "There," he said with a chuckle and pointed at copies of his two Nobel Prize winners. "Miss, see these, here? Those are mine. Do you know them?" If she'd ever been to high school, she must have.

He pulled one out, turned it over and showed her the back cover photo of a much-younger version of himself. Her eyes went wide and she picked up her phone.

Within minutes, waves of obsequious staff swarmed him—taking his coat, bringing him coffee, inquiring as to his every need while guiding us into the inner sanctum. Once executives had learned Demetrio Luminoso *himself* had just pitched up, with a new novel and without agent representation, they fell all over themselves courting their reclusive star, whom most had never previously met.

"It felt like they had been waiting for me," Demy commented. In fact they had, for fifteen years.

Responding to his absolute star power and the marketability of this historically important new work, the manuscript was rushed into print. The publisher waived all usual constraints and bumped other schedules aside, authorizing an *anything-goes* budget.

His editor urged him at an early meeting, "Mr. Luminoso, please immediately secure representation."

"Agents are like prostate exams, Dash," Demy told him with a sigh, winking at me. "Unpleasant but probably necessary."

"Yes, but considering all the legality to come," his editor continued, "with movie rights, international sales, licensing possibilities, speaking engagements and more, you'll need one who is a very strong lawyer. You don't want to handle any of that yourself."

Demy agreed.

Pre-sale orders soared to unimaginable heights.

On launch day, front page excerpts appeared in the world's most prestigious newspapers: *The New York Times, The Guardian, The Sydney Morning Herald, Le Monde* and others. Opinion-leading periodicals like *The Economist* and *Der Spiegel* ran special sections with full-chapter previews. London's *Financial Times* judged it "the most important work of fiction (in both artistic and commercial terms) in the last hundred years." "A wonderment," proclaimed the BBC. *The Times of India* cheered: "Move over, Hemingway, Fitzgerald and Joyce. This is the *Luminoso Era*." Bidding for serialization rights was astronomical. Film rights would, no doubt, break the bank.

A third Nobel already a certainty.

Demy told journalists, "I just feel blessed to be able to lay this, my gift, at the feet of humanity."

His thousand-page tome rocketed up international bestseller lists right from day one and stayed on top. It was proclaimed a book for the ages, the crowning achievement of a scintillating career, the quintessential Luminoso literary miracle.

Impossibly, my mentor's stratospheric success eclipsed his own previous achievement. He had vanquished his fiercest competitor: himself! My spirits elevated, also, knowing my role as midwife in this literary birth would not go unnoticed.

Universal praise proclaimed the novel vital while artistically sumptuous, exploring grave human issues in a story laced with darkness, romance and redemption, all spun in the glory and elegance of Demy's signature writing style. The work was transcendent and seemed almost an impossibility. It was beautiful and eternal, as important as humankind itself.

    This master, at the height of his powers, evoked themes of Life, Death, Morality, Love, Evil and Redemption, in a story played out by flawed and tragic characters, set within the living hell of a WWII concentration camp. Those fearing a bleak and ponderous work (a 'serious' story, heavy with morbidity and sadness) were happily disappointed. Evil incarnate was certainly on display, in all its horror, but the triumph of love and life was the book's uplifting message, transporting readers into pure bliss.

    Demy took a sabbatical and I joined him on his yearlong global book tour, gliding through a universe of celebrity and privilege. There were cocktail receptions at the White House, visits to the Vatican and trips to European capitals. Artsy, well-moneyed host organizations sent private jets to fetch us. Cologne and Tel Aviv, in particular, couldn't get enough of us. He delivered speeches before academia and dined with presidents. Even China, then transitioning from Mao to Deng Xiaoping, wanted to host Demy.

    He received honors from the Queen at Buckingham. "You write like the best of *us*," she complimented. "There must be a British branch on the Luminoso family tree."

    "No, Your Majesty, at least it's never been admitted." He winked.

    We ran from dawn to dusk on pure adrenaline. My mentor's handsome face constantly appeared on television and magazine covers. No longer just a literary rock star, he had transformed himself into The Beatles *plus* Elvis and Sinatra, all at once. As the living legend of the arts, he commanded extraordinary appearance fees.

    In short, it was all stunning and quite wonderful.

    Naturally, too good to last.

A tiny voice (one as inconsequential as a mosquito's whine) launched a global controversy the media would soon dub *Il Plagioso Luminoso:* Luminoso's Plagiarism.

In those very first days, when the first whispers arose, before it could blow up into a worldwide scandal, Demy dispatched me to West Germany on an emergency fact-finding mission.

Okay, research assistant, go research this mess.

I caught a midnight flight to Frankfurt and ran down most of the salient points in a few days. It was already clear that disaster was looming and would only get worse.

While waiting for my flight back to Logan Airport in Boston, I phoned Demy to brief him. My thought was to give him the highlights right away and full details later, in person, after he'd calmed down.

His voice crackled over a bad line. "I still don't understand, Dash. Who in hell is this Wolfgang Gerlach-Klein?" He sounded incredulous and victimized, pounded by the growing daily parade of news stories since I'd left, as the cataclysm was developing. "Never heard of him."

"That's because he's just a college student, Demy. And that's just his German pen name. Roughly translates as *"The Little Spear-Thrower."*

Demy grunted. "How fitting. So, a little spear has skewered me?"

"The college is fiercely protecting his identity and keeping him anonymous. Only one professor (not identified, either) even knows who he is."

It was utterly amazing that a mere student newspaper article had gone viral and stormed the global world of letters. But the revelations were *that* explosive and their target *that* world-famous.

In early coverage of the scandal, The *International Herald Tribune,* a beacon of global journalism, reminded readers how another recent controversy (that Beatle Paul was supposedly dead) had also been launched by a mere college essay. That silly hoax alleged the singer died and was replaced by a look-alike and the rumor flew on the wings of the musician's enormous popularity. Humankind can be insatiable when the theme is celebrity somehow gone wrong.

In Demy's case, everything was triggered by a freshman essay in a junior college literary magazine in a small German town. The flimsy publication had been run off on a copying machine and stapled into booklets, with a print run of less than 200, so the publication hardly existed. By all rights the essay should have never circulated beyond the author's own household, much less go planetary and threaten literature's reigning icon.

I gave it to Demy straight. "I read an English translation, Demy. Less than 1,000 words and replete with spelling and syntax errors. But it makes a strong case, nearly airtight, that you're a plagiarist."

"But Dash, that's utter nonsense!"

"Yes, and of course we both know that." It felt like being awake during a nightmare. "Yet what's so awful (and amazing) is how it does seem to prove beyond all doubt, that much of your recent story was stolen."

Demy's angry voice knifed through the static. "But we both know that's impossible!"

"Indeed. I was there beside you, all the way." I knew his innocence, beyond all doubt. "Still, the essay identifies too many eerie and undeniable similarities between your work and a slim German novella, published decades earlier in Switzerland. The only possible explanation is coincidence—enormous, incredible and repeating coincidence. Which seems an awfully weak explanation."

The 1950s book had long been out-of-print, so I'd not yet located a copy. But from all reports, it was a poorly-written little romantic novella, a tragedy that deservedly never gained traction with any readers. The unconvincing work was stillborn and hardly sold and quickly faded into insignificance. Forgotten by the world after a short print run.

The current worldwide controversy almost didn't even happen. The German college student, the *Little Spear-Thrower,* only stumbled upon a copy of the novella at a used book stall by sheer accident. Could have easily moved on to the next rack. But instead he picked it up and the back cover blurb struck him because it sounded so similar to Luminoso's latest masterwork, discussed just that week in his Modern Literature class. He recognized an easy killer essay topic and snapped up the book.

It still seemed impossible such a random event could lead to the demolition of Demy's literary career.

In contrast, Demy's work was classical in both its beauty and power, infinitely artful in its exploration of the very issues that define humanity. Yet it was undeniable the two stories were essentially one and the same, though executed by authors commanding vastly different talent levels. The same essential characters (though under different names) drove both stories. Remarkably similar plot-lines unfolded and the works both wrapped up with a similar multi-layered resolution.

Common themes, twists and character dynamics ran in parallel within both—the setting in a Nazi concentration camp; doomed lovers trapped in an impossible triangle; two prisoners and a self-loathing guard (the woman's secret childhood sweetheart); the extermination of a rival; a pregnancy and questions about the baby's identity; the soul-destroying choices forced upon the mother.

All there, in both works.

I flew home, anxious to brief Demy, but also struggling to process the bizarre situation's contradictions. One thing I knew for sure: Demetrio Luminoso was no plagiarist.

We met for breakfast at the student union. Over bagels and coffee I explained how, with just a little luck, the entire mess could have ended before it ever began.

"It's just a podunk school, Demy, and nobody ever reads its low-circulation annual literary journal. But this year, for some reason, the college ran a tiny ad in its school paper to tease a shocking new discovery about a world-famous author. That ad didn't even name you, Demy."

Demy just stared into my eyes, no emotion visible. "Anyway, a bored journalist in Cologne was skimming periodicals and spotted the item. He phoned the school on a whim and asked for a copy."

"Just my luck." Demy took off his black specs, sighed and rubbed his eyelids.

"Based on that, the newsman wrote just a brief piece but added a significant detail: your name."

Demy chuckled sadly and shook his head.

Everything caught fire once the weekly 'Leisure & Arts' section editor at the *International Herald Tribune* spotted *that* item. "She knew cultural dynamite when she saw it and assigned a writer to investigate, resulting in a splashy weekend feature. All the wire services picked it up and the story spread around the globe: *Nobel Laureate Luminoso—Literary Genius or Thief?"*

Demy's proud cult of literary snobs refused to let the allegation go unchallenged and by fighting back had amplified the debate, strengthening the heresy. Like a tiny snowball tossed by a child from high atop a mountain, it rolled steadily downhill and relentlessly gathered mass and speed, transforming into an icy monster that crushes everything at ground level.

The global media feasted, an echo chamber that repeated and reinforced the story. Proud news organizations asserted ownership by rewriting the scoop from fresh angles, always picking at the scab and keeping the wound raw and the scandal alive. This artistic morality play became the *only* story media deemed worthy of coverage.

As high as Demy had once soared, his stomach-churning plunge was even more astonishing. Having already amassed as many adversaries as admirers, a sea of hacks and failures also gleefully piled on.

My soul ached.

Demy all but disappeared and we did not speak for weeks. Finally one morning he summoned me to his campus office.

I sat down amid the familiar mess, piles of books and stacks of dusty periodicals lining the walls. Crumpled balls of yellow legal sheets lay on the floor beside the wastebasket. His desktop ashtray overflowed.

His personal condition looked no better. His eyes were baggy and blood-shot and his breath smelled of alcohol. He looked like the aftermath incarnate of prolonged heavy drinking combined with no sleep.

"Just one thing, Dash." His voice was low like distant thunder as he rubbed his face. "I need to hear only one thing."

"Anything, sir. You know that."

He snorted a sad laugh and sighed. "*Anything,* he says. Right. So then how on earth could *you* allow this to happen to me?"

Me? That didn't register. What did he say?

"How could you, of all people, have possibly missed it, Dash?"

Wait, he blaming *me* for this disaster? Either I couldn't understand or my mind stopped processing inputs. I had no words and could not speak so I just shrugged. A blinding insight hit me a moment later and I totally got it. He was, of course, correct.

"Dash, I absolutely relied upon you. *You* were the one spending untold hours in libraries (for two years!) checking facts and researching every angle from the historic to the psychological. *You* should have come across everything ever printed that related to my story's subject matter."

"I agree." Silence filled the room. Suddenly, as the owner of this catastrophe, I felt mystified and ambushed. "But I can't explain it. I don't understand it either, Demy, but I also wonder did *you* ever—"

He cut me off with a snarl. "What? Are you wondering if I actually *did* it? Plagiarize the story? Steal and claim it as my own?"

He glared at me and squeezed a fist. Then he unclasped it. "So go ahead if you like. Ask me."

This was getting ridiculous.

"Come on, Demy, stop it already. I don't have to ask. I *know* you."

I sensed that on top of my apparent failure to protect him, I'd now done irreparable damage the last remaining fragments of our relationship, just by alluding to that ultimate question about his integrity.

"Nevertheless, Dashiell—"

Dashiell? I hadn't heard that from him in years.

Oh boy.

"—just in case, perhaps deep down, you still do wonder? No, I never had even the slightest hint that inept novella existed. Don't read German anyway. However, I must admit that as coincidences go, this was a real stunner." He smiled a horrible grimace. "My hypothesis is that, given the hellish situation of a love triangle in an extermination camp, there is a single, 'superior' story that tends to force its way forward above all others. It naturally follows. Building upon that same foundation, a failed Swiss writer erected a pitiful structure. But from that same starting point, I imagined a monumental work—about people, the evil they do, the salvation offered by love. How death can even be superior to life poorly lived. And *that* story, Dash, is authentic and art and mine alone. Best creation of my entire life."

I gazed upon the broken genius. He appeared shrunken and soft, wobbling between anxiety and depression. The contrast with his past self (all confidence and charisma) was impossible to ignore. "But now because of this . . . because of *you*, Dashiell . . . I am damned."

CHAPTER NINE
Falling Star

It was indeed my job to protect Demy's work from factual errors and glaring contradictions, so there was no arguing otherwise: I was undeniably on the hook, with him, for this mess. I'd become our expert on all things about Germany and the Holocaust era and read every publication that even remotely touched upon the period.

In reality, it would have been virtually impossible for *anyone* to have discovered that tiny precursor novel. Deep down, maybe Demy knew that, too. And the German student finding it was only serendipity.

But none of that mattered now.

Our relationship unwound and we met less frequently, having little reason or desire to do so. Rumors were flying that Olde Albion planned to protect its reputation by severing Demy's position. He preempted that insult by resigning in fury.

Vacating that cozy university cottage, he and Evangelina loaded a rental trailer and moved to a small farmhouse in Upstate New York.

And with that our contact totally ceased.

I became dispirited and lost all interest in academia and literature, pulling back from social interaction. No more classes, campus walks, or snacks at the student union. I sat around in my studio apartment, unshowered and nibbling on spongy slices of cheap white bread. I binged on all-night TV and must have seen every Three Stooges or Andy Clyde comedy short ever filmed.

An envelope turned up one day in the mailbox. It was from Marielle, returning a slim bracelet and a few baubles I'd given her (as if I wanted any of those things back). She'd actually dumped me several months earlier while Demy and I were off globe-trotting, so this was just the finishing touch. It didn't hurt much then but now, alone and pathetic, it stung. *That's just perfect,* I thought. *Kick me while I'm down.*

Life as I knew it seemed over.

A little door at eye level slid open with a wooden squeak, like at a speakeasy, and revealed a gray-haired old man in semi-silhouette behind a cloth-covered grill.

"Go ahead, my son," said the raspy voice.

I don't really know how I wound up at the school chapel, but the familiar, sweet fragrance of incense and candle smoke seemed to calm me, Dash the former choir boy. I spotted the little red light glowing above the confessional box and after the drape was pulled open and a girl came out, I went in.

"I don't remember too much how this works, Father."

"Not a Catholic?"

"Long ago. Not anymore."

"Then you must really be lost," the priest chuckled.

But for me, his humor missed the mark.

"Lost? Yeah, I sure am." My voice cracked.

The old priest sighed. "Sorry, I see. Why don't we try and find you then? What brings you here, my son?"

"Dunno, Father, but can we just talk? Maybe get some advice?"

"Ah, just so happens those are my specialties. And for new customers, for a limited time only, there's a special discount rate." He wheezed out another quiet laugh. This guy really seemed corny; but I was starting to like him, sort of. "Just go ahead and tell me whatever's on your mind."

Out poured my story, wandering as far back as Hong Kong and The Slug. For good measure, I also made a few sad stops along the way for my parents' deaths and the stolen inheritance. But above all, it was the Demy debacle that had crushed me, a fall from too great a height.

"Father, it was like I dropped a fly ball in the bottom of the ninth in Game 7 of the World Series."

"Lucky that life isn't like baseball, son. As far as God is concerned—"

"Please don't," I interrupted, "tell me about God." I didn't much care for how He was treating me lately. Or my friends.

"Sorry, but in life, it doesn't always matter so much that things work out, just that you keep on trying. The important things are what's inside your soul: your motivation and beliefs, your intentions. That accident with your writer friend was truly awful but surely nobody's fault. Certainly, not yours." He sounded quite sure of this and much more convincing than when I told myself the same thing.

"But I've ruined my life, Father. Everything is over."

"Goodness." The priest coughed and his rosary beads rattled. "What are you, mid-to-late 20s?"

"Yeah."

"In that case, you've only ruined *a little bit* of your life. Maybe 20, 25 percent. No biggie." He chuckled again. "See?"

I started to have second thoughts after this comedy act. What kind of priest was this? "Listen, Father, I am totally alone in the world, broke, and have no future."

"I see." He sighed. "Your path is uncertain and all relationships are gone. You have no direction, no constraints. I can understand why this troubles you."

I perked up and raised my head, trying to see him better through the screen. "Please, father . . ."

"Like everyone, you're terrified to confront (maybe for the very first time) the very possibility of *total freedom*."

What?

Such total bullshit. The old fraud didn't know what he was talking about.

"Okay, thanks anyway," I said and jumped up. I tossed back the curtain and stormed out of the chapel.

I woke the next morning after a surprisingly sound night's sleep, got up and fried some bacon and eggs. I showered off weeks of accumulated crud.

I didn't know why, but things seemed different. My mind tumbled with crystalline realizations. After so much had gone wrong, it was against the odds that could continue. Maybe the future and its unlimited options would be okay.

I shook my head and picked up a nostalgic souvenir from my desktop, a small Chinese *chop* hand-carved from marble. Bought it at the Stanley Market in Hong Kong. It left me wistful, reminding me of better days. The stone block stamped my name in Chinese ideograms though, for all I knew, might have actually said something like *Shit-eating Foreign Devil Boy.* But no matter.

As I thumbed the cool smooth stone, memories began to flood back from my international past. All my losses of the past decade morphed and softened into a feeling more like a release, of burdens being lifted.

I understood. It was as clear and powerful as a blinding sunrise.

I was totally untethered and adrift, but in a good way. The old priest was right. I was young, alive and totally free. A global citizen with nothing to lose. A planetary vagabond. My future didn't even need to involve the USA.

A strange new ambition seized me—to stop torturing myself with unanswerable questions and instead flee this nightmare. The world was huge. I could return to my international roots and just do a Ken Kesey. Get on the road and have an adventure. With an entire planet beckoning, choosing a destination would be both exhilarating and daunting.

How did one decide such a thing?

I trotted over to the Olde Albion college library.

"Here you go," said the grandmotherly desk clerk. "I use these myself to plan out dream vacations. Only dreams, of course."

She began stacking up thick black binders on the counter. Each contained several years of *National Geographic* magazines. They were dusty and smelled old and vaguely foreign. I grabbed a binder at random and started to browse. It was from the 1950s and from it, I drank in a deluge of exotic photos and lost all track of time. My pupils dilated for hours over scenes of spectacular blue-green mountains, foamy seascapes, lush green jungles and stunning, tan ethnic breasts.

At first the abundance of options left me dazzled. But after wading through a decade of glossy periodicals, I booted Africa and South America from further consideration. Although fascinating and colorful and fizzing with amazing cultures, they also demanded ultra-rough travel. Not right for me, just now.

After I marched onward into 1960s magazines, Europe was next to drop from consideration. After all, if I was seeking change—jarring change—then why would I travel to see fat, prosperous white people eating sausages? For that I could just as easily head back to Illinois. Also, traveling through Europe would burn through my savings too fast.

That left Asia and the Middle East and by the time I finished another binder, Asia had won. Hands down. Why? Well, I was young and virile and those pictures of Asia's women settled everything.

"All done?" The grandma librarian smiled as she gathered up the binders. My fingerprints decorated their dusty covers. "So, where will it be?"

"Asia, ma'am. Anyplace but Hong Kong, I guess."

"You don't like Hong Kong?"

"I do, but that's rather a long story." As much as I had loved the place, it was time to tread new ground, not relive the past.

An electric thrill percolated through me. Footloose and young, I would leave adverse fortune behind and reinvent myself. This would be a journey to rediscover my soul and my global roots. There would be no demands, schedules or expectations as I just vagabonded across Asia for a few months . . . or would it become years? I planned to stay in constant motion and crisscross the map. My direction each day would be chosen by the prevailing winds and my morning moods.

But within that enormous Asian landmass, I needed a precise landing spot. I decided to let Fate decide, by going with the most economical transport option and preserving my nest egg.

"Ma'am, are there back issues of the *Sunday New York Times*?" I'd spent many leisurely Sunday mornings with coffee and a Danish and the Times and remembered the travel section, always replete with ads.

She sent me to a far corner, where I studied myriad black-bordered classifieds stacked in columns and blaring cheap travel options. There were come-ons for economical charters, courier flights and package tours. One in particular seized my eye, its line drawing depicting a propeller plane aloft and dragging a banner:

"International Travel! Absolutely Cheapest Airfares! Regular Departures to Bali - Singapore - Delhi - Hong Kong!"

Hmm: Bali?

Now *that* sounded cool. A quick return to the *National Geo* cinched it. A cover story about that magical Indonesian island exploded with impossible images, an orgy of culture and color. Bali offered frantic cremation ceremonies, gyrating local dances, idyllic sandy beaches, spooky monkey forests and phenomenal temples. One photo showed an iconic hilly island temple, poking up from the churning sea. A twin image, the same view shot at low tide, showed a dry path to the island magically appeared.

The charter flight seemed the right price for a cheap, magical wormhole. I would enter at an American airport and pop out on the other side of the world, in a mystical Asian fantasy-land.

I withdrew all my money from the student credit union (a whopping $4,000 squirreled away from the grad assistant stipend) and hauled everything I owned off to a dingy campus thrift shop. I doubted poor people really needed my crappy used stuff, but freeing myself from the weight of possessions was astonishing.

I felt giddy and light, almost able to levitate.

I was totally stoked and heading for Bali, gem of the Indonesian archipelago.

Book Three

Backpacker in Bali
Indonesia, 1979

CHAPTER TEN
Welcome to Bali

Cramped charter flight to Denpasar
Island of Bali, Indonesia - 1979

An overly-loud announcement boomed through the cabin and jarred me awake. "Time to buckle up, folks, and bring those seat backs upright. We'll be on the ground shortly in Denpasar." The long charter flight to Bali had been a stratospheric tuna can, but at least it *did* reach the promised destination with (as an added bonus) no *water landing.* I spent most of the flight awake and bouncing through Pacific turbulence while studying a dog-eared budget travel guide, squinting in low cabin light.

My expectations ran sky-high after reading all the raves about Bali, alleged as one of the planet's few genuine remaining miracles. Despite a constant assault by boorish tourists and their corrupting cash, the place somehow had fended off materialism and modernity. Bali promised a joyful swirl of cultural surprises as it broadly infused art, dance and sacred ritual into everyday life.

I cinched my seat belt tight and anticipated the glorious arrival so vividly described in my yellow paperback budget travel book: coming in low over the azure sea to thrilling vistas of a brilliant lime-green island, palm-dotted and ringed by sandy beaches, with deep blue and purple volcanoes brooding in the distance.

But when our plane dropped its flaps and began to descend, none of us vagabond gap-year travelers or hippies saw any of that. Just black. It was 2 a.m. when we bounced hard off the tarmac and sped down the runway, braked hard and skidded to a halt.

We queued up in the arrivals hall and the wait began. I noticed a vague sweet odor and asked the tired-looking young man next to me in line. "Hey, buddy, any idea what that smell is?"

"You vill become used to it," he said with a sharp German accent. "The aroma of Bali is palm oil and coconut plus at the airport a bonus: the scent of jet fuel." He sniffed impatiently and looked at his watch. "These Indonesians, so disorganized. They act like they have all night."

"Well they do, you know," laughed a slim youth standing nearby, tan with long blonde hair that cascaded in greasy twists tamed under a purple headband. Patches of the Brazilian flag decorated his backpack and from his wrists dangled string bracelets of feathers in brilliant red, yellow and green.

Amid all this instant intimacy, a freckled California girl then started to lecture me on the love-hate relationship between Indonesia and its super-economy visitors, all the penniless, unscrubbed youth arriving daily and ready to buy some flour sack clothes at the beach markets, score some local hash and dab on aromatic oils.

What was with all this sudden familiarity and friendliness? I guess none of us felt like strangers. All being in the same boat made it easy to talk, like freshman orientation week at college, when everyone undergoing the same situation was open to making friends. "See those guys?" she said, pointing at the uniformed *Imigrasi* agents who frowned as they studied the twisting lines of happy-go-lucky Westerners. "Happy to take our tourist dollars, but they'd rather have our parents in these lines, not their doped-up kids."

A young Frenchman joined in. He modeled a marvelous tasseled buckskin jacket, a la Roger Daltrey at Woodstock. "Now begins the challenge." *Zee chahlange.* "Subsist as efficiently as you can and extend your tourist visa as many times as possible. Quite *fantastique*, this game." *Zis game.*

"Until you run outta money?"

He smiled. "In this game money is the major challenge. But *c'est simple.* Perhaps teach English or sell *un peu de* hash." He shrugged. "But the authorities want you to spend it fast and just go home."

The feathered Brazilian, smelling of patchouli, moved closer. "You are American? Don't worry. You will soon see, my friend. This fraternity of backpackers all help each other with tips, warnings, and information." He explained that for budget travelers ad-libbing their way across Asia, each day presented a fresh adventure but many of the same faces. Shoestring tourists traveled the same routes, visited the same temples and beaches and frequented the same fleabag hotels and eateries. Notes were left on public bulletin boards about dangers or soft touches lurking on the road ahead. There were immigration offices notoriously hard on visa renewals; small hotels that pilfered from guest bags; and venues where the pickpocketing threat was high. New scams constantly arose to target tourists.

This smorgasbord of footloose international youth sat in small clusters on the hard concourse floor, chatting and entertaining themselves as they killed time waiting for a passport stamp and entry into Bali. Guitars were strummed and cards slapped onto the dusty linoleum floor. When an occasional unlucky visitor was pulled from line for a private interview, rumors flitted around the arrivals hall like small birds, spreading horror tales of *Imigrasi* extortion.

Another ninety minutes and I cleared passport control with no drama. At the baggage carousel a ruddy young Swiss in a blue bandanna was clearly still rattled and complaining to anyone who'd listen. When he reached the immigration desk, agents had ordered him to a back room. "They found an *unfortunate problem* with my travel documents," he said, stroking his red goatee. *"Your passport expires in five months so you cannot enter Indonesia."* The six-month cut-off seemed suspicious and flexible. "They sweated me for an hour before offering two choices: the dawn return flight to Zurich or purchase a *special exemption* for $125, cash. I paid."

A bone-thin girl sauntered over, dragging tattered bell-bottoms on the ground. "They got me too. *Insufficient travel funds*, surely a made-up law. I didn't have enough money to enter Indonesia. As if. '*Sorry, miss, you must take the dawn flight back to LA.*' I freaked out for two hours until we worked it out. I bought a special waiver for cash to enter Indonesia, with $300 *even less* money."

Every backpacker seemed to have different and ingenious bureaucratic scam stories to share, most concluding with the unwitnessed purchase of a special license in a backroom cash transaction. Passports were stamped on the sly, no receipts issued and (with business concluded) authorities reverted to their genuine, warm-hearted Indonesian nature. The traveler was often sent off under a deluge of cheery smiles and offers of assistance.

Hours after landing, I finally dragged my duffel bag in the dawn light to the airport curb. I had no clue what came next—where were those *National Geographic* beaches?

A Euro-hippie knelt there to cinch up her backpack so I asked for help. She smiled. "Kuta beach, love, it all happens there. Follow me. I'll show you. We just flag down a *bemo*." She waved and a large unmarked van pulled up. We climbed in.

All the seats had been torn out and replaced by two long benches. The van bounced up and down rutted asphalt roads and left the small capital, whizzing past green rice paddies that looked like steaming mirrors in the orange-streaked dawn. Riders jumped on or off every few hundred meters so we seemed to make only halting progress. But we eventually rattled into a tiny beach town that was little more than a collection of ramshackle wooden buildings lining a single intersection where one dirt road headed toward the beach and the other, inland, paralleled the shore.

After the long trans-Pacific journey from the other side of the planet, my body clock was upside-down and I was utterly fatigued. If a case of jet lag could be fatal, this might be it. I could hardly think straight or even focus. "Get off here," smiled the Euro-hippie girl, "or anywhere that feels lucky." *Ha.*

Despite the early hour Kuta was already buzzing with hordes of motorbikes and small transport trucks overflowing with passengers. As a beach resort for impoverished vagabonds, Kuta seemed to mainly offer disorganization and pandemonium as their prime attractions.

I climbed down into the chaos, feeling weak and dizzy. The noise, dirt and disorder were overwhelming. Clouds of dust boiled up all around me. Amid the blare and smoke, vendors constantly came up from behind like tag-teams pestering me to buy crappy little carvings, shiny rings or *batik* cloth. I was the town's freshest target, another stupid American.

My first impression of Kuta was clear, as in: *Oh shit, what have I done to myself?* I had managed to trap myself in some squalid foreign place with disease probably ready to strike, floating in on every breeze. Could this miserable place *really* be Asia's premiere beach capital for penniless wanderers, surfer dudes and lost hippies?

Despite my brain fog, I knew it didn't matter. I was already there. Kuta Beach, Bali, at the far terminus of the *Great Overland Hippie Trail* that linked Asia and Europe, would serve as my reintroduction to Asia. I'd already once mastered the easy role of pampered expat child in exquisite Hong Kong, so now it was time for the totally unstructured experience of Asia on the cheap.

CHAPTER ELEVEN
Paladin Kelley

My body clock was shattered and my mind melting. Jet lag had me feeling dizzier and more confused than ever before, destroying all ability to think. It was all I could muster just to retreat to a small roadside cafe with a dirt floor, where I hid at a plastic table with a pink tablecloth and bought some iced coffee.

It was amazingly delicious, sweet and strong. I chugged down this black magic and immediately ordered a second before belatedly wondering if the water might be tainted.

Wake up, Dash. Of course it is!

Could one get dysentery from coffee? If so, I'd soon find out. Deciding it was already too late, I settled back and enjoyed the sweet beverage.

Two tourists strolled into the cafe, arm in arm, almost exuding the air of proprietors as they nodded and smiled at the few customers. They waved at the cafe's sole employee, a combination waitress/chef, and then (to my total surprise) marched past an open table and sat at mine.

"Join you?" purred the delectable blonde with a fetching accent. Her partner winked at me. Normally, I would have been on my guard, but today I was grateful, as a little lost backpacker sheep in desperate need of help. "You're new in Kuta, *oui*?"

"Yeah, just got off the plane. I'm Dash. American."

She smiled, knowingly, at her partner. "See? I told you."

I sipped more iced coffee. Maybe I was just thirsty, but the stuff was phenomenal. Best ever.

"She's Angelique and I'm Kelley. But most folks around here call me *Paladin.*"

I chuckled and could see why—he bore an eerie resemblance to the 1950s TV star who played a cowboy mercenary in *Have Gun, Will Travel.* Kelley's face was a younger version of that rugged, charismatic actor, right down to acne scars, bulbous nose, thick mustache and cruel eyes. The hip, young, backpacking crowd lounging around Bali quickly dubbed him *Paladin Kelley* or variations: *Paladin, Kelley* or PK. No one knew his family name.

"So, how's vagabond life treating you, so far?" Kelley fired up a *kretek,* the local Indonesian cigarette laced with cloves. "Geez, I love these buggers," he said, exhaling a cloud of thick, sweet smoke in a series of perfect rings. Angelique applauded.

"To be honest, I . . . I can't even think . . . this damned jet lag." I put my head on the table to stop the world from spinning. They exploded in laughter.

"Fuckin' A! Been there, amigo. But you're not even a *baby* backpacker. You're like an infant, a newborn. Lucky we spotted you. Traditional for old hands to take newbies under their wing."

Old hands? Maybe this was some of that backpacker fraternity I'd heard about. Help, about to be served up. In order to prompt their stories, I gave them a quick version of my background: Moderate Bluffs, Hong Kong and college. Unable to focus or talk very well, I left out a lot.

"What about you, Paladin?" Great nickname.

"I was a croupier for five years at a seedy casino in Reno. Dealt blackjack and sometimes worked the stick at the craps table."

Angelique called out for three more iced coffees. *"Sila, tiga kopi es!"* It was definitely helping my jet lag. I stole another glance at her. What a knock-out: those cheekbones, pouty lips, blonde ringlets and stunning figure. Impossible blue eyes. Just sitting there, quiet and demure. What was her story?

"Lots of money at those tables." Kelley rubbed his thumb and finger in the universal *money* gesture. Yep, I could really see it now: just give him a black hat and he's *Baby Paladin.* "Winners and losers and always drama. Plus incredible women, of course. Hookers, girlfriends and sexy check thieves."

"Checks?"

"You customers usually call them *chips*."

"Ah."

"So a year ago, I hit the road and began overlanding through Asia. Started in Hong Kong and then spent a good long stretch in Thailand."

"Nice temples and stuff?"

"So they say, but I was mainly whoring." He leaned closer and lowered his voice. Angelique appeared to not be listening, anyway. "Naturally, caught a dose of the clap there. Beautiful ladies in Thailand, for sure, but . . ."

His story was perking me up. I could envision myself traveling like him, a totally free spirit. Minus the VD, of course. "Where'd you go next?"

"Then on to Burma."

"Whoa, cool." I'd read about that hermit kingdom, ruled by a crazy military junta and trapped inside a 1960s time warp.

"Yeah. Well, I followed the infamous special instructions for budget travelers entering Burma. Bought a carton of State Express 555s cigarettes and a bottle of Johnny Walker Red at the Bangkok airport duty free. After landing in Rangoon, I nearly had to fight off airport taxi drivers demanding my contraband. One took my goodies and gave me enough rumpled Burmese money (it's called *kyat*) to fill a paper bag. Lived large off that, a whole week, which is all the country gives tourists. Sweet people, those Burmese, but their government is nuts."

Kelley continued down the Malay Peninsula, took a ferry across the Straits of Malacca to the Sumatra's jungles and then crossed over to Java for some volcano-hopping and temple visits. After a year on the road, he finally plunked himself down in Kuta to recuperate.

"So now," he said, gesturing at the divine Angelique, "I am studying French. Met her here." She wrinkled her nose, fake-scowled at him and rose to pay the bill.

"So, Kelley . . . why Asia?" Maybe I hoped to hear corroboration for my own fuzzy decision.

"Simple, babe: sex and drugs. Plain and simple, only good reasons to come here." I wasn't going to judge him. As a healthy, unthinking, testosterone-driven young man, he probably qualified for the standard wild oats morality waiver. What impressed me was that, after a year of travel, his nest egg was still mainly intact. That sounded like magic. "How did you do that?"

"Patience, little one. So much to show you." He chuckled, rose and waved me to follow.

The two began to lead me down a forest path that wound away from the main drag. Far ahead I could hear the surf crashing but couldn't keep my eyes off the undulating, slightly mysterious Angelique. *Extraordinaire!* We strolled under a lush canopy of coconut palms past small floral offerings in tiny baskets that just appeared on the path. We finally reached a compound behind a primitive wall.

"Welcome to *Losmen Wayan*, Dash. Your new home. Simple and safe, rooms for pocket change."

CHAPTER TWELVE
The Losmen Wayan

Losmen *Wayan* was an ultra-simple hostel, a long concrete building shoe-horned into the walled compound of a Balinese family. A half dozen austere guest rooms sheltered side by side under a long thatched roof. Each contained a small bed, a dark wooden table with candles (no electricity) and a squeaky cupboard. Windows opened onto the breezy cement veranda where each room also had a small rattan table and chair.

I sat outside my door and enjoyed watching timid Balinese pigs tussle and frenetic chickens meander about. The lush forest canopy soared high overhead. Tiny children chased a scrawny goat about the compound. The host family kept a fire permanently burning in the yard near their hut, mainly to boil water.

I did the math and converted the daily charge for my room and breakfast, from Indonesian *rupiah* into dollars. Including unlimited hot tea, at any time, it was about a buck a night. That meant I could crash in Kuta for (hmm, let's see) fifteen, maybe twenty years?

Financial concerns? Zap. Gone!

Kelley patted his stomach. "And the brekkie here's great. Big bowl of black rice pudding with banana slices and hot tea. Everybody sits outside their rooms in the morning, a good time to scope out the guests and check out newcomers."

One of the family's children grabbed my hand and pulled me out back, to show me the simple outdoor bathroom facility, what Indonesians euphemistically call the *kamar kecil:* The Little Room. On a cement slab sat a *mandi*, a tub full of water for splash baths. A small multi-purpose hole was cut into the concrete floor, to drain sewerage and bath water.

The little boy demonstrated.

"Like dis!" he squeaked, pantomiming bathing using a plastic dipper, fishing cool water from the large barrel and splashing it around.

"And like dis!" he laughed as he play-acted squatting and defecating into that little hole.

Now that's just impossible, I thought. *No way can I shit into a little hole in the floor.*

But my tiny guide dismissed my concern with a laugh and gave me a thumbs-up, implying I'd soon become a champion marksman, able to pop that target every time.

Another surprise was the absence of toilet paper. He communicated somehow that clean-up was achieved via dippers of cool water sluiced down one's backside, while scrubbing with the left hand.

I returned to the veranda to find Paladin and Angelique already gone. I stowed my gear in my petite concrete room, put on some flip-flops and a swimsuit, and headed down a small forest trail toward the beach.

All was cool, breezy and green on the jungle path, with the only sounds that of trilling birds and distant waves crashing. After several hundred meters, the trees thinned out and then parted to reveal a vast, perfect crescent beach of white sand beneath a brilliant blue sky. Breakers offshore churned creamy white foam and waves gently lapped on the sand. Vendors looked friendlier now, no longer a nuisance, as they balanced wares on their heads and puttered about, darting between blankets and folding chairs where tourists dozed. Local villagers sauntered up and down the beach to offer *batik* or massages, cheap jewelry and postcards or anything else the sunbathers (both Westerners and wealthy Asians) might desire.

Despite my jet-lag dizziness I began to feel almost euphoric, bewitched by the idyllic tropical scene. I plopped down and sat on the sand facing the sea. A small boy instantly appeared, lugging a large perspiring orange metal cooler. He dangled a soda can in my face and grinned saying something like *Tuan wahnnn cohl dreeeen*? Man, that Indonesian language sounded funny . . . but then I realized he was speaking English. Sort of.

"Yes please. A drink." I gave him a couple loose coins, not yet knowing denominations, and that flash of silver triggered an avalanche of seaside marketers. A gaggle of vendors descended upon me like a flock of pigeons pecking at fresh breadcrumbs, but they were friendly and we enjoyed the pantomimed bantering and laughed a lot. A haggard-looking old woman offered me a massage right there on the beach. Hard to say no when she was already vigorously kneading my shoulder muscles with her strong, hard-skinned, bony hands.

Might even help with the jet lag. But even if it didn't, well, what was a dollar?

Welcome back to Asia, I thought. But after an hour, the overpowering urge to sleep was on me again. I returned to the *losmen* and soon was unconscious.

I woke around midnight and sat up the rest of the night, my body clock totally buggered, I reread my worn Asian budget travel guide by candlelight.

When dawn's light began to penetrate around the edges of the shutters and under my door, I moved outside to the veranda, where the show was already underway. Clucking chickens chased each other across the pounded dirt and docile pigs nosed about, endlessly searching for food. Two mangy dogs dozed by the entrance to the family hut, looking all-but-dead except for the occasional, well-aimed tail flick when a fly landed on a damp canine nose.

Smoke curled from the roof corner of the family pavilion, not much more than a hut of woven reed stretched over a bamboo frame. But as I watched, an entire extended family emerged for the morning: grandparents, seven children, the owner, his wife and several adults, probably siblings. How did they all fit? Guest valuables were stashed in there for safekeeping (no hotel room safes here) so I surrendered the brown envelope with my life savings in travelers' checks, just trusting the arrangement was secure.

Birds flitted about the jungle canopy overhead and twittered as guest room doors began to swing open, one by one, and travelers emerged. Some hurried off for a morning piss and quick splash bath. Others, perhaps after too much *tuak* (a local rice wine) the night before, just yawned and fell into their veranda chairs, awaiting the delivery of tea and rice pudding.

Angelique floated out onto the concrete deck. She was draped in a long silky wrap that hugged her curves and fluttered in her wake. Paladin followed, stretching out both arms and yawning theatrically. "Yeah, babe," he crowed to no one in particular, "good firm Balinese mattress. Like a rock. I slept *baguuuuus*!" He looked at me. "That's the *Bahasa*, Dash. Learn that word right away, means *real nice*." He raised an eyebrow and tossed a chin toward Angelique, gyrating off to the loo.

Yeah, Paladin, you lucky bastard. I'd be grinning, too.

At first their pairing seemed a little odd. She was an absolute stunner, smoking hot, whereas (gotta say this) Paladin was less than physically attractive. But right from the start I'd already felt the power of his charisma, which was indeed overwhelming. He was bright and funny, endlessly energetic and immediately captivating. I suspected few could resist his charm and that people would desire his approval, just enjoying being in his presence.

Amid the incessant racket of neighborhood roosters, a crowing competition that surrounded us, more of the neighbors woke and came out from their rooms.

Two Australian surfer dudes, looking unspeakably *chill*, introduced themselves: Tony Fisher and Bob ('Waves') Cosier. They regularly visited this world-class surfing destination and desired no more from life than the next great wave. Tony was a welder from Brisbane with the California beach bum look down pat: lean, tan and well-muscled, with his long golden locks tied in a ponytail and his batik tee-shirt artfully-torn. He wore bell bottoms with frazzled edges that rested atop truck-tire rubber sandals.

His friend, Waves, worked as a pressman. Hard-bodied and tattooed, day and night he wore the same loose pair of batik swim trunks. A half dozen silver bangles jingled on his wrist and a bauble dangled from his ear. A beaded leather headband held his shoulder-length brown hair in place. Inked on his forearms were large, three-dimensional tattoos in blue and red: *"Still"* on one arm, *"Alive"* on the other. Across his shoulders and back stretched a wave cresting in watery fury above the caption, *"Surf's Up"*.

"We come when cash and work cooperate," Waves said. After a few weeks surfing, life at the print shop and factory was again bearable. "*Losmen Wayan* is our second home and the boss, Wayan, is pretty bonza, mate." The family granted them total access to the compound, even the family hut.

A chubby, dimpled Chinese man in flip-flops padded out from the room next door. He was short and plump though not obese, with a bowl haircut above a round face, round head and round gold-framed glasses with thick lenses. Wrapped in a *sarong* probably bought at the beach he looked older, maybe his mid-thirties. He planted himself on the concrete veranda and began rolling through an odd routine of calisthenics and stretching exercises. Though it seemed he was making them up as he went along, his round, compact form moved smoothly and with confidence from one to the next. He caught me watching and smiled.

"For my back," he said.

Those stretches couldn't ever possibly help anyone.

"Important to exercise and stay fit," said the funny little fat man, who then lovingly patted his pot belly.

There was something amusing and endearing about the little guy and his goofy exercise program. I just nodded back and dug into my pudding and bananas.

"Anyway," he continued, undeterred, pulling one arm behind his back and then the other, "I am P.Y. Lee. Family name *Lee* (Chinese, naturally) and the initials are for my given names. But you should just use my nickname. Everybody does."

"And that is . . .?"

"Little Fatty." He smiled.

I snorted out some tea and coughed. "You kidding?"

"No. But actually, it sounds better in Chinese."

"Hope so."

"*Fatty* because when I was a baby, I *was* chubby."

I noticed he was quite serious so I stifled an urge to laugh.

"And *Little* because, well, I haven't grown much, ever since." He flashed a disarming smile and then jerked a thumb over his left shoulder, adding, "And I'm from Malaysia." (As if that tropical nation was just over there, over his shoulder and behind our dormer, somewhere in the coconut trees with the stray monkeys.)

Hmm, Malaysia? That explained a lot. The former British colony had a lot of spoken English and his accent reminded me of a Malaysian Chinese kid at HKIS. Touch of a Brit accent mixed incongruously with a staccato Asian cadence. Choppy intonation with familiar English words stressed on unexpected syllables.

Little Fatty paused his exercises. "And what about you?"

"Just call me Dash. From world-famous Moderate Bluffs, Illinois." Little Fatty just smiled, waiting. "Bet you don't really know where *that* is?" But he kept quiet and just grinned, nodding slightly and waiting me out. Funny guy wasn't going to admit any ignorance. I ended the standoff. "It's sort of near Chicago."

"Ah yes, Chicago! I know. Al Capone, isn't it? The *Windy City!*" One of the children delivered Fatty a bowl of black rice pudding. He frowned. "Ugh, this brekkie not so good, *lah.*"

"I like it a lot." This first morning it seemed delicious. "Just hope it doesn't turn my shit black." I smiled.

"No," Little Fatty said, missing my humor and shaking his head very serious. "No it won't. Don't worry. Myself, I prefer *nasi lemak.*"

"Did you say Nazi?"

"No. *Nasi*. Rice." He grinned. "*Nasi lemak* means 'fat rice.' Popular Malaysian dish with coconut rice and curried chicken, spicy *ikan bilis*, even a fried egg. Hey, later I can take you for a *real* breakfast as my welcome to Bali treat for you. At *The Hibiscus*. Civilized food: fruit salad, eggs and toast, good coffee. What you *gweilos* call brunch, isn't it?"

Gweilo? I remembered that Chinese word from my Hong Kong days: *foreign devil*. Could be an insult, but context was everything and I knew he was just being friendly, using it as an affectionate tease.

Something about Fatty connected with my expat youth, and I sensed we might become good friends.

A thin, dark man in a tattered white undershirt sauntered out to greet his breakfasting guests.

"There's Wayan," Fatty said, "head of the family. Our landlord. This is his daily ritual—about all he ever really does around here. At the *losmen* his fierce wife does all the heavy lifting." Wayan padded over to Fatty, shook his head and then demonstrated the proper way to knot a Balinese *sarong*. "There! Now Mr. Fatty look handsome, like Bali man."

Above Wayan's smile hovered alarmingly bloodshot eyes, all burst capillaries and angry red sclera. Heavy drink seemed the logical explanation—either that or he had conjunctivitis or had been sticking pins into his eyes.

"Balinese men enjoy their *tuak*," Fatty whispered. "Watch, later this morning, he'll disappear down the *gang*, that dirt alleyway. Every day his friends gather at the local cock fighting pit to drink and bet." Feathered gladiators and drink? My landlord's life sounded good.

"And Mr. Dashiell, *selamat pagi!* Good morning." Wayan was onto me now. His English was limited and halting but then again, my *Bahasa Indonesia* was nonexistent. I vowed right then to master the basics, fast. "Welcome to Bali! Maybe today you send postcards to America?" I could barely concentrate on his words, hypnotically staring at his bloody eyes.

"Um, postcards? No, not yet."

"Good. Because post office closed. Maybe never open."

"Hmm?"

"Somebody die." He shrugged and, having imparted this wisdom, walked away. Smiling wide he headed off to visit Paladin and Angelique.

"Fatty, what the heck was that all about?" This Bali place really *was* kinda different.

The Malaysian paused in mid-stretch and giggled. Before I knew it, I was laughing too. "Dash, he tells that same story to every new arrival. That postmaster died years ago and the tiny, one-man local post office went *habis*. Finished. Anybody's guess why Wayan still feels this is breaking news."

None of that concerned me, though.

I had no one back home to write. I wasn't even sure where *back home* was, anymore. If some coconut truck squashed me flat on some equatorial highway, there would be no place for authorities to ship the pancaked body.

It was a sobering thought. Here I was, completely alone in the world, with no back-up. Yet I felt quite okay. Things seemed to be working out.

CHAPTER THIRTEEN
Little Fatty & the Surfer Dudes

I should have known it just from his nickname: Little Fatty *really* knew food. Our brunch at The Hibiscus later that morning was an utter treat. Just off the beach path, the little restaurant squatted cozily under the trees, tucked deep in the leafy foliage like an organic part of the forest. A blackboard announced the day's specialty in orange and blue chalk: monster fruit salads of papaya, banana, mango, melons and coconut, mixed with nuts, doused in sweetened condensed milk.

"Fatty, this is amazing. Like munching tropical delights inside Tarzan's own jungle hideaway."

"See?" He nodded. "Fatty knows."

The small white stucco structure was open, airy and bright. It lacked a roof and depended for protection upon the thick forest canopy high overhead. Green branches and fronds hung down and poked through windows.

Serving as waitresses were little angelic nymphs in sarongs, mere innocents no older than eight or nine. They hauled in colorful platters from a kitchen hidden away somewhere out back. The arrival of each grandiose meal seemed miraculous.

One little pixie approached our table and stood there awaiting our orders. She looked nervous, her eyes big. One arm stretched behind her back to clasp the opposite elbow as she teetered from one foot to the other. She smiled but looked terrified. The menu was only an approximation of English (which she didn't speak, anyway) and nothing was ever written down. Surely this couldn't work.

"Ahn for kohl dreen, Tuan?" Those mysterious words rode a sweet, high-pitched, sing-song voice.

"Sorry?" I smiled. My newcomer's ears weren't tuned yet for local pronunciation.

Little Fatty patted my shoulder and chuckled. "She asked about your drink."

"Oh. Iced coffee?" Already my go-to beverage.

As she spun and started to skip away, Little Fatty cried out, *"Maaf, puan! Sila berhenti!"* The angel flitted back. *"Dingin sekali, tetapi tanpa es."* Fatty smiled.

"Dash, Indonesian is almost the same as Malay. Told her very cold but no ice. Bottled water is usually safe here, but street vendors sometimes just refill old plastic bottles. The Hibiscus probably uses genuine purified water, boiled, but why take a chance on your first day?"

We relaxed and watched the jungle path outside. Lithe Balinese maidens, probably in their twenties, pitter-pattered by, carrying little offerings. They wore cheap flip-flops and were wrapped in tight sarongs. Fresh-cut orchids or frangipani decorated their hair as they floated along, the embodiment of grace.

Little Fatty read my mind. "Forget it, Dash. Sure they're beautiful. And also very good. Female beauty in Bali is both physical and spiritual."

Sounded like a wonderful combination to me, a healthy young American male in heat.

"Women here are religious and honorable and dedicated to their families. You will even see ten-year-old girls with an infant brother slung over her hip, helping mom keep the sacred law that a baby not touch the ground for its first 210 days . . . a full Balinese year." Fatty shrugged.

"So are local women off limits?" They looked great.

"Not officially, but your interest is unlikely to be reciprocated. They come from a vastly different world and culture. Many still live in candle-lit huts with no running water. Their religion is unique and beautiful and all-consuming."

He had a point: beyond physical attraction there seemed little basis for a deep tourist-local relationship.

"But don't worry, so many other women here you'll never be lonely. An ever-changing sea of beautiful tourists as well as working girls from Java, Singapore and Thailand."

Our fruit salads, eggs, toast, and iced coffee appeared. Like I said, a miracle.

As we ate, Little Fatty shared more background. "I am a small businessman, a typical Overseas Chinese and pretty successful so far." Fatty owned gas stations at the southern tip of the Malay Peninsula. Also a small fleet of tank trucks to distribute diesel and kerosene to industrial customers. "I'm a family man too." He and his wife, Nancy, had a small daughter.

So I wondered what he was doing on this bachelor outing to Bali. Why was he staying in a rock-bottom dwelling like *Losmen Wayan*? Surely he could afford better. And what did that mean, "typical *Overseas Chinese?*"

"I was working too hard and just needed a break. So Nancy issued me a vacation visa but no pink ticket." He winked.

"Wait. Pink ticket?"

He laughed. "Sorry, a local joke. Means I can have fun but must behave." His spouse sounded accommodating, as I would learn were many Asian wives . . . but not *ridiculously* so.

We continued to monitor traffic on the dirt path. Then, as if Fatty scheduled it, the Balinese maidens were replaced by a sumptuous buffet of international females. Fatty called out the nationalities: Europeans, Japanese, Americans, Southeast Asians and Chinese. Each was charming in her own way; some with boyfriends, and others paired with girlfriends or traveling in female packs.

Twenty-four hours had passed since I'd arrived in Indonesia and I was still adjusting. But my eyes were sloughing off their dependence upon the tidy parallel and perpendicular lines of the West and I was getting more comfortable with friendly tropical chaos.

"So Fatty, what about the other guests at *Losmen Wayan*?"

"Good folks. Like the American and his French girlfriend."

"Paladin Kelley."

"Right. A lucky fellow." We both silently appraised Angelique. Though at the apex of European female desirability, she was already taken. You didn't mess with a friend's good fortune, not even a brand-new friend.

I picked at some juicy papaya and sipped the potent coffee. Tropical birds flitted about and nestled in the restaurant's beams. A large green and yellow parrot squawked from one corner and off in another, a massive creature with huge claws (perhaps a type of local eagle) stood within a large steel loop, chained by one leg. The child waitresses called him *Hanuman,* after the irrepressible monkey god of Hindu mythology. Something suddenly set Hanuman off and the huge white creature exploded in panic, jumping, flapping and squawking, a frightening display of desperate kinetic energy. Unfortunately, his furious activity only twisted and wound his tethering chain around the metal loop.

The chain constantly clanked and feathers fluttering through the air, destroying the small cafe's peaceful atmosphere.

Three small boys materialized in torn shirts, short pants and bare feet. Somehow linked to the cafe, they were armed with specialized tools for this recurring emergency: a broomstick and some wire coat hangers. Slow and cautious, knowing how to avoid getting pecked, they coaxed the frightened eagle to hop onto the broomstick and then worked the twisted chain free by using hangers to poke at and untwist the tangle. Toiling in a quiet and patient process, they whispered advice to each and clucked at mistakes. Eventually, the bird's leg was liberated. We politely clapped and tossed the boys a small tip. Free entertainment for the brunch crowd.

Fatty laughed. "Know a lot about Bali?"

I shrugged. "Almost nothing."

"Crazy place but you'll learn fast. Monkey forests and monkey gods. Trance dances and live volcanoes. Mythical creatures appeased by pretty little girls or floral gifts left on the ground. Spirits all around. Dollar hotels and gruesome motorcycle accidents. Clanging exotic music and beer bars full of boorish Aussies. Hookers from Java. Amazing and cheap art." He shook his head. "Quite the place."

"Been here a lot, Fatty?"

"Ha! Many times. But this visit is almost done. Even Nancy has her limits so I must scurry back to JB. But she can't complain. At least I did it cheap-cheap—you know, stayed in a losmen."

"What's JB?"

"Johor Baru. Capital of Johor state at the bottom tip of Malaysia. Just across from Singapore Island, *lah*." He smiled on the 'lah'.

Lah? What was that?

We settled the bill (less than a dollar each for a stomach-bursting brunch) and then strolled down the path toward the beach.

"Hey!" Little Fatty yelped and grabbed my arm, pulling me aside. "Careful. Didn't you see it? You nearly stepped on that offering." Down on the ground by my foot was a little flat tray woven from lime-green palm leaves. It contained fruit, flowers, and a small piece of shimmering embroidery. Also a lit candle and a coin. Fatty explained it was all a miniature offering for some mystical entity, perhaps a Hindu god or local animist spirit.

"Whew, guess you must've saved my life there, man." I was joking but he gave me a funny look.

"Maybe yes! Don't fool around, Dash. You never know." His stern tone melted away and he smiled again. "Anyway, let's check the beach. Maybe surf's up or, better still, bikini tops down."

Over the next week we became friends as Fatty ran me through Asian backpacker basic training. The guy was intelligent and warm-hearted with a sense of humor that tickled me. Our backgrounds diverged so markedly that our personal stories fascinated the other. But his always seemed to top mine.

One day while watching Balinese tykes on the beach hustling drinks and selling individual cigarettes, I reminisced about selling raffle tickets as a boy for my little league baseball team, to adults in front of the local bank.

Fatty topped that. When he was a boy in Kuala Lumpur, aka KL, the Malaysian capital, he hawked little dittoed sheets with lottery results for a couple cents each. He worked late into the evenings at smoky bars and street restaurants.

When I admitted over beers as having lost my virginity only in college (a brief, drunken party liaison with a sexy stranger), he was genuinely shocked. Then he outdid me with his personal ribald tale of being deflowered in a KL brothel at the tender age of thirteen.

But in the end, Fatty won the all-time storytelling championship with the tale of a childhood tapeworm. "I was only nine and very little. But the worm was big. Like this." He spread his arms open wide. "Over one, maybe two meters long!" He giggled and shivered. "The doctor was an old Indian man smelling of curry, with orange saffron stains on his gown. He made me eat medicine at home to kill the worm. Then I returned to his office. He made me bend over and—owww!—so very slowly he pulled the dead worm out from my bum!" I had nothing that could ever top that and knew it was time to surrender.

"So what about the other *losmen* guests, like those Aussie surfers . . .?"

"*Fair dinkum*, mate." Fatty winked. "Good men. Tony and 'Waves' take me to Kuta beach bars, and Morgan, their biker friend, is a cool dude, too. We all sit on cheap rattan chairs under thatched ceilings and drink and window-shop. The catalog of female tourists changes nightly!" A wide grin split his face. "What's more, they even promised to teach me to surf!"

Once word spread that Fatty would soon leave, we all spent the remaining evenings together, including the Aussies. Cheap dinner at *Mama's* smorgasbord one night or at the *Bamboo Den* the next. Then, off to a beach bar where we would browse the newest arrivals, viewing through a male alcoholic haze that made all women more attractive.

One night we five commandeered a corner table at *Kartika,* the latest beach hot spot boasting the most muscular sound system on the island. *Kartika* pumped out a late-70s disco baseline that physically hammered the drunken crowd into blissful oblivion.

We spotted Paladin and Angelique at a far table and waved them over. He carried over two chairs, a big grin slapped on his face, with Angelique trailing.

"Hey, bro!" he yelled over the thumping beat, "Guess what we're doing?" I could barely hear him. Luckily the music then paused. "We're heading out soon. Leaving Bali."

Oh no, not them too?

"We're heading for Europe overland by motorcycle."

Now *that* was impressive. "Wow. Sounds pretty wild, Kelley."

"Fuckin' A, Dash. We'll cycle across Java and continue across Sumatra or catch a ferry direct to Singapore. And then we head for Penang off western Malaysia."

I could imagine myself roaring overland on a bike, the wind in my face while green and glorious Southeast Asia unwound beneath my wheels. "And then after that?"

"I forget."

"No offense, Kelley, but that's not much of a plan so far." As a specialist in poor planning I knew mediocrity when I saw it.

Kelley grunted a laugh. "People do this all the time, Dash. It's easy. We'll meet folks coming from the opposite direction, from Europe, and get advice on what's ahead." Despite having just arrived in Bali I felt the slightest tickle of a new travel itch.

Angelique sat quietly and sipped her beer until finally interjecting with calm confidence. "Dash, after Penang we bike up through Thailand. We'll dispose of the motorcycle there, *n'est-ce pas?*"

"Right," Kelley said. "And then it's buses and trains to the subcontinent, where we can get happily lost for years. Colossally great place. Cheap, too."

"I hear Nepal is legendarily cool." I was becoming really intrigued.

"Worth a half year all by itself. Packed with good food, cheap drugs. Nice place to recharge. But the bad news is how some portions of the *Great Overland Hippie Trail* are now shut down. Asshole Ayatollah blocked the route through Iran. And Afghanistan must be avoided—Soviet troops there, warring with armed *mujahedeen* freedom fighters. But once we get past the Middle East, somehow, we'll hop a ferry to Greece."

"What, no USSR?"

"Nah. Bypass all that Russia and Iron Curtain crap. And once aground in Western Europe we'll hitchhike to Paris and I'll deliver my lady to her home."

Kelley and I retreated out back and released parallel streams of beer into the darkness, blindly shooting at chirping and buzzing insects.

"But seriously man, what about you and Angelique? Planning to stay together?"

Kelley laughed. "Come on, who knows? But by the time we arrive in Paris, six months or six years from now, we should really know each other good." He smirked and shot an elbow into my ribs. "Maybe her parents won't like their little princess hooking up with some vagabond from Reno."

Back in the bar, we found Angelique playing a drinking game with the Aussies. The loser chugged, and so far she appeared to be winning. As for me, I wanted to know more about overlanding to Europe. "So Paladin, you must be pretty good on a motorcycle."

"Me? Nah. But lots of small easy roads here in Bali, to practice."

The Aussies heard this and slammed down their glasses, hooting in derision. Morgan, an avid biker with full sleeve *Harley Davidson* tattoos on his forearms, seemed especially agitated.

"Paladin, ain't you seen enough Bali biking spills yet, mate? Tourist rents a bike, gets just half an hour of training and heads off to explore the island. Bad plan, uglier results. Biking here's no simple piece a piss."

Angelique frowned. *"Mais oui,* I too have seen this: *beaucoup* de blood."

Paladin smirked. "Y'all are making too much outta nothing." He turned to Angelique. "It'll be great, babe. We'll be fine. Time of our lives."

Morgan the biker drained his beer. "Listen, I once seen a fella in *Brizzvegas*—"

"Where?" Little Fatty squinted at Morgan.

"In Brisbane, you wanker. Anyway, fella came up a real gutser. Bloody oath! He skids a good fifteen meters, skin and insides scraping the pavement. Just lay there, all raw meat and bones sticking out."

Tony piled on. "Truth, mate! Also seen it, right here in Kuta, a wowser spin-out on gravel."

Kelley had enough. "Fellas, stop stirring the shit. You're scaring the mademoiselle."

"Ah, go root yer boot," laughed Morgan, draining his mug.

The disco music resumed pounding. I gulped my beer and bobbed my head with the beat. A warm beer cocoon was enveloping me and I felt good. The sweet heavy odor of burning ganja drifted through the bar.

The eclectic crowd was young and fairly attractive. Women everywhere. At a nearby table four burly men with dark hair and stubbly faces like Bluto were draining potent shots of clear liquor and swearing earthy curses in an odd guttural dialect. They constantly stole glances at a table with three women who shrieked like hyenas while tossing back tequila shots. Down in front, a half dozen goofy-drunk American kids in jeans and baseball caps were nearly falling off their chairs.

That's when I spotted an interesting couple tucked away in the back and keeping to themselves. Were they Chinese? The guy was nondescript but she was utterly magnificent—long raven hair, dark fiery eyes, sensual lips and high cheekbones. Bearing and attire like a fashion model.

"Whoa, guys: look back there: who is *that*?"

Waves roared with laughter, drunk out of his mind. *"Whoa*, he says? Dash, you little cunt, didn't know you were into Chinese guys."

I tossed a balled-up napkin at him. "Waves, you shithead, you know I meant the girl."

The music started to thump the Bee-Gees at us, even louder, and Tony leaned closer, yelling in my ear. "Yeah, mate, I noticed her, too. A real ripper, hey?" He waved the barman over and palmed him a folded square of Indonesian rupiah. We waited a minute and soon had an answer.

"Waiter says that sheila over there is called *Fiona Lo*."

But Little Fatty—no pink ticket—could care less. After chugging down several mugs of beer he had turned an amazing crimson. Tingly drunk. He pounded the table. "Hey, you fellows promised to teach me to surf. And I'm leaving in just a few days."

"You, surf?" Tony grinned. "Bad plan, mate. You'd wobble right off the board."

"Nah," Morgan rejoined. "He'd be deadly stable up there. Like a nun's nasty."

Waves yawned. "So then it's settled: *manana,* our favorite Chinaman rides the waves. Deal?"

"Deal," chirped Little Fatty. "And you too, Dash."

As for me, I was busy stealing glances back at the red-hot Fiona Lo. "Huh, what? Surfing?"

Native to inland cornfields, my strict personal policy forbade dangerous play on turbulent bodies of water. So balancing my body atop a waxed moving plank was absolutely forbidden. Don't get me wrong, I *loved* all those 1960s Beach Boys pop hits, but that was as close as it got.

"Nope, gents, I'm passing—"

They all began to shout and bang fists on the table, spilling beer while chanting my name along with Aussie oaths. Angelique's disappointed look settled it.

Outvoted (and against my better judgment) I was soon laughing and committed to a surfing lesson.

CHAPTER FOURTEEN
Little Fatty's Surfing Lesson

The tide tables called for optimal surfing conditions after 10 a.m. We all woke around midmorning, choked down some aspirin for our hangovers and then wandered down to the shore. Tony approached me, his blonde ponytail tied tight and dangling. "You too, Dash. Gotta rent a board and get up on some waves."

"No way, buddy. Body surfing is good enough for me."

He made a disapproving noise, but I waded out to waist-deep water just beyond where waves gently broke and there tried to ride atop the incoming waves, floating atop the salty azure warmth. In just a few minutes I mastered it and was able to body-surf nearly all the way to shore. Fun at first, it soon bored me.

Tony, Waves and Morgan escorted Little Fatty further down the beach where higher, more powerful waves crashed. First they had him just lay on the board on his stomach and paddle to get in sync up with incoming waves. He clearly wouldn't be standing up, anytime soon. Everyone enjoyed this, especially Little Fatty, and the Aussies took turns tutoring while the others surfed.

Lean, tan and well-muscled, their tattoos blazing, they were agile and masterful commanding the watery turbulence, willing the sea's power to lift and propel them. Waves showed off by riding inside the tubes of occasional, particularly monstrous breakers. To me, it almost seemed surreal. Were they incredibly brave or had their deep experience eliminated any real danger? By comparison, my body-surfing was mundane and all that effort, swimming to catch up with cresting waves, had already tired me out.

The sun was already high overhead and baking me. I'd had enough. Just slip away? Why not? They wouldn't miss me.

I rode my morning's final wave toward shore and stood in thigh-deep water, the cool waves sloshing against my back. I surveyed Kuta's gorgeous golden crescent of beach backed by a rising green wall of lush coconut palm trees. I scanned the beach and confirmed all the usual sights. Sunbathers lay on towels and glistened from coconut oil. Vendors balanced multi-colored stacks on their heads. Little nymphs skittered about selling postcards and bewitching visitors. A flock of leather-skinned, grandmotherly masseuses hovered, awaiting business. Small dark boys with pencil-thin limbs lugged orange-rusted ice chests, hawking soda.

But then I saw something else, something marvelous and altogether unexpected: the stunning Fiona Lo. Second time I'd seen her.

She was standing in the shade of a palm tree, slim and elegant in a crisp white expensive-looking beach outfit. Nothing like those batik rags sold for pennies on the beach. Even though she was a fair distance away I could see her lips were perfectly painted in a purplish-red gloss. She was rhythmically flicking a small sandalwood fan to cool herself while she strolled a private section of the beach, exclusive hotel property hived off by a small white picket fence and patrolled by guards. Compared to my buck-a-night digs at *Wayan's*, her residence looked luxurious and ostentatious, the apex of local resort comfort. Nice, but for me a waste of limited funds.

Fiona daintily applied suntan lotion and then reclined on a lounge chair under a large round nipa palm-style canopy. Her floppy white fashion hat and over-sized sunglasses made her look sultry and adorable. All but hypnotized by her mystery and beauty, I drank in the intoxicating sight (I admit it, she *endlessly* fascinated me) and only snapped out of my daze when I realized she was staring straight back at me.

I'd been visually consuming her, ravenous as a wild animal.

What must she think?

Nothing good, that's for sure. Unsmiling, she continued to stare at me as I stood frozen in thigh-deep water. Then with a mind of its own, my hand decided to wave.

Stop it, you idiot! What are you doing? The move was ridiculous and I instantly regretted it, that little flick of the wrist. A quick and sappy little *hey, how-do-you-do?*

She didn't respond, like she didn't see it, though she did. She abruptly looked away and buried her nose in a book.

Nice. She thinks I'm a creep.

So much for *that* opportunity. Good-bye before anything could even begin.

I shuffled out of the water and climbed up the beach, turning toward the path leading through the woods back to the *losmen*. Having botched my chances with Fiona, I just wanted to go back to the shady courtyard and nap or watch the chickens play. The sun was now really frying my back and shoulders. I noticed the Aussies had a similar idea: their morning swim was already finished and they were ahead of me, up at the opening to the jungle path. They jumped and howled and slapped hands in self-congratulation over their success that morning in taming monster waves.

But where was Little Fatty?

I turned back toward the sea and spotted him all alone out there, doggedly trying to master surfing. Such persistence! But wait, he had no board. Was he trying to body surf? If so, he didn't get even the basics: he was too far out, where the incoming swells rolled in high and were far more dangerous. Instead of trying to float up top, swim and catch a wave to ride upon, he just stood there, regularly disappearing under monstrous walls of water crashing in over his head.

Each time he briefly reappeared he waved his hands.

What's that idiot doing?

Then I realized the idiot was me. Little Fatty wasn't surfing, he was in big trouble and trying to survive.

Those assholes! Why'd they leave him all alone like that? And why'd he stay out there by himself; we'd heard every year a considerable number of tourists perished off Indonesia's beaches. Kuta was notorious with tides there playing havoc by creating a drifting sandy bottom, unpredictable undertows and instant underwater ditches. One could easily stumble into a sudden pit or be dragged out to sea. There were no lifeguards.

He seemed to be getting smaller, shrinking now to just a pinkish blob in a red sun cap, farther offshore, sporadically bobbing up to the surface. He waved frantically until being consumed by each successive towering wave. His mouth moved but all sound was masked by the wind's strong hiss and loud slapping waves.

Now, being raised in the Illinois cornfields, I was much more of a farmer than a swimmer and life-saving had never been one of my specialties. But lucky for Little Fatty I wasn't thinking, just reacting, and was immediately on the move.

I ran out into the water far as I could and then began to swim, battering at the water, fighting it. (Like I said, no swimmer.) After what seemed forever I stopped to check but saw I hadn't gotten much closer to him. I realized he was drifting further out to sea. Great.

Already exhausted, I pushed myself onward and after an interminable effort eventually got closer. "Hey!" I screamed at him. "Fatty!" He wasn't too far away but didn't respond.

When I finally pulled up beside him he seemed half-conscious at best and must've already swallowed a lot of water. I looked back toward the shore .It seemed a mile away. And below us, the bottom might be a thousand feet down. I had no idea what to do next. So just like in the cartoons or comics (where I learned many of life's greatest lessons) I hooked an arm around his neck and began to sidestroke both of us back toward shore.

Once we were both somehow afloat, atop the surface, it surprised me how peaceful everything suddenly again became. White birds hovered overhead, circling us and calling out. The setting was beautiful, noontime on a sunny day in Paradise: deep blue water, the green island and its golden beach in the distance.

I wasn't confident but some of my fear was abating. If I took my time perhaps I could regain some strength. We could always float. This all might work out.

We made slow but unmistakable progress, side-stroking and then resting. Eventually I began to see individual palm trees again, not just the distant mass of tropical forest. Experimenting, I tried to stand and found the water was neck-deep. We were close to safety!

So, it surprised me when the hardest part came only now. While floating on the surface my chubby friend had been remarkably buoyant, almost weight-free. But now his weight worked against me. Closer to shore the waves towered and tumbled over us and alternated with the angry, treacherous undertow that tried to pull us back out to sea or into a deep underwater pit. I suspected this was about where I first spotted him, where he lost control.

The undertow was massive.

I held fast onto my unconscious friend, fearing that (incredibly, seemingly so close to safety) he might now drown by breathing in water. I hoisted him up as much as I could above the onrushing waves, trying to keep his head above and only lowering him while resisting the powerful backwash.

It was a bizarre stalemate: we were stuck, unable to move forward toward the shore and fighting being relentlessly worked back out to sea by the brutal riptide.

It seemed a lost cause.

"We may be done for, buddy," I mumbled, though he was out cold. I was totally spent, having exhausted the last of my strength just trying to stand our ground. It all seemed horribly unfair, like a trap. Though I felt no real panic (too busy) I realized we were both about to die. My fatigue would eventually doom us both. It felt ironic and surreal as all hell. Dying in paradise.

You kidding me, God? It all ends like this?

If I were to just let Fatty go, I might still be able to swim to shore and save myself, but that option never even occurred to me. Inconceivable.

Just as I got close to surrender, too dead tired to keep hoisting Fatty and then fighting off the merciless undertow, an especially powerful wave knocked off his red and white cap. It bobbed on the waves and floated away toward the shore.

Like a message. At last, I understood: as long as I fought the backwash, the sea inevitably *would* kill us both. I needed to go *with* it. That was our only chance.

I wrapped an elbow under Fatty's neck and trusting this was right, leapt up with a wave, laying us both out horizontally, hoping we could get up top of the water again and float. I began to side-stroke madly, swimming for our lives. My bemused fatalism of moments ago was gone, there was no more chuckling over divine ironies—this was some serious shit. I swam as hard as I could for as long as I could (probably only a minute or two, I suppose), giving it my final, ultimate effort.

Everything I had left.

I was finally spent so it was no longer in my hands. I stopped swimming and tried to stand. The water was just below my waist and we'd escaped the deadly undertow.

It was over.

I slung Little Fatty across my shoulders and began to trudge up the steep banked shore. Vendors spotted us and dropped their wares to sprint over while the entire beach exploded into action. Gesticulating wildly and gabbing, several lifted Little Fatty from my shoulders and carried him ashore. Two hulking Europeans (funny, I'd never seen them before or again) walked me up onto the beach, my arms draped over their shoulders. Other tourists spread a large blanket in a shady area under the coconut palms and laid me down.

Overcome by exhaustion and emotion, more tired than at any other time in my life, I just collapsed.

I awoke with my head pounding and nose burning from a crushed ammonia capsule held under my nostrils. I learned later the doctor had buzzed down from Denpasar via motorbike taxi, carrying the tools of his trade in a small black vinyl case.

"You're lucky," he said in simple *Bahasa*-for-tourists. "No real harm. You're mainly just totally fatigued. Eat a hearty dinner, get a good night's sleep and you'll recover fine." Little Fatty, however, lying on the blanket beside me, was far worse off. Alive but in deep shock.

He'd ingested copious amounts of sea water into his lungs and stomach. The medic nodded at him and tsk-tsked. "He was probably inhaling seawater before you reached him. Without you, he's a dead man. So you're a hero." Funny, but I didn't feel like one, just myself, impulsively and recklessly trying to help a friend.

Fatty shivered under a rainbow-colored pile of beach towels. He sobbed and coughed up blood before beginning to dry vomit. "He was puking seawater before. Now he's empty. That's good," the doctor said, putting his stethoscope back into his bag. "Outlook good for recovery after a few days' rest." He jotted down a prescription and warned us to watch for danger signs that would require immediate hospitalization, like heart palpitations or pneumonia symptoms.

"Beware of a *second drowning,* on land."

"Huh?"

"Sometimes fluid collects in the lungs. Very dangerous."

My thinking continued to clarify and my focus broadened. I realized we were the center attention of a vast beach crowd that encircled us, buzzing as they watched the doctor perform his magic. My friends from the *losmen* stood above us, looking concerned. I still felt weak and ready to pass out again, my head throbbing like a ticking clock.

And yet despite all that, a rush of adrenaline spiked in my bloodstream and jolted my heart the moment I spotted her. There was Fiona again in her sexy white beach outfit, standing at the back of the crowd but (damn it!) leaning close to that fellow again. Her Chinese boyfriend. But at least she look concerned about me. Boyfriend or not, when our eyes locked and she blasted me a radiant smile. Those bright eyes, perfect teeth and sexy lips! I tingled as a buzz of electricity coursed through my entire body and my mind raced.

But when I looked back up again just moments later, she had already gone.

My entourage escorted us back to the *losmen*—Paladin, Angelique, Wayan's family and those worthless surfers from Oz.

Wayan's wife and mother-in-law tucked Fatty and me into our beds and began to pamper us, Bali family-style. Every hour light snacks or local drinks arrived. The eldest daughter, teenager Ketut, spent long periods mothering me. She fanned me, sang songs and showed me picture books about the Ramayana. She regularly dosed me with *jamu*, a local herbal remedy, Orang *Kuat* (Strong Man) brand.

I was out of bed by day two but Little Fatty needed longer to recover. I was happy to sit at his bedside, talking and whiling away hours. His strength slowly returned but he was prone to occasional fits of emotion. I understood—after all, for all practical purposes he'd been a dead man . . . until being saved by the most unlikely of heroes.

"I just can't stop thinking about it, Dash. Why did this all happen? Were you *sent here* to save me?" I had no answers. "I owe you my life. We will forever be linked."

"Aw come on, Fatty—maybe you didn't die because it just wasn't your time."

He sniffled, tearing up again. "I was totally helpless. Unable to save myself."

I just grinned and poked his arm. "Hey, maybe someday you'll repay the favor."

"Yes! But it's not funny, Dash. This is a profound debt, one I can *never* fully repay."

"Stop all the *repayment* nonsense, Fatty. You owe me nothing. We're friends, that's all." He dabbed his eyes, listening. "Sometimes friendship can be a funny thing." I shared the story of my failed relationship with my mentor, Demy.

Little Fatty nodded. "Someday he'll surely forgive you."

I castigated our mutual friends, the Aussies. "How could they have left you all alone out there?"

"No, Dash, it was all my mistake. Not their fault. They're good mates." What a great guy: heart as huge as an elephant.

On the fourth day after the incident Little Fatty pronounced himself better and climbed out of his sick bed. As if to prove all was well, he resumed his morning stretches and tucked into two bowls of black pudding and bananas. And his recovery had arrived not a moment too soon. He was booked to fly home that day.

"Dash, if I can ever—"

"Yeah, yeah, I know. Just shut up already."

"But I *really* mean it!" He handed me a scrap of paper. "My contact details. Hang onto this. Maybe when you get tired of bumming around you can come live in Johor, be my business partner, or at least use my home in Malaysia as a base for more of your bumming."

"Hey, don't be so judgmental."

He laughed. I folded the paper into a little square and tucked it deep inside my wallet and promised to not forget. We both knew our bond was unique and unbreakable. This odd, aggressive and clever Chinese entrepreneur had been a fascinating companion, energizing me with fresh and unexpected perspectives, many in conflict with my narrow American mindset. I probably *could* learn a lot more from Little Fatty.

Around noon we hailed a *bemo* at *Jalan Legian* for the airport run and amid laughs, a brotherly hug and much pounding of backs, said our good-byes. He climbed aboard and the vehicle ground its gears and lurched forward. He looked back and mouthed at me: "Don't forget."

"Okay, okay," I mimed back.

As the *bemo* pulled away, spitting smoke and noise, it belatedly hit me. Something about Fatty reminded me of my old friend at HKIS, Jackson Toh.

Great guys, both of them—but would probably never see either of them again. Ever.

CHAPTER FIFTEEN
Ubud Fantasy

With Fatty gone I retreated to a dirty roadside cafe for scrambled eggs and some sweet milky iced coffee. First I sat quietly and watched the show stream by, the never-ending flow of Kuta's impecunious travelers. Then I pulled out the slim blue booklet from my hip pocket, the same *Bahasa* tutorial carried by every shoestring traveler on the archipelago. The cartoon on the cover showed a princely *wayang kulit* shadow puppet exclaiming *"Bagus!"* Nice!

Language practice was easy. Warm-hearted Indonesians loved nothing better than when foreigners tried to learn their practical language. At the least provocation Indonesians would shift into teaching mode and impromptu lessons break out in taxis, coffee shops or shopping stalls. With just the slightest effort you couldn't miss quickly mastering the essentials.

Glancing up from my book, I spotted a familiar couple off in the distance. Paladin Kelley was plodding along with his slightly bow-legged gait while Angelique glided beside him. I could see their eyes light up when they spotted me and headed over.

"Well, our little swimmer boy is looking better," Paladin said.

I grinned my thanks. "Yeah, Kelley, but Fatty's gone. Just left."

"Good for him, a full recovery. And such a sweet man." Angelique glowed in her long gauzy linen dress, batik headband, beads and bangles. Sensual beauty like hers made even hippie glitter-glam look sexy. "But Dash, have you heard the news? Soon to come . . . in Ubud . . ."

She paused dramatically and yes, it *did* irritate me.

"There will be a *cremation!*"

A cremation? Well, whoop-de-doo. My non-response did little to dampen her enthusiasm. She was nearly gasping with delight.

"The ceremony will be *formidable!* For a very wealthy and powerful man." Her eyes twinkled as the cultural side of Bali infatuated Angelique as much as surfing and the bar scene bewitched those Aussies. Every night she tracked down a dance performance and dragged Paladin along. He never complained, actually, and told of chilling trance performances he'd seen with costumed demons and deities or hallucinatory exhibitions by divine nymphs and mythical creatures. I saw a *Kecak* dance once, viscerally exciting and unforgettable with something like 150 men stripped naked from the waist up and sitting in concentric circles. They rhythmically shouted and clapped and flailed their bodies in unison like some monstrous serpent. Fucking amazing.

Well, by now, even I knew gaudy cremation ceremonies stood at the very apex of Balinese social, religious and cultural life. Supposedly must-see stuff according to my little travel book.

And when the event was being bankrolled by a wealthy family, a five-star event was likely.

"So, man, we're going." Paladin seemed infected by Angelique's excitement. "Want in?"

"Yes, *mon cher*. You *must* come." Angelique squeezed my arm, pouting again. Fetching but I didn't need the tease.

Kelley just laughed.

I'd already heard so much about cremations it was probably time to see one. And with Fatty gone I could use a diversion.

The rooster alarm clock woke us early. We flagged down a ride to Ubud and expected to reach the glorious arts town in Bali's central hills by mid-morning.

According to the grapevine, festivities would start around noon. We stood in the back deck of an open-air truck for the bumpy ride north, assaulted on all sides by the verdant island's magical vistas. We were surrounded by steep ravines and misting mountains and passed through green valleys sculpted with lush rice paddies that climbed hillsides like wide, curving stairs. The water-filled valleys sparkled and glistened in the sun while being trodden by massive, slow-limbed water buffalo, knee-deep in muck and pulling plows.

Several times we passed a prototypical Balinese postcard image: withered old village duck herders driving their flocks. These rail-thin, bare-chested men walked behind battalions of forty or more ducks, all marching down the asphalt road in orderly lines about three abreast. There was a pleasing suggestion of organization and rank, like a duck army. The herder guided his flock by dangling a white cloth off a long bamboo pole, ahead of the birds, which they followed. Most mornings, duck herders and their fowl shared the same highways as trucks and gleaming Mercedes limos that flashed dangerously close by.

We arrived at Ubud to find a leafy dream of quiet lanes, serene roadside temples and artisan workshops. Idyllic and untouched. I'd expected cooler temperatures at this higher elevation, but the day was heating up, anyway. The streets already teemed with a mixed crowd of several thousand, both Balinese and tourists. There was a slightly manic tone in the air as all savored the build-up to the ceremony. The tiny burg was already overwhelmed.

Paladin steered us to an open-air stall for the first of the dozen colas I would consume that hot day. Angelique sipped sweet mint tea as we sheltered in the shade and watched the burgeoning crowd.

"This ceremony will be *magnifique.*" Angelique smiled and launched into an unsolicited lecture. "The dead man was a very rich *Brahmana*, a high religious leader."

From my yellow travel book I already knew Bali had three other castes. The *Sudras* were commoners. *Satrias* were royals and nobles. And *Wesias* were warriors.

"Fine, Angie. But what's with that huge bull statue over there?"

"Mais oui, Dash. The bull structure." *Zee bool structoor.* "Also the bamboo tower, there. Like a pagoda. You see it, *n'est-ce pas?"*

I nodded.

"The bull is the sarcophagus for a male *Brahmana.* For a woman, it would be a cow."

"Okay, cool. Nice lecture." I yawned and nudged Paladin, who winked back. "What about the other castes?"

"Royalty get a winged lion but for commoners, a remarkable creature."

"Yes?"

"An *elephant-fish.*"

"Naturally." I chuckled and Angelique scowled back. "So what's the deal with that cool pagoda with seven-decks?"

"It represents the cosmos," she said curtly.

"Ding-ding-ding! Correct answer! And the young lady wins this *wonderful* prize." I handed her my empty cola can. Paladin shot me a look to stop teasing already. He probably worried he'd be punished later as a proxy for my sins.

The crowd noise began rising, with a gaiety and party atmosphere that seemed weird and out of place. I mean, wasn't this a Balinese wake? Many of the revelers looked tipsy already. Not totally blasted yet but hey, the day was still young.

This was unlike any funeral I'd ever seen before. It was a celebration, a jubilee with hordes spilling out into the streets to laugh, flirt and dance.

Perhaps the Balinese were onto something here. I remembered the pain of that entire grisly ritual when my mother died: the painted-up body at the wake, the mournful requiem mass. Yeah, this was much better.

We killed time wandering around cozy artisan shops, admiring intricate but inexpensive carved wooden sculptures. There were fantasy bird-like monsters called *Garudas;* mythical long-haired *Barong* creatures carved from dark mahogany; and the melding, intertwined faces of the *Ramayana* lovers Rama and Sita emerging from a single ebony block.

"So, Angelique, some guy died . . . why all the joy?"

She nodded, obviously lying in wait for my obvious question. "Dash, in Bali they believe people have *three* bodies. A physical one, a soul and one's thoughts."

"Thoughts?" *Nonsense.* "How can those be a body?"

She sighed. "*C'est simple.* When you dream, don't you sometimes wander about? It's like that. *That* body, those thoughts." She raised her eyebrows and I answered with a nod that I was with her so far. "The physical body is least important of them all, and only its destruction can free the soul to travel to heaven and rejoin the cycle of reincarnation."

"Okay, great." That was already enough for me, but the lesson continued.

"When Balinese die, families temporarily bury the bodies until later when they can cremate the remains. It's expensive so village folk 'save up' bodies for economical mass cremations. However, this man was rich and important, so his cremation is extravagant. The family pays for the food, decorations and liquor."

"Free booze?" Now *that* sounded better.

"Not for tourists, of course. But *brem* rice wine here is already cheap and delicious. And this whole show today in the streets is free for all of us."

The noon start time came and went but nothing happened.

Finally, as if a secret signal flare had been shot off, the crowd began to amass near the bull sarcophagus and cremation tower. For a better view, gawkers perched on walls or climbed into trees or sat atop cars, trucks and bullock carts.

Abruptly, a *gamelan gong* orchestra began to hammer out a clanging, bittersweet, rhythmic melody that fortified the growing atmosphere of mystery and anticipation.

"Geez, this is getting freakin' unreal, Paladin." Everywhere I looked was a boiling sea of bodies, thousands throbbing along with the *gamelan* and its insistent chiming cadence. The clove smell of *kretek* and sweet incense filled the air and amplified the mood.

While taking in the sheer spectacle unfolding before me, I happened by chance to glance across the road and my gaze was irresistibly drawn to and riveted upon a single figure.

There she was again, looking radiant and magnificent as usual, while trying to stay shaded and avoid the crowd. Leaning against a large, sarong-decorated stone statue that guarded a temple entrance within a courtyard was the one and only, Fiona Lo.

I urgently scanned the crowd everywhere and saw no boyfriend in tow.

She's alone?

Hey, I gotta go!" I called over my shoulder to Paladin and began to weave through the crowd to cross the street. "Catch you later."

Paladin shouted over the din. "Wait, Dash! Where will—"

"I dunno," I yelled back, moving fast. "Wherever!"

I saw Angelique looking perturbed by my unscheduled departure, but I had to reach the other side before the elusive Fiona disappeared again.

Fiona was leaning against a massive sculpted stone creature, sipping lemon tea from a small foil pack. She didn't see me approach. A sudden uproar from down the street made her flinch. Family members began to spill out from the dead man's residence, hoisting the fabric-wrapped corpse high overhead, turning the body this way and that, like pallbearers gone berserk. Some dropped away as new participants joined in amid the noise and chaos.

"They are trying to confuse the dead man's soul." My voice was loud and authoritative. "So it won't be tempted to leave his body and return to the family house. Never a good thing." Angelique's little tutorial on the cremation ritual only moments ago had come in handy. I liked appearing knowledgeable.

Fiona turned toward me, her face blank and questioning until she recognized me and brightened. "Ah, the beach hero!" She moved closer. "But nearly killed yourself in the process. Courageous but inefficient if two die instead of just one."

"Zero dead is best of all, of course. That was my plan." I winked, bluffing courage. She smiled back and her radiance melted my composure. Up close like this she was even more stunning than I recalled. My mind all but went blank.

Her features were perfect: lovely dark brown eyes above pronounced cheekbones, a porcelain complexion, and silky black hair flowing down her back. A rosebud mouth with beautiful lips. But her teasing tone made me feel unsure, even a little foolish.

I hoped approaching her like this wasn't a mistake.

"Yes," she said, "I know. They pass the corpse around. Family and friends are performing a service and honoring the deceased. Others are repaying debts."

I basked in the hypnotic warmth of her attention. She seemed friendly, but also proud and knowledgeable. A tiny bit stuck-up. I wasn't sure yet how to read her, but perhaps she liked me. Did I detect a teensy vibe of mutual attraction?

"So," I said, "you enjoying the cremation so far?" I immediately regretted sounding stupid and shallow. Good one, Dash.

She nodded, her brown eyes large. "The best is yet to come. Wait until they hoist that body onto the tower with seven roofs and march to the holy place. Then load the body into the bull and set it all on fire. Thrilling!"

Again (and silently grateful for Angelique's tutoring) I had a rejoinder. "But always obeying, of course, all the key restrictions on lighting that fire, right?"

"Restrictions?" Her eyebrows briefly knitted. Caught her off guard.

"You know, like no use of unclean devices like matches or cigarette lighters."

"Um, maybe a candle, perhaps?" She was still off-balance.

"Best is a magnifying glass to achieve ignition via pure energy from the sun."

"Ah, yes. Very good!" She approved. "So, sir, um—"

"I'm Dashiell X. Bonaventure II."

"I'm impressed," she said, slightly bowing in mock deference.

"But just call me Dash, like all my friends."

"Oh I see. And I am to be one of those many friends?"

"Yes, dear. Sorry, but it's mandatory."

She chuckled. "Fine. And I am Lo Ting-ting, but go by *Fiona*." I laughed. "What?"

"Your names. Good choice sticking with Fiona. I mean, *Yo Ding-a-ling?*"

"*Lo Ting-ting.*" She feigned dismay. "You're quite the flirt, Mr. Bonaventure; so I suspect you are an American."

I laughed. "Oh, so we're all brash and flirtatious? Okay. But what about you? You're definitely Chinese but I'm not sure which *flavor*? From your speech, certainly not from Singapore."

"Singaporean? No, *lah*." She laughed. "But I'll save you some guesswork. We're from Taiwan." Ahah, that explained a lot, like why she dressed so well, looked so prosperous, had such a fair complexion, was so well educated and spoke such good English.

I moved carefully toward the most crucial issue of all. "So, no escort today. Where's your boyfriend?"

"What, you mean Harry? He hardly goes in for this sort of thing."

"Stayed back in Kuta?"

"No, actually he's off on a one-week motor-coach tour through East and Central Java. A few nights in Jogja and Solo, visits to *Borobudur* and *Candi Prambanan,* dawn on horseback down into the volcanic crater of Mt. Bromo."

"Surprised he didn't take you."

She chuckled. "I plan to give those experiences the time they deserve. I'm in no hurry but Harry must head home, fairly soon."

My heart leapt at the prospect of an unencumbered shot at this enchantress. "None of my business, but—"

"Uh-oh."

"—I'm astounded Harry would leave you here, all alone." In my book it was never too early to start throwing dirt at a rival. "Now Fiona, if you were *my* girlfriend—"

"Oh, dear, just listen to you!" She shook her head but hid a smile behind her lovely hand and a sandalwood fan. She softly tittered with delight.

Before I could recover, a fresh commotion erupted in the street. Harsh clanging metallic tones pounded my eardrums anew and announced the funeral was underway. The fast rhythmic clanging of the *gamelan gong* impelled the crowd into motion.

The tower and sarcophagus began to rise and lurch, moving side to side, swerving wildly and threatening nearby observers. A line of women carrying offerings led the procession, trailed by family. All gripped a long white rippling cloth that was tethered to the cremation tower. The bamboo pagoda floated high in the air and, along with the bull sarcophagus, led the way for thousands of excited spectators. The unsteady tower swayed and lunged, its massive weight pressing down upon the bearers, who yipped and hooted to urge each other onward.

The enormous assembly seemed to ride atop the flood of bodies as it slithered its way through the village. Fiona and I fell into place alongside the massive crowd, pulled along by their frenzy and deafening uproar. Opportunistic, I grabbed her hand, tight, to ensure we weren't separated by the jostling masses. She gripped back.

Bottles of fermented palm sap and rice wine moved from stranger to smiling stranger. I took a swig from one and the yeasty alcoholic flavor tasted somehow *healthy* to me. Fiona wrinkled her nose and refused the bottle. I passed it on.

The procession stalled at an intersection blocked by a haphazard web of power lines hanging low across the road. While amused bystanders cheered them on, a squad of nimble youths (armed only with thin cloth gloves for insulation) snaked their way up the roadside poles and unhooked the lines one by one, lowering them to the ground. This feat looked not only tricky but downright *fucking dangerous.* Shinnying up those electrical poles, the kids could have gotten their guts fried by the 220 volt local current, necessitating a fresh round of cremations. Soon the procession resumed. The delighted crowd clapped and surged behind the sarcophagus.

"Up there," Fiona said, pointing ahead at higher ground, "must be the cremation site." The crowd poured into the area. A good five thousand or more massed there, agitated and impatient for this holy barbecue to start already. Showtime seemed imminent. So naturally, at that precise moment, a violent tropical downpour began to pummel Ubud. Fat, heavy raindrops blasted down from a leaden sky that only moments earlier had been brilliant blue. Spectators dashed for safety, including the dead man's family and bearers, the clearest sign nothing would be happening soon.

From our position on the outside edge of the crowd, Fiona and I moved fast. We grabbed a table at a small snack stand under a tarp canopy stretched to a tree. We bought drinks and a few packs of biscuits.

"That is *not* a good thing, for the dead man," Fiona opined. "People in Bali read *signs* into everything. To us it's just rain. But the Balinese will long remember how a storm materialized from a perfect blue sky, delaying the rich man's cremation. They will speculate what it meant. Perhaps he wasn't so blessed after all?"

This was my first chance at conversation since my botched *'If I were your boyfriend'* comment, so I tried to tease out more information from Fiona. Nothing to lose.

"Just hope it's not also raining too badly in East Java. I mean, where your boyfriend is."

She sighed and narrowed her eyes in mild irritation. Evidently, I was *that* transparent. "Dashiell, I suppose I should be flattered. But if we are to have any sort of relationship, you really must try to stop being so boring."

"Boring, me? Okay, but then *you* need to start calling me *Dash*, already." I sipped my cola and said no more, not wanting to jinx anything. She really *had* spoken about our future relationship, hadn't she?

"I suppose then I should tell you about Harry."
Oh, shit.
"You see, Dash," she purred, "Harry's my brother."
Her brother!

My heart, earlier smashed thin as a pancake, re-inflated and began to happily pound like a big bass drum.

I had the clear impression my life was pivoting into a new phase, one hopefully including a new relationship that might be downright beautiful.

CHAPTER SIXTEEN
The Fabulous Fiona Lo Ting-ting

The news stunned me but Fiona only shrugged her gorgeous shoulders. "How can that be," I demanded, "that Harry's your *brother?*" This turn of events was stunning. "Why, all along I thought suave ol' Harry was—"

"Yes, I know: my *boyfriend*. That was the plan. Safer if all you ravenous backpacker studs thought that." She giggled. "And would you believe we're twins?"

"Nope, now that's just impossible, Fiona. You're *way* better-looking."

She sighed. "Actually, Harry's quite handsome, in a *spoiled-Taiwanese-rich boy* sort of way."

"If you say so."

"Dash, you wouldn't believe how women back home chase him. It's disgusting. Sheer lust! Their clothes just drop off, almost of their own accord. Harry lacks for nothing in terms of female companionship."

The storm continued to piss on down and lash Ubud in watery violence. Other revelers took refuge wherever they could, bunched shoulder to shoulder under trees or leaning in under canopies of little shops.

Fiona flashed a coy grin and leaned closer. What was that, her scent: like vanilla and cinnamon? I was ready to consume her, right there.

"I was a Fine Arts major," she went on.

"Figures."

So the grand cultural tour of Asia had been her idea for a graduation gift. They'd take in religious arts and dance in Indonesia; the Shwedagon Pagoda in Rangoon plus Burma's the thousand temples at Pagan; Cambodia's mind-blowing, mammoth Angkor Wat (if entry was possible); and the Taj Mahal along with the subcontinent's myriad other glorious sights.

"But," she said with a frown, "my father refused." He was a domineering Taipei business titan accustomed to getting his way. "But as his cherished princess, I held my ground. I inherited my father's strength and stubborn streak. We bumped heads for months. Finally, a compromise."

"Travel with Harry?"

She smiled impishly and nodded. "My baby-sitter! But worth it. Father agreed to pay for a year-long, all-inclusive luxury tour. Completely regimented and safe with five-star hotels and spas, gala celebrations."

"So what are you doing in low-budget Kuta?"

"Dash! Who wants to be trapped in a pampered geriatric entourage and delivered safe to each location, right? In being strictly monitored and protected from danger, real or imagined, one misses all adventure and genuine experiences . . . the only real reasons to travel, no? Like this cremation, for instance. On a fancy tour, it wouldn't be possible to get here. Cremations occur with little notice. To partake, one must be nimble and flexible."

"Good point." But I was thinking, *and I'll bet she's nimble and flexible.* Her delicious, warm scent was distracting me again. Now did I smell notes of coconut? Good lord, the woman was hypnotizing me. Either that or I needed some dessert.

I tuned back in to her story.

". . . so Harry and I cashed in the prepaid luxury tour and headed off on our own."

"And what about Daddy?"

"None the wiser. Still thinks we're on the *Emperor Package* with Asia Platinum Tours."

"Sounds chic."

"Nothing but the best."

Fiona was sensuous and sassy, headstrong and intelligent. And there was that spectacular package, too.

"But Dash, our own version of a one-year grand tour is far more adventurous. With economy lodging and cheaper travel options, we're making father's money last, too. "

I chuckled. "You call *that* economizing? That's no buck-a-night *losmen*."

She made a face like there was a bad smell. "For Harry? Oh, please, Darling."

"But you're missing cultural highlights like hole-in-the-floor shitters and dueling courtyard chickens."

"A pity."

Then it was my turn. I provided an over-condensed version of my story.

"But then what, after all this, Dash? You can't just wander around for the rest of your life."

Why did people keep telling me that? Actually, why not just wander? At least till the money runs out. I just bounced my shoulders at her and deflected. "But what about *your* future plans, Fiona?"

She winced. "Already scripted out, both for Harry and me. Once we return home we take over a few branches of the family business, to train and learn. Over time our portfolios will expand until eventually including everything. Initially I get our fashion house business, all the big-flash brands in all the Asian capitals."

Considering her exquisite taste and strong fashion sense, that seemed like a good plan.

"I also get the food service business." She listed the names of famous food franchises. "All of them, ours, chains in all the major Asian cities.

"Nice. And what about our ladies' man, Harry?"

She detailed how the future division of the Lo family business aligned with then-prevailing sexual stereotypes. Harry was to command the industrial and real estate sectors, along with a construction business that dominated Asia, propelling great glass towers into the sky and striping the continent with superhighways, toll roads and bridges.

"Harry will also oversee the entertainment ventures," she said. "Mother's little joke is to call those businesses father's *little hobby*. Chains of movie theaters, private television networks, motion picture studios in Taipei and Hong Kong . . . but, best of all, a string of posh Chinese night clubs all across the continent."

"Chinese night clubs?"

"Every large Asian city has them if there's a significant Overseas Chinese population. They pour bottles of XO brandy or blue label scotch down the gullets of businessmen and overcharge like crazy. Across much of Southeast Asia the singers on stage are often Taiwanese. Malaysian men love them and the Singaporeans go crazy-*lah*. Many say Taiwanese women are among the loveliest in the world. "

I looked at her. "And modest, too."

She stared back deep into my eyes and didn't miss a beat. "Well, do you agree?"

I chuckled. "Well my sample size is far too small to extrapolate—"

She frowned.

"—but from what I've seen so far, the women of Taipei seem like goddesses."

Beaming a male-melting smile, she reached out and squeezed my hand.

"Dash, I have such a good feeling, a *special* feeling about you. And I am almost *always* right about people."

My heart jumped.

The infatuation was mutual. So back in Kuta we spent every waking hour together, strolling through affection's sweet garden, constantly delighted by our *yin-yang* complementarity. One's sweet usually offset the other's momentary sour.

Bali's rich culture provided an irresistible backdrop for deepening romance. Ours steadily grew, overwhelming us both. We spent hours in each other's arms and toured sights like temples, volcanoes and art performances. Hand-in-hand we'd jumped off a cliff and were floating rapturously down toward a heavenly valley far below, paying little mind to the future.

Harry only mildly protested at first. But as the love affair lingered his concern intensified, eventually morphing into anger. This for him was clearly an unwelcome complication.

He began to constantly hover and his intrusive guardianship began to exhaust us both. We toyed with the idea of traveling onward together.

"After all," she pouted, "I *am* an adult. In my twenties." I thrilled at the idea of becoming her protector and travel companion but foresaw problems.

"Harry's bad enough, Fiona, but what about your father?"

"Don't worry. He's far away, in Taipei, and probably little he could do once he learned the truth." She shrugged and smiled. "Harry might even cover for us, just a tiny while. *Maybe.*"

Now *that* I doubted.

We were powerless to resist the intoxicating idea of escaping together and traveling overland. Singles often paired up on the road, driven by romance or practicality. Sometimes single women even joined platonic males for travel safety. But our merger for the road would encompass it all: adventure, security, love and sex. We began to fashion a plan, borrowing Kelley's idea. The first stage was to head west across Java on two wheels, following the winding ribbon of blacktop, 600 glorious miles twisting past volcanoes and shimmering rice fields.

"Imagine the wind blowing through your hair, Fiona. Endless sky overhead. Total freedom to embrace every new sight or experience travel has to offer."

Kelley had already located a motorcycle rental agency in Denpasar and one could for a fee drop-off the bike in Jakarta at the western end of Java. It wouldn't be cheap (after all in Indonesia, only tourists did this) but the cost was reasonable. Comparable to a domestic air ticket.

Adrenalized, we filled our days planning the trip. Other than anticipated hostility from Fiona's family, my only concern was rustiness riding a motorcycle. "Just a minor consideration," I reassured her. "I rode motorbikes back in college. Just need a little practice to refresh my skills. They say you never really forget."

Fiona grew lovelier by the day and I needed to possess all of her. There was never enough. I was utterly infatuated and constantly daydreamed about our sweet future together.

I was investigating motorcycle rentals in Denpasar when unfriendly knuckles poked me in the back. After a few semesters of martial arts training at Olde Albion, in such situations I was zero thought and all reaction.

Jumping and pivoting in a single motion, I landed in a defensive crouch and ready to strike, my arms raised and fists at the ready. I relaxed when I saw who it was.

"Harry! Hey, man, what's up?" My first reaction was to be friendly and try to schmooze him—after all, I *was* entering a serious relationship with his sister.

But he was all cold fury. "You!" he hissed. "Don't give me that crap."

For the past month, while Fiona and I were bewitching each other, Harry remained a disapproving and ever-watchful presence. He maintained a distant reserve and we hardly ever spoke. Maybe he hoped our fling would burn itself out but each night when I brought Fiona back from dinner or a dance performance, there he was, staring out the window at their beach hotel. When we swam or sun-bathed, he monitored us from the shade of a tiny drinks shack. To escape his scrutiny, we often hid away at my dingy *losmen* room in rapturous afternoons of sensual indulgence. Fiona was an exotic gourmet feast and I couldn't get my fill.

Harry's hands were balled into fists and sweat beaded on his forehead. "Time you cooled it with my sister."

"Come on, Harry." I straddled a woebegone motorbike. "Fiona is an adult. Can make her own decisions."

"See, you don't get it. I am *telling* you. Stay away." Dude was furious. Blood pressure looked jacked. Made no sense to me.

"Hey, try and relax, man. You're out of bounds on this."

"No, you—" he poked my sternum "—are the one intruding."

Okay, maybe their all-powerful father entrusted Harry with his sister's welfare but he was taking this *way* too seriously.

"*Dashiell*—that's your real name, right?—you are interfering in something much larger and far more important than your little life." He closed his eyes and paused for a breath. When he resumed, his tone had moderated.

The guy was no dummy.

"Try and understand. Soon Fiona inherits a colossal fortune, a continental business empire, and her life is already scripted out. Those plans don't include a silly young Yank."

Silly? My temper started to flare.

"Believe me, as one of Asia's richest and most powerful men, there's no way my father will let her stay involved with the likes of you. No offense. But he already has her marriage planned out, and mine too. Alliances to deliver commercial or political leverage. In our world there is simply no room for silly romantic entanglements."

There it was again: *silly*. Clearly no respect from this guy. But he also seemed completely unaware of our plans to leave soon. Fiona had kept him totally in the dark. Good girl.

"Well, thanks for the heads-up, Harry, but let's allow Fiona to call her own shots. Okay?"

He shook his head. "Listen, friend. Putting my father's interests at risk is a dangerous game. He can be brutal. You have no idea."

"Nice guy, huh?"

"Actually, for those whom he loves, truly the best. And Fiona is the center of his universe. You don't mess with that. But for the likes of you—"

"Dirt, I know. Oh right—and *silly*. Yeah, I already got that."

"Listen, I'm just protecting my sister, as my father demands. And right now that means preventing mistakes like you. So don't you go and fuck up my future, too."

I feigned being a bit chastened, to buy time. "Okay, Harry, you've really given me a lot to think about." But inside, I knew it was time to leave with Fiona, and the sooner the better. Before her dictator brother caused trouble.

CHAPTER SEVENTEEN
Motorcycling to Europe

As Harry continued to lurk, he'd soon confirm Fiona and I were heating up, not cooling down. We needed to step up our getaway planning. And yet it still unsettled me, in a thrilling way, the day she blurted out her audacious suggestion over a lunch plate littered with spent satay sticks.

"I say let's just leave right away. Okay?"

"Absolutely! I agree. Soon as we can." But this sudden jump to warp speed worried me we might overlook something critical.

"Harry is being totally unbearable, Dash. It's taking all my willpower to not just snap back that we *are* going and he *can't* stop us."

Oh boy—now *that* would be a bad move. "Okay, then, time to get ready."

"Wonderful." She smiled lovingly. "What first?"

"Well, gotta cull our stuff down to one backpack apiece, max. That's all we can carry."

She shot me a sly, smoldering look. "But darling, my unmentionables alone will fill one . . . and trust me, you really don't want to miss any of those."

My cheeks burned but I blustered on. "You just pick out the best ones, Honey, and tell me about the rest."

"Okay," she tittered, "but your loss."

I shrugged. "Next, about money—"

"Harry tends to all that."

"Then you need to get your share, much as you can. And be careful. Don't tip him off something's up." She bit her lower lip and stared at the ground in thought. So that would be a challenge. "As for me, I've got a pad of traveler's checks in my money-belt. I'll cash a few right away."

"Right. What else?" She was beaming. Our adventure was starting and Fiona was loving it.

"I'll get the motorcycle. The rental fee isn't bad but the deposit for distant drop-off is fairly serious cash. We'll share that. Another reason to get your money."

"And what about maps?" She played with her satay sticks.

"We'll just wing it at first and follow road signs. But we've also got *this*." With a smirk I pulled out my dog-eared, yellow paperback guide. "And we'll check the tourist bulletin boards around Kuta for fresh info. Maybe get a current map at the Denpasar book stall."

We vowed to make steady progress each day and move ahead faster.

"Let's meet Paladin and Angelique for dinner," Fiona said. "Get an update on overlanding to Europe. They've been researching that for a while."

"Great idea. Oh and one more thing." I coughed, suddenly a little uncomfortable. "We should take a short practice ride, a little motorbiking refresher."

Her eyebrows flew high. "What? I just assumed (you being a guy and all) you were already good at that."

Ouch! That stung. "Well, Fiona, it has been a few years. A short ride around Bali will be fun anyway."

She nodded. "Okay. But just a quick trip. Visit some temple towns."

Our plan was coming together. And with each task ticked off the list, we were that much closer to our romantic overland escape.

Late the next morning, Fiona waited in the little book store in downtown Denpasar while I visited the small motor repair shop.

A hand-drawn sign in the window read *Sepeda Motor untuk Disewakan*: Motorcycles for Rent. Every surface inside the shop was caked black with grease and dust. Junkers of every description lie scattered around the lot out back: rusting motorcycles, small trucks and old, semi-demolished cars. In a far corner a car's front axle was propped up on two cracking cinder blocks and a mechanic lay underneath, sweating and naked but for a pair of shorts, putting his life at risk with every twist of the wrench.

I called out: *"Selamat pagi!"* Good morning. *"Apa kabar?"* Literally: What's the news?

From under the car a voice rang out with the standard reply: *"Kabar baik!"* News is good!

A small dark man with flashing eyes hopped up, wiping sweat from his forehead. *I Made Wirtha* (his name, according to the shop sign) was a one-man wonder who repaired, rented and sold vehicles. Yes, he grinned, he could rent me a bike. By the hour, day or month. Drop-off in Jakarta or even Bangkok? No problem.

He wheeled over a rusting, grease-covered Triumph 650cc motorcycle, more than enough power for two riders. I briefly wondered how this classic but bedraggled British bike had wound up in Bali in the first place. Perhaps we'd ride it back home to Europe, after its years in Asia.

His *Bahasa* flew by fast but I followed along okay. That was pleasing. He demonstrated the gear shift pattern and pointed out the reserve fuel tank switch.

I motioned at the empty space where an emergency toolkit once nestled but he just laughed, implying I wouldn't need it.

In my beginner's *Bahasa* I indicated I wanted the bike only a few hours, perhaps till late afternoon. He pursed his lips in thought and then charged me twenty dollars in *rupiah*, paid up front.

"Any additional deposit?"

"No need," he said, surprising me with some simple English. "*Tuan* sign paper. Nobody steal bike of Wirtha shop." Maybe I looked confused because he added, "Bali very small."

I started to fish out my driver's license but he waved that off, too, with a chuckle and went off to fill the gas tank from a large smudged plastic container. He spilled nary a drop. Then he signaled I could leave already and crawled back under the car to get back to work.

Just like that, for the first time in years, I found myself perched atop a motorcycle. When I cranked the handlebar grip to feed some gas the bike roared, the power between my legs surprising me. As I pulled out onto the street everything felt natural and easy: indeed, you don't forget. Everything came right back.

As I rolled down the small island capital's main drag, small shops and restaurants swept across my field of vision, streets bulging with tourists and sarong-wrapped women, school children and uniformed soldiers. The deep growl from my dual exhaust pipes announced my presence to those pedestrians. After the oppressive tropical heat, the cool breeze generated by motion felt luxurious.

I approached the bookshop and pressed the horn button. The funny little *beep* that issued forth surprised me.

Fiona came skipping out of the shop and squealed with delight. A wide grin adorned her pretty face, perfect in its symmetry, set off by a dimple on each cheek. She wore the latest fashion craze for our ride, tight designer jeans (first time I'd ever seen those) and swung a leg over the seat, settling in behind me. She wrapped her arms tightly around my waist and nuzzled her chin against my back.

I gunned the engine and off we went.

Our practice route promised a pleasant jaunt down winding asphalt roads to *Klungkung*, an old royal capital about twenty-five miles to the east, famous for the entrancing ceiling murals at its open-air palace courthouse on an island in a pond choked with lily-pads.

I continually braked and accelerated to pass standing buses and avoid bullock carts lumbering down the middle of the highway. We constantly swerved and slowed to miss ubiquitous potholes. Small boys ran out into the road, crossing at random, and Mercedes sedans occasionally roared past us, rich Chinese businessmen hurrying off to their next deals. Overall it was a good test ride, perfect for practice, and our spirits ran high. Stopping and starting, it felt like a game with which we soon grew comfortable. Rather than becoming frustrated we mastered the constant maneuvering and rhythm of this mode of travel, anticipating and smoothly overcoming obstacles.

I smiled and wondered if perhaps I was becoming more Zen lately, more easy-going and Eastern in my outlook?

The gentle, comforting pressure of Fiona's slender hands clenched in front of my stomach kept me present in the moment. I drank in the entire experience and thanked providence for my current streak of good fortune. In between rural villages, the traffic thinned out and on both sides of the highway, verdant rice paddies glistened in the sun. It was a tranquil, picture-postcard setting.

My brain flooded with endorphins and I buzzed with pleasure. I leaned comfortably into the curve as the road drifted slightly right, heading toward a bend through a thicket of trees.

At first my brain couldn't quite process the flurry of odd perceptions that flashed at me, nearly all at once.

First I spotted something odd up the road, something flapping and waggling. Moving toward me and dangling like a little flag. A fluttering white cloth.

It made no sense but I realized it was hanging from a long bamboo pole and my eyes then locked onto a slim, wizened old man, holding that pole in outstretched arms. He wore no shirt and his head was wrapped in a soiled rag.

This perception seemed near-hallucinatory and fully blossomed the next instant.

Marching out ahead of him and following his dancing white flag, approaching me and now swinging into full view around the bend in the road, was an army of fifty or more brown and white ducks, all waddling in formation. They quacked and bounded down the asphalt road like avian soldiers drilling in fluffy, feathered uniforms.

The innocent creatures probably sensed impending disaster just a heartbeat before I did, so their panic came first. All the simulated military order crumbled as they began to flap and squawk and a few succeeded in taking flight. But most of them just bounced and tripped against each other, creating a scrambling mess blocking the road.

And now I was already nearly on top of them.

With no time to think. I jerked the motorcycle handlebars to steer clear but it was already too late.

And that one bad move only destabilized the bike.

My world exploded into a chaos of squalling cries by the birds, wings flapping madly and feathers flying everywhere. I collided with perhaps a dozen of the unfortunate creatures, each impact feeling surprisingly heavy, like being pounded by a club. Their bodies ricocheted in all directions. The old herder screamed out and dived off the road for safety.

I tried to brake but that just made things worse. The cycle, having already lost its grip on the road, began to skid and swerve atop stray pebbles and gravel. I held on for my life. The machine felt angry, thirsting for blood and possessed of its own mind and intentions.

Careening toward the road shoulder, the machine began to increasingly lean over and enter into a tilting spin while still sliding forward. I screamed out – *Oh my God, no! No no no!*—but no sound issued.

Stony shrapnel and metal pieces began to cut into my skin as I spun along the ground but I felt no pain. Everything seemed shifted into slow-motion, but was still happening way too fast for pain. Surreal as a bad dream, strange and astonishing, all this felt like an eternity but probably took only a few seconds.

The last I remember was the menacing thicket of trees roaring up at me. I reached for Fiona's hands at my waist but they were gone.

Then everything went black.

CHAPTER EIGHTEEN
Rumah Sakit Denpasar

I emerged from the blackness and at first only sensed some kind of throbbing, hovering presence amid the brilliant light. There were no shadows in this world, only a pleasant muffled hum and blinding whiteness.

As my head continued clearing, more started to come back to me. Realizations broke against one another like waves splashing across the beach of my consciousness.

Abruptly, I became aware of myself as a sentient being and of the passage of time.

The questions began.

But where . . . how . . . ?

Gulping for air, I gazed up and saw a young nurse in a crisp white uniform and smart domed cap. As she leaned over me to adjust a tangle of plastic tubes and wires, I inhaled her fresh clean soapy scent. She cranked knobs, adjusted counterweights and made refinements to a mechanical pulley.

Then she spoke. She was asking if something was okay. But is *what* okay? And what language was that? And how did I know it?

I tried to smile and say thanks but my mouth didn't work and only a dry, throaty hiss emerged. Regardless, it seemed to inspire her. Excited, she summoned a doctor.

I looked up at the large white ceiling fan buzzing softly overhead and realized that must have been the humming energy source. That initial, comforting Genesis-like presence.

But back to the nurse and all those tubes and contraptions. Pulleys and counterweights, for what?

Where was I?

I tried taking a census of body parts but couldn't turn my head, which was propped up and somehow immobilized. My eyes darted side to side but if I'd broken an arm or a leg, I couldn't tell yet.

Then I began to understand. The euphoria was due to heavy sedation. I was doped up outta my mind. What were they pumping into me?

Groggy memories began to flicker like a small candle on a far windowsill. Confused thought fragments sparkled and tantalized, but lay just beyond reach.

Uh, wait. There was something else. Something about what … a motorcycle?

That's when it all began to race back.

I remembered losing control. A spin-out? The dam then collapsed and returning memories began to flood down upon me. I'd been motorcycling somewhere. Bali! The duck herder's white flag.

I remembered the horrible, sudden collision with all those poor creatures, their panic and flapping of wings, the clouds of feathers as my bike spun out and skidded across the road and down into a wooded thicket.

I flashed on my mother's death, similar circumstances years ago, in a frozen Illinois cornfield.

And then arose the most critical memory of all.

I hadn't been alone.

Though immobile and previously mute, a raspy cry issued as panic exploded within me.

"Fiona!" What had happened to her? I searched my memory, but couldn't recall hearing her cry out. I couldn't recall hearing anything. Had it all occurred just too fast for her to even react?

I tried to remember last feeling her arms around my waist, during the accident, but couldn't.

How long had I been unconscious? Days?

The petite nurse interrupted, feeling my forehead and shining a light in my eyes to check the pupillary reflex.

"*Bagus!*" she said. Fine. "*Tuan kembali.*" Sir has come back.

I easily followed her simple *Bahasa*. No tenses, gender words, prefixes or suffixes. Trying to speak, I croaked out, "*Dimana ada saya?*" Where am I? I sounded as raspy as a ninety-year-old man.

She giggled. "*Tuan ada disini.*" Sir is *here*.

In my confused and weakened state I was no match for a playful nurse. "*Nona, apa tempat ini?*" Miss, what is this place?

"*Ini rumah sakit, tuan, di* Denpasar." A hospital, sir, in Denpasar.

At least the conversation was waking me. Out of the corner of my eye I could now see my left arm in a plaster cast and elevated, supported by a pulley device. I tried to peer around and assess other injuries, the best I could, and spotted my right foot in a cast, also elevated. Everywhere else was an acre of white adhesive tape wrapping me up like Boris Karloff in *The Mummy*.

I gathered she must've taken special care of me, her unconscious pet patient. Considering the sponge bathes and whatnot, she now knew as much about me, physically, as Fiona. And she also knew everything I needed to know about my condition.

What about Fiona?

That realization excited me. Probably made me seem suddenly anxious because she started to stroke my forehead and mutter soft, calming words while her other hand flew up toward valves on the nest of tubes snaking around my bed.

And just like that, that same wonderful warmth as before began to return and percolate throughout my body. All the crisp lines delineating my room began to fuzz out, in the most pleasant way.

Oh, no! . . . .. Ah, yes . . . she's putting me under, again.

My last waking thoughts, as long as I could hold onto them, were about the accident. What had happened to Fiona? I wasn't thinking straight. Should have asked if there was another tourist in the hospital, a pretty Chinese woman?

It was already too late. A thin rivulet of drool leaked from the corner of my mouth and puddled on my hospital gown. I didn't care.

The last I could recall, the nurse wiped my mouth with a cotton ball, readjusted my pillow and switched off the light.

I drifted in and out of sedation for days, aware of neither time nor pain. But each time I revived, the euphoric blur faded faster and reality reconstructed more quickly. Maybe they were reducing my dosage?

Unable to think clearly, I mindlessly studied the austere hospital room, counting chip marks on the dirty concrete walls or scuffs on the linoleum floor. The room's single window was always latched, keeping it warm and stuffy inside. My budget travel guide had warned that Indonesian hospital care didn't match the quality back home but was cheap. And for broken bones and the like, more than sufficient.

I ordered my drugged brain to try and remember, next time the nurse returned, to ask about Fiona. Was she perhaps in the next room? Nursie would know.

I pictured my reunion with Fiona and felt a momentary thrill. We would abandon motorcycling forever and resume our travels via cheap and safe public transport. Wander Asia by bus or train, taxi and ferry.

One afternoon when my mind seemed its clearest yet, I sensed something odd, like I was not alone. This first emerged as intuition but crystalized into certainty. Somehow I knew someone was in the room with me. Watching.

There, that noise again, what was that?

It was a soft tapping sound, like someone testily rapping a pencil on a table top. Was I imagining it?

I struggled to speak through lips of jelly. Even on reduced dosage the sedative was still in control. I finally managed to hiss out, "Is someone there?"

Footsteps shuffled toward me from behind and I expected to see the nurse but prayed to instead see Fiona's perfect face swing into view.

Instead, the menacing countenance of Fiona's brother appeared. His face stopped just inches from mine.

"Harry," I croaked, "it's you." My throat hurt as I spoke.

The underlying resemblance to his twin sister was apparent, though in an angry, brooding, anti-Fiona sort of way. Symmetrical but opposite. Distorted.

He just scowled.

"I asked them to phone me as soon as you came out of the coma." A cruel smile masked his face. "You know how easy it would be to just kill you, right now? Just turn off a machine, mess with your medicine lines. And there's always this." He held up a pillow. "In your face. The local doctors would never know."

That was crazy talk and my heart started to race. I whispered, "But what about Fiona? Is she—?"

"Ah, good! Concern. So touching." His face twisted. "Too bad it comes too late, only after you risked her life on a junk motorcycle. No helmets, a dangerous Indonesian highway." His face was glowing crimson. "You fucking bastard."

"Please, Harry . . . is she okay?"

He spat out a scornful laugh. "She was pitched into the air and skidded across the pavement. Broken bones, and massive internal bleeding. They found her at the base of a tree."

"Oh my God." Sedated or not, my heart tried to thump out of my chest. I could picture it all. *Dear, sweet Fiona!* Tears filled my eyes and I couldn't breathe. But all that only fanned Harry's rage.

"You miserable son of a whore . . . but yes, she's still alive. If you can call it that.'

Thank you, sweet Jesus.

"And is she . . . here?" I pictured her room, just down the hall.

He leaned closer and exhaled a stench of cigarettes and garlic at me. His pitiless eyes glared through black spectacles. "Here?" A cruel laugh. "Only briefly. She's long gone already. And you'll never see her again. We'll make sure of that."

He growled a low sound, not unlike a wild animal. "It was my fault for not stopping you two right from the start. So naturally Father now holds *me* responsible. Rightly so."

"Sorry, but—"

"Shut up! You can't even begin to understand *my* loss. My entire future. My father is close to writing me off. He's furious! So as horribly as Fiona was injured, you also managed to colossally fuck me up." He saved his cruelest blows for last, detailing Fiona's injuries, the harm I had personally caused to my beloved. "You worshiped my sister. Remember her lovely face? Well half was scraped away against the asphalt road, right down to bone, flesh removed from an entire side of her head. One ear was never found." He began to tear up, more in anger, but fought it off. "Her injuries were horrendous. She was literally beaten to a pulp. All her beauty destroyed."

Harry drew in a slow, deep breath.

"From Taipei, father immediately took charge. No way would he trust Indonesia's Stone Age medical care. He immediately arranged an ambulance jet to medevac her to Australia. She's in a Darwin hospital right now, still being stabilized. Father has assembled a team of specialists to attend to her, best in the world, and flew them in from London, Sydney and New York. As soon as possible, they'll transfer her down to Sydney for the extended recovery process—plastic surgery, reconstructions, fittings for prostheses, physical therapy, all that. The physicians say she'll be fighting back for years."

I felt searing pain but also empty inside. My love had been sentenced to live a nightmare and though it was totally an accident, I felt responsible. It all seemed so unfair and my injuries by comparison seemed insignificant.

"Harry, please believe how sorry I—"

"You *should* be sorry. Changes nothing." He fake-smiled an insincere grimace at me. "But relax. I don't need to kill you. Father is busy at Fiona's bedside in Darwin, but he'll take care of matters, soon enough."

Surely this gangster revenge talk was just Harry being melodramatic and trying to scare me. Well, it was working.

He read my mind. "Don't doubt it for a moment, Dash, it's real. You destroyed his baby princess so Father will extract serious payback."

In a case of the world's best timing, my pet nurse entered the room dragging clouds of soapy floral scent with her. She smiled and pointed at the wall clock, pantomiming that Harry's visiting time was over.

"I'm done here anyway." He picked up his things and slowly started toward the door.

I called out in a soft croak. "But Harry, please! Tell Fiona I love her . . . and how badly I feel . . . and apologize to your father, too. Believe me—"

He paused at the door and sneered. "Oh, I *believe* you but your grief doesn't mean shit. And soon you'll be absolutely, *totally* sorry. Father has some rather nasty, violent friends who owe him favors. Get me?"

He walked out.

Comprehending nothing, the sweet young nurse appeared happy to be left alone again with her favorite patient. She padded over, sat on my bedside and began opening the valve on my sedation line.

"*Selamat tidur, tuan,*" she breathed. Good night, sir.

After a few more days the hospital stay was really starting to wear on me. My guilt over Fiona's injuries was a constant weight, along with steadily growing fear her vengeful father might soon turn up.

Even the small solace of that cute little nurse's ministrations ended; she was reassigned and ordered to stay away from the young *orang putih*.

To top things off, they cut way back on my painkillers. They gave me just enough to lie there, conscious and brooding. Just my thoughts and the ceiling fan.

I needed to heal quickly and get away.

The replacement nurse was brawny as a sumo but quite educated and tasked with weaning me from that morphine regimen. Thus it was good-bye to the friendly, warm rush spreading through me every four to six hours. And with my meds knocked way back, pain started keeping me awake at night.

On the plus side, sumo nurse could communicate better and provided a full inventory on my injuries. I'd been in a coma for days and, at least at first, it was feared I might not make it.

My left forearm was broken and right shin fractured, explaining the plaster casts and elevation devices around the hospital bed. I'd lost sizable patches of skin from my legs, back and sides. Regarding all those tubes, one delivered painkillers and another was for an antibiotic cocktail to stave off infection. The prevailing logic in Denpasar regarding antibiotics seemed to be the more, the better.

Fine with me.

And yet another line was my nutrition drip. Indeed, I couldn't recall having eaten since I'd been there.

She held up a mirror and the side of my head looked pumped full of air. Real beauty of a black eye too.

But despite all that I was lucky compared to Fiona. Would I ever get a chance to apologize? How could I ever make amends? As much as my physical injuries hurt, the emotional pain surpassed that.

Sumo nurse nudged me awake.

"*Sudah sepuluh hari, tuan,*" she said. Already ten days, sir. "*Teman-teman kamu datang.*" Your friends have come.

Friends?

I shivered to picture Harry and his monstrous father or his henchmen ready to descend.

But to my eternal delight, in breezed Paladin Kelley and Angelique. He shot me one of those patented Paladin smirks (*well, look at you!*) but she just sniffled and some smeared mascara streams ran down her cheeks.

They were less efficient than Harry and only tracked me down days later.

"You disappeared, Dash. Wayan was kinda freaking and asked if I'd be paying your bill." Kelley chortled. "Fat chance!"

Angelique patted a kerchief to her eyes. "Oh, Dash! You look horrid." *Aw-reeeeed.* "I'm so sorry."

Kelley fired up a *kretek* right there in the hospital room and clove-scented tobacco smoke began to sail up into the ceiling fan. "We just assumed you were shacked-up with that righteous Fiona, maybe at her hotel. But after a few days not seeing you around Kuta, we guessed maybe you headed out, overland."

He held up a finger. "Ah, but then I saw my little motorcycle shop fella and he was whining about a crash that wrecked one of his bikes. Some *orang putih* was injured plus a girl. Bingo! This Denpasar hospital was the first place I looked . . . and whaddya know, here you are, all drugged-up and bloody."

"Not as druggy as before. They're starting to get stingy."

The two seemed overjoyed to find me and offered help.

"Thanks, guys, I'll be okay. Just tell Wayan to hold my room and don't worry about the bill. I'm recuperating fast as I can. Back on my feet soon."

Kelley chuckled. "Ah the wonders of Indonesian medicine."

"Evidently."

I shared the wretched tale of Fiona and her injuries, plus her embittered and vengeful family.

"Then better get your ass outta here ASAP, Dash. If you were in better shape, you could even leave with us. We're heading off to Europe in another day or two."

"Cycling?"

Kelley nodded.

"Needless to say, be careful."

Kelley flinched. "Gotcha."

We at last came to final farewells and acknowledged (without harping on it) we might never meet again.

"But life is funny, man." Kelley grinned. "Maybe someday you'll cruise into a casino and there I'll be, dealing blackjack or running a craps table." He grinned broadly, his mustache rising. "Just wink that you recognize me, amigo, and get ready for the lucky streak of your life! Paladin gonna bury his buddy in chips."

I laughed. "You'd do that for me?"

"Well, for the usual cut, of course." He smiled.

"Sure. Penny on the dollar, right?"

He shook his head and laughed and moments later they were gone. The aroma of *kretek* and Angelique's perfume lingered in the room as I drifted back off to sleep.

My circadian rhythms were all screwed up. I slept during the day and due to my reduced painkillers was up at night, suffering.

Late afternoon one day, I again woke to that *not alone* feeling. Was it intuition? Maybe just brain processing sensory input at the subconscious level—barely-heard sounds or someone's body heat being sensed?

Whatever, I knew somebody was in the room with me.

Please, God—not Fiona's father or his muscle.

The brace restrained my head so I couldn't turn and look. My small attempt at motion triggered an immediate response as I heard the metal chair behind me scrape on the linoleum and someone stand up. Footsteps approached from behind.

Crippled and weak, bed-ridden, I was in no shape to deal with a revenge-seeking billionaire or his hired thugs. I'd only be safe once I'd put a continent between myself and that man and his angry son. I bargained for mercy with any higher powers that might be monitoring patients in the Denpasar hospital.

When the mystery visitor came into view I gasped.

"What . . . how did you . . ." My words came rasping out, tangled and breathless.

It was Little Fatty.

He laughed and raised his hands overhead, interweaving and cradling his fingers, as he feigned beginning yet another series of his bizarre stretching exercises like at the losmen. I burst out laughing, which only shot bolts of pain up and down my body.

"Good Lord . . . it's my little buddy, the bore of Johor! Chinese contortionist and champion swimmer."

About a month after nearly drowning, Fatty looked very well. But he'd returned to Malaysia so how on earth was he back in Bali? Just seeing him was like a happy hallucination. He nodded and winked at me and spoke in his clipped accent, dripping with *Singlish* slang.

"All last week, Dash, entire world go mad, *lah*! Everybody in Bali want Little Fatty! Police, US consulate, awful Denpasar hospital and what-not. After your accident, Fatty suddenly become rock star."

"I don't get it. Why you?"

"Aduh! No talking, Dash, please just listen to story. Police search your wallet and discover man with no family, home or friends . . . except one. Stuffed deep inside your wallet they find little scrap of paper with address and phone of Fatty, in Malaysia."

"The one that you—"

"Shush!" He play-scowled. "Anyway, considering all your mounting bills, medical and legal—"

"Whaddya mean, legal?"

"Shh!" Fatty held a finger to his lips, overly dramatic and stern, his eyes opened wide. "The Bali authorities redouble chasing Fatty and his money. They demand I pay all your bills." He bent over laughing. His eyes twinkled through bottle-thick spectacles and his chubby rounded cheeks dimpled. "I mean how can, *lah*?"

"But what about all my money? My traveler's checks? I had them with me. Had just taken from safekeeping with Wayan since we were getting ready to leave."

"Funny, but nothing found at crash site." Fatty sighed. "So, welcome to Asia."

My chest clenched. With no cash I was finished.

"So you give authorities big headache, Dash: penniless foreigner with expensive problem and no back-up. Hospital fees and damages. Many dead duck and unless you pay duck herder, after you heal, you go straight to jail. Not so nice there, maybe." He shook his head. "So they phone Fatty in JB so many time! They worry. *Mat salleh* in coma many days but no visitors."

He stared into my eyes. "Of course, I tell them truth, Dash. No choice! '*What, my friend, that mat salleh? No lah, how can?? Perhaps gweilo pick Fatty pocket, get my contact details that way.*'"

The short man rose from his chair he pantomimed washing his hands. "So anyway, my *gweilo*, best of luck to you."

I had to admire his act. "Hah! Well screw you, too, Fatty."

His façade broke a moment later and he returned to my bedside, chuckling. "Fatty pretty funny fellow, no?" He patted my shoulder.

"Oh, you're good, *Mr. P.Y. Lee*. Real good." I tried to reach out and poke him with my better arm, but thick bandage wrapping and a brace hampered movement. He just clucked and smiled.

"So anyway I tell them, '*Yes, of course is my friend, and Fatty will pay all miserable bills and hustle fat little self back to*

Bali.' But *aiee-yah*, wife very upset, *lah*, until I share secret story of near-death of Little Fatty, Surfer Boy. Then I buy air ticket and ask friend to watch over my business, please not rob. *Aduh*, so many headache, just for *gweilo*. But Bali people now happy and tell me, '*No hurry, and Fatty take time—Dash going nowhere soon.*'"

He shrugged.

"I arrive and first resolve legal problems. Pay off duck man: not too bad, only two hundred Malaysian ringgit." Less than a hundred dollars. "And once I start to pay your debts, other Balinese find *me*. Fellow in greasy shirt turns up with hand out for *moto-cy* you destroyed. I pay $500 U.S. Not too bad, I guess."

A rush of gratitude overwhelmed me. My dear friend had returned to help. Although initially thrown together by random circumstances, Little Fatty and I had become closer than brothers. After the incident at sea he would never forget his obligation to me. Just as I would never forget what he was doing for me now.

But still crushed by guilt over Fiona's injuries, I questioned if I even deserved such a good friend's love. I poured out my pain to Fatty, who sat quietly next to my bed. He nodded as he listened to my grief and made reassuring sounds. After I had talked myself out, he rested a reassuring hand on my bandaged shoulder.

"*Aiee-yah*, Dash, why so much talking about *fault* and *guilt*? Nobody at fault, that's why is called *accident*." He bounced his shoulders. "You only want love for Fiona, isn't it? The way I see, you are *both* victim."

"Yes, but—"

"Both are adult and make decisions. But was an *accident*. If must blame, fault is probably old duck man."

Maybe. But still. . .

"Why on road with so many duck, hey?"

"But Fatty the poor dude just wanted to walk his flood to a nearby rice paddy, I suppose. Catch a meal and a swim."

"Right," Fatty nodded. "But then, *ac-ci-dent*."

Next morning, Fatty bounded into the hospital room, his spirits pumped by news. "Dash, despite you still look like plate of scrambly eggs (heavy with *gweilo* ketchup) hospital want to discharge you."

I couldn't believe it. "Great but I still hurt all over."

"Yes. Happy time over, Dash. No more drugs inside ugly *mat salleh* body. Soon feel just like old self—but with multiple fracture, black eyes, and sutures."

"Whew." I frowned. "That's a relief. I feel better already."

"Serious, is good news—soon you can travel, though no more *moto-cy*."

What would I do next? Spend a month recuperating at the primitive *losmen*? That sounded like prison, maybe even a death sentence by making it easy for Harry's father to find me.

Little Fatty read my mind and his next words shocked me. "So no other choice, Dash. Come to Malaysia to heal. You must! Rest at my home in JB. Nancy will fatten you up with *nasi lemak* and *bak kut teh* . . . delicious Malaysian health food. Pork and broth, chicken curry, eggs, coconut steamed rice." He rubbed his bulging tummy and laughed.

"I don't think—"

"Exactly your usual problem, Dash—no thinking. There's nothing to think. Come rest in Johor, weigh future options. Besides Fiona's father wants to kill you, hmm?" His eyebrows rose. "Malaysia is far away. We'll hide you." He laughed. "And maybe you can try your hand at business. Become my junior partner."

That was a laugh. Run a business in a foreign country? But Fatty didn't seem to be totally joking.

"Well, Fatty, that's an absolutely amazing idea but I don't know."

"Otherwise, you can continue to backpack and hide from world. Stay in dollar-a-day beach huts and screw dollar-a-night hookers. But would that really make you happy?"

"That's a trick question?"

We both laughed.

"You'd enjoy it for a while, Dash, but it goes nowhere—we both know. You can stay in JB long or as short as you want. Maybe only just a couple years." Fatty giggled. "But honestly, is a very nice place and my wife is excellent cook. I put bed in empty room where you can heal. Sort everything out."

No question the offer had considerable merit. Actually live somewhere exotic, set down roots and even work—why not? Happy memories from my expat days back in HK supported the idea. And Little Fatty was offering me the semblance of a family.

He kept on selling. "Besides, it's the least I can do. Remember, I still owe—"

"Stop it, Fatty, there's no debt. You owe me nothing. We're just friends."

"Exactly my point, too."

I realized he'd won this debate.

"As your friend, Dash, let me help. It will be easy for me and fun, too, like having a brother in my business. We will haunt every banana leaf curry restaurant in JB and go to night clubs. It'll be great. And your visa is easy—just regularly cross the causeway into Singapore and come back. Your tourist visa renews each time."

"Is that legal?"

"Yes though frowned upon. But don't worry, I have friends at JB immigration." He nodded, a glint in his eye.

The hospital released me two days later. The bill tallied up to a tenth of what I expected. Fatty paid in cash.

My two nurse friends appeared heartbroken. The younger, besotted beauty openly sobbed as they rolled me to the front door and down a ramp, where I got up onto crutches. Sumo nurse just smiled and shook my hand. It hurt.

Little Fatty rented a taxi for the day. First, he hauled me back to the losmen. Wayan showed absolutely no surprise to see me, as if I'd just returned from a half-hour walk. He poured hot tea and helped me slowly maneuver into my concrete room. Fatty propped me up in the bed and handed me over to Wayan's family for care.

"I am off to Denpasar to make arrangements," he said. "Back by nightfall. And tomorrow we leave on a direct flight to Singapore. From Changi Airport we'll taxi across the causeway into Johor Baru." He spoke so matter-of-factly, his tone indicating "no major deal," that I had no chance to tense up.

Deep down, though, I could sense something enormous was underway.

Book Four

The Floating Diamond
Straits of Malacca, 1980

CHAPTER NINETEEN
Welcome to Johor

Arrival at Little Fatty's
Johor Baru, South Malaysia - 1980

After several hours on Air Indonesia we landed at Singapore's Changi Airport and hailed a creamy blue taxi. It sped us across the velvety smooth ribbons of asphalt lacing this modern urban island, until we reached the north shore causeway link with Malaysia. After perfunctory customs and immigration formalities, we drove across onto the verdant Southeast Asia mainland.

Our taxi nosed through the noise and bustle of downtown Johor Baru before heading toward the city's outskirts and a green, comfortable-looking neighborhood dotted with small cement homes. Cars of all kinds crouched behind each low-rise bungalow's gate and hinted at each household's economic status. There were Volvos, occasional BMWs, and many Toyotas, but the majority were *Proton Sagas*, the Malaysian national car. "Actually," Fatty shrugged, "is just a re-badged Mitsubishi."

We pulled up at his house. A gorgeous midnight blue Mercedes sedan sat in the driveway.

"Wow, Fatty, that's a beauty!"

"You expected something less?" Fatty winked, dimpling his cheek. His precious toy was a decade old but fully restored to near-mint condition. It exuded the appropriate aura for him, of prestige.

Funny, I hadn't really noticed that before, this apparently intense drive of his for wealth and social rank.

After the taxi halted, a pert and diminutive Chinese woman swung open my door and reached for my hand. "Hello, Dash, and welcome! I am Nancy. I'm with that fellow over there, the bad swimmer." She smiled and cocked her head in Fatty's direction. He nodded back.

Behind Nancy a tiny angel in a tailored silk jumpsuit hid and held fast to her mother's calves. "And down there, that's our little Ayna." The two-year-old was an utter darling, a pixie with bangs and dimples like an animated doll.

The house looked attractive in stuccoed white with an orange tile roof. Whitewashed security walls, topped by embedded shards of broken glass, surrounded a compact compound filled with abundant vegetation that created the sensation of a luxurious tropical garden—especially the grassy retreat out back where the family raised orchids and tended a small vegetable garden.

I followed Fatty, hobbling slowly on wooden crutches he'd purchased for me in Denpasar. My broken arm made movement doubly difficult. He led me to a small storage room that had been converted into my bedroom. At a glance, it looked stark, a simple bed surrounded by shelves stacked with household goods.

Maybe Fatty read the concern in my face. "Never mind, Dash," he said, leading me out back, "because here's where you'll spend most of your time the next months, healing." He swung the back door open and a green refuge delighted my eyes. A simple patio deck was at the center, well-shaded by palm trees. And leaning against the high white perimeter wall were banana and mango trees heavily laden with fruit. A large cardboard carton sat atop the wrought iron and glass table. "And look here, what I buy for you!" Fatty giggled with excitement. "A new chaise lounge. Will soon have permanent imprint of Dashiell backside, so we can never forget you."

What a friend!

But I was so exhausted that after a quick early dinner I collapsed into the back room bed for a nap. I was immediately out cold, sound asleep despite my continuing pain.

Deep into that first night at Fatty's, a howling voice boomed out and shocked me awake. "Whoa!" I hollered, "What the hell?"

Seconds later Fatty shuffled in, wearing flip-flops and a purple silk robe with a golden dragon embroidered across the back. "Sorry, Dash, forgot to warn you about the *muezzin*."

"The what?" I rubbed my eyes.

"The neighborhood Islamic holy man. The mosque is quite nearby." He pointed out the window. "That's the recorded call to prayer over a loudspeaker."

"But why—"

"Five times every day he reminds all Muslim faithful of their duty: '*Come to pray. Come to salvation. Allah is most great. No God but Allah.*' Like that."

"Fine but it's 3 a.m."

Fatty chuckled. "Don't worry, it's almost over. And soon you won't hear it anymore." And he was right—it was like living near railroad tracks and not hearing the trains. It would take only a week for my cerebral filter to permanently tune out the holy racket.

Unable to sleep any longer I hobbled my way to the backyard garden and Fatty followed. A beautiful smell scented the air.

"Frangipani," he said, helping me onto the yellow lounge chair, now unboxed and smelling of new vinyl printed with gaudy red flowers.

"Frangi what?"

"The flower you are smelling. Many frangipani trees in our neighborhood. Release their perfume at night."

"Nice, but doesn't make up for the abrupt 3 a.m. wake-up call."

Fatty smiled. "Malaysia not bad for a *gweilo* American. Former British colony so English everywhere." He handed me my tattered yellow travel book. "Tomorrow job is you read Malaysia chapter. Learn quick." I nodded. "But for now, I give you Fatty Short-Cut Version. Okay, *lah*?"

"Okay, *lah*."

"Good, your first *lah!*" He patted my shoulder. "First, we call this town JB, capital of Johor State, which also has its own sultan, palace and holidays." I nodded. "Next, we Malaysians come in three flavor: Malay, Chinese and Indian."

"Complicated. Does everyone get along?"

"We do now. But population mix is not a naturally peaceful one."

"How so?"

Fatty sighed. "We are quite different. Consider. Malay are half the population, rural Muslim folk who live in small villages and grow rice. We Chinese are one third and city people. Commercial: we do business. And the Indians are just a sliver, one tenth of population. Mainly Tamil Hindus. Arrived in 1800s to work at British colony plantations for rubber and palm oil. Much better life than back in India."

A night bird trilled out a sweet tune and bats looped down over Fatty's tree tops. A noise behind me startled me: Nancy arrived with a platter of tea and biscuits and quietly sat down to join us.

"Dash receiving first lesson about Malaysia," Fatty said. Nancy nodded.

"So, Dash, as long as Britain ruled colony until 1957, everything under control. But after independence, natural friction and resentment grew until all hell blow up in 1969. Terrible race riots."

What, here? It shocked me to hear that—the place looked so mild and the people, sweet.

"Many Chinese died at the hands of angry Malay mobs. My uncle . . ." Nancy's face went dark.

"But why the hatred?" I didn't understand.

"My people were seen as oppressors," Fatty explained. "Although in the majority, the Malays saw themselves as economically disadvantaged compared to us Chinese. It's true, we are a clever minority. Easy to blame. Our businessmen seemed too rich and powerful and dominated the economy."

"Jealousy." This story was getting interesting.

"Yes, but more than that. I admit it was hard for a non-Chinese to compete with us. Our culture of family help, capital sharing and cooperation is a great advantage, spurring business success."

"So how did you achieve today's racial peace?" At 4 a.m. I was wide awake now, sipping hot black Chinese tea from a tall clear water glass. Grounds accumulated at the bottom like coal cinders, but the tart flavor was so refreshing. And once this raised a light perspiration, I could feel cooling breezes.

Nancy refilled my tea. "A deal was struck, Dash, to guarantee Malaysia's peace and prosperity."

Fatty jumped in. "Understandings, written and unwritten, were reached about how the economy and power would be shared in the future."

"Cool."

"First, the *written*. Something called the *New Economic Policy* was set up and over following decades would steer ownership of the economy into Malay hands. The NEP established preferences favoring the Malays for hiring, education, equity ownership in companies . . . all that."

"And what about the *unwritten*?"

"We Chinese would be left alone and given free rein to do our business, though increasingly large tracts of the economy were cut off from us. Government tenders and so forth. But we're a confident sort and were okay with that, especially considering the bloody alternative."

After 1969, that made sense.

"So, Dash, basically the *bumiputeras* (another word for Malays, meaning 'sons of the soil), with half the population, obtained absolute control over the national government. And the Chinese were left to our own commercial devices. The out-gunned Indians received table scraps."

"What also helped," Nancy added, "was that in recent years, Malaysia became rather wealthy. Not only palm oil, tin and rubber, we now have a lot of oil."

"Massive offshore reserves." Fatty smiled. "Did you know we are in OPEC? True. So, with a fast-growing pie, divided amongst only 13 million people, we are all doing okay. Despite an unlevel playing field."

It sounded workable. "But still, don't you resent being cut off from opportunities, just because you are Chinese?"

Fatty chuckled and shook his head. "Cut off? No, *lah*! That's what *bumi* partners are for."

I had a lot to learn.

Every day I sat in the small backyard, cozy in the chaise lounge or a rattan chair with my broken leg elevated, and read old British novels or listened to shortwave radio broadcasts.

The continuous, sweet trilling of tropical birds serenaded me in the background. I devoured each issue of the International Herald Tribune, imported daily across the causeway from Singapore. But thick black-pen markings by Malaysian censors frustrated me.

I saw maids arriving and leaving neighboring houses, usually Tamil women or Sumatrans (likely undocumented). Surprising conveniences abounded in the Johor suburbs, like food vans that regularly roamed the streets along with an army of snack vendor carts. More than once I hobbled out to the front after hearing one of them signal to customers with a unique signature call like whistles or the clicking of musical sticks.

Ayna was shy at first when wandering out back and would keep the foreign guest at a distance. But she eventually warmed to the stranger and lost all fear of Uncle Dash. No longer running away when I called her, she would happily play beside me for hours with her dolls.

Every morning Little Fatty left around dawn and returned just after nightfall for dinner with the family. We would chat about the day over simple but mouth-watering food. Nancy worked afternoons as a real estate agent and sent Anya off to a nursery. On the way home she purchased delicious carryout dishes from the town's seemingly endless options like monstrous barbecued pork ribs one night, fish head curry the next. Malaysia's cultural mix made it a gastronomic paradise, with Chinese herbal stews, crispy stir-fries, tangy chutneys, fresh fish dishes, succulent and exotic fruits, Malay rice cakes, Indian desserts . . . and on it went.

One night over curried shrimp and samosas, Fatty began tutoring me on his business. "I own a small chain of three gas stations and operate the biggest one myself," Fatty explained. "Famous brand—British Oil."

"Why not *Petronas*, the national brand?"

He laughed as if that was hilarious. "Come on now, Dash, do I look like *bumi*?" His voice changed. "Remember? Little Fatty is Chinaman!" He raised his eyebrows as if to ask *are you following*. "Maybe Fatty needs to become a better teacher."

We often discussed plans to explore Malaysia together once I'd fully healed. My hosts tempted me with stories of fine beaches, offshore islands, cool green hill stations and funky, vibrant cities.

"And our holidays, that's the best part." Fatty grinned. "The calendar is jammed! Every few months a festival shuts down the country for a week. Instant vacation! And it's our national duty to celebrate the other groups' holidays, also." Fatty winked. "Chinese New Year comes first, in January or February, with fireworks and family gatherings, huge multi-course meals, and costumed performances. Giant dragons dance and bounce down village lanes, with cymbals clanging."

"I remember from my Hong Kong days."

"Good! Then comes the Malay festival of *Hari Raya*, after the month-long Ramadan fast. Another week of non-stop celebrating. And last comes the Hindu festival, *Thaipusam*. Same extravagant, general idea." Fatty's face came alive with excitement. "We will go to Batu Caves outside KL to see the procession of entranced devotees. Thousands mass to see this, holding candles and gathering in dark stinky caverns. Smell of bat droppings mixing with incense. Why? To see zoned-out Indians with skewered cheeks—but no blood! And they hang weighted objects off their chest and stomach, with fishhooks. *Aiee-yah*!"

"Geez, what's with that, Fatty?"

"Crazy stuff. Transcendent for the religious but, for the rest of us, a freak show. Stunning and even a bit frightening."

Nancy then left us alone, so I seized the opportunity to seek counsel on an issue still gravely troubling me.

Fatty listened with knitted eyebrows. He shook his head. *"Alamak,* Dash! Again with Fiona? *Tsk.* How can, *lah*?*"*

"Sorry, Fatty. Never mind." I regretted revealing my continuing secret worry.

"No, Dash, *you* never mind. Time to face reality, brother. Past is past and for you, Fiona is past. No more lovey-dovey time." I felt my cheeks burn as I just stared at him. "Dash, we speak the hard truth. This one time. Okay*, lah*?"

"Sure."

"You and Fiona, that never made any sense, did it? Everybody said same thing."

"Everybody?"

"Paladin, Angelique, the Australians . . ."

"Nice to know."

"Relax. *Truth*, remember?" Fatty nodded and I nodded back. "She's a Taiwanese heiress. Money like Rockefeller. Crossing her father and throwing away life, privilege and wealth. Okay, but for what . . . my *gweilo* boy here?" He smirked. "How can, *lah*? I think maybe you both were caught in strange, crazy hormone adventure."

I wouldn't put it *quite* that way but perhaps he had a point. Still . . .

"Remember what I already tell you at hospital, Dash. *Accident* is nobody's fault. Both are adult. Both make decision. So now, all the time, stop thinking about this. Let guilt go away."

If only!

"Besides, Fiona eyes open now, too. No doubt. I think not angry, maybe, but no way does she need my boy Dash anymore." He raised a lecturing finger. "And if you try to see her, father and brother chop Dash into thousand tiny pieces. Chop-chop-chop!" He mimicked a wok chef mincing pork. "So best to just forget."

"Well, Fatty, that's kinda tricky. Wish I knew how."

"Just keep self busy. Turn off mind." A chorus of evening insects serenaded us and the mosquitoes were starting to bite. I lit a repellent coil to smolder and drive them away.

Maybe he was right: stay busy, but how? One way popped into my mind and before I knew it, I heard my words spilling out. "Fatty, maybe it's time I tried working with you?"

A broad grin split his round face and he slapped the table. *"Aee-yah!!* Great, Dash, that's just great! Early tomorrow we start to teach you the business. You come along to my petrol stations." I didn't want to disappoint him, but the idea already sounded less than thrilling. Hydrocarbons, fuel pumps and lubrication? Hoo, boy. But maybe the sheer novelty would keep it diverting, if not entertaining. At least for a short spell.

"First I take you to my *big* station," he said. "Show you opening procedures. Then we'll drive to the other sites." Local laws, he explained, forced gas stations to all close by sundown, around 6 p.m.

So then what was he up to each night after dinner, when he went back out "to work"?

Fatty didn't strike me as a "woman-on-the-side" type of guy. But you never knew.

Little Fatty was already out on the back patio by 5 a.m., running through his stretching regiment. The bustle of activity in the neighborhood at that hour surprised me. The small road out front was alive with people—couples strolling, hand in hand, in the predawn coolness, while others bicycled, jogged or exercised with their pets.

"We shift outdoor activity to the cooler morning hours to beat the steamy equatorial heat," Fatty said. Tropical birds sang along with morning prayers that drifted in from the nearby mosque. We breakfasted on bowls of thick chicken-flavored rice *congee*, a porridge topped with savories like *ikan bilis* (tiny dried anchovies), peanuts and chunks of salted duck egg.

At 5:30 sharp we hopped into the Mercedes and drove off into the predawn darkness.

"I arrived in JB fresh from college, Dash, and had nothing. Bugger-all. But before long I purchased a crumbling little gas station from an old Indian fellow who wanted to retire." Fatty clicked the turn signal. "Struck a good deal for both of us." Fatty signed a promissory note committing to five years of generous monthly payments, simulating a pension benefit for the elderly man.

Fatty worked tirelessly to repair the site and cultivate sales. He knocked on neighborhood doors to solicit business and extended credit to small workshops and commercial fleets. "By year two, I turned the corner. The business started to spin off cash so the local bank was happy to finance my second. I revived that one the same way."

I began to see my friend in a new light. He was a genuine entrepreneur: your typical ambitious, aggressive and hard-working Overseas Chinese businessman. "Nice story, Fatty, and congrats."

He laughed.

"But wait that was just the start." He then entered a lucrative sideline. "I started to find real estate sites for new gas stations and flipped them to big companies like the national oil giant or slower-moving multinationals." A motivated deal-maker like Fatty easily ran circles around cautious salary-men. "There are always problems for them, Dash. Maybe a land parcel is perfect but zoning is wrong. Or the owner doesn't want to sell. When a big oil company runs into that, they drop the site and move on. But I can make things happen (there are so many ways!) and transform cheap farmland into valuable commercial property." His eyes were gleaming. He clearly loved this. "It's like striking gold! I don't even need my own cash up front, as long as I time all the payments to happen simultaneously. The inflated final price paid by the huge company covers everything."

Proud of his success and cunning, he grinned. Fatty made money from nothing other than effort and intelligence.

"So I was on my way. But then came my big break. Look, here it is! *Mega-Star.*" Fatty steered the Benz into an enormous gas station, a true monster. Even I immediately saw how unique the location was, as the very first property passed when one exited Singapore and crossed the causeway into Malaysia.

"My filling station is the first chance for wealthy Singaporeans to buy fuel at our delightfully cheaper prices here in oil-rich Malaysia. Nearly every inbound car stops to tank up."

We entered the sales office and Fatty scanned the front page of a morning tabloid. "Great!" He pointed at a headline that gas station hours might change. "More hours, more money. And it's more than just a rumor. The laws *will* change and soon."

I tried to look intelligent. "So awaiting a city council vote?"

Little Fatty burst out laughing and spilled his tea. "Ah my poor naive *gweilo* friend. So much to learn. No, the delay is for negotiations . . . between our causeway stations and greedy government officials who want a share of the windfall. And as always, they want too much." Maybe I looked shocked. "Dash, that's just how the world works here. But my partner is handling the bargaining for our side and he's *really* good. Persuasive."

Partner? First I'd heard of that. Who was that?

We watched his manager, a middle-aged Malay man in a tidy uniform, run smoothly through a list of pre-opening procedures. He wielded calibration sticks that looked like enormous wooden rulers and dipped them into underground fuel storage tanks to double-check inventory levels and confirm meter readings. Once all was ready, he threw a master switch and at precisely 6 a.m. the station sprang to life. The street sign flickered on and fully illuminated. Inbound cars immediately began to turn in, as if drawn by a powerful magnet.

"In all of Malaysia," Fatty said, shrugging, "only one location is better."

"Where?"

"Over there." He pointed with his chin at the rival station across the road, where every car *leaving* Malaysia filled up to the brim before entering higher-priced, higher-taxed Singapore. "They say," he winked, "that local royalty is involved in that one. A fellow who opened a station right next-door might get himself killed, or at least put in prison." Little Fatty laughed. This previously-hidden entrepreneurial side of my friend fascinated me. Fatty showed me his other two stations, smaller ones, and issued instructions to the managers before we headed back to Mega-Star.

All that week I sat in the Mega-Star sales office, hypnotized watching the busy forecourt through the glass. Vehicles continuously streamed in and out, nearly all bearing Singapore plates and driven by Chinese families, Tamils, Malay truck drivers, even Sikhs in turbans. This unending procession past Little Fatty's gas pumps seemed unexceptional at first glance but was a thing of true commercial beauty. He was turning a profit on every liter sold!

I began to absorb gas station basics and was surprised how, rather than boring, it was actually fun in a way. Like learning a new game. I enjoyed bantering with the staff. Most were slight and dark-complexioned, illegal immigrants from Sumatra who clearly found interesting this pink foreign friend of the big boss. The women were generally demure but at times brazen and locked eyes with me in a hot gaze, perhaps floating an offer. Needing no warning of potential complications down that road, I would just smile back and look away.

One afternoon I sat in the air-conditioned sales office and watched Singaporeans pumping money into Fatty's bank account. He surprised me.

"Okay, Dash, I think you're now ready to meet my partner."

"Ah, the mysterious negotiator?"

"Ha. Yes, but it's no joke. He does a lot more than that. You don't think I achieved Mega-Star all by myself, did you?"

Well yes, actually, I did.

"But Fatty, why complicate things with a partner? I mean look at this place! Banks will give you as much money as you need!"

"You Americans!" He shook his head. "Not always just about money, *lah*! Partners bring much more to the table."

"For instance . . .?"

"Take this land for instance. Do you think it was easy to acquire?"

"If you had the money."

"But *everybody* has money, Dash. That's not special." He sighed and gave me another pitiful look. "And now, so many would like to steal this jewel. My partner helps protect it."

"Steal, how? You own it, right?"

He feigned disbelief and took a deep breath. "So many, too many ways to steal it. Any government official, even small fry from some tiny local office, can issue harsh new regulations and threaten the business. The lowest agent from the roads department can order constant pavement repairs out front. Block all my customers! Or heavy taxes can be levied. What if some ambitious immigration officer swoops down and raids me, takes away all my workers? There are endless legal ways (or otherwise) to force me out."

I was shocked. Could governmental power be wielded so easily here for personal gain? Did this sort of thing happen everywhere, or did Southeast Asia perhaps have some special competence in such black arts? The message hit me hard and again reminded me: I had a lot to learn.

Little Fatty was on a roll and kept tutoring.

"And that's just the government. Local gangsters might also desire Mega-Star. They can visit and destroy our equipment. A bomb! Or sometimes the owner-operator can die in a suspicious traffic accident, or maybe fall from a great height, eh? And there's always the straight-out shooting of an owner at his station. It looks like robbery. Probably his heirs will be more amenable to a new business partner. More likely, they'll want to sell the business altogether."

I stayed silent but my sober face probably told him this was all registering.

"Some threats aren't as dramatic but just as effective. A predator can slowly choke the business: start a rumor the Chinese owner is anti-Islamic. That drives away half the customers, the Malays. Or if the owner was a Malay, the rumor could spread word he disrespects Allah's laws and drinks liquor or commits *khalwat*."

"Call what?"

"No, *khalwat.* Means 'close proximity'. Islamic religious police can a Muslim found alone with the opposite sex, if not the spouse." Little Fatty smiled. Was he being ironic? "So you see? Unlimited number of ways a business can be attacked." He raised his palm, waving off concern. "So a powerful partner can protect us. Time for you, my *gweilo* friend, to meet *my* partner. My *boss* and protector." He rubbed his hands in delight. "Tonight we will drink XO brandy with my elder brother, *Snakehead Goh.*"

"Your elder brother?"

"Not really. Just an expression."

"*Snakehead?*"

"Chinese nickname."

Indeed, an interesting evening beckoned.

CHAPTER TWENTY
Snakehead Goh

Fatty expertly maneuvered through the tangle of JB narrow side streets. His Mercedes dodged potholes in the darkness and swerved around straggling pedestrians and small push carts. At the fringes of town we sped past palm oil plantations, trees flashing by and faintly illuminated in the car's high-beam side-splash.

"Why don't you hire a driver, Fatty? You can afford it, easy."

"True. And I prefer the freedom of driving myself. But soon I must hire a driver, no choice. Image, you know? People starting to tease."

Huh, what people? Why does a mere gas station operator, however successful, need to impress anybody?

Fatty smiled. "Anyway tonight you meet an important man."

"Snakehead."

He nodded. "My dear friend. And hopefully yours too, soon."

He briefed me as he drove. Snakehead was born in a sleepy south Malaysian town, only son to a small-time merchant family. His parents, dreaming big, scrimped and saved and denied themselves everything in order to send him off to university in Sydney, Australia. He studied engineering and followed that up with an MBA in Singapore.

Fully armed for Southeast Asian business warfare, Snakehead returned to Malaysia rather than battle a flood of cut-throat Chinese businessmen in Singapore. He settled in the Wild West town of JB, ready to build his fortune. "He made connections, one by one, thanks to hard work and overwhelming charisma." Fatty smiled. "But charming as he was, Snakehead always stayed humble. No opportunity was ever too small."

Pragmatic and unfettered by ethical constraints, Snakehead's only rule was to always turn a profit for his partners.

"Always! So his reputation spread and opportunities began to seek *him* out, more than he could ever pursue." He mastered myriad ways to lubricate the machinery of business success, practical arts like how to facilitate government approvals; forge powerful partnerships; and even smooth the ruffled feathers of beaten rivals.

"For Snakehead, there are no *permanent* business enemies, only *temporary* competitors. He stays adaptable and avoids lasting rivalries. Always ready to create new partnerships for new deals, often with former opponents."

"So he's now some kind of regional business superstar, I guess?"

"Absolutely. Owns a galaxy of businesses: import/export, commodity trading, oil sales, real estate, you-name-it. Snakehead controls the regional supply of high-grade rice from Burma and never runs short when others do." With nary a permanent business foe, the longer he was active, the broader his alliances grew. "By now he's a true force of nature in the Southeast Asia business universe."

"Impressive."

"But still he stays disciplined. Every day Snakehead pores over newspapers, searching out new ideas and opportunities. His creative mind recognizes new emerging trends before anyone else."

I smiled. "So no offense, Fatty, but why did some Chinese business god hook up with the likes of *you?*"

Fatty giggled and continued driving. We were entering another urban area, but where the hell were we? Seemed like the back end of nowhere.

"Funny story, Dash. When I first arrived in JB fresh from college, I had only a degree, ambition and my energy. And every day I wandered the streets and observed. I talked to strangers at fruit stands and small noodle houses, always smiling and staying humble. Making myself approachable. *You never know*—that was my motto."

Fatty turned on his wipers after a sudden cloudburst. "One night, I was eating chicken rice at a cheap roadside stall. A taxi driver sat next to me for his dinner and we chatted. He asked me friendly questions. *'So, where are your people from?'* 'Kuala Lumpur' I said. *'No,'* he replied, *'I mean where in China?'* I explained my Teochew ancestors were fishermen and traders who migrated from South China, a century ago." Fatty reached across the front seat and poked me. "Now listen to this. Then this simple cab driver says, *'So you should probably go visit the JB local Teochew clan house. Meet your countrymen'.*"

Little Fatty slapped his forehead. "*Alamak*, Dash, of course! How did I ever miss that? Even a dirty-shirt taxi driver knew better than me and he was right. That was how I could meet other Lee's. Business folk, maybe even relatives."

"What's a Teochew clan house?"

Fatty rushed ahead with his story, his voice excited and rising. "Dash, my Teochew people are a commercial powerhouse across all of Malaysia, Singapore, Indonesia and Thailand. So I visited the local *kongsi*, a gathering place, the very next evening and fell in with a friendly group. We played *mahjong,* smoked and drank tea, all fellow entrepreneurs in a safe and friendly atmosphere. We chatted about horse racing and Malaysian politics. I took it slow and just concentrated on making some friends."

Later that evening a large impressive man joined us. He was friendly but projected the unmistakable air of the ultra-alpha male. "They all smiled and deferred to him. Poured his drinks and lit his cigarettes. They offered snacks to him first." Fatty grinned.

"Snakehead?"

"Yes. He visited the clan house every night after his dinner. The next few evenings we chatted and determined our great-great-grandfathers on our mothers' side came from the same village in South China. We weren't related, but it was still an important connection. We had great chemistry and became friends. Regularly met for lunch, dinner or just drinks. Before long Snakehead was parading me around town as his new protégé."

Droplets splattered the windshield and Fatty turned on his wipers. His high beams cut through the night to illuminate a ramshackle urban area. Where were we?

"He viewed me like a clever younger brother, just starting out, and commended my early efforts and initiative. He doled out ideas and shared contacts. Our personalities just clicked. We had the same sense of humor and appetite for the same foods. Even found the same type of females attractive."

"So you two are alike."

Fatty laughed. "Not really. So many differences. He is big but I am small. He is slim and muscular and I am fat. He is older but I am young. He is very handsome but Little Fatty is just, um, so-so. He was already a big success but I was just starting out. Snakehead was a happy bachelor, like a bee buzzing from one fragrant flower to the next, while I was already newly married and a dedicated family man. In so many ways we were opposites but together made a good team."

This was when Little Fatty finally confided how Snakehead had helped direct him toward his first gas station deal and negotiate it with that old Indian man. "And once I got it fixed up, it was Snakehead who pushed me to expand and add a second site. But—" Fatty seemed to inflate with pride "—it was *my* idea, after a few more years, to build that monster gas station at the Singapore causeway."

"You? Really?"

Fatty smiled. "Yes! Not him. But impossible to execute by myself so I gladly shared. Snakehead leapt right in, excited, and demolished all political and commercial road blocks. He knew whom to pay and how much. Also distributed some minority equity positions to important partners. Nobody dares mess with us now—Snakehead's protection is bulletproof."

Tick-tick-tick sang out the sedan's turn signal as Fatty steered onto an entry ramp climbing up into a concrete multi-story parking lot. "Okay," he chirped, "we're here!" It looked like a dilapidated shopping mall—already closed, too. It was late.

"*Here?* Where are we, Fatty?"

He grabbed my arm and squeezed. "Listen hard, Dash, this is important. If Snakehead likes you, you can join our big new project. It's a huge deal that can set us all up for life."

I guess Fatty just liked and trusted me. (Saving a guy's life will do that.) But for some audacious new venture, why might Snakehead ever agree to bring aboard a business neophyte like me, and a *gweilo*, to boot?

Round and round the Mercedes corkscrewed up the narrow concrete ramp past empty, pitch-black floors in the parking garage. At 10 p.m. the shopping mall had already been closed for hours. We emerged at the very top level into a brightly floodlit area stacked thick with luxury cars of all makes and models.

Chauffeurs loitered around, smoking cigarettes and looking smart in tailored tan safari suits as they leaned against shining vehicles with Malaysian or Singapore plates. They read newspapers or gambled in small clusters, tossing down playing cards and crumpled, colorful currency onto overturned cardboard boxes.

Far off at the opposite end of the lot, a large blinking neon sign blared words in a rainbow of color, beckoning entry to the *New World Night Club.* The sign assaulted the eye with harsh phosphorescent green, lipstick pink and iridescent purple. Just above the club's name in English, massive golden Chinese ideograms writhed against a bright red background and stood out like the sun. Down below, a modest third deck (looking almost like an afterthought) appeared in *Jawi* script for Malay customers. There was no Tamil version.

After our crawl up through the murky blackness, this overall explosion of bright light and raucous color surprised and delighted me.

Fatty grinned. "Welcome to business heaven."

We slammed our car doors and with a bounce in our step headed toward the glowing gateway. Music throbbed through the cement walls. Drivers looked up from their newspapers or wagers to smile at Little Fatty, clearly well-known here, a respected little kingpin. But when their eyes then flicked over to me they laughed and muttered: *"Aiee-yah, gweilo!"*

Safe to assume not many Westerners hung out at the New World.

Inside we waded through a buzzing crush of people who packed the well-lit lobby where lush burgundy velvet curtains framed the walls. Many customers appeared fresh from dinner, some already drunk. Fat and austere-looking Chinese club managers pranced about in stiff white dress shirts and black bow ties, directing traffic. Rouged women in over-the-top, flashy dresses (showing way too much skin) laughed and smiled, looking like over-ripened prom dates.

I trailed behind Little Fatty's grand entrance, watching as he greeted staff in the antechamber and shook hands with friends. Off to our right two broad doorways revealed an enormous darkened room where loud music issued forth from a floodlit stage. A female singer was yowling a 1950s-style Chinese torch song, backed by a middle-aged combo with clarinet, sax and keyboard.

Near the center of the lobby stood the floor manager, mopping his brow. He spotted Little Fatty and his face split into an enormous smile. Greatly animated, he waved us over. After they shook hands and chatted in a Chinese dialect, the manager discreetly pocketed a small, folded-up square of cash. Then in a grand, sweeping gesture he pointed into the noisy ballroom toward the stage. A minion with penlight instantly appeared and led us into the cavernous room.

It was ice-cold in there and at first the entire place seemed hidden in blackness except for the over-illuminated stage. Slowly my eyes began to adjust and I started making out dozens of tables surrounded by sofas and easy chairs.

Our guide with his tiny dot of red light directed us deeper into the room until we at last reached the very front (a premier table location for super-VIPs only) where elegant-looking people crowded a double-sized table. Its glass top groaned under the weight of ice buckets, bottles of liquor and plates of snacks, bathed in colored light overflowing from the stage. A mirrored ball overhead slowly spun, a Roaring 20s throwback that occasionally drenched the room with dizzying, uncountable dots of light.

Up closer the singer on stage looked pretty, a Chinese woman poured into a slinky red brocade dress and wearing overdone make-up. Gorgeous despite extraordinary eyebrows thick as black caterpillars. Overall, she looked much better than she sounded.

Fatty nudged me and gestured down the table. That's when I first spotted our host. Snakehead Goh was no doubt paying a monstrous tab to entertain this large group. He spotted Little Fatty and winked, walked over and patted him on the back. Then he shot a quizzical look in my direction as if to imply: *What's with the gweilo?*

Snakehead was a tower of a man, atypical for Chinese, massive and well-built. He sported the bearing of a natural athlete. Lean and muscular with a V-shaped physique, his narrow waist and hips accentuated his wide shoulders. Gold-framed glasses perfectly highlighted a handsome face with high cheekbones and dark, clear eyes flashing beneath a full head of bushy, silver hair. He was undeniably handsome and exuded unlimited confidence and charisma.

After watching only a few minutes, I could see Snakehead was a born charmer, easy-to-laugh as he chain-smoked and schmoozed his way from one guest to the next, always appearing to deliver the right comment or interesting story. He threw back a prodigious amount of scotch, drinking with each guest, chugging full glasses with just a splash of water. In just the hour I watched, he easily downed a dozen drinks with no sign of intoxication.

Little Fatty gently elbowed me. "We'll get him later. Don't worry, plenty of time. For him now, first things first: he's hosting important contacts."

Fatty gestured toward one of the guests. "See that *bumi* over there? Big man in the government." He meant the elegant Malay man with a neatly-trimmed Van Dyke beard and wearing expensive-looking ethnic attire, topped off by a *songket*, the traditional black velvet hat. Whenever he cracked open his diamond-studded golden cigarette case, a pretty Malay hostess lit his cigarette, constantly leaning close and laughing at his jokes while pouring non-stop refills of XO brandy. *"Bumiputera,* remember? Means 'Son of the Soil' in Malay."

"But doesn't Islam forbid him from drinking? And what about that *khalwat* thing? That religious police stuff—"

Little Fatty chuckled with an impish grin. "Stop, Dash, stop it already." He sighed. "Almost like a little baby, *lah,* too much to learn! Those are laws *outside*, maybe, but not inside *Chinese* night club." He reminded me of our complex entry, winding up through the darkened car park. "Makes it easy for someone hidden in a car behind dark glass—say, a Malay government official—to slip in or out. Also makes surprise police raids difficult." He shrugged. "But we already pay police to stay away, anyway."

I was learning. *Unenforced* laws, no problem.

"Besides, Dash, *who* would inform on him? Not us, his business partners. Nor anyone else. All the others here are probably just waiting for the right moment to make his acquaintance, also."

Fatty paused for emphasis and imparted an important lesson. "For the powerful here, Dash, laws are never barriers, just inconveniences."

After playing host for another hour, Snakehead finally sat at our table. A magnetic and commanding physical presence, he seemed even larger up close. He mumbled a private comment to Little Fatty and they both chuckled.

Then he faced me and spoke in perfect English, with the mildest trace of a classy accent. British, but not quite. "So you must be the hero, Dashiell Bonaventure. Saved my little brother's life." When he smiled, he radiated near-tangible waves of power and charm. "Welcome to JB, my friend."

I stumbled for words. "Uh, should I call you Mr. Goh . . ."

He snorted a rich, bassy laugh. *"Aduh*! We're friends now so use *Snakehead,* a good translation of my Chinese nickname." He leaned closer. "But let me tell you my *real* name, this one time, then you can forget it." He and Fatty both grinned. "As you know, the family name is *Goh*. Like in *Go Away*." He laughed. "Unfortunately my given names are Fook Yu." His eyebrows danced. "Imagine how funny *that* was for my English-speaking friends at university in Australia."

"Sorry? I don't—"

"*Goh Fook Yu.* Get it? At first, they called me *Go Fuck You, the Chinaman*."

"Oh geez," I groaned. "Sorry. That's bad."

He stared deep into my eyes as if looking for something, then grinned. "Nah come on, it *was* rather funny. Had I let it bother me there might've been a problem. But I took it like a man and thereby joined their brotherhood. I was bigger than most of them anyway and trained in martial arts since childhood. People learn to only cross me once." His eyes glowed with an angry confidence. No doubt a dangerous foe. "Before long everyone learned it was far preferable to be my friend. So *Snakehead*, my true nickname since childhood, caught on instead."

I decided to be careful. "Because like a snake, you move smoothly and strike fast?" Fatty laughed and clapped his hands. Snakehead looked at him and snorted.

"Good guess but wrong. I was circumcised for health reasons, so in grade school the other boys said the cap on my penis looked like a snake's head. I don't know about that but they loved to tease me. After I got older my plumbing filled out pretty well and the brothel girls would gossip about *my snake*. Harmless chit-chat. But it spread to other customers and that, more than anything, made the nickname stick. Been Snakehead Goh, ever since." I chuckled.

"But I like your theory, too, Dash. Because I *am* quick to strike (like a viper) when a business opportunity arises or retribution is demanded."

We clinked glasses. After a brief recounting of the Little Fatty drowning story he left us and headed back to the large sofa facing the stage. Hostesses poured him and his guests glass after glass of peaty, expensive scotch.

Once the performance ended, the musicians filed away but the singer sashayed down the front steps to sit beside Snakehead. She smiled brightly and stroked his arm while he seemingly ignored her ministrations and continued chatting with business associates.

"That's his hobby," Fatty confided with a giggle. "Collecting beautiful nightclub singers, usually Taiwanese." The circuit inevitably channels performers through Singapore and from there, it is just a short taxi ride over to JB. Pampering weeklong affairs with Snakehead are in demand. His reputation for charm and generosity has spread far and wide across the region. "They seek him out."

We left the club well after midnight. Little Fatty took me for what he called *breakfast,* theoretically to settle our booze-soaked digestive systems. At a roadside restaurant we ate soupy rice *congee* and delicious *bak kut teh*, a fragrant herbal broth with ribs and chewy chunks of pig intestine. Driving home around 2 a.m., Little

Fatty sang Chinese opera along with his car stereo. I'd never before seen him this happy. Then he told me the good news: Snakehead approved of me.

"Just like that?"

"Just like that. So now comes something quite wonderful." He clearly intended to tantalize me—and succeeded.

This unexpected turn of events had me feeling a bit like *Dash in a Tropical Wonderland*.

CHAPTER TWENTY-ONE
The Tropical Princess

All the next day Little Fatty seemed on edge, like he had a secret. That night we closed down the gas stations, wolfed down a quick dinner with his family, hustled back into the Benz and sped off.

"So, more nightclubbing?" I'd really enjoyed the setting, drinks and excitement of it all.

"No, *lah.*" He winked. "Maybe a boat ride, okay?"

"You kidding?" I didn't like the idea of going out to sea in the dead of night. Nor, given his recent history, should Fatty. "Sounds like a waste of time—"

"Trust me, Dash, and just go with this. Tonight we get a peek at the spectacular future."

Such melodrama.

I sighed and sank back into the soft leather seat and watched dark shapes outside flying past windows: regimented forests of palm oil plantations and swaying groves of sugar cane. Finally Fatty steered the car off the road and began to slowly plunge through a wall of overgrown vegetation.

What was he doing? There was no road but the car kept slowly nosing forward and lurching down and up through deep ruts while bushes, branches and tall grass swished and scraped against both sides of the car.

"What the hell, Fatty? You're ruining your baby's paint job. This car's no jeep. "

"Actually we *are* driving on a path." He shook his head. "But it's really overgrown. Later, we fix." He smiled and the Benz crawled forward through the vegetation. "And don't worry about the paint. Soon I can buy a dozen Mercedes. You too! Convertibles or sports cars, all new."

We seemed in the middle of nowhere and soon, no doubt, to be stuck axle-deep in muck. "So to repeat, Fatty: What the hell?"

"This is all private, undeveloped shoreline property, Dash. Outside JB and well-hidden, as you can see. And just ahead of us lay untold riches." The thicket of weeds and small trees finally opened onto a cleared area covered in gravel. The sea was up ahead where the headlamp beams illuminated a large concrete dock, impressive and new-looking, poking its long nose out into the water.

"Hey, my *gweilo* brother, see all those twinkling lights across the channel? Singapore is very close."

Black outlines of slow-moving vessels floated past, crisscrossing on the water. Small fishing boats putt-putted by, riding low and heading home laden with the day's catch.

We got out but Little Fatty left the engine running and headlights lit. Impossibly thick clouds of flying insects immediately clustered around the headlamps and within the light beams. I'd never seen anything like it.

The sudden crackle and crunch of gravel behind us announced the arrival of a gorgeous cream colored Rolls-Royce emerging from the jungle. As it pulled up behind us, its light beams swept the area. A uniformed chauffeur in white gloves and cap popped out, swung open the rear door and the imposing figure of Snakehead emerged with a leather portfolio tucked under one arm and a sweater loosely twisted across his shoulders, prep-style. In my short time in Johor Baru, I'd already learned that despite the equatorial heat, it was easy to catch a chill in the overly cooled offices, restaurants and shops.

"Ah, brilliant. Both already here." He checked his watch, shook it and made a face like it was lying. "But where are the others? We *did* say 10 p.m., no?"

Little Fatty placated Snakehead with a mild face and a small shrug of the shoulders. "Maybe a few more minutes, chief."

He turned to chat with me, clearly to avoid the impatient Snakehead. "In the tropics, Dash, it's nearly impossible to keep a place like this clear of weeds. Our crews have been continuously hacking away but plants keep retaking the land just as fast. That's okay, for now. Good camouflage." He was making no sense.

We stood and waited—for what, I didn't know—engulfed by a thick humid odor of vegetation mingled with the dank rotting smell from nearby mud flats. Vessels glided by on the black glass surface in front of Singapore's twinkling lights. Finally, a soft buzzing sound in the distance began to cut through the droning chatter of insects.

After a while, I made out the running lights of an approaching vessel. The launch quickly closed on us and, at last, sliced an effortless semicircle to smoothly park beside the cement pier. Professionals at work. Long and low slung, the yacht was a rich man's elaborate toy built for speed, comfort and style. A bilingual name decorated the bow: *Sheung Shui*—The Rising Star.

After the crew tied up at the concrete dock a young man bounded down the gangplank and approached us on the dock. Smiling and smooth-mannered, he projected a youthful energetic aura that was irresistible and infectious. "Gentlemen, greetings! My dear friends, Little Fatty and Mr. Goh—sorry, I mean *Snakehead!* Welcome, always an honor!" He drew in a deep breath of the thick moist air and smiled. "Beautiful evening for our little voyage, isn't it?"

He glanced at me and looked momentarily puzzled but didn't miss a beat. "And you too, sir, are most welcome. I am Gary Tan, your host this evening."

Fatty pulled me aside and quietly briefed me.

"Dash, that charismatic young lion is heir to the entire business empire of *Eastern Ferry & Bus (EFB)*." Fatty's eyes were wide. He explained how the Tan family, from their headquarters in Singapore, dominated mass transport across all of Asia. Their enormous bus fleets maintained a choke-hold on urban mass transit while their navy of ferry boats plied coastal waters across all Southeast Asia, Japan and South Asia. "Something like several thousand ferries and eight thousand buses. Gary's aunt is *the* Madame Emerald Tan—"

"*The?*"

"Respect, please, Dash! Dried-up old super-bitch but *aieeyah,* so powerful, just the same. Shriveled and riding a wheelchair and infamous for her horrible temper and deep into her 80s, that granny still rules her empire with a harsh whip hand. Personally built EFB from scratch after her husband mysteriously died, half a century ago."

Nice.

"Mysteriously?"

"And never remarried. But from a modest start, the widow sent off family members, one after another, to penetrate national markets in Asia. Each early success funded even more expansion."

"Virtuous growth cycle."

Fatty nodded and raised a finger, as if instructing. "And to this day, all those national companies are still owned by EFB, Madame Tan's holding company in Singapore, and still managed by their aging original founders."

"They sure know how to enjoy their golden years, eh?"

"Ha! But think how amazing the future must look for an up-and-comer like Gary, only son of Madame Tan's sole younger brother, now deceased. Gary is just back to Singapore from MBA studies in the UK, ready to ease into the family business."

"Got it made."

"Maybe. Madame Tan knows that despite all that prestigious education, Gary knows fuck-all about the *real* Asian business world and how things really work." Fatty smiled. "So I think she cleverly chose this assignment as a test. His first job at EFB is to be front man on a daring potential project with Malaysian partners. That's us. Massive potential, but quite separate from the rest of the family business."

"In case he fucks it up."

"Correct."

"A test."

"A big one—and he knows it."

If Snakehead and Fatty were trying to tantalize me with their secret project it was working. By now I was dying to know what was going on.

A second man stood beside Gary and chuckled. Locks of curly black hair danced across his forehead. "I'm Lim Chi Kwok," he said with a heavy Singaporean accent, "but just call me Tommy." He shook my hand and flashed a brilliant smile.

"Tommy's overseeing Gary's training," Fatty whispered, filling me in. Tommy, the font of excruciating but funny jokes, boasted a vast network of friendly contacts: businessmen and sailors, police and military, nightclub operators and bankers, expatriates and locals. Tommy had in fact been Snakehead's conduit to the Tan family for this audacious plan. "They met a year ago, in a nightclub," Fatty explained, "and stayed in touch. Snakehead knew the value of a solid contact at EFB. Tommy no doubt prized Snakehead's reputation as a stellar business partner."

Snakehead scanned the dock and looked visibly irritated. "So where are all the others?"

Gary grinned. "Already there, sir, on board. They are waiting for *us*, actually." Tommy smiled uncomfortably and motioned us onto the launch. "We'd better move, gentlemen. Never smart to keep *CBC* waiting."

CBC? Now I wondered who this impatient CBC fellow was, and why he obviously made all the others so nervous.

We climbed aboard the sleek yacht and it sped off into the night. A trio of perfumed smiling attendants, poured into and bursting out of sleek black sequined dresses sidled up and offered drinks and hors d'oeuvre from gleaming platters. The vessel accelerated with impressive g-force and amid the hiss of agitated water, knifed its way across the strait's dark waters, leaving the lights of Johor and Singapore behind us. It leveled off at high-speed for a well-cushioned ride, the ultimate in shipboard luxury presented in glass, chrome and butter-soft leather. I didn't know where we were going or why but savored the entertaining mystery of it all. I knew this was both my friends' way of luring me into some earthshaking project so all soon would be revealed.

Snakehead and Little Fatty stood at the bow, the wind in their faces, and peered ahead into the pitch-black as if looking for something. Acting jovial, I put my arms up around their shoulders. "So, gents, what now? Are we going for a swim?" They both laughed, but then Snakehead, his eyebrows high, looked at Fatty.

"You mean he still doesn't know yet?" He chuckled.

Fatty shrugged. "No time, *lah*."

Snakehead put a large hand on my shoulder. "Ah, my newly adopted *gweilo* little brother. Tonight your life changes, in a most agreeable way." I stayed silent and let that promise hang in the air. Might as well give them space and let them pace out their surprise, they were enjoying it so much.

Fatty poked my shoulder and pulled me aside. He spoke quietly. "Now don't screw this up, Dash. I told Snakehead how clever you are and hard-working. Oodles of *gweilo* brilliance. An asset to our project. So, in other words," he said, grinning, "I lied. Don't make me look bad."

The launch was a true champion and moved like a rocket as it skimmed its way atop the water, leaving frothy entrails and rolling clouds of mist in its wake. After several minutes Snakehead raised his head and pointed with his chin. "See it ahead out there, Dash, that little dot of light?"

It was just a flicker on the horizon, like a distant candle.

But as we approached, the tiny point of light eventually grew and transformed into a huge and well-lit vessel, massive and substantial and rising out of the water four floors high, anchored in the middle of nowhere. I guessed we were somewhere in international waters, twenty, maybe thirty miles offshore from

Singapore. Probably beyond the territorial claim of all three adjacent nations—Malaysia, Singapore and Indonesia.

As we slowed to approach, I saw other expensive-looking yachts and speedboats, each rivaling our *Sheung Shui* in luxury, tethered to and dwarfed by the huge vessel. I wondered which one belonged to the frightening and cantankerous *CBC*.

Gary abruptly materialized beside me, as if from nowhere, and pointed at the massive vessel. "So how do you like her? What you expected? A high-capacity, high-quality ferry, her current name is *The Tropical Princess*. You can of course change that." He winked.

"Yes, rather impressive." I let him talk.

"Flagged out of Panama. Built in 1958 so as vessels go still almost *new*! Less than 20 years old. About five hundred feet long and 15,000 tons displacement and 7,000 tons net tonnage. But most important for your purposes, her capacity: she can safely transport as many as 1,300 people, including crew."

What did a gigantic used ferry boat have to do with me?

Gary kept spinning his pitch and seemed to not notice my befuddlement. Or if he did, he didn't care. I was already starting to like him. "Plenty of space for cabins, restaurants, a sizable kitchen. And the car parking area below can be converted for other entertainment purposes. More than enough space."

"I hope so." I tried to appear not *completely* ignorant. Little Fatty and Snakehead walked over and exchanged amused looks, having immediately picked up on my plight.

Gary plowed ahead. "If I may ask, sir, how many tables are you planning?"

Tables?

He didn't wait. "I'm sure plenty for baccarat and for roulette. We Chinese love those two. No doubt you've been up to Genting Highlands outside KL and saw how popular roulette is in Malaysia."

"Not yet."

"Anyway you'll need blackjack, too, just like in Vegas."

"Of course." I smiled. Snakehead and Little Fatty also nodded.

"But don't waste space on craps tables. We Asians *do* love playing dice but our own version. *Sic Bo,* the game of big/small"

"I don't know it."

"Three dice inside a covered container are rolled. Bets are taken on the total: high, low or whatever. The dice are uncovered, the winners cheer and losers groan. Imagine it: one hundred times per hour! One, two, three, bets down, and *boom.* Payoffs and losses. Crowd goes wild. Exciting and a fast game, big house percentage, so a big moneymaker for you."

Snakehead cut in.

"Our floating fantasy land will provide a convenient opportunity to gamble for millions in the region, starved for that. We won't make much selling food or rooms, but some clients may demand it so we'll allocate a little space, but only after ensuring enough tables. Gaming always comes first."

Good God. They were planning a monstrous, floating casino! Everything was starting to register and my brain felt ready to explode.

Snakehead's idea was pure genius: a massive offshore gambling boat in international waters, beyond the reach of authorities but just a figurative stone's throw away for millions of gambling-crazed Asians. I also sensed its legality was questionable so this might be dangerous.

And remarkably, my new friends were inviting me along for the ride.

We climbed up the gangway and boarded *The Tropical Princess,* stopping briefly at the lowest deck of the massive luxury ferry, where cars could drive on and off. From that vantage point the vessel seemed even more immense and impressive. The parking area was as wide as a football field and fifty percent longer.

"Please hurry, everybody," Gary said, "CBC and the rest are already waiting in the ballroom." He led us up a flight of stairs and through the ship, tossing out nuggets of info like the potential for gaming rooms here or a restaurant there.

A pair of heavy dark glass doors parted to reveal a spacious, high-ceilinged ballroom. We strode briskly toward the front stage where a group had already assembled. Our heels clicked atop the shiny wood parquet floor. Snakehead hugged one man and slapped the back of another. He nodded at a shriveled old woman in a wheelchair. Gruff laughter echoed through the empty chamber.

So these must all be the partners.

Little Fatty hung back, wearing an overly wide smile. Snakehead was clearly in charge. "You two," he barked at us, "get over here. Some regional celebrities for you to meet." The charming crowd-pleaser of the other night had completely vanished. Snakehead was now all business.

The ancient-looking woman in the wheelchair was rolled close. "Men, please meet Madame Emerald Tan, in all her glory! Chairman and CEO of *Eastern Ferry & Bus*. She's also Auntie to Gary." Gary, standing nearby, smiled.

I shot my most ingratiating grin at the old crone but she remained stone-faced and frozen. Did she disapprove of a *gweilo* being here? But then I noticed Little Fatty was getting no love, either.

Gary wheeled her away.

"Intro already over?" I mumbled to myself.

Snakehead heard and addressed us in a low tone. "Listen. Her friends call her *Emerald* but for you two, it'll always be *Madame Tan*. Okay? Unless she invites more familiarity."

"Fat chance of that." I said with a wink at Fatty. But he looked much more serious now and just shrugged.

Snakehead went on to explain how the Tans had sourced the ship and would provide marine operating know-how for the venture. Their fabricators would fit out the vessel and oversee its conversion into a floating mega-casino. The entire downstairs parking area was to be walled off into rooms for gaming tables and slot machines. The Tans would also second experienced staff from EFT, including a captain and crew, the safety master, everything.

"Also, it goes without saying EFT and the Tans maintain impeccable relationships with the area's marine authorities." Snakehead grinned. "Critical."

"Very handy," said Fatty, nodding.

Snakehead lit a cigarette. "I suspect you two may never see the old bat again, anyway. Tonight was her look-see to meet all the partners, first time assembled. This is the go or no-go time. And if Madame Tan is comfortable, she'll hand off all future liaison to her nephew, Gary, and Tommy Lim."

Next Snakehead ushered us over toward a squat, heavyset Chinese man who seemed to frown at everybody—even Snakehead. The man seemed fierce and miserable, perspiring in his ill-fitting suit. His hair was brushed forward in a failed attempt to conceal a receding hairline.

"Fellows, this is the famous Mr. Chong Beng Chuan. But you can call him 'CBC' like everyone else."

Ahah, so this was the cantankerous CBC that made all the others so nervous. I wondered why.

I smiled when we shook hands but CBC seemed lost in thought and didn't even seem to notice me. He looked unhappy to even be there and kept casting furtive glances over toward Madame Tan, wicked witch of Asian transport. Perhaps had the two bumped heads in past business endeavors? But perhaps this opportunity was just too huge to miss and worth making peace with a former rival.

The hostile man glistened in clothes that stretched tight. His shirt buttons were ready to pop as he noisily sucked on his teeth and smoked nonstop, lighting new cigarettes from embers of their predecessors. A dissipated but overtly sexy-looking woman squeezed close to him and gripped his elbow, stroking his upper arm. Hot twenty years ago, now she mainly appeared desperate underneath over-applied make-up, eyelids black and purple with mascara. Her ears and neck sparkled with diamonds.

"CBC is a brilliant businessman. Famous of course, everywhere in Asia." Snakehead was ostensibly speaking to us but loud enough to ensure CBC heard the flattery. But the man just sighed with displeasure. "Having admired CBC for so many years, we were thrilled when he agreed to consider our venture." Snakehead aimed a deferential smile at the rough-edged businessman and then turned back to us. "CBC owns the region's largest oil distribution company, more powerful and extensive than even the multinationals. His many *other* business lines will also be useful to our project."

Snakehead finally walked CBC over toward the bar and left us behind. Then Little Fatty leaned over and whispered the truth to me. CBC was some kind of Asian-style mafia don, infamously violent and quick-tempered, with a criminal network spanning all of Southeast Asia.

This capo's tentacles maintained a choke-hold on oil markets across Southeast Asia, especially southern Malaysia where he illegally smuggled diesel ashore at secluded beaches, avoiding duty and taxes. His syndicate also ran a massive theft ring that bribed drivers and siphoned oil from petroleum tank trucks traversing the peninsula. His portfolio also extended into vice— loan-sharking and prostitution.

"CBC will provide cheap fuel for our floating casino. And," Fatty said with eyebrows rising, "he will oversee various other activities on-board like girls, money-lending, narcotics, a massage parlor and a small nightclub. His boys will also provide, um, the *security* on board."

Woe be to any gambler who did not pay off debts incurred at our tables.

Snakehead finally returned.

"Ready to meet one more? This partner is one of the most powerful men in Malaysia." He ushered us over to an elegant Malay gentleman in an immaculate tailored suit and black felt *songkok* velvet cap, who had been quietly standing off to the side. Two brutes hovered close by, clearly his bodyguards.

"*As salaam alaikum,*" Snakehead said to the Malay with a slight bow.

The handsome man touched his heart and replied: *"Wa alaikum salaam."*

"Men, let me introduce *The Sheikh.*" His actual name was much longer but I immediately forgot it. He was quite striking. Thin, long-haired and suave with a Van Dyke goatee.

We shook hands and after saying 'hello' Snakehead squired the man away, just like that.

"Fatty, these lightning intros are making me dizzy."

Fatty snorted a quiet laugh. "Sheikh's role is to provide *air cover* with the government," he said. "He's a fast-rising political star, nationally-known and often on TV delivering firebrand speeches. He's moved through a succession of senior government posts and accumulated an enormous real estate portfolio along the way. Land parcels all up and down the peninsula, hidden behind a slew of front names."

"Wow."

Fatty shook his head in admiration. "Wow indeed, *lah*! Everyone says Sheikh's goals are to become the Prime Minister and also Malaysia's wealthiest man. He is well on the way. His wife is a member of royalty, spectacularly attractive. Two children, too, despite a widespread rumor he's bisexual."

"Who cares? Different strokes."

"Not in Malaysia. Homosexuality is forbidden by law and dangerous here. Sometimes used to put political enemies in prison."

Once the others left on a brief ship tour led by Gary, Snakehead returned, beaming. "Looks like our alliance is formed and the deal is done! The Sheikh was the last one to confirm." Fatty and Snakehead shook hands and grinned like school kids.

"Sincere congrats, gents," I said.

"All the partners are crucial, Dash, but especially Sheikh. It may be no surprise that he *owns* that five-mile stretch of coastline where we boarded the launch tonight. Location for our first dock, right there: close enough to the Singapore causeway with plenty of room for parking but hidden from prying eyes. And Sheikh's political protection will provide a bulletproof shield—no problems for customers coming or going to the casino ship via our high-speed launches."

Fatty chimed in. "I've heard he already has extensive undertakings protecting coastal landing spots for CBC's smugglers." Snakehead nodded.

That's when I suddenly realized something. "So the other night at the nightclub, that *was* him . . .?"

Snakehead smiled and raised a finger. "But be forewarned, boys: if things go against us, Sheikh will (in an instant) publicly disavow us and transform into a highly visible opponent."

"Well that seems awful wrong."

"Forget about what's fair, Dash. Just how it is."

And it was even worse. The Sheikh (unlike all other partners) would contribute no cash to the project and only provide his land via a lease arrangement at a friendly but commercial rate.

Snakehead summoned me and Fatty out onto the rear deck for privacy. He waved the approaching drinks hostesses away. "Now listen carefully, Dash." His voice was firm but confidential. "I am the founder, lead partner and CEO of this venture. Totally *my* baby, put it all together, myself. Assembled the team of partners based upon their specific capabilities and influence. Fatty here is my number two, the general manager, and will own a share."

I opened my cards. "Snakehead, I know zero about the gambling business. Closest is when I bet on my Chicago Bears and lose money."

"Bears?"

"American football, but never mind. The point is that I don't see how I fit into this picture. I've got no money and don't bring anything to the table."

Fatty snickered.

"Your role, *gweilo* boy?" Snakehead smiled and shook his head. "Your role is to be our most trusted lieutenant and closest ally. Someone whose loyalty is unquestioned. Oh, you're bright so you'll do fine. And you'll learn all you need to know, soon enough. It will be hard work but the most fun you'll ever have in your life."

I smiled to signal interest but stayed silent. Kept listening.

"While the Tans are physically building-out this vessel into a floating casino, we three must build the operation and staff the casino. We'll need to obtain expertise, right from the ground up. Assemble a management team, hire floor men and croupiers, staff for the back office and cash operations. Everything. We'll poach *existing* expertise since growing our own would take too long."

My heart raced as I listened.

"So the three of us are leaving tomorrow. An exploratory trip to regional casinos in KL, Manila, Macau, Seoul. Advance scouting before we begin raiding personnel."

Later as the *Sheung Shui* jetted back toward Malaysia, all partners on board appeared giddy with dreams of staggering casino wealth. Even bitter old CBC.

And as for me, I was tingling with excitement. I'd been totally blindsided by the sheer scale of Snakehead and Fatty's grand plan . . . and their offer to me. This was potentially as exciting as when Demy's rocket ride had taken off and we toured the world.

They wanted an answer and nearly immediately. And I could think of plenty of reasons I should probably say no.

But still . . . holy shit!

By 2 a.m. we had arrived ashore and were back at Sheikh's overgrown lot, sitting in Fatty's sedan. The engine idled and the air conditioner blew an icy breeze against our damp skin. Just a minute's walk from the dock coated us both thick with sweat. Fatty sat at the steering wheel and softly giggled to himself.

Our astonishing new prospect left us both dazzled. The entire evening had seemed surreal as a fantastic hallucination.

"Like printing our own money, Dash. We Chinese are all mad to gamble, you know, just who we are. Millions of us are nearby and starving to try our luck. But there are no casinos! Only a distant few in the region." Best was a jungle hillside resort an hour or so outside Malaysia's capital. But for a Singaporean, it took hours to reach Genting Highlands, including a flight to KL and a nausea-inducing drive over twisting mountain roads.

"And Macau in South China or Walker Hill in Korea are too far away. Those shitty little casinos in Manila don't really count. Cheat you there, anyway."

Snakehead's scheme would break new ground. Everything first class all the way, just a pleasant hour's trip from Singapore and Johor in Southern Malaysia. It would be a large fully *professional* casino plus staterooms, bars, quality dining, massage parlor and a small nightclub. And VIP lounges for ultra-high-stake gamblers.

"Snakehead was worried, his idea seemed too good to be true." Fatty smiled, raising his eyebrows. "He engaged Singapore's top law firm. They confirmed that beyond the territorial waters of Singapore, Malaysia and Indonesia, those nations had no authority. The venture had the right to anchor and operate a business, but there was a catch." Fatty shook his head and sighed. "It probably would violate border laws, transporting gamblers to and from our ship. Malaysia could claim the gamblers had illegally left and reentered their sovereign territory, with no passport formalities."

"Bummer. So we're cooked." I sighed. But never much lusted for riches, anyway.

Fatty laughed. "Oh, no! Just like *gweilo* to give up like that. Answer is easy. We will call our shuttles one-hour coastal 'cruises to nowhere' Domestic sightseeing trips that supposedly *never leave Malaysia. Voila*, no need to stamp passports. Of course is make-believe, but gamblers are happy to wink and go along. So for insurance, we must identify and pay off all potential troublemakers at *Imigrasi*. Snakehead's department."

I chuckled. *The nerve!*

But Fatty's tone darkened. "Best to be clear, Dash, before you agree to join. We *are* vulnerable to significant legal risk, and depend upon our partners' blue-chip contacts for survival."

The opportunity seemed imperfect but doable, bizarre yet fantastic: a floating casino in international waters? Nobody was going to get hurt but we'd all get rich.

A miraculous opportunity was dropping into my lap, helping friends while at the same time gaining immense wealth while dodging gangsters, hookers and corrupt politicians all part of the mix. You couldn't make this stuff up.

Maybe, for once, I was due for some good luck? After the theft of my inheritance, the disaster with Demy and, worst of all, the Fiona tragedy.

So before Little Fatty even put the Benz into gear, I told him. "Anyway, Mr. PY Lee—you can count me in."

Fatty punched the air and grinned.

CHAPTER TWENTY-TWO
High Seas Gambling

The next six months flew by and driven by dreams of limitless wealth, the partners all executed their specialized roles at breakneck speed, with all of us running on pure adrenaline.

The Tans acquired a fleet of shuttle launches to run customers between Johor and the casino and sent the huge ferry into dry-dock for customization and fitting-out as a floating casino.

The Sheikh and CBC greased all relevant authorities.

Snakehead, Fatty and I roamed Asia to recruit casino and hospitality management professionals who in turn hired and trained floor men, pit bosses, dealers and so forth. Construction on our docking area in Johor moved briskly forward: clearing once and for all the nefarious weeds, paving a private road and building a comfortable waiting room facility for customers.

In six months' time, *The Diamond Floating Palace Casino* was ready to anchor on the high seas, just thirty minutes offshore, and start printing money.

But would the gamblers come?

Our questionable legality precluded any advertising or publicity campaigns. But word of the casino flashed across the region and right from day one, players descended *en masse* upon our gaming paradise to pack our tables. It was astonishing, not just instant success, but more like a miracle.

The Diamond was huge, beautiful and modern—prime luxury all the way—and our "Voyage to Nowhere" shuttles left the dock in Johor every hour on the hour, stuffed with ebullient gamblers buzzing with an endorphin overload.

Authorities generally ignored it all, to our delight. They clearly welcomed this new honey pot that directly benefitted them also, as CBC regularly greased a host of powerful politicians and higher-ups in government ministries.

Soon, though, emissaries from lower levels of government departments in all three countries started visiting the ship. They arrived daily with hands open and insatiable greed. We paid modest handouts to them and never looked back.

Casino operations were at first limited to evening hours since we'd assumed our clientele sweet spot was male and thus working during the daytime. But the pent-up gambling lust of area housewives stunned us and soon forced *The Diamond* into round-the-clock operations. Many women were pleased to send their husbands off to the office, kiss the children good-bye at the school bus stop and then catch a launch out to The Diamond to gamble away the afternoon playing *Sic Bao*.

During the daytime we closed the specialized attractions aimed squarely at their husbands: the night club, prostitution services and bars. This worked out well since even hookers and bartenders needed to sleep. Then each night, after the women retreated, the ship morphed into a male heaven on the high seas.

Fatty and I stood on deck at the back, jammed among a pack of gamblers staring off into the black at the tiny spot of light on the far horizon. "Approaching always gives me the chills," I said. "Every time."

"Me too, Dash. It's pure electricity. The buzz of money."

While the engines sang in a high smooth whine, the dot of light steadily enlarged until transforming into a gaudy, iridescent rainbow of color. As we closed in, the casino vessel revealed itself as a fantasy world bathed in neon purple, green and hot pink, throbbing with noise. Fiery red signs promised sensual delights and beckoned gamblers, who responded like Pavlov's dogs. Their excitement rose to a crescendo as the shuttle tied up.

Fatty and I knew to stay back and stand aside when the gangplank clanged down. Each time, crazed gamblers pushed, shoved and shouldered each other aside in their haste to enter nirvana. Often some were injured slipping and falling within these small stampedes. But they always waved off medical care, not wanting even a moment's delay to their arrival at the tables or perhaps with a favorite courtesan.

Across its four floors of activity, *The Diamond* easily absorbed a thousand customers at a time, with every seat constantly filled and every table jammed.

Rows of additional players stood behind and reached over shoulders to bet, slamming down towers of chips onto the green baize tables. In a Western casino, such non-stop nudging and contact might trigger fist fights. But in Asia, it was unexceptional—everyone needed to get their bets down, no?

Our clientele continuously turned over 24/7 so the casino actually served many thousands of gamblers each day. And since even the smallest fry brought several thousand dollars to wager, usually losing, we soon found ourselves swimming in cash.

Frightening thugs from CBC's criminal empire always loomed in the background, providing security and keeping the peace.

They monitored *everything*, including heavy winners and losers, targeting the latter for loan offers at exorbitant rates. They also oversaw the shipboard flesh trade. Wrapped tight and bulging in pink, gold or silver sequined dresses, their team of hookers cruised the tables, their heavy perfume mixing with thick clouds of cigarette smoke.

Thanks to CBC's harsh justice, shipboard pickpocketing was nonexistent. Our very first week at sea, two slick-handed cads were caught and tossed overboard. Word spread fast.

Most of the casino's tables were devoted to baccarat, a quick and easy game with high bet limits. Gamblers bet on a 50/50 proposition: which of two dealt hands (one called "Player" and the other, "Banker") would win with the highest total up to nine, something like the children's *War* card game, but on steroids.

Often the entire table wagered in unison, following the same hot streak. Dizzying sums were won or lost. Posh VIP rooms on *The Diamond* catered to ultra-high stakes players with the highest credit lines and wagering habits, absolute *whales* like Indonesian timber tycoons, Malaysian royals and Chinese billionaires, betting tens of thousands on a single baccarat hand with nary a second thought.

Ooi Soon Fok, a Malaysian high-stakes gambler, boarded *The Diamond* several nights a week. Back ashore he ran a bookmaking operation on Malaysia's national four-digit lottery, earning him the nickname *Eddie Numbers*. One night I watched Eddie ride a sizzling baccarat streak, winning bet after enormous bet, all on the Player hand. I was fascinated to watch, up close, this unique Chinese cultural drive, this passion for gambling, as Eddie tested his fate and tried to force favorable outcomes.

Hopping early on the Player winning streak, he won a dozen consecutive Player hands, pyramiding his bets. When a disappointing Banker win finally broke the streak, Eddie jumped right back on Player and won another fifteen consecutive coups. A crowd of hundreds gathered, pressing close and envying his nerve and the mountain of colorful high-value chips stacked in front of him. Other players followed his lead, trying to ride his luck.

"I wonder," I asked Snakehead as we watched, "if Eddie's personal good luck *caused* this streak? Or did he just happen to spot it early and stay with it?"

"Nobody knows for sure, but doesn't really matter, does it?" Snakehead jotted down notes and calculated what Eddie's run was costing the house—us.

Every bettor waited for Eddie to place his wager (Player, of course) and then followed. They pushed gaudy towers of chips out onto the green felt. A mass of others standing in back desperately crowded forward and reached over seated players, slamming down stacks of chips.

Once all bets were down Eddie then put on a show. VIP baccarat traditionally allows the two highest bettors (one each for Player and Banker) to turn over the hands dealt face-down. Eddie turned this into a spectacle as the chattering, joyous audience held their breath.

"But in the process, he's destroying the cards." I complained, trying to think like an owner and hoping Snakehead would approve.

But he just harrumphed me. "Dollar for a deck of cards, Dash. Least of our concerns."

Eddie would tease open each Player hand in a virtuoso performance. Laughing and calling a play-by-play for his audience, he charmed them by at first just barely bending the card corners up to steal a peek underneath. Then with a loud comical voice, he began to provide a running commentary on the developing baccarat hand as he pressed and squeezed the cards, slowly peeling corners or edges up off the felt, revealing more and more of each card and deriving additional clues on the hidden card's value. The crowd roared at his jokes.

"Wish I spoke Chinese."

"In a bawdy, funny way, he just announced how many legs the cards have."

"Legs?"

"That's the pips or spots at the top of the card. If he sees a single leg, in the middle at the top, that means two or a three. If no legs, it's an ace. But if there are two legs, one at each corner, it can be *anything* else."

"Seems complicated."

"Only a little. Players like Eddie will crumple and bend the cards beyond recognition, looking further for hints and announcing their deductions as they accumulate, bit by bit." Occasionally, Eddie stopped and sat back upright, his voice soaring as he teased the crowd of fellow bettors, fanning their hopes and lust for the win.

The rabid audience responded with comments and curses, anxious or assisting.

He's making a lot of puns. Curses and crude jokes. For gamblers this is as entertaining as a talented sports announcer calling a high-stakes prize fight."

Amid this sizzling atmosphere the entire crowd won again and again, drunk with the infectious joy of a win streak that was making them all rich. *Together*. Even to a *gweilo* with no bets riding and missing all the Chinese commentary, it was thrilling, even if only in an odd way.

However, all streaks end.

This one did after a new gambler joined the table, a blonde Western woman who sounded Australian. We'd not seen her on board before. Not a working girl. She placed a minimal bet on Banker, in direct opposition to Eddie and the horde, and the crowd grumbled. But Eddie just smiled and waved off their concern. But with the sole Banker bet at the table, and no fanfare, she blithely flipped open three consecutive hands with *natural* nine's. Automatic winners. Eddie's magic was officially over and the streak was broken.

She gathered her tiny winnings and dropped the chips into her purse, smiled and headed for the slot machines. The crowd's angry rumbling grew louder after she wandered off.

"Eddie took us for a quarter million U.S. dollars tonight," Snakehead said. "And his fellow players? Smaller bets, so all together probably another $100,000."

Snakehead looked at the gloom in my face and laughed. "Dash! Come on. Of course it stings, a little. But never forget: it's only a loan. Eventually it all comes back, plus a profit."

I didn't know about that. "How can you be sure?"

"Laws of pure math."

"Well, I was an English major."

"Then just trust me." Over the long run, the laws of probability were inexorable. "The game's design guarantees our profit. So big wins like Eddie's can be our best possible publicity.

We can't advertise so the next best thing is to have the gambling grapevine rave about *The Diamond.* That our games are fair and big money *can* be won here."

Though *The Diamond* was massive, all space was still carefully allocated and followed a clear pecking order: gaming tables came first, then slots and only then, places to drink or eat. We decided staterooms were a waste of precious space and besides, a sleeping gambler wasn't at the tables. Never good. So we ruled out hoteling and settled on providing just a handful of luxury suites, reserved for our super VIPs.

But even the most crazed gambler needed an occasional break so we provided a nightclub, a few restaurants and a spa.

Our Golden Moon nightclub specialized in over-priced brandy and under-clothed performers. Six Taiwanese women performed nightly with a small band and rotated through theme shows that determined the type of music and skimpy costumes eventually stripped off: *Arabian Nights; Charms of Ancient China; Springtime in Paris; Mysterious Africa;* and *Hawaiian Holiday.*

Our food outlets mainly targeted clientele from Singapore and Malaysia.

Snakehead convinced a popular Johor restaurateur to open a floating branch of his *Mother Chee's Curry House.* Chee was short and harsh, so obese as to be nearly round, and hardened by years dealing with hard-ass characters who hung around his shop. His fish head curry was beloved by tourists, small-time gangsters and high-level businessmen alike. It was said he was called 'Mother' Chee not for maternal, home-style cooking but because he was just a miserable motherfucker. But all agreed his food—brewed in large vats of spicy brown-yellow coconut curry sauce with okra and eggplant, submerging large red snapper heads—was the *Mother of All Curries.*

His small restaurant in JB did frantic business day and night with tourist buses lined up for the genuine cultural experience of dislodging sweet meat from beneath fish cheeks and mopping up savory gravy with chewy bread or rice.

Chee, himself a degenerate gambler, was already aboard our vessel several nights a week so when Snakehead offered him a sweetheart deal, he didn't need much convincing. The floating restaurant would help offset his inevitable gambling losses.

Our second shipboard restaurant was *3-M Noodles,* another cozy space catering to another local food fetish: thick, chewy Hokkien noodles in a lively broth. "Mimi" Mee was a wizened 63-year-old widow with a tiny diner in JB where (to her everlasting good fortune) Little Fatty and I often hung out. After a quick and easy negotiation, Mimi agreed to close her shop in JB and reopen *3-M Noodles* on *The Diamond*, which also became her new home.

She slept on a small cot in the kitchen. In the process, we inherited a hovering auntie and became instant targets for her incessant, well-intentioned pecking.

"That shirt no clean, Little Fatty," she would say. "Bad image, *lah.* Your wife no good." I was also a target. "Dash, you make careful. Many bad woman on casino boat. You still clean young man."

It was a strange life. Half the time I, too, slept on board, taking over a tiny back room. Other nights I went back to Little Fatty's when I needed more sleep (the boat was always noisy, a constant party). I never paid rent to anyone, ate for free and was pleasantly surprised every month or so when Snakehead casually sidled up and handed me a thick stack of Sing dollars or Malaysian Ringgit. "Here's your share," he would say, making no effort to hide my bundle from others' view. Walking around with a fat, bulging wad of cash in a gold money-clip, I couldn't help but feel rich, blessed and happy. Heady stuff for a young man not yet even thirty.

The arrangement seemed utterly informal. As special assistant to Snakehead and Little Fatty, I felt some pride in my role helping build the venture though there was never any mention of my becoming a partner or getting an equity share. But I felt well-compensated and was satisfied.

Frankly, I had no real need for cash anyway. I wanted nothing and had nothing to spend it on.

Early on, Snakehead and Little Fatty kept me close under wing and assigned me work on specific projects, each as a learning experience. Although lacking their authority, by my proximity to them I was on board a man of *some* stature. And as management's lone *gweilo,* I was inevitably under constant observation. Nothing hostile, mind you: I was just *different* and therefore a curiosity. Watchable.

Staff didn't always quite know how to deal with the young Western member of the powerful triumvirate. So I made many acquaintances but few true friends.

At first the working girls targeted me. "Hey, Mr. Dash," they would call out, beaming as I approached and winking to insinuate a freebie might be available.

Snakehead sorted me out, early. "Don't get entangled with any of the girls on board," he warned, "or you'll be out. Take those urges elsewhere."

I totally got it. So when the flirtation started, I'd mutter "Ladies" with a smile and keep walking. The cool responses slowed all that down until they eventually solicited me no more frequently than sailors from the engine room or waiters from the Chinese restaurant.

The women, controlled by CBC's syndicate, were of many ethnicities and conducted their business in the few empty VIP staterooms or in the spa. They included a fair-skinned Chinese woman with silken black hair from Suzhou, who moved like a soft breeze; sweet, soft-spoken Thai women with mocha complexions from Chiang Mai; a towering Russian blonde from Vladivostok; and Zubaidah, a veteran sex worker from Surabaya.

One could tell the Indonesian was once highly attractive but had deteriorated after working so long in a hard line. But with enough mascara, powder and lipstick, some of her considerable past appeal could be temporarily restored, especially in dim light. Zubaidah haunted the gaming rooms and watched for chip stacks that grew or declined fast, knowing winners might want to celebrate and that losers often needed consolation.

One weekend a trio of freelancing Thai women boarded the ship and worked without CBC's approval. The three, under the names of *Ning, Neng* and *Nong,* drew a lot of attention for their fair skin, lean frames and beautiful, piercing smiles. And then they suddenly disappeared.

"One of CBC's goons," Fatty confided, "locked them in a storage room and forced them to talk. They were actually transvestite gambling addicts and pickpockets on the run. A month earlier, they'd fleeced the wrong target (son of a Bangkok crime lord, *aduh!*) and fled Thailand."

"Then what?"

"Well a quick phone call to CBC's associates in the Kingdom revealed there was a fat bounty on them. So after taking photos as proof for the cash CBC's men roped weights to their heels and tossed them overboard, a mile off *The Diamond*."

I shuddered. Fatty frowned and put a hand on my shoulder. "CBC is no joke, Dash. A bad man, like I keep telling you. Be careful."

One evening an irate Tamil man marched up to me. "You must be in charge," said the short man, demanding to see management. He insisted on compensation for a case of venereal disease allegedly contracted on board the casino boat. My reaction was straightforward.

The nerve of this asshole!

I left him with a complimentary drink at the bar, told him to wait and furious, went to see Fatty.

"This asshole got himself into trouble by injudicious screwing. So Fatty, I say we tell him now he can just go screw himself, too."

Fatty smiled and shook his head "You tell this to Snakehead yet?"

"No, but—"

His eyes brightened. "Thank goodness. Now, about your idea, my *mat salleh* friend: No way!" He sighed "Just cut him a generous check, enough to cover the doctor bill and his antibiotics."

"But this clown—"

"Dash. Please just try and understand. It's only another investment and a very cheap one at that. We can afford to be generous."

I suppose I really did still have a lot to learn. And over time, I did.

They made me a troubleshooter and I worked to solve all manner of problems that beset casinos. Common sense solutions usually worked best.

As I built up experience in gaming operations, Snakehead and Fatty threw ever more new challenges at me. The more I achieved, the more their reliance upon me grew. Some issues were just an afternoon's diversion, while others required a small team and months to crack.

I soaked up all manner of hands-on experience. I learned how to best schedule croupiers and work shifts in the cash room. I interviewed new hires and walked the ship daily maintaining the safety and cleanliness checklist. I worked in the counting room.

I became increasingly comfortable with my role and this business, on the way to maturing into a legitimate casino executive.

Casino gaming is a *people* business so customer complaints and staff issues abounded. There were howls about dealer payoff errors, obnoxious drunks and fights between players. We closely monitored staff relationships. To head off collusion, we watched that dealers, floor managers and pit bosses never became *too* chummy.

Once I mastered the broader outlines of casino operations, they started pairing me on managerial assignments with Gary Tan, who also brought book insights from his MBA training.

We teamed up on a trip through Europe and reviewed well-run gaming houses to garner insights that might improve *The Diamond's* operation. We brought back a system of overlapping process checks to ensure all player cash drops made it into the table slots and onward to the cash room, with nothing "lost" en route.

We looked into ways to squeeze more gaming tables onto our limited shipboard space and rescheduled for more frequent shuttle runs. We studied but rejected adding more shuttle dock locations, fearing the threat of increased exposure to onshore authorities.

An early modest investment in security cameras for our cash room later evolved into a comprehensive "eye in the sky" system monitoring our gaming tables. It paid for itself by heading off fraud.

And a true real estate master, The Sheikh, tutored me when he came on board several times a month, visits that usually signaled a government problem requiring *special attention*. Sheikh always left with a small suitcase stuffed with currency from the casino safe. I wondered if CBC and Sheikh always actually paid out all that slush money. I didn't fully trust them but that was Snakehead's call, whose business sense I did completely trust.

Once we commissioned some university professors to develop a statistical control system that compared actual table outcomes against what probability theory predicted should happen. We spent hours poring over those results, looking for shortfalls. Snakehead *loved* that.

"Dash, when a player keeps winning, beating the probabilities, something is *always* wrong. It's just math." Probability-defying results, when they persisted, always triggered deeper investigations.

One evening, Fatty, Snakehead and I took a private launch into Singapore. Ostensibly just for dinner, but I knew they wanted to talk about something.

"*The Diamond* is blowing past even our rosiest projections." Fatty shook his head in wonder. "Unbelievable."

But oddly Snakehead's face was grim. "So what do you think our biggest problem is now, Dash?"

"I guess spending all that lovely money fast enough, chief," I said with a smile. "Man only lives eighty, ninety years."

Snakehead grunted and Fatty shot me a quick warning look. I clammed up. "It almost sounds impossible," Fatty said, "but actually we are generating too much cash, too fast."

I immediately grasped the problem. "Security, right? We are a vulnerable target, out on the high seas."

"Exactly." Snakehead's his face warmed to me now. "Pirates, gangsters or government authorities all have us in their sights and we need to do something. Any ideas, Dash?"

By now, a year into the venture, I was getting pretty good at this kind of stuff. Toss a problem at me and, sometimes, ideas came. This was one of those times.

"Maybe we start pushing players to establish credit lines with us and make deposits, in advance. Discourage them from bringing cash to the casino at all, or as much as possible. Then, it'll already be safe in our bank account, onshore somewhere."

Fatty nodded. "Not bad for a *gweilo*, eh, chief?"

We sold this idea to our gambling clientele by harping on convenience and security. "Mr. Seow," our typical pitch went, "no need for you to travel to and from *The Diamond* with dangerously large sums of money." To our delight, all our regulars began to open accounts with us, backed by large initial deposits. They also executed *markers* payable to *The Diamond Floating Palace*. These were bank checks or pre-approved wire transfers that we could cash, any time a player exhausted his normal credit and failed to replenish it in five business days.

The result? Our venture quickly accumulated a monstrous deposit base. We spread that across a team of banks in Singapore and JB, backed-up by a Swiss bank in Geneva. Our many accounts had unremarkable, numbered names like *FD1, FD2, and FD3*.

Once credit operations were fully underway, we would cut checks from "Diamond Investments" and transmit them to winners from our Orchard Road office within 24 hours of a gambling session. Wire transfers were immediate. Yet despite all that, our *physical* cash kept piling up. There was non-VIP play, the daytime housewives and so forth.

We assembled stacks of currency packed into bricks and stuffed them in a huge walk-in safe in our armored counting room. Armed men stood guard. Eventually the stubborn cash glut (the very best type of bad news) forced us to start conducting dangerous stealth runs, physically transporting cash to banks onshore.

These cash blitzkriegs always occurred in the dead of night, their timing totally at random, via high-speed launches filled with gunmen, speeding direct to private docks in JB or Singapore near our banks. No passports stamped. It was all highly illegal.

But *The Diamond's* enormous deposit base made us by far each bank's top customer, so they readily accommodated our demands for abrupt, after-hour visits. What else could they do?

Whenever we unloaded cash in JB, The Sheikh arranged airtight cover for these missions with a crew of fierce-looking Sikhs in turbans always standing guard. In Singapore, Madame Tan arranged for a few dozen off-duty police to stand by, overseen by CBC's thugs.

CHAPTER TWENTY-THREE
Literary Redemption

Gary handed me a stack of publications. "Here you go," he said, "this week's supply." Gary and I worked well together for years, but we were an odd pairing. He was a wealthy young Asian commercial hot-shot, heir to the Eastern Ferry & Bus empire, whereas I was a penniless, motorcycle-wrecking, ex-literary wanderer from rural Illinois.

Gary was always maneuvering and cultivating relationships and locked up a spot in my heart, early on, by hand-carrying international magazines and newspapers to me (uncensored!) from Singapore.

Spending as much time as I did on The Diamond, I devoured the regional news weeklies for English-speaking elites: *The East Asia Review,* an esteemed pioneer published by British journalists in Hong Kong; and *Southeast Asian Weekly,* the newer and sensation-seeking upstart produced by an Australian team in Singapore.

I fanned out the stack of magazines on an empty dice table but before I could even thank Gary, a face smiling out from one of the covers stunned me like a physical slap.

Suddenly dizzy, I collapsed into a chair.

"Whoa, Dash, steady there." Gary put a firm hand on my shoulder. "Here, drink this."

I sipped some cool water, caught my breath and nodded I was okay. But upon sneaking a second look, another electric jolt of recognition pounded me.

It *was* him.

Demy.

The cover feature stories were about Demetrio Luminoso, the mentor I'd unintentionally betrayed. I flipped through the stack and noticed many magazines had similar cover stories. All were probably rewritten from the same originating source, perhaps a *New York Times* article.

The gist was that the literary world appeared ready to grant absolution and once again embrace its banished genius. *"Literary World Forgiving Prodigal Genius?"* teased the *Southeast Asian Weekly*.

The stories reported a movement underway amongst literary elite (like university professors, reviewers and critics) to pardon Demy for his accused past plagiarism.

A consensus was gaining support that prior to writing his magnum opus, Demy had surely been unaware of the weaker and inconsequential predecessor novella. Despite the undeniable parallels, Luminoso's work was so transcendently superior it seemed a near-profanity to compare the works.

Perspiration beaded on my forehead. I breathed deeply and willed my heart to slow. Why had my past hunted me down like this, to again remind me why I'd fled the U.S. years so long ago? This abrupt reminder why I'd disappeared halfway around the globe felt cruel and unreal.

I'd never really completely forgotten the Demy mess, but became adept at ignoring. Now I realized unforgiven guilt probably never goes away. Pushed to the back of mind it might fade from view, but was always lurking.

A flash of insight and I knew what I needed to do for closure and my own peace of mind.

"Gary, a favor?"

"More cold water? Sure. You still don't look so good."

"Ha, no, it's this story. I'd like to meet the writer." The byline said *Robert Branch, Singapore*. "Maybe with your connections—"

He shot me a warning look. "Careful, buddy, our casino venture and publicity don't mix. Best to steer clear of journalists."

"Yeah, I know. I'm not *stupid*." I smiled. "Just a personal interest and absolutely nothing will endanger *The Diamond*. I swear."

"Okay, but step lightly." He jotted down Branch's name. "Consider it done." He gazed over and smiled. "You're looking better now. Scared me there."

"Forgot my breakfast, I guess." I winked. "And hey, can you hook this up with Branch, soon as possible?"

Later that night, Gary phoned with results. Fast, even for him.

"Dash, tomorrow we're buying that writer lunch at *The Raffles*. Big fan of free meals. You'll can take it from there."

The journalist was a large puffy man with graying hair, a walrus mustache and bloodshot eyes. He inhaled food at the iconic Singapore hotel restaurant like it was his last meal, or else his first in a week, gulping down beer and spilling food everywhere. His booming voice was spiced with an Aussie accent and colorful Oz jargon.

When we walked back to the magazine's office, Gary (his mission accomplished) took off.

Branch's desk was unimpressive, jammed into the corner of a cramped newsroom bullpen. I took a chair. "How does one get a job like this??"

"Been a *journo* on the Asia beat over two decades," Branch smiled. "Started in Nam for a Sydney paper but the contract wasn't renewed. Maybe overly-enjoyed Saigon a bit, hey? Anyway, hunted around and tucked into this little spot on the rewrite desk when the brand new *Southeast Asian Weekly* opened."

"Is it hard?"

"Hard as sleepwalking. I browse the *NY Times, The Economist, Daily Mail* and bugger-all to mine them for stories.

Liberate news and convert into our own. The pay is piss-poor but it's an afternoon's work per week, at most. Indeed, mine is a special skill, mate. Still . . ." He shrugged.

"I saw your name on that Luminoso cover story for the current edition."

"Yeah? If you say so. Don't really recall. Just another rewrite."

I tried to target any flickering embers of his former journalistic ambition or integrity. "Mr. Branch, what if a worldwide scoop were to drop right into your lap? And every news organization in the world that picked up *your* original story personally credited *Robert Branch*."

He smiled, bemused.

"Mate, you misunderstand. Nowadays, I'm just a re-write *yobbo*."

"Listen, sir, this is important." I leaned closer. "Luminoso's downfall due to plagiarism was electrifying. Global news. But nobody ever knew the full story. Turns out entire mess was really the fault of an assistant, a little pipsqueak who failed to do his job properly. Demy never knew about that other book. He was never warned." I was getting passionate but Branch stifled a yawn.

"Ace story, mate. But what's all that to do with me?"

"Well, sir, the shitty little pipsqueak was *me*. I have the inside story and want to tell it, now, exclusively. First time ever. Will be huge."

Something flickered in the writer's eyes.

"Luminoso was my mentor. Magnanimous, he protected me and never revealed any of this. Even when his integrity was under attack, his masterpiece degraded and his literary career all but blown up, he never deflected the blame onto me." I found myself shaking as I spoke this long-buried truth and only now realized I'd been unconscionably self-centered and always remained focused upon my *own* personal loss, not Demy's.

Branch led me into a small private room off the newsroom floor and away from the bullpen. He turned on a tape recorder, opened a notepad and listened. For the next several hours, the story spilled from me in vibrant detail. Though rusty in his reportorial skills, Branch peppered me with occasional helpful questions whenever I lagged, helping tease out color or solidify my narrative.

Finally, I had nothing more to say and he closed his notepad.

"So, that's real *bonzer* stuff, mate. Spiffy. How can I reach you for follow-up questions and what-not?"

"Quite impossible, sir." To protect *The Diamond*, I could allow no trail so I lied. "Right now, I'm in the middle of an overland trek across Asia. Just passing through Singapore for a day and spotted your Branch story on a newsstand. Wanted to come clean."

"Ah, lucky that." He frowned momentarily and then his face brightened. "But perhaps your Singapore friend can contact you on the road?"

"No, sorry. Great fella but he's just a casual acquaintance. We only met for the first time last night. Shared a couple beers at a bar in Orchard Towers."

Branch grunted and shook his head. "Well until we can confirm this stuff, nothing gets printed. And without your help that'll be more difficult. But not impossible."

The next day, a desperate Branch sent urgent word via Gary to clarify some confusion in his notes. I called from a pay phone in Johor. "You were lucky to reach me, Mr. Branch, this final time. I'm waiting for my steamer right now. Leaves at dusk for India."

I sorted out his questions and said good-bye.

Then the waiting started.

It seemed forever but *nothing* happened. After six non-eventful weekly issues, I stopped watching the *Southeast Asian Weekly* and regretted pinning any hopes on a booze-soaked writer. One morning, just as I was weighing the idea of mailing my first-person story to the *New York Times* or *The Economist,* Gary phoned.

"Dash, looks like you're famous!"

Branch had come through.

His scoop in *Southeast Asia Weekly* went on to trigger a worldwide sensation. News organizations across the planet piled on, picking up and quoting his story. Some tried to take it further by contacting Demy, who flatly refused to speak on what was reported. Branch himself had secured Demy's only on-the-record comment by phone, just before his story hit print: "Well, if that's what Dash Bonaventure said, I won't dispute it. He's an honest man."

The media blitz appeared from out of nowhere and seemed to boost my status among casino staff to mini-celebrity.

Gary was as excited as me.

And Little Fatty lauded my honesty and loyalty to Demy. "And nice how he kept *The Diamond* completely out of it. Eh, chief?" But Snakehead only shrugged.

I had been very careful with Branch and left no tracks. There was no way imaginable for the story to somehow be linked back to me at our floating casino. *The Diamond* was safe.

None of the other partners—CBC, The Sheikh, and Madame Tan—betrayed any interest or emotion, whatsoever. Who knows? Maybe they didn't care about Western literature or just didn't read the news. Covering all contingencies, I reminded Gary to remain evasive should Branch ever contact him again. "Nothing good could ever come of it."

"Okay, *lah*. But no need to even tell me, Dash." The smooth Western-educated Chinese businessman cleared his throat and rasped into an imaginary telephone. "*Solly, Mistah Blanch, but Mistah Dash . . . he gone.*"

CHAPTER TWENTY-FOUR
Unwelcome Attention

The shipboard buzz triggered by the Demy story eventually calmed down and my work consumed me again. By now, I'd been aboard *The Diamond* four years and had become the ultimate shipboard rat, spending my every waking hour wandering the vessel, cruising the casino floor, working projects and cajoling customers. I went ashore only a night or two per week and slept at Little Fatty's house in JB, just to get away and retain my sanity.

Otherwise, I was a devoted casino executive dedicated 24/7 to *The Diamond*.

I'd discovered an innate common sense ability and connected with this particular business. I loved the vibe, the people, and the challenges. My confidence grew.

The fellow in the mirror, staring back at me each day when I shaved, had changed. I looked lighter and more mature, thanks to my hairline beginning to recede by my mid-30s. And thanks to my pattern of working nights and sleeping days, paralleling the casino's activity, my complexion was now more sallow compared to the tanned, wind-burnt fellow who'd arrived from Bali years back.

A golden period for me ensued, the next four years aboard *The Diamond*.

I worked on major projects. One of my favorites was to create a database on our players. In the mid-to-late 1980s, we were a pioneer with this. We kept gambling profiles on our players, their birthdays, names of wives or girlfriends, favorite brands of liquor or cigars. We tracked their favorite games and pace of play. We recorded their detailed win/loss history, by visit. It was a pleasant coincidence that personal computers and workstations were just emerging, so we purchased a score and hired a team of young Singaporean MBAs to maintain our spreadsheets.

At first, we didn't realize how powerful this tool could be. But we learned one Chinese New Year, after holiday overcrowding threatened to capsize *The Diamond* with two thousand souls jammed on board.

To prevent any chilling reoccurrences, we used our database to create a gambler loyalty program and during major holiday periods flipped this on/off like a switch to limit casino entry to only our loyal, premiere customers.

Fatty and Snakehead liked my common sense approach to problems. "You think like a *gweilo*, Dash," said Snakehead.

"But your heart has now become Chinese, I think," added Fatty.

My stature was sealed the day I permanently solved that vexing *too-much-cash* problem.

The plan I pitched to Snakehead was straightforward. "Force the banks to swallow the risk," I argued, "and make *them* come *here* to collect the cash."

Snakehead narrowed his eyes in skepticism. "And how will they do that?"

"Well, I don't really know—"

"See?"

"—but that's their problem, no? Just watch, every last one of them will compete for the privilege of handling our cash. We are *that* important a customer. And whoever won't, they're out."

The concept was audacious and even a bit arrogant.

But it worked.

After eight years prowling the casino floor, one becomes very close with the regulars.

One night after 3 a.m., the crowd had already thinned and Eddie Numbers was holding down his usual lucky spot (seat number eight) at a near-empty baccarat table. Like many in the East he believed the number eight to be lucky because the word in Cantonese is a homonym for *prosperity*.

I was overseeing the floor, doing my usual rounds, and plopped down in the seat next to him. I liked the guy and always tried to exchange a friendly word with him. Good customer relations.

"So, how the cards treating you tonight, Eddie?"

He made a sour face, like the croupier had just released a giant cloud of flatulence.

"So far, Dash, luck no good." He'd battled choppy shoes all night, unable to catch a streak. He leaned closer and his expression changed. Conspiratorial. "My luck bad," he hissed, "but still maybe better than luck for *Diamond* casino. No?"

That was odd.

I smiled and patted his forearm. "Eddie, you *always* win and take casino money." A flattering lie. "But don't worry about *The Diamond's* luck. We'll win money from other players."

He shook his head and sighed. "I mean bad luck *business problem* for casino."

Now he was confusing me. "Sorry?"

"Illegal casino like *Diamond*—"

"Hey!" I chuckled. "Illegal? Let's say we're *innovative.*"

"Okay *lah*. But bad publicity never good."

Bad publicity?

Little transpired across the region that escaped Eddie's view. His bookmaking network spread its tentacles across Malaysia and Singapore, with runners maintaining warm relationships in offices and restaurants everywhere. He motioned me closer.

"My worker, Siva, he hear something bad." Eddie meant Sivaraja Che Johani, one of his agents, had snagged a hot rumor while making his rounds. I'd met Siva before. He was a flashy and ambitious young man of mixed Indian and Malay heritage. Siva always seemed to be working angles and looking for advantageous information: stock tips, fixed horse races, whatever.

Eddie said while collecting bets at the *Southeast Asian Weekly* office in Singapore, Siva was pulled aside by a friendly client and, in an empty meeting room, privately learned some sizzling news.

"Siva say story coming soon in big magazine. About *Floating Diamond.*" *Froating.* He stared hard into my eyes, maybe looking for surprise. But I was too shocked to even react.

"But Snakehead and Fatty already know this, yes?"

I was frozen, too nervous to make the wrong move. Feigning knowledge would seem to confirm his rumor. But admitting ignorance would make us look uninformed, especially the big boss—and Snakehead never liked to look a fool.

When I finally spoke I kept my face blank and voice calm. "Eddie, better that you focus on your baccarat. You've already missed a trend! This shoe, the *tie* bet is coming up every fifth hand!" Ties paid off eight-to-one.

It worked.

Looking irritated or surprised, Eddie grinned displaying tar-stained teeth and lit another cigarette. "*Tie* bet no good, Mr. Dash. Just lose money faster. So maybe Dash stick to casino job, not betting. Okay, *lah*?" He turned away and directed his full attention back to his gambling.

I stood up, brushed the cigarette ashes from my coat and briskly walked to the back office.

"*Aiee-yah!*" Snakehead hollered, slamming an angry fist against the desk. "That would be a disaster. This casino is no secret, of course. All Singapore knows. But once the media starts making noise all our legal cover will evaporate. Politicians whom we pay for protection will have no choice and blind eyes will be forced to see. They will be compelled (to themselves survive) to attack us. And our venture will die."

The threat of a story seemed plausible. Several dealers and cash room workers that week had already received odd phone calls at their homes. Their wives took down messages. From some magazine. Of course none phoned back, but all were spooked and reported it at work.

"So, which magazine. Supposedly?" Snakehead drummed his fingers.

"*Southeast Asian Weekly.*

"Same rag that briefly made you a little famous, a few years ago?" I nodded. Snakehead inhaled deeply and sighed. "I remember there was a writer—"

"The drunken Aussie? Branch. Wonder if he's still there."

"You better pay him a visit, Dash."

"Hmm. Good idea, boss." *No, maybe, not really . . .*

"Move fast but carefully and try to find out what's going on. If this is true, there's no time to lose." Snakehead patted my shoulder. "But keep this totally quiet. Just between us."

"Plus Gary. He's my liaison with Branch."

Snakehead pondered a moment, looking unhappy. "Okay, but that's all."

We agreed on a game plan. Gary would stay quiet at first while I did all the talking. Later, he would do the heavy lifting.

I barely recognized Branch's work station, no longer a small desk in the bullpen. Propelled by my Demy exclusive, his career had taken off like a rocket.

He now occupied a spacious, well-appointed private office with an oversized desk of tropical wood topped with tinted glass. Behind him awards jammed the wall, saluting recent victories by the magazine's new investigative team, which he led. At the far end, a comfortable leather sofa squatted between carved mahogany tables littered with cultural artifacts like miniature etchings in smooth ebony, antique opium pipes, jade carvings and bejeweled ornaments.

A massive painting of the Li River's other-worldly landscape near Guilin covered an entire wall.

Branch rose and waved us toward the couch.

More than just his workplace had changed. I could hardly recognize this svelte, updated version of the journalist. He now appeared elegant and well-groomed in an expensive, vested dark blue suit. His Italian designer tie alone probably cost more than my entire outfit. His former walrus mustache had narrowed down to a wispy line, like an old film star: he was channeling Errol Flynn. Success had totally revamped him.

"Ah, Mr. Bonaventure. Lovely to see you." Even his accent and vocal mannerisms had gone uptown. "And charmed to see your friend, again. Mr. Foo, wasn't it?" He smiled solicitously.

"No. Gary Tan."

"Of course." Branch waved the tea lady into the room. She pushed her cart alongside the sofa and laid out three settings with sweet biscuits on the long glass-topped coffee table with ornate carved legs. Out in the bullpen a team of six journalists (his investigators) watched intently as their boss gave these visitors the deluxe treatment.

"So look at you! You look well, Mr. Bonaventure, all fit and tanned. Lovely suit, too. Quite different from last time. How time flies! What is it, a year or so since that literary story of yours?" Branch smiled.

"Nearly four. But thanks to you it had the desired effect for Demy." My confession had thrown gasoline onto a fire already raging through the literary world.

"And, well, I also benefited, mate. So I am beyond satisfied and grateful . . ." His voice drifted off as he swung his arm and slowly panned the office and beyond in an *all-of-this* gesture. He smiled and shrugged, looking nearly embarrassed. "You certainly disappeared, Mr. Bonaventure. Hope your Asian vagabonding was enjoyable. And I'm glad to see you back in the area."

"My round-the-world backpacking finally ended so I now live in the USA. Just here on vacation and wanted to check in with you, pay my respects."

"Of course. Anyway, anything else I can do for you?" This new, higher-status version of Branch appeared to already be wrapping up our visit and this part would be delicate.

"Not for me actually but Gary. He has a question about a possible investigation your magazine may be conducting on a business in the area."

Branched laughed. "An investigation? Yes, well we only do that . . . continuously." Chuckling, he pointed through the glass at his team of journalists, who swung their heads down to study papers on their desktops. "These days my team does *only* original reporting." His rewrite days were over.

Gary cleared his throat. "Well, sir, there is a silly rumor—I feel foolish even asking—about a gambling ship supposedly somewhere in the region. International waters somewhere. Anyway, silly, I know, but . . ."

"Hmm." Branch's eyebrows rose and his smile evaporated. Lost for words and looking noticeably uncomfortable, momentarily he stumbled until regaining his footing. When he finally spoke, his tone was abrupt and all business. "Now Mr. Foo—"

"Tan."

"Yes." He coughed. "Obviously we never discuss ongoing investigations. So if we were indeed conducting such an investigation (and I am *not* saying that, neither yes or no), I would be unable to answer any questions. Confidentiality and what-not. You understand, of course."

Gary nodded.

This abrupt, total stonewalling seemed a very bad sign. The glad-handing friendly Branch of just moments earlier had disappeared. Something clearly seemed afoot.

"Mr. Branch, please don't misunderstand. I personally have *nothing* to do with any such rumored ship," Gary continued. "Mine is only a *business* curiosity. A story like that might very remotely affect my other interests. That's all, so . . ."

I took one last shot and gave Branch a chance to deny it all.

"Gary, it's no surprise Robert's magazine can't waste resources on far-fetched rumors like imaginary casino ships offshore—"

"Mr. Bonaventure, please!" Branch's face was flushed bright pink. "There is nothing further we can discuss. Nothing at all. This matter is closed." He forced an uncomfortable smile. "And remember. I have neither confirmed nor denied anything, mate. Right? Ethics, you know."

The tea lady suddenly returned, as if responding to an invisible signal that the meeting had ended. She began to collect our half-filled cups of coffee and tea, rattling the silverware. Branch stood up, giving an unmistakable signal, and started herding us toward the door. "Do call again, won't you?"

Gary and I found ourselves in the reception foyer so fast, being hustled out of the building that it felt like a scene from an old comedy movie when they toss people out into the street and then sail their fedoras after them.

"So what do you think?" Gary said, with a smirk.

"Same as you, probably."

"That he seemed awfully nervous, that chap?"

"Yeah. And as soon as you asked your question, he was no longer my oldest, best friend. Wanted our asses outta there, pronto."

"Quite the glorious heave-ho," Gary agreed. "Something *must* be up."

"Without saying anything, he told us everything."

Gary nodded. "I liked him better as a big, sloppy drunk."

Back at *The Diamond* my report infuriated Snakehead. "Damn it, why don't you *gweilos* stick together?"

"*Gweilo* solidarity is not a real thing, boss. Besides he's an Aussie and I'm a Yank. Not the same."

Snakehead raked fingers through his thick, silver locks and rubbed his forehead, thinking hard. "Hmm," he muttered to himself, nodding. "We have a problem named Robert Branch . . ."

CHAPTER TWENTY-FIVE
Gold Bars & a Check

From that day on, we intently screened all media, not just the *Southeast Asian Weekly,* for anything even remotely hinting about our casino. Gary became the top volume customer at his local Singapore newsstand. Every day the wizened Indian operator gathered up one of *everything* to hand over. We pored through it all, imagining angry headlines (*'Floating Scandal: Authorities Ignore Illegal Offshore Casino'*) that could force our shutdown.

Instead the news remained innocuous and we were happy to be disappointed. And in another positive sign those phone calls ended, the ones disturbing our casino staff.

So it seemed Eddie Number's rumor had it all wrong. Or perhaps had Branch's investigators run up against a dead end? Nope, that seemed unlikely. After all, it would have been easy to land an undercover reporter aboard *The Diamond*. A thousand Singaporeans did it every night.

Or had Branch called off the hounds out of friendship, or perceived debt, to me? Fat chance.

We could only assume the more likely explanation that the protection we purchased from authorities via CBC and The Sheikh was just working. It made sense that while nosing around, reporters might have run into political heat. Wasn't that why we were paying all that money? Or had the clout of our partner, dowager empress Madame Emerald Tan, cowed the Singapore press?

Whatever the reason, no story appeared. With each passing day the threat ebbed and things felt safer. The mood seemed to brighten on board and eventually all was forgotten, like a nonsensical bad dream.

I continued to stay overnight at Fatty's once a week, almost like part of the family. One morning there it was just after 5 a.m. and Fatty was already out with Nancy, walking in the morning cool.

I picked up the newspapers from his mailbox (*Nanyang Siang Pow* in Chinese, *The Star* in English, and *Berita Harian* in Malay) and took them out to the back garden. It was my custom to sit at the patio table and take my morning coffee while browsing the papers.

But glancing down at page one headlines, something made me cough and spit coffee out my nose. All three had a photo of CBC. And the banner headline in *The Star* made my heart leap: *Massive Oil Theft Ring Preys on Malaysia and Singapore.*

My spine tingled and I sensed trouble, big trouble, though not fully understanding why.

Our partner and crime titan was coming under direct attack. This was the last thing any of us could have expected. I had no idea how CBC's woes might affect the casino, but it sure couldn't help. Danger seemed to threaten like a dark wall of thunderheads off in the distance that might roll in at any time.

Little Fatty glistened with light perspiration after his morning stroll and entered the garden smiling. He peaked over my shoulder and his face suddenly went blank. "Oh, my," he said, clicking his tongue, "this is bad. Very serious."

He briskly strode to a table in the entryway and picked up his wallet and car keys. "Come on, Dash, let's go. *Cepat, cepat.* Quick, quick. Into the Benz. We need to immediately go see Snakehead, in private."

At 6 a.m.? Whatever. He made a quick phone call while I slipped on some clothes.

His chauffeur hadn't yet arrived for work so Fatty took the wheel of his magnificent new Benz, a stunning sedan in flamboyant creamy purple that floated across the roads. Its suspension was amazing and seemed to levitate over the pot-holes as we sped off to Snakehead's palatial estate just outside Johor Baru, hidden in a still-jungled area.

Though I'd known Snakehead the better part of a decade already, this was the first time I'd see his home.

Two armed Sikh guards in turbans flung open the sturdy black wrought iron gates and directed us up the circular graveled drive to a magnificent old whitewashed colonial house.

Snakehead, wearing vermilion silk pajamas (a huge dragon embroidered across the back) and rubber flip-flops, stood at the front door. He held a rolled-up newspaper and absently swatted it against his side while quietly muttering. I'd never seen him so anxious.

He nodded, turned, and marched us out onto an airy veranda. His servant, in a black and white uniform, laid out two more breakfast settings on a large glass-topped rattan table. At least the morning was beautiful: a lovely dawn was underway with soft breezes, birds singing, and the air cool and fresh.

"This," sighed Snakehead, motioning at the tabloid paper atop the patio breakfast table, "is as bad as it gets." He'd only seen the article minutes earlier, after Fatty's phone alert. He lit a cigarette and barked out an order to another servant. "Blue label and three glasses. Water and ice. Fast."

"Booze at 6:15?" I teased, hoping to lighten things. "*That* bad?"

No smile came in return. Snakehead looked serious as death and intimidating as hell. The scotch arrived and we clinked glasses before taking a gulp.

"At least no mention of the casino." Little Fatty was trying some optimism.

Snakehead frowned. "True, so far. But with CBC one of our partners, an owner, this by definition *must* impact *The Diamond*." The handsome, silver-haired man poured more whiskey. "And once the media free-for-all breaks out in earnest, centering on

CBC, the *Diamond* connection will inevitably attract attention. With dire results."

All three papers' stories were based upon the same damning news story broken by the AP, based on a sensational investigative piece just published by *Southeast Asian Weekly*.

So it *was* Branch, after all.

As reportorial assassination jobs went, it seemed a *tour de force,* with considerable color and impressively detailed inside information on vice kingpin Chuah Beng Chong. Our CBC.

The impressive mechanism of his oil theft syndicate was laid out in bloody detail, a full description of the daily pilfering of oil from hundreds of tank trucks that moved between the Singapore refineries and storage terminals and gas stations of Malaysia. The process was efficient and regimented, down to a science. Secret compartments were built into many trucks to retain fuel for later theft, after delivery had supposedly emptied the trucks.

There were also maps showing a network of jungle pull-off locations that facilitated theft from trucks that lacked such hidden compartments. Those just parked there and in minutes had valuable petroleum product siphoned out and replaced with cheaper substitutes. The thieves were as educated in oil industry operating standards as company petroleum engineers, which ensured that resulting product adulteration or shortages remained low enough to escape scrutiny.

The newspaper article also included maps of the sea routes used by CBC's oil smugglers. There were estimates of product volumes and a chart calculating the government's huge tax losses, a tactic designed to infuriate not only government ministers but also the average Malaysian or Singaporean taxpayer.

"The Sheikh won't like this either," Snakehead mumbled, pointing at the map showing landing spots—all no doubt on the Malay official's land.

At least *The Diamond's* jetty location was not shown.

Snakehead whistled a low tone, impressed. "But the sheer scale of CBC's operations. Whew! I never suspected. And as for your buddy, Branch: that's some amazing reporting, no?"

I didn't like that. "Whaddya mean? He's not *my* buddy."

Snakehead didn't seem to hear. "Look at all the story's detail! The oil theft network, the smuggling operations, the duty evasion. And for good measure, the juicy details about CBC's loan-sharking and whore running. Wow."

"*Alamak!*" Little Fatty chimed in, nodding. "Our CBC's been a very busy boy, *heya*? What a businessman!"

"So our partner is in a world of trouble now. No doubt. This was a first-class hit piece," Snakehead said, scratching his head.

I was glad my friends seemed to be regaining their composure and becoming more resigned to the situation. "And lucky for The Sheikh too," I added, "not being identified or highlighted as part of the smuggling."

Fatty shook his head. "Be clear, Dash. Sheikh was never the target, nor us. He'll be okay. This was aimed squarely at CBC, almost like an attempt to destroy him."

"Poor guy," I said. *Poor evil, ill-tempered, corrupt, scary, mafia-type guy.*

I demurred but Snakehead poured himself another drink. "Hah, Dash. Save your pity, CBC doesn't want or need it. He will survive, no worries." The dashing man slapped at a morning mosquito, leaving a small blood-stain on his white silk pajama sleeve. "But good God, at least for now he's lost massive face." Snakehead stage acted a shiver. "He must be absolutely furious! Unable to even think straight and ready to lash out, hard, at any possible culprits. And worst of all his payments to authorities must now multiply. All sorts of headaches. Overall for CBC, a very expensive mess"

That all made sense.

"So it's best," Snakehead said, smiling, "that we all keep our distance from him, at least for now."

"I certainly agree with *that*." I chuckled.

Little Fatty and Snakehead exchanged odd smiles.

"Glad you understand," Snakehead said, his voice lowering, "because in your particular case—"

"In *my particular* case? No, I don't have a case."

"—because in *your* particular case, there probably isn't enough room in all of Southeast Asia to keep you safe from CBC."

What?

I looked over at Little Fatty, who just bounced his shoulders in one of those little *What-can-you-do?* Shrugs.

"Listen, Snakehead, this CBC mess has *nothing* to do with me. No more my problem than either of you." They stayed quiet with faces blank and let me vent. "I don't even know that fucking CBC's real name—Ching Bong Chong or whatever. And I don't even care." Snakehead started to grin, which only made me angrier. "So again, why's this about me, at all? I'm no leak or informant."

The two exchanged a look and something unspoken seemed agreed upon, on the fly. Little Fatty, my closest friend, took the lead.

"Listen, Dash, CBC is violent and dangerous." Fatty's eyes were wide. "The guy's unstable and a real criminal."

"This is news? I'd already sort of guessed that, Fatty, what with his vast continental crime organization and, you know, all those thieves, hookers and killers he employs." I shivered a bit inside to remember the times that CBC's thugs had meted out brutal punishment in providing on board security, putting weights on the ankles of victims and just tossing them into the sea.

Little Fatty sighed.

"Right now, Dash, this situation is dangerous for *everyone*. But for you it's a million times worse."

"But I had nothing to do with the news story. You both *know* that, right?"

"Of course we do." Little Fatty took in a calming breath. "But what *we* think doesn't matter. While what CBC thinks is a life-

or-death consideration. And he no doubt is certain *you* were the writer's source."

"Why? Just because I'm a *gweilo* like Branch, so we naturally stick together?" I spat out the words. "How can anyone even suggest that?"

"Little Fatty is *suggesting* nothing," Snakehead interjected. "It is absolutely certain CBC already has ordered gun-sights trained on you. He knows, as we all do, that you once fed information to that journalist. Remember? About your literary friend?"

"Years ago." I couldn't believe this. "So that's some pretty weak-assed shit, Snakehead."

"Please. You turned that Australian journalist into a regional media star and *nobody* on *The Diamond* missed that." Sounded like Snakehead was getting hot. "At the time it was quite dangerous. There was *huge* concern among the partners about you and the media. Both CBC and The Sheikh both wanted you *out*."

Out? I shuddered, understanding the euphemism. "But nobody told me—"

"It was better you didn't know," snapped Snakehead. "And we *handled* it. But this new problem is far worse because you visited Branch again, just a few months ago."

"At *your* request!" My heart was pounding. "About the rumored casino story, remember?"

"Of course. And it all worked out fine. The expose we feared about our venture never reached print."

"Yes, though I did nothing."

"Perhaps so. Yet within a week, not a single croupier or cleaning maid on *The Diamond* was unaware there'd been a big *gweilo* summit in Singapore." I felt dumbstruck. "Nothing remains secret here for long, Dash."

In a flash of insight, I understood what had so spooked Branch during the visit.

His team must have been deep into investigating their grand expose on crime boss CBC and so were aware of the rumored floating casino connection. But that would have been just a minor element in the much larger *crime lord* story.

And when Gary asked his casino question, only remotely touching upon CBC, the journalist panicked and shut down the meeting. Too close to home.

"So CBC is aware Branch and I recently met and already assumes us to be chums. So now, when this scoop comes out about his entire sleazy operation . . . I am the number one suspect. Winner in the guessing game of *Who's The Rat?*"

"Jackpot!" Little Fatty gave me a playful poke. "You really went big-time, Dash. Your own personal enemy is one of the most feared men in Asia, a real shoot-first and *maybe* think-later kind of character."

"Great."

Snakehead put a hand on my shoulder. "But put yourself in his shoes, Dash. Exposed and humiliated, his entire life is suddenly a mess. Authorities about to come at him from all sides. Ones he's been paying off will abandon him or, at best, jack up the price for his protection. And all because of some miserable *gweilo* he wanted to bump off, years ago."

"Oh, shit."

"Yes," Fatty said, nodding, "is *very shit*, indeed. CBC is probably so furious, cannot even think, *lah*. To him, you must die. Unfair? *Fair* is not his consideration. *Innocent?* Same-same. No need for CBC to confirm anything, just boom, a bullet behind your ear." Little Fatty wiped his brow and neck with a table napkin.

Snakehead shrugged, his face grim. "And that ear-bullet is just if you were lucky. More likely his men take you somewhere and extract a confession. Your demise would probably be as painful and prolonged as possible, to mirror the distress CBC think's you've caused."

Then he abruptly brightened a little, winked and hoisted his glass. "Well, anyway, cheers!"

Little Fatty shook his head. "Come on boss, let's remember Dash's feelings."

But I knew they were right.

Snakehead looked me straight in the eyes. "Okay, Dash, relax and keep breathing. Naturally I can explain all this to CBC, that you're no traitor. I can smooth his feathers."

Snakehead, my guy!

"Now that's more like it."

"But we'll also have to help him sort out his own problems. Can't have one of our *Diamond* partners drawing high heat from authorities and the media. It may take time but I'm sure all can be resolved."

I started to feel my blood pressure easing off. Snakehead Goh (my wily unofficial Chinese godfather) would fix everything.

"Wow, chief. Thanks! That's a relief." I smiled and sipped my dawn scotch whiskey. I noticed how delicious it suddenly tasted. "So anyway, what's next then?"

Snakehead's visage remained impassive. "Well for one thing, you need to leave Southeast Asia, that's for sure."

"What?" That came as an absolute gut punch.

A hint of a smile softened Snakehead's grimace. Pity? "My little brother, you need to get the hell out." His steel-cold eyes bored into mine as he poured three more drinks. He raised his and clinked it against mine, still on the table, and then he tossed in the killer: "And you'd better make your getaway fast, too—like today. Better yet? Right *now*."

I started to hyperventilate.

"But I . . . I . . ."

My temper and confusion were rocketing and I was unable to think straight, much less talk.

Snakehead looked wise and cool and read all this. He raised his palms at me to signal calm. Little Fatty just stared at the floor, unable to look me in the eye.

Leave the region? The idea stunned me and I struggled to even begin processing the concept. It seemed a load of pure bullshit, just *too* crazy.

But Snakehead kept rolling along. He started riffing on plans, moving fast. "Okay. So I'll arrange your air ticket. First class all the way. Onward to where, Chicago, I guess? You said you were from somewhere in rural Illinois, right?"

This was getting way too surreal and my stomach was going all queasy.

"Probably," Snakehead continued, exhaling cigarette smoke that made his breath visible, "that will require connections, like via Hong Kong, Japan and Hawaii. Then on to LA or San Francisco." Quite the internationalist, Snakehead knew this stuff as well as any travel agent.

"Wait a minute, chief. I—"

"And no stopping back at Little Fatty's place, on the way. Not for *anything*. And certainly not at *The Diamond*."

"What?" The lump in my throat was swelling and choking me.

"CBC moves fast. We may only have an hour or two at best to make you disappear."

That did it. Now I was really ready to puke. This sudden new reality hit me like a sledgehammer and I fought for control.

"Dash, Dash . . ." Snakehead smiled and put a hand on my shoulder, squeezing a little. "Relax. Directly from here we'll send you across the causeway, straight to Changi Airport by limo. You'll catch the first flight out of Singapore, probably one bound for Hong Kong. You'll be safe."

I saw his lips move and heard him talking but things stopped registering. A burning orange sun was climbing into a brilliant blue sky and birds in trees near the Snakehead's veranda sang sweetly, oblivious to my distress. But his maid, doing the morning wet mopping, recognized all the signs. She quickly dumped all the soapy water from her bucket onto the grass beside the tiled patio and slid the plastic container under my chin. Just in time to catch several upchucked scotches and last night's dinner.

Snakehead shook his head.

Little Fatty couldn't help smirking. "Sorry!" he apologized with a giggle.

No denying I was really in trouble. All those blood-chilling stories about CBC and his thugs played out in my imagination. What might happen to me, if my friends hadn't been there to save the day?

Snakehead continued conjuring plans on the fly and ticked points off a mental list. "Now as to critical financial matters, Dash, like your cash and banking situation. Where is your account, in JB or Singapore?"

"Neither." Confusion darkened both their faces. "Actually, all that cash you gave me, I never spent. Didn't need anything. So I just squirreled it all away at Fatty's place. In the ceiling of my room."

Little Fatty's eyes popped wide. "You *broke* my house and stored money in ceiling?" Then he burst out laughing. "*Aiee-yah!* Dash, you damned crazy *gweilo*! Too risky, *lah*! What if bandits find?"

"True. Like a fat little, non-swimming Chinese bandit?"

We all burst out in laughter, destroying some of the tension. Guess I was finally relaxing, being able to banter like that. "Don't worry, Fatty, I didn't break anything. Just move that corner ceiling tile and you'll find eight years of cash, all there."

But Snakehead had no time for further delay.

"Please pay attention. The clock is ticking! Next thing: what about your passport?"

"Right here," I said and tapped a back pocket. "Always in my pocket. Always." I'd never trusted it being out of my possession.

"Excellent," Snakehead said. "Now wait here and give me twenty minutes." He scurried off. I nibbled on some plain white rice to settle my stomach. Fatty just kept joking about all that cash secretly stashed in his ceiling and what a rude house guest I'd been, destroying his house.

Snakehead came strolling back in twenty minutes, like clockwork, already freshly showered and dressed in his usual immaculate business attire.

He picked at his fingernails as if cleaning some missed bits of dirt lodged underneath. Then he handed me a wooden cigar box and an envelope.

"Okay, my *gweilo* little brother, here's the only luggage you need for the trip." He winked.

"What, cigars? How can, *lah*?" Fatty smiled at Snakehead. "Hope they're at least Cubans, chief, not some of that Manila shit."

Snakehead's no-nonsense confidence was infectious. I knew he'd handle everything and felt my spirits starting to cautiously rise.

Maybe it *would* all work out.

"You've no time for any other way, Dash, so trust me. *This* is everything you need." He patted the box. "Clothes and all the rest, you can buy later. Now head straight for Changi, immediately (the limo is on the way) while Little Fatty and I head to *The Diamond* to begin damage control."

I nodded. "Okay, chief."

"We must assume CBC's men are already watching for you there, also at Fatty's house. Possibly already on their way here, too, but I doubt CBC would have the nerve to fuck with me like that."

I saw fire in Snakehead's eyes. One tough hombre.

"So when they start asking about you we'll just make excuses. You're sick, at the doctor, whatever." He smiled and shook his head. "Don't look so worried. Just go. It'll all be fine."

I started to ping them with my questions.

"But how do we stay in touch? How will I know when it's safe to return?"

They looked at each other and then me. There were no possible answers, only silence.

We all realized this was probably an ending and amid shrugs and smiles, burst out in testosterone-fueled laughter at the ridiculousness of it all. A maid approached and politely mumbled something to Snakehead. The limo had arrived.

"But this box and the envelope, chief, what—"

"Listen, Dash. Must be four or five hundred flights a day leaving Changi, going everywhere in the world. So once your flight takes off, not even CBC can track you. You could be anywhere. Wheels up and you're safe."

"Okay but . . ."

"And just in case, here's insurance for your safe passage through Changi. Shouldn't be any trouble, but you never know." Snakehead handed me a small sealed brown envelope with Chinese ideograms scribbled on the front. "That says *Mr. Loh Ah Sah*. Head of airport security. He's an old friend and he owes me."

My nerves were crackling but Snakehead's steely resolve that this would work helped tamped down my nerves. I trusted him.

We all shook our heads in disbelief. The two of them pounded my back, ushered me toward the front door and pushed me toward the waiting limousine.

"Now just go!"

I sank deep into the luxurious leather back seat of the Benz stretch limo and as it pulled out of Snakehead's estate, I opened the cigar box.

A fat white envelope was on top and after slitting it open, I counted fifty-five crisp US $100 bills. Wow. Way more than enough for a plane ticket.

And at the bottom of the currency stack was a freshly-cut check made out to *Dashiell Bonaventure II,* and drawn on Snakehead's bank in Singapore. The amount penned in blue ink astounded me: $500,000 Singapore dollars (at the current exchange rate, more than U.S. $200,000).

Whew, that *way* more than compensated for the cash stash left behind in Fatty's ceiling. I was suddenly a wealthy young man.

Still inside and filling the box, I found a stack of five thin rectangular parcels, individually wrapped in newspaper. They seemed abnormally heavy. I peeled open the corner of one and was assaulted by the sudden, hypnotic and obscene beauty of gold. Those dense, weighty and glistening oblong plates of brilliant yellow metal were pure gold in bulk form. Peeling away more newsprint, I uncovered an embossed stamp that indicated 24 carat quality, the highest possible.

Each bar was a full kilogram in weight, 2.2 pounds. In total, I had nearly eleven pounds of pure gold!

The pleasingly heavy metal bars shone like the sea glinting at sunrise.

It was bewitching. For the first time I could suddenly understood why misers and others down through the ages had so obsessed over this magical stuff, lusting for its power and its promise of safety.

Gold solved all problems, so it was a favored store of value and flight asset for the Overseas Chinese. These kilos were probably from Snakehead's own personal cache, buried somewhere on his estate: insurance against the improbable day when banks might fail him but he needed immediate access to wealth. Ever since Malaysia's bloody race riots in 1969, many Chinese lived in fear of a recurrence, however unlikely. Snakehead must have vowed (still remembering that horror from his childhood) to always protect himself against that risk.

I remembered his dirty fingernails. He'd personally dug these up for me.

I did the math and the stash of pure gold that nestled in my lap was worth a cool $65,000 at the then-official rate of US $400 per ounce. I re-wrapped the bar in its newspaper and shut the box.

Whether it was the gold or Snakehead's infectious confidence, I began to feel optimistic while once again abruptly heading off into the uncertain future.

I could handle this.

I wondered if it was even legal to transport gold like that. I didn't know. It was probably dangerous as hell, regardless. And probably why Snakehead gave me that envelope for the airport security chief, in case I got pulled out of line for questioning.

My limousine pulled up at Changi Airport in Singapore and a team of skycaps descended. Considering the Johor plates they probably expected to see Malay royalty or a rich politician emerge. Instead out pops Dash, unshaven and a little buzzed already from morning scotch, in dirty jeans with a cigar box under my arm.

They signaled the limo driver to pop the trunk. "Is your luggage, sir, in the boot?"

"Nah. I'm traveling light today," I smiled. "Just these cigars."

Adrenaline coursed through me as I walked into the terminal and searched for the check-in counter. My flights were already reserved so the tickets would be awaiting me. I just had to pay.

I stepped up to the Air Cathay counter and a comely clerk, wrapped in a luscious green and purple *sarong kebaya,* smiled. I guessed that her considerable beauty was the result of a mixed heritage, dollops of Malay, Chinese and Indian.

She penned final details onto my multi-page ticket folder and stamped each page before detaching a carbon copy for the airline. Then, before handing me the ticket pad and boarding pass, she asked: "And how will *Tuan* be paying today?"

I pulled out my deck of mint U.S. hundred dollar bills and her green eyes grew huge and round, white expanding around the irises.

"Hopefully U.S. cash is acceptable, miss?"

"U.S. dollars? Oh yes, *lah. Always can,*" she purred while reaching out a lovely manicured hand.

I hit her palm with fifteen crisp Benjamins.

Book Five

Celestial Winnings
Macau, HK, Taiwan etc. 1988

CHAPTER TWENTY-SIX
Glitzy HK Reunion

Air Cathay first class cabin
35,000 feet above the South China Sea - 1988

Snakehead's words echoed in my memory. *Wheels up, and then you're safe.* I smiled, feeling thankful and almost giddy. Nestled in luxury nearly seven miles up, in my lap I cradled that wooden box with a fortune in gold bullion.

And in my pocket was tucked a check for more money than I was able to imagine.

With my sudden escape, the entire day had had a surreal and dreamlike quality to it but every bit was real. That now included fetching stewardesses sashaying up and down the aisle in *sarong kebayas* so tight they looked spray-painted on. Endlessly smiling, they delivered snacks or refilled my champagne flute or adjusted the blanket on my lap.

I sipped my drink, nibbled on curry *samosas* or shrimp crisps and wrestled with choices. Fillet mignon or Chateaubriand for lunch?

But as I shut my eyes, weightier issues descended upon me. Like what would I do with the rest of my life? The sudden loss of my recent lifestyle, all of it, came as a severe blow. But still I couldn't help but overflow with gratitude toward Snakehead and Fatty, who'd saved my life and staked my future.

Other insights emerged.

Almost like stepping out and hovering somewhere beyond my own existence to review Dash Bonaventure, I realized I'd been experiencing life so far like a series of thundering waves to surf.

The first breaker was my expat youth in Hong Kong, ending with that disaster with the odd kid, The Slug. Then came the rise and fall of my relationship with a world-famous writer. The next wave carried me to Bali, those crazy few months that ended with an absurd, red-hot infatuation with Fiona and the motorcycle crash. And then a long ride (eight full years!) as an executive on *The Diamond*, a massive, illegal casino twenty miles offshore from Singapore.

Each time I'd managed to regain my balance atop the next wave and ride it until it too abruptly disappeared in foam or crashed onto hidden rocks.

So what would come next?

No hurry to decide, but I mused about holing up in some remote mountain cabin (Wyoming, say, or Montana?) to finally start writing a novel. It was a pretty dream: I'd burn aromatic wood (chopped myself) and tend a small vegetable garden along with a simple chicken coop. Live off eggs and veggies. Drink a lot of fresh cold mountain water. There was more than enough money from Snakehead to survive a decade of publishers' rejection letters, so I could take my time.

Pleasantly buzzing from the champagne, my mind continued to drift. Could I resume my relationship with Demy? Perhaps more as colleagues this time, no longer that master-serf stuff. First become a new breakout literary star, I guess.

I mused about all the unpredictable twists my young life had taken and wondered about old friends. Paladin, Chickie, Fiona, all the others. Where were they now and how were they doing? In that moment, I missed them all, remembering them all as they had been. And as I had.

Just as I was drifting off, lulled to sleep by the alcohol and the parade of my foolish thoughts, a sharp bell pierced the cabin hiss and the pilot's plummy, British-accented voice boomed over the loudspeaker. "Ladies and gentlemen, we'll be arriving in Hong Kong in just a few minutes."

The cabin burst into action: flight attendants scurried about to close cabinets and collect snack plates and cutlery. The plane's flaps descended with a thud and our air speed dropped with a jolt. We began to noisily veer toward the green hillsides of Kowloon. First-timers on board gasped but I just chuckled, remembering well the infamous Kai Tak landing.

And there again were all those laundry poles, sticking out from windows of gray residential blocks we seemed intent upon hitting.

It seemed a lifetime since I'd lived there as a naive expat kid. How had twenty years changed the place?

I stared out the window as the aircraft taxied down the narrow landing strip. Gray, mammoth Kowloon looked cold and super-urban and lacked the comfortable, welcoming vibe of Singapore. But I knew this only meant my eyes still needed to readjust to first sight of my former home.

What an incredible city! My heart soared with nostalgia and before the plane even docked at the gate I'd already decided. I'd take a one-day layover in Honkers.

After all, Snakehead had assured me I'd be safe just as soon as I'd left Southeast Asia. And hell, I paid cash for a full-fare, no-bargaining ticket. Surely there would be *zero* restrictions on making changes.

The pert Chinese clerk in a flirty little purple cap at the airline counter inside the terminal smiled as she amended my ticket. "And we'll get your bags off the connecting flight, sir."

"That's okay. I have none."

She looked confused but smiled as she handed me off to an even more solicitous female attendant, who booked me a deeply discounted hotel layover rate at the colony's most famous, super-luxury hotel in *Tsim Sha Tsui*. Kowloon side of the harbor.

"And may I provide any other assistance?" she purred. "Tourist maps or shopping tips . . . *anything* at all?" Did I catch a suggestion there?

"No really, I'm fine." I smiled. "But thanks."

"Are you sure?" She was smoking hot and her eyes gleamed as they bored into mine. Normally about now, a young man's gonads would commandeer all rationality. But instead, my practical side elbowed its way to the front of my mind.

"Actually now that you mention it, yes, there *is* something."

"Wonderful!" She adjusted her cap, looking expectant.

"I need a phone number."

Her smile grew even wider.

"I need help locating someone." If she was disappointed she hid it well. "Not even sure if he is still in Hong Kong but his name is Jackson Toh."

She flashed a sudden weird expression before turning to her assistant and snapping off a string of questions in Cantonese. (*"Blah-blah-blah* Jackson Toh *blah-blah-blah?"*). She gazed back at me with a smile that would melt a rock.

"This this friend of yours, sir, Mr. Jackson Toh . . . is this the famous Toh Chi Wah? A Macau princeling, the son of the Macau gambling king, Toh Thian En? Mahjong parlors, casinos, all that?"

"Well, he did say his father was some kind of Macau big shot, back when we were kids together at HKIS."

Her eyes sparkled. She seemed *really* impressed with my guy, Jackson.

"Well, sir, if your friend is still in the region, your hotel concierge can easily track him down."

The elegant hotel lobby shimmered with chrome, mirrors and glass, highlighted by a garish red and gold color scheme. A bubbling fountain sprawled in the center, surrounded by scores of potted palms. After check-in I visited the concierge desk tucked away in the corner.

By reputation, this hotel would part the seas to meet any reasonable customer request (and even unreasonable ones, too).

Two men working the desk were dressed like generals in glitzy, impressive uniforms festooned with gold stars, medals and epaulets. They recorded my request and guaranteed a positive result.

I showered at my penthouse room and changed into new clothes purchased at a chic menswear shop in the swank hotel arcade. Then I headed down to the lobby for a late afternoon taxi tour to reacquaint me with Hong Kong.

But on the way one of the concierges caught my eye.

"Mr. Bonaventure, everything is already arranged," he said, his teeth gleaming. "We contacted Mr. Toh's business office in Macau and, as it happens, he is here in Hong Kong today. He would be *delighted* to meet with you and suggested dinner at nine. We have taken the liberty to book a prime table for you at our hotel's famous Imperial Phoenix restaurant. Three Michelin stars, you know."

He'd already earned himself a massive tip, upon my check-out. "Will there be anything else, sir? Any way to perhaps make your evening even more enjoyable?" Now he was insuring his mega-tip. "Perhaps a pair of lovely escorts for you two gentlemen? Or else we can book your *second place,* for after-dinner entertainment?"

I demurred, rendering profuse thanks. If Jackson had any other needs or ideas, he was more than capable.

Tingling with excitement, I canceled my taxi tour and headed back to my room. In only a few hours, I'd again see my boyhood friend, right there and in the flesh.

Jackson *Freaking* Toh!

It would be the first time I'd ever seen the world-renowned Imperial Phoenix restaurant. Asia's undisputed champion big-flash venue with gourmet food rated a ten on any five-star scale. Dad used to often host big flash dinners there for business.

The setting was classic and exuded wealth and luxury. Large circular tables covered by crisp white linen were surrounded by high-backed ebony wood chairs, all on a polished parquet wooden floor that glistened like Victoria Harbor on a sunny day. Off to all sides were massive pillars of warm brown wood hung with lacquered scrolls with Chinese inscriptions in gold leaf. Balconies cantilevered out overhead and offered exclusive, totally private dining areas. On sparkling white walls, expensive silk tapestries depicted red dragons floating across blue silk skies or proud pagodas standing tall against golden backgrounds.

Performers in silk costumes were tucked off in a far corner and played traditional Chinese instruments, weaving an exquisite aural backdrop.

Reservations there were typically wait-listed for months. But (in nothing short of a social miracle) the concierge was able to use the omnipotent Toh family name to jump the queue and snag us a table that same day. Prime location too. I was impressed.

A glossy travel magazine on a cocktail table in my suite explained that people visited The Imperial Phoenix to dine but even more importantly *to be consumed* by others' eyes.

Any night, diners might include the British Colonial Governor, ambassadors or film stars (from Hollywood or Bollywood), even an entourage from the General Secretariat of the China Communist Party.

I entered shortly before 9 p.m. and found every table occupied, other than the one reserved for us. Supervisors and waiters hovered and glided about the room, looking sharp in blazing white tailored dinner jackets and silk gloves. As they perfectly attended to every customer's needs, their demeanor was always distinguished and respectful. The room buzzed with percussive gales of loud, effervescent Cantonese chatter, making it hard to even hear the music.

I wondered how Jackson would look. Changed, certainly, but how much? As for myself, I still looked pretty much the same, maybe a little worn, perhaps, but not haggard. Years of squinting in the bright tropical sun had creased my face with fine crow's-feet lines that radiated outward from my eyes. My hairline had levitated a bit northward and I was far leaner, any excess weight burnt away by years of irregular eating and long stretches of adrenaline-fueled activity. With no wife or mother to remind me—*Eat, Dashiell!*—I tended to forget about food.

Plainly speaking, hanging around casinos is not conducive to good health. I probably took in a couple packs of Camels each day in secondary smoke.

Two unusual characters in dark business attire marched into the restaurant foyer, broadcasting an air of authority and hinting at danger. The beefy one's suit was ill-fitting and looked several sizes too small. The other was a wiry bald bantam, slim and glittering with gold. He wore rings, a bracelet, shiny glasses and even his gold front teeth glistened. His suit hung on him looking baggy and a few sizes too large.

The burly one shouldered past the *maître d'* and waddled at a no-nonsense pace over to my side of the room, looking right and left. He cruised the room perimeter and briefly stared at each table before returning to the foyer and nodding at his partner.

That's when the slim man took charge. Beaming a broad, golden smile he placed a friendly hand on the shoulder of the restaurant's gatekeeper and spoke with great animation. The *maître d'* carefully listened and nodded with obvious respect. All three looked over at me across the room then shrugged, laughing. The small man gave his partner a go-ahead sign. He went outside and returned moments later, followed by a much younger man.

Despite it being two decades since we last met, I recognized Jackson at first glance. His hairline was a little higher but he'd remained high school slim. No longer wearing an HKIS uniform, he was draped in a dark, elegant three-piece silk suit, deep blue with dignified pin striping.

"Jackson!"

We embraced, pounding each other's back. I jabbered away and told him how much I'd missed him. He took a playful shot back at me for my falling out of touch.

"Takes two to not write, man," I said, grinning. "Hey, your bodyguards tonight look a lot more serious than your minders back in HKIS days. Heavier heat."

He flicked his eyes toward the security detail and laughed. "Their names are *Cobra* Ang and Mr. Kong."

"Cobra must be the little guy, the one in charge?"

"Good guess."

"And all just to protect your rich ass, huh?"

"Like back at school. But nowadays I need security far more." He shrugged. "Ang is way more dangerous of the two."

"No way." I chuckled.

"He's a martial arts master but only uses that if he lacks a proper weapon. Ang is usually like a regular little mobile armory with knives, a revolver and what-not. And big ol' Mr. Kong over there, he's more about deterrence."

"Quite the threatening presence."

"Tears people in half," Jackson laughed. "So watch it!"

My old friend leaned back from the table, reeking of wealth and class. He shot his cuffs and expensive jewelry flashed: diamond-studded cufflinks and a gem-encrusted investment grade watch. Probably worth more than my old family home, back in Moderate Bluffs. His shirt was tailored from fine Egyptian cotton, brilliant white and starched crisp.

He caught me staring at the logo repeating on his silk rep tie. "That's the crest for LSE, Dash." I squinted in confusion. "London School of Economics."

Smooth, confident and relaxed, Jackson pulled out a smoke and offered me one. What the hell, I accepted. He flicked a diamond-studded gold lighter engraved with his initials.

"You seem quite the big deal now, Jackson. Scary bodyguards and special treatment here."

"Come on, Dash. I was *always* the spoiled little rich kid with a security detail, no?"

"Funny but I never really paid it much mind."

"I know. That's why we were able to become such buds."

He was right.

"Anyway, remember my father?"

"Not much. Just something about Macau casinos. But the airline hotties at Kai Tak just about wet their panties when I dropped the Toh family name."

Jackson grinned. "Since the 1960s, Dad has owned half of all legal casino gambling in China."

"Wow."

Jackson no more than flicked an eyebrow and a team of waiters in white tuxedos materialized. "Quick-quick, men, XO and water. Two doubles." Bottles of liquor, crystal cocktail glasses, ice and water rolled up on a trolley and moments later we hoisted our glasses.

"Here's to our future," Jackson said, his eyes alive. "Together. Massive prosperity, shared by true friends."

I had no idea what that was about.

We clinked glasses, read each other's eyes and then in unison yelled at the top of our lungs: *"Yaaaaam sennnng!" Drink it all, bottoms up!* Nary a head turned in the fancy restaurant as we two buddies chugged brandy the Chinese way.

Jackson signaled for refills.

God, it was great to see him again.

"Anyway about my father? He's more commonly known these days as *David Toh*. His company is *Jewel Mountain Jogos*. (That's a Portuguese word for *gaming*.) For generations, our family ran little *mahjong* parlors in Macau. But in the 1960s, the government awarded a private gambling monopoly. Dad sued and he won! As a result, he received the only other gambling license in China and opened a few small casinos. Compared to the original licensee, he was like a small dog waiting patiently under the table for scraps."

"A small-time operator."

"Yes but of course everything is relative. And by playing it cool, Dad became one of the richest men in Asia, with half the action in Macau."

"Making you the junior *Mr. Golden Boy.*"

"Don't be a jerk." Jackson feigned irritation but then smiled. "The Macau duopoly has remained hospitable. Occasional friendly dinners. Dad just stays out of their way and has free reign with his casinos and mahjong parlors. His are the smaller, seedier spots, but Macau folk like them."

I started to understand why Jackson needed heavy security. Kidnap him and the potential ransom could break a bank.

"So Jackson, exactly *how* did your dad—"

"Dash, don't ask. I really don't know how some of these things are done."

I suspected he knew more than he was saying but just sipped my brandy and waited.

Jackson leaned in closer. "Okay, I imagine he probably struck some deals. Various partnerships to split the gaming proceeds, payments for protection, you know."

"Partnerships? With Macau government insiders perhaps?"

"Maybe. I mean, how did he possibly ever win that lawsuit, resulting in his license?" Jackson rolled his eyes.

"True. So who do you think gets greased?"

"Nor sure, but it's helpful to have friends in the police, but also with the triads." He sipped his brandy. "I'd only find all that out, for sure, when I fully join the family business, for good. If and when."

Also wasn't sure what *that* meant. He seemed to be sharing an awful lot, almost too much, like he wanted to involve me, somehow. But that was impossible.

Wasn't it?

Our dinner was a long, boozy, dozen-course Chinese extravaganza. Phenomenal cuisine arrived in squadrons of silver platters manned by waiters who uncovered them with flashing, synchronized drama.

But even more delicious was this rekindling of our friendship, dormant almost two decades.

I lost count how many times we crashed brandy glasses and knocked back chilled liquid fire. And each time, as if by magic, our brandy glasses instantaneously refilled.

The alcohol did its work. When Jackson demanded a full catch-up from me since our HKIS days, I was ready and spilled out my story in breathless detail. Everything. The rise and collapse of my literary life with Demy; vagabonding across Indonesia, including the rescue of Little Fatty and the near-fatal motorcycle crash, as well as Fiona's tragedy; my unplanned casino career in the Straits of Johor; and just this week, as an exciting conclusion, my name topping the hit list of a Southeast Asian mafia chieftain.

"Whoa, stop it, man. Just stop!" Jackson pounded the table in delight. "So overall you're saying not much has happened—"

"Yeah, just the usual."

We'd picked up just as before, finishing each other's sentences and providing punchlines.

"You know, Dash, you're like a walking advertisement for good luck. The Karma Kid—saving lives and getting saved. You know?"

"I don't know if I believe any of that karma stuff, Jackson."

"Regardless. And you've been out here so long, you no longer really even think like a *gweilo* anymore, do you?"

He was right. I no longer judged a lot of the things I saw in Asia that once would have really offended my Western sensibilities. Different strokes. I was no longer really Western anymore, but not quite yet Eastern. Mid-Pacific, maybe? Yeah. Just call me *Pacific Dash*.

Jackson was rolling. "But a bad idea, Old Man, making enemies with the likes of CBC. Chong Beng Chuan is a *famously bad* man." Jackson smiled. He seemed to find this entertaining in some comical, disbelieving, *oh-my-goodness* sort of way. "But don't worry. Long as you are with me, you're safe. CBC's arms aren't long enough to reach all the way up here and mess with somebody under Toh protection. Besides, we have Cobra and Kong. They could take on the entire North Korean army and win. So a crew of CBC goons? No problem." He chuckled and sipped his brandy and water.

"But go on, Dash, and tell me more about this floating casino venture. Up here in the gambling capital of North Asia, we don't hear so much about it."

I realized The Diamond, for all its success and the riches it generated for us, was just small beer compared to Macau's lucrative gaming market.

Jackson lobbed a series of questions at me about *The Diamond* and the roles I played. It almost felt like he was testing the depth of my knowledge about the business. An odd excited look illuminated his face as I poured it all out in excruciating detail.

As he soaked it all in, thinking hard, his eyes flicked right-left-right-left in rapid motion. I'd forgotten all about that disconcerting quirk, which always signaled when Jackson was focused ultra-deep in concentration. Like a sign: *The computer is running.*

When at last I finished, he drew in a deep breath and nodded to himself, as if reaching personal agreement with some secret decision. He folded his hands on the white linen tablecloth and looked toward me with the utterly earnest expression of a dear friend. "Oh, how I envy you, Dash."

Golden Boy envies me? That's a laugh.

"All this time you've been wandering Asia, bonking Taiwanese lovelies and inventing the floating casino business. But I've mainly just been a school boy. Achieved nothing, really." He softly clicked his tongue in disapproval. "Did my undergrad studies at the LSE and then an MBA at Harvard. Spent summers interning at Pop's office, getting some exposure to the family business, mainly on the legal side. So then I spent quite a few years at Yale law, admittedly taking it rather slow, with some gap years in there, too. Delaying the inevitable, I suppose." He sipped some ice water. "But now the point is I can no longer delay the inevitable. With schooling and preparation over, it's time for me to join the family business, in earnest. Select a desk and sit there, quietly, the next thirty years as *David Toh's son*." He pictured something and shook his head. "Well, no effing way." He sighed and picked up the mirrored ice bucket from the trolley and stared into it for the longest time, stirred and twirling melting ice cubes with a chopstick.

I finally tossed a fried peanut at him. It landed on his shoulder, like a little tan ladybug. "Yo, Jackson! Come in please! Where'd you go, just now?"

He looked up and grinned, reached out and grabbed my arm, hard.

"You won't believe this, Dash, but I was envisioning *our* future together. You and me! Wouldn't that be great?"

Our future? Um, no, don't think so. My best plan right then was to hightail it out of Asia and head for a cabin in the Rockies. Stay alive. Those plans didn't include this old friend.

He waved a hand and a waiter set up another round. Jackson pushed another heavy crystal tumbler at me (brandy over ice with a splash of water) and clinked my glass. "So anyway, good son: chin-chin, *yam seng* and all that rot."

A strange fire sparkled in his eyes. Something was going on in that brilliant mind.

As we left the restaurant around midnight he crooked an arm around my neck and pulled me close in a fraternal hug.

"Can't tell you how happy I am to see you, Dash!" He grinned. "You *do* believe in fate, right? Well, it must be fate or karma or whatever, why you've appeared here with me tonight."

It was well past midnight and time for sleep but my childhood friend had other ideas.

Cobra Ang and Kong rode with us in the chauffeured Bentley and dropped us at the Shun Tak ferry terminal in Western District, where we boarded a jet foil for the forty-mile cruise across the Pearl River Delta to Macau. Whirring engine noise flooded the red and white vessel's cabin as it raised up upon its blades and sped off at high speed, like a boxy water-skier.

And even at this late hour, the boat was packed.

"Always like this, Dash," Jackson bubbled. "Hongkies are always nipping off to Macau, around the clock."

He had insisted I accompany him but refused to say why. Considering the tiny Portuguese colony's reputation for vice, perhaps he wanted to buy me some *desert*? I pictured a sugary blonde tart from Vladivostok.

He hollered in my ear over the jetfoil's engine roar. "You can't leave for America tomorrow, Dash. I've got to change your mind."

No chance. "Forget it, Jackson. I'm flying out, early afternoon."

"We'll see." He smiled, looking confident.

Fifty-five minutes later we stepped from the ferry's air-conditioned chill into Macau's warm damp night. Back on Jackson's home turf. The air seemed almost too thick to breathe and his gold specs immediately steamed up. He cleaned them with a handkerchief and mopped his neck and brow.

I started to hail a taxi but he laughed and pulled my hand down. A dark sleek monstrous limo with black-tinted windows pulled up: Jackson's.

Wow, he had multiple teams of bodyguards, chauffeurs and armored luxury vehicles in both Hong Kong *and* Macau.

We sped down the main drag toward the colony's gaudy flagship casino that sparkled in the night and somehow resembled a gigantic neon-and-concrete pineapple.

"All of Macau's five major casinos and Dad's minor parlors are tired-looking and dirty. But with millions of crazed gamblers just a short ride away across the Delta, the tables are always jammed. Why spend on maintenance? And with Macau too tiny for expansion (just eleven square miles), the casinos just milk the situation and count their money."

We shuffled down a gangway at the base of the giant electric pineapple and entered a maze of confined spaces. Hallways and gaming rooms were jammed with bodies, smoke and noise. No place for the claustrophobic.

Perfumed women at roulette tables shrieked after wins. Others sang out demands upon the Fates, trying to will specific winning numbers or colors to appear. HK businessmen, bald and glistening in rumpled suits, having stolen a few hours to dash across the Delta, cursed and hollered as they slammed down tottering stacks of chips onto the green felt tables.

I rubbed my eyes. This dwarfed our floating casino in every way.

"Geez, Jackson, this is freaking crazy!"

"Wonderful mess, no?"

"I can't even remember how we got in here, Jackson, much less how to get out. The corridors, the twists, the turns . . ."

"*Feng shui*. All by design, to maximize the casino advantage. Gamblers' money can't easily escape."

"Never thought you were a Tao *wind-water* kinda guy, Jackson. They teach that crap at LSE?"

"Hah. Casino old-timers like my dad believe it. Guess it can't hurt."

We shouldered our way through the crowd and moved from one gaming room to the next until finally emerging onto a corridor that circled around a retail arcade. As we walked clockwise around this perimeter, approaching from the opposite direction was one breathtaking woman after another, clicking toward us in silk stockings and stiletto heels. Jackson elbowed me and nodded at the international smorgasbord of Chinese, Vietnamese and Indonesian working women. All made bold aggressive eye-contact, soliciting business. The air was thick with a mix of floral perfumes, gamblers' tobacco stench and body odor.

"Guys call this *The Racetrack*." Jackson shrugged.

"I can see why." The all-business, assembly line nature of it was unsettling, certainly compared to the relaxed haggling on Kuta's dusty back lanes.

Jackson led me up a flight of stairs to a landing where we could look out over the main gaming floor. Nearly 2 a.m. but a sea of bodies packed the broad room. The tables were stacked side by side like eggs in an enormous carton, every one jammed with raucous players. The place rocked under a blue haze of cigarette smoke that hovered overhead.

"See that dealer?" I pointed down at a tall bald Chinese croupier in tuxedo vest, dealing blackjack. "He's cheating. Tipping his cards to somebody."

"Really? You tell?"

"Come on, Jackson, I've been in this trade for years now. Seen it all." Then I gave him my reading on which tables were most profitable and even estimated hourly cash drops.

Jackson smiled brightly. "I knew it. I just knew it!"

"Hmm?"

He just shot an enigmatic smile back at me. "Follow me, Dash, and all will be revealed."

He led me to a small table in a coffee-and-sweets shop deep inside the casino building, where Jackson barked out an order in Cantonese. The waitress brought over plates of sweet rice-cakes and cups of dark coffee. We dove in.

"Dash, bear with me. First a little history."

I tried a cloyingly sweet rice cake and washed it down with some black coffee. "Okay, Jackson, your show. Shoot."

"The two European colonies on the South China coast (Hong Kong and Macau) have always been inextricably bound. HK is large, rich and British. Great harbor, hub of North Asia. Macau is the poor cousin, much smaller and Portuguese. Shallow harbor. But when the sanctimonious Brits outlawed gambling in HK in the mid-1800s, Macau found its *raison d'etre*."

I fought off a yawn. 3 a.m. was closing in. Why the history lesson?

"For years, the Macau casinos chugged along, living off the Hongkies and generating enough cash for its operators and the politicians. But greedy for more by the 1930s, the brainstorm was to hire middlemen on commission to promote more gambling. Mainly a failure. So in the 1960s the government made a bold move and passed the casino licenses over to private interests."

"I know. Like your father." Impatient and getting tired, I smiled and rose from my chair. "Well that's all great stuff, Jackson, but I'm flying out in twelve hours and I'm bushed. So, no offense, but are we going to a brothel now or not? I figured that was the *exciting future* you were hinting at, earlier."

"A brothel?" He burst out laughing and shook his head. "Oh Dash, dear old boy, how I've missed you!"

CHAPTER TWENTY-SEVEN
Dead Chip Dealers

Jackson laid a hand upon my shoulder and pushed me back down into the chair. "Dash, please, humor me and just listen." I sighed, knowing my brainiac friend from high school was probably about to open my unseeing *gweilo eyes* to something.

"Jeez, man, okay."

"Remember all those seedy guys down on the casino floor carrying little leather bags?"

"Sure. I guess they were loan sharks." Scores of them slinked from table to table, never gambling and their eyes always darting to and fro, until they stopped to lean in to chat with a player. "Their leather bags contained chips or guns. Maybe both."

Jackson smiled. "Astute! Great guess but wrong. That was a trick question. Actually, most of those slime balls are *dead chip dealers—"*

"Looked plenty alive to me."

"Dead *chips*," Jackson emphasized, "not dead *dealers.* Their bags were full of high-value *dead chips.* Those are dealers, on the hunt."

"So, like I said: loan sharks." I looked at him funny and Jackson laughed.

"No. They are front men for *dead chip* businesses. Something that creates an astonishing opportunity for the two of us, amigo. Right now."

Us? Hoo-boy, I was afraid of something like that.

Jackson sipped his coffee and nibbled a baked almond confection. "A decade ago, this concrete pineapple casino when new was the 'must-see' spectacle of North Asia and gamblers flooded in. The operators were raking in the money until disaster struck."

"Government canceled the casino duopoly?"

"Almost as bad: the HK ferry boat operators declared war."

Okay, now *that* was unexpected.

"Every ferry was sailing from HK, packed, with people almost riding on the rooftops like an Indian passenger train. Macau tickets became a hot commodity with long waitlists. Every sailing was selling out, far into the future, so a genuine transport shortage developed. The ferry operators realized they had a choke-hold on Macau gaming and got greedy. They began holding seats back and even canceling sailings, allowing them to jack up ticket prices even more."

"Squeezing casino activity."

"Big time. And then ferry ticket scalpers jumped in, making things even worse. They snapped up the limited ticket supply and hiked prices even higher."

I nibbled a coconut macaroon. "So lemme guess. The casino bosses sent in their triads to firebomb the ferry offices in HK, something like that?"

"Dash, that's only in the movie version." Jackson smiled. "Not real life. The casinos solved this peacefully, by inventing *dead chips*."

"This must now be getting to the part where I hear how this all affects our future."

"Correct. You see, like magic, dead chips enabled ferry operators to share in casino profits. An incentive to *promote* Macau's casinos, rather than choke them."

"All interests aligned. Good." Where was Jackson's story going?

"Dash, they call those special chips *dead* because they cannot be cashed in, only be played at the tables until they are absorbed. The ferry operators earned a 0.7% commission putting dead chips into customers' hands. And the ferrymen didn't even have to pay, they just borrowed the dead chips."

I immediately understood the math here. What sounded like a piddling commission was actually a *huge* payoff. For instance, in baccarat the casino retains, like clockwork, about 2.6% of all money gambled. So that dead chip commission was generous, handing over about a fourth of the casino's take to the ferry operators.

But why should I care?

"Jackson, thanks. Great story and all but it's getting late . . ."

He shot me a frustrated look and raised a hand, ordering me to halt.

"Their plan succeeded, Dash. The transport squeeze ended and new agents were created to grow the casino business." Jackson tapped my hand and cleared his throat. "Now listen closely, here is the key: after a decade of dead chip sales, nobody has ever done it right, yet."

"Hmm?"

"All the potential is just being wasted. All the ferry operators did, as new agents, was send their slimy bag men into the casinos to sell dead chips to gamblers *already* playing there."

I stopped him. "Sounds like a lousy deal for the casino, Jackson. Surely the intent was to use dead chips *outside* and promote new visitation by gamblers, right? Customers *already* in the casino should buy normal chips at the cash cage. When they buy dead chips, it's almost like existing casino profit is being stolen."

Jackson grinned. "Exactly! You're totally getting it, lad." He jumped to his feet, seeming awfully juiced up. "That's margin cannibalization and the casinos hate it. Dead chips drain away their existing profit and also subsidize a negative element in the casinos." Jackson sipped his coffee. "The whole ferry crisis is ancient history now. Long forgotten. So to put it bluntly, the gambling duopoly is

VERY open to change." His face grew deadly serious. "And *that* opens a massive door for the two of us, my *gweilo* brother."

I kept listening.

"We two can deliver the future, Dash . . . and in the process become enormously, outrageously fucking rich!"

Okay, so now he had my full attention.

We went outside and began to stroll down the main drag, neither of us any longer aware of the time. (It was 4 a.m.) Jackson's crew of bodyguards and limo trailed at a short distance.

Jackson was selling, hard, and I admit his idea was beginning to elevate my interest.

He waved a hand and his limo drifted over to pick us up and speed us to Jackson's luxurious apartment.

We sat at the sleek island table in his magnificent kitchen rendered all in white and stainless steel.

"The casino bosses are sick, Dash, of it all. Sick of the seedy dead chip thugs in their casinos, draining profits. Sick of no growth. They are ready for serious change and are kicking around fresh ideas. Government is on board, too." He rubbed his hands. "One of those ideas is to invite outside parties—like us!—to own and operate our own VIP rooms inside the casinos, under contract."

"How's that work?"

"Well, we'd get a quarter of the casino's revenue on every dollar wagered in our VIP rooms."

"One quarter?" I made the connection. "I'll bet it's via dead chips."

"Of course. But this time the casinos will acquire *new,* incremental business, and not cannibalize existing profits." He pulled a slim metal calculator from his suit coat pocket and started punching buttons. "I've already done the sums, Dash, and they're staggering."

I looked and his numbers seemed far too good to be true. "If that's for real, Jackson, why haven't others already charged in?"

"Simple!" Jackson's near-manic laugh shocked me. Adrenaline was roaring through him and I'd never seen him so excited. He grinned with eyes large and hands shaking ever-so-slightly. "It's because we are the very FIRST!" He paused to let that sink in. "First! In everything, Dash, there always has to be *somebody* who is first. And astounding as this may seem, this one time, for this new opportunity, we are the ones: *First!*"

With that near-crazy grin, he stared into my eyes.

"How, you ask? Well, thanks to my Dad we are early and on the inside. Very soon others will also see this opportunity, but for now . . . it's only us."

"You're saying we have the absolute mother of all temporary, first-mover advantages?"

"Utterly once-in-a-lifetime stuff, Old Man. I've already begun negotiations and my father has already recused himself. He had to agree in advance to accept whatever deal his duopoly partners struck with me."

Jackson took off his suit coat and rolled up his sleeves. "Now there will be a huge deposit required, of course. And I could borrow all of it from my father. But I prefer to see you also having to go all-in on this, Dash, alongside me." He smiled. "I mean that big payday you got from that Straits gambling boat."

There goes my nest egg.

He outlined his vision for what would come to be known as the Macau VIP junket business. The casinos would hold our deposit for security and loan us dead chips for the VIP 'whale' gamblers we brought to Macau. Over and over again. The math was complex, but that 0.7% commission on table action resulted in us capturing 40% of the VIP room's actual profits. Another 40% went to pay the Macau taxes, leaving 20% for the casino itself.

"Seems a great deal for us and the government, but not so much for the casinos."

"Wrong. They'll love it. Our VIP rooms will dramatically boost overall gambling activity, with no effort on their part. And they benefit other ways, too."

"Like?"

"Well, we take on all the credit risk for our whales, so if a gambler doesn't pay his losses, that's on us."

"Don't care much for that part."

"Don't worry. There are powerful tools, plenty of ways to collect."

I laughed. "Ah, listen to you! My part-time Chinese gangster buddy."

"If so needed? Yes." He smiled back.

"I don't know, Jackson." Just picturing myself involved with those sleazy, vinyl zipper-pouch guys made me shudder.

Jackson raised his hands in *faux* surrender. "Dash, this simply can't miss! Until now the dead chip partners have had no imagination and limited their own opportunity. We'll change all that, be professional and organized and actively hunt down whales (gamblers with monster bankrolls) and import them to our VIP rooms. And as first to market, we will perfect this and *own* the casino action for hordes of rich, new customers."

His unrelenting enthusiasm was getting me. "We're going to revolutionize this game, Dash. It'll be like major league superstars playing against minor leaguers."

I flashed back to see my friend again as on that first day, the shy teenager at the HKIS gym with a binder full of photos.

"And we won't just succeed, Dash, we'll skyrocket! I have loads of ideas. Train and run teams of recruiters on the ground. Passive investors can help underwrite our business—it will grow so fast, we'll need more cash. We'll expand and set up more and more branches to find big-time gamblers everywhere in Asia and bring them to Macau. The opportunity is unlimited."

My head was spinning. Jackson had been working hard to develop this I couldn't shoot any holes in it. He had covered everything.

"The way I see it, we start in Hong Kong, where all the early, easy opportunity awaits. Then we ramp up by moving into Taiwan, the second best venue to harpoon our whales. And just down the road comes Southeast Asia, Japan and what-not? Someday, we will even move into Mainland China (biggest prize of all) once their laws are relaxed."

Jackson's live-in chef, roused at 5 a.m., poured us coffee and prepared us omelets, crepes and bacon.

Already losing my ability to resist, I summoned up some lingering concerns.

"But Jackson, why would a super-VIP gambler want to put himself into our hands anyway?"

He smiled. "Easy. Total luxury and ease. Sumptuous rooms, the best food, world-class 'escorts' and first-class travel options. Our business will provide *whatever they want,* including (maybe most important of all) a credit line. And if we move fast, for a while we'll be the only game in town. We start with a pair of VIP rooms and expand to five in a year. Then ten or twenty or more, the next few years. No limit to what we can achieve."

It was tempting, no question, and I was wavering. So Jackson took his best shot at closing the deal.

"Dash, imagine a nice big juicy number in U.S. dollars. Then multiply that by a hundred." He chuckled. "That's how seriously obscene our moneymaker will be. Our annual income should reach $10 to $20 million."

Sheezus!—$20 million?

"Shit, man, every bloody year: $10 million apiece?"

"No, Dash. That's $20 million a year for *each* of us. Maybe more."

That gaudy number exploded in my head left me woozy. Jackson laughed, pushed another coffee toward me and placed my hand on the cup.

Less than 24 hours since I'd fled Johor I could have never anticipated that by seeking out an old high school buddy on a whim, I'd again be blasting off into the stratosphere and riding another of life's surprises.

"Jackson," I warned, "you know I'm no business school grad."

"You graduated from the floating school of casino management." He smiled. "Plus you have common sense, Dash, and my complete trust. I can easily teach you anything else you need. And the rest, we hire."

I nibbled on a sweet. The coffee was helping clear my head. "You're usually one not given to exaggeration, Jackson."

"Never."

"And this would be unprecedented. Historic."

"No shit."

"Just think: two guys from HKIS, changing the world!"

He shrugged. "Dash, it honestly can't miss. Right idea, right time and place. All that."

It was genuinely irresistible. But I still had one remaining concern. "But Jackson, remember: I've got this problem with CBC–—"

He smiled. "Don't worry. Trust me. We can handle that."

We? Who was that? Jackson's father and who knows whom else? But I totally trusted him so it didn't matter.

We shook hands.

CHAPTER TWENTY-EIGHT
The Gweilo Casino King of China

We named the company *Celestial Winnings VIP Services* with a registered legal domicile in the Grand Caymans and our headquarters in a penthouse high above Hong Kong's Central District. We also maintained a smaller office in Macau itself.

A fast start in Hong Kong was crucial to propel our exclusive club for high-rollers and set the stage for expansion into Taiwan, Southeast Asia and Japan. Mainland China, much later.

So we charged furiously ahead, making up much of our business model as we went along.

We lusted to track down every platinum-class gambler in HK, the type of player who could sustain a monster loss one weekend but bounce right back the next and return to the tables.

We began by paying generous bounties to cleaning ladies and trash collectors across the colony who late at night would sift through 'office waste' for us, *recycling* prospect information from bank documents, finance company accounts and luxury goods sales records. Real estate development offices turned into an utter gold mine for us, providing names, addresses, and credit information on the Territory's wealthiest residents. We even obtained confidential membership data from the hallowed British turf club, hoping many would prefer to play Macau baccarat than bet on horses at Happy Valley.

One night while Jackson and I worked late, as usual, and our secretary entered wearing an odd look.

"What is it, Mei?"

"Mr. Dash," she said, bemused, "some ladies are here to see you."

I shrugged an okay and in marched a half dozen sweaty cleaning ladies from Pokfulam with their hair tied up in rags. Each lugged a couple heavy cardboard file boxes. I recognized the ringleader, an especially ambitious and productive source for us.

"We find, boss." She grinned and wiped perspiration from her forehead. "Good for you, *heya*?"

Jackson chatted with her in Cantonese and his eyes widened. "She says they found all these stacked up outside an office building in Central, being tossed out. You think? Ha."

"So what are they?"

"Pure gold, Dash! Customer data from the HK promo office for Las Vegas' biggest hotel/casino operator." As our bounties went, those cleaning ladies really cleaned up that night.

Until well past 3 a.m., we pored through a treasure trove of critical detail on HK blue-chip gamblers. Their Vegas credit lines, visit frequency, levels of comp pampering and extended support. *Everything*. We instantly knew exactly the level at which our program would blow away all existing competing offers.

The names kept gushing in and it almost seemed too easy. Many of our new clients volunteered their friends, additional diamond-quality leads, begging us to allow their wealthy playing partners to join the elite ranks of *Celestial Winnings*. And no wonder: there was nothing else quite like it, an exclusive club where premium-level gamblers were treated like royalty.

We leased helicopters for private courtesy shuttles to and from Macau, with our choppers lifting off any time a passenger was ready to go. Jackson's powerful father obtained (I can only imagine *how*) passport control authority for us, on both ends.

Our fleets of stretch limos stood always ready, day or night, to fetch clients to or from our heliports in HK and Macau.

Upon landing in Macau, a luxury limo whisked our players to hotel suites or straight to our VIP rooms. We specialized in accommodating abrupt, unplanned arrivals and even stocked fine casual clothing and accoutrements in each high-roller's sizes, waiting for them in their suites.

Simply put, we satisfied their every need.

Beyond the instant luxury transport and posh accommodations, we also provided anonymity and, most important of all, an instant gambling credit line, available on demand, at our VIP rooms. In the form of *dead chips*, of course.

So once an HK gambler had established himself as one of our clients, all normal complications and impediments for an impromptu Macau gambling run vanished.

We were aggressive and sought out any opportunity. One time both Jackson and I visited a famous real estate tycoon at his ornate offices high above Victoria Harbor, in a building named for his family. By sheer coincidence, his picture had run on the front page of that morning's *South China Morning Post,* tucked under my arm.

"Thanks, gentlemen," said the magnate, "but why should I join Celestial? My secretary can already arrange everything." His eyebrows raised.

Jackson smiled. "Of course she can, sir. But picture this. It's the end of a long day and you've been spearheading real estate deals and billion dollar developments. And on a whim, you decide you'd love to get away and unwind a bit in Macau. Dinner, then perhaps a little baccarat? Perhaps other enjoyment. As a Celestial Winnings client, a simple phone call arranges *everything*. Minutes later our limo will whisk you to our private rooftop heliport in Central. And twenty minutes after that, you are in Macau with a limo and hotel suite already at your disposal. Even clothing, tailored precisely for you is waiting and always ready, on demand. You travel secure and anonymous, all the way, in luxury and comfort. Everything you might require is already provided. Credit line, meals, refreshments . . . perhaps some feminine pampering?" Jackson winked.

"Well you do think of everything, that's for sure. But nonetheless, my girl can arrange a helicopter and hotel for me, if I want."

"But there's so much more, sir. You need not carry a dangerous, large sum of money. Your playing stake. And don't forget, within our VIP rooms you have total privacy and anonymity. And unlimited table stakes. Whatever you need."

"Hmm." The tycoon was visibly wavering.

"And later, we seamlessly zip you back home to HK. You can even leave all your winnings in your Celestial Winnings account (no need to fuss with that) so no one is any the wiser how you spent your evening. Not your business partners, nor the media, nor your secretary . . . and certainly not your wife."

It *was* perfect. The real estate magnate thought only a moment longer, tapping his pen on his desk pad, and then nodded. He smiled the familiar grin of a new client.

Thanks to Jackson's impeccable business sense, we were pioneering an entirely new field. It became known as the *Macau junket busines*s.

His foresight had been impeccable, that by starting fast and expanding relentlessly we could build a lead inevitable copycat competitors could never close.

We mastered the process of seamlessly delivering gamblers to our VIP room gaming tables, staked to the max by our streamlined credit system, and babysat them at our leased luxury hotel suites. Food, booze, women . . . whatever they wanted was all on the Celestial Winnings tab.

And between junket trips, we nurtured these coveted relationships by staying in frequent contact and keeping them thirsting for more action, itching for their next trip back to the tables.

The Macau gaming duopoly had indeed required a huge initial deposit from us, consuming my entire nest egg. But Jackson paid a far larger amount, so we were fairly communistic in establishing 50/50 partnership. From each according to one's means. Jackson borrowed an additional $3.5 million from his father, easily paid back from the first year's cash flow.

The deal was sweet as nectar. Jackson's advance info, as pipelined straight from the inside, had been accurate. The gaming revenue was split 40/40/20 between us, the tax man and the casinos.

For their part, the casinos hired the dealers and actually operated the rooms. We paid all recruitment and travel expenses like helicopters, jets and sumptuous hotel suites, F&B.

Celestial was not 'the house' but still pocketed 0.7% on *every* dollar wagered, win or lose. So we rooted for our clients to win, knowing that any winning episodes by our whales inspired future visits and reduced our credit concerns. By the way, credit turned out to be a far weightier expense and consumed more of our attention than we'd ever anticipated. Debt collection was a constant challenge.

Our business grew as fast as we dared to allow. According to plan, our initial pair of VIP rooms expanded to five in less than a year, doubled and then redoubled.

And in less than twenty-four months, we locked down HK's full potential and established an unassailable position and reputation. The moat surrounding our business was wide and deep, thanks to our head start and fierce client loyalty.

Celestial Winnings became synonymous with the luxury VIP gambling junket in Asia. Continued growth in Hong Kong became automatic as new, elite high-rollers found *us* and begged for admission.

Our personal bank accounts became swollen with cash.

I must admit during that first year, despite Jackson's assurances all would be okay, I still found myself glancing over my shoulder and looking for South Malaysian hit men. But at some point it became clear I'd either been forgiven by CBC or forgotten. Jackson's contacts had fixed things and the *how* didn't matter, leaving me free to immerse myself in the daily puzzles and challenges of reinventing Asia's gambling business.

CHAPTER TWENTY-NINE
Paladin Rides In

During those first few years, I personally visited our VIP rooms each night to schmooze clients and ensure each was enjoying the highest quality experience possible. Before going in I would fully prep on their personal details from our files: their businesses, names of family members, personal interests, and recent luck at our tables. My goal was to make each feel recognized and special, one of our most valued clients.

Over time I memorized hundreds of faces and names and even recognized the sound of their voices.

One evening while on the way to our VIP room and passing through the casino main gaming floor, my attention was drawn by the staccato interplay of two raised, angry voices. The first voice was shrill and spat out ire in English (perhaps an American tourist?) while the second harangued back in Cantonese (likely a croupier or another gambler). Such incidents were common enough so I was inclined to ignore it. What occurred outside our VIP rooms didn't involve me. None of my business.

And waiting for me *inside* our VIP room were several of our bluest blue-chip customers, awaiting some personal coddling *a la Dash*. The VIP room doors slid open and just as I was about to enter those posh, chilled, subdued confines, I heard that English voice again.

It stopped me in my tracks. Something about it sounded oddly familiar.

Out of curiosity, I gazed back across the room and was dumbfounded to spot a familiar ruddy face, rumpled with acne scars, along with a bulbous nose and a thick, cowboy-gunslinger mustache. That familiar stew of homely features which, when taken together, created a somehow arresting and charismatic visage.

It was my old friend, Paladin Kelley!

I hadn't seen him in maybe ten years but there he was, snarling and irrepressible, standing nose-to-nose with a baccarat croupier. Security had already encircled the table and was closing in while other gamblers were stepping back to distance themselves from the trouble.

I walked over from behind and laid an arm around Kelley's shoulders. Security, seeing me, immediately backed off.

Startled by the contact, Paladin turned to me and his eyes popped open. "Oh my freaking God in heaven," he roared. "It's, um . . . *The Dash Man*!"

He burst out in that familiar mad laugh, suddenly oblivious to all the melodrama engulfing him. With my free hand, I snapped my fingers and motioned for casino security to disburse.

Once the angry croupier saw Kelley's powerful friend, he dropped all his attitude and quietly resumed dealing.

"Whoa, how'd you pull off *that* shit, man?" Kelley chuckled, his eyebrows knitted in confusion.

I pounded his back. "Heh, never mind for now, buddy. A better question, Paladin, is how are *you* doing?"

Probably not so good, based on appearances.

"Great, great," he said. "Well, been better, but still . . ."

My old Bali backpacking buddy looked grizzled and drawn and appeared decades older. What happened to him? He exuded a gambler's sour stink of nervous perspiration, alcohol and stale tobacco. He seemed dissipated and smaller. Weaker. This was not the bold, charismatic gadabout of the past—something was very wrong.

Taking him into a VIP room was out of the question, in his current condition, so I guided him to a small cocktail lounge. We parked at a small table and called for drinks. He quickly drained a couple whiskeys.

"So wow, what's it been? Ten or twelve years? You still with that French chick, the blonde—"

"Angelique." His voice rumbled. Edgy.

"Yeah, right. Angelique."

"Take a good look at me, Dash, and think again. That little Parisian angel spread her wings and flew away, years ago."

"Sorry to hear that. You two seemed pretty good together, least for a while."

"We wandered around Southeast Asia and through every dumpy fly-blown town in India. Got up to Tibet. And then a nice long stay in Nepal where we smoked a lot of hash, gorged on fresh-baked pies and homemade ice cream. Heaven's rest stop along the Hippie Trail, that's Kathmandu."

As I'd heard. "Okay so then?"

"Well our timing stunk. Just as we were ready to shoot across Pakistan and Afghanistan, cross through Iran and reenter Europe, everything basically shut down."

"Jeez."

"All hell broke loose, what with the Russians invading Afghanistan and the Ayatollah going nuts in Iran. So the route to Europe was shut down." He lit a cigarette. "So we returned to Kathmandu."

"Long stay?"

"About a year for me." He sighed, letting out a stream of smoke. "Maybe only a week for her."

"Oh crap. What happened?"

"Well, turns out she was as clever as she was pretty." Paladin lit a fresh cigarette from his stub. "She wanted to get back to France real bad, and accurately evaluated the situation. She would need a traveling partner *upgrade*." This one fleeting moment, Kelley displayed his pain, only this once. "Flat-out dumped me, man, to hook up with some suave Persian dude."

"Wow, that's cold."

"Yeah, but smart. Jahanshah could get her across Iran, his country, and then home to Paris. Handsome bastard too. I guess she used him, just like how she'd used me." He smiled. "But Dash, while it lasted I *really* did enjoy being of use." Traces of that old Paladin Kelley smile emerged.

"So I was alone and pretty pathetic. It's embarrassing now, just to think about it. Crashed for a half year just smoking hash and *schtupping* Kathmandu working girls. Sometimes slept for days and was basically always stoned. My head never really cleared."

"Well you always said you were here in Asia only for the sex and drugs. Seems you've finally gotten over that."

He snorted a bitter laugh. "Fella gets tired of getting beaten up by local thieves."

I began to understand why he looked so bad.

"After Nepal, I headed back into India, this time to Goa in the southwest. And guess what I found there? Casinos!" His voice became theatrical, like a bible-thumping preacher. "*And so, it came to pass that young Paladin Kelley once again took up gainful employment, dealing blackjack in the dusky casinos of Goa.*"

He chuckled. "Spent a couple years at it, off and on, built up a little stash again, finally enough to put an end to this vagabond adventuring. I caught a train to Calcutta and booked a cheap steamer there for Singapore. Planned to go home to Reno."

"Then why you here now, making trouble in a Macau casino?"

Behind his squinting eyes and washed out smile, a little of my old travel pal was showing through again. "Won't b-s you, Dash. All this travel shit has totally burned me out. I just wanted to get to Singapore, travel cheap up through Malaysia and Thailand and then catch a cheap flight out of Hong Kong, where air fares are a bargain."

I nodded. "Reasonable plan."

"All was good right up until southern Thailand. I got sidetracked there at some offshore islands—Samui, Phi Phi and Phuket. Started living large again: drugs and women, midnight raves on the beaches, boozing. Put myself in harm's way and whaddya know, harm found me. Robbed twice and beaten to a pulp once. By the time I straightened out and resumed my trip home, I was broke by the time I reached Hong Kong."

"Kelley, don't tell me you're trying to *win* your airfare home at a Macau casino?"

"Guilty as charged."

Real bad plan. I just looked at him.

"But don't forget, Dash, as an experienced dealer, I *know* how to win. Knowledge shifts the odds in my favor." He read the doubt on my face. "And it was working all right, until I ran into this crooked baccarat dealer here. Snake was cheating me."

"Ah."

"Dealing me stiffs, seconds, to bust me."

That explained the explosion: a desperate, slightly unhinged player berating a dealer (who *may* have been cheating him).

I poured more whiskeys. "Okay Kelley, my turn now. Sit back and listen. Happier ending."

Curious, he grinned and sat quietly, draining drink after drink and chewing on ice cubes as I told my story. He laughed at the right parts. His face changed from initial doubt to bewilderment to, eventually, vast amusement.

"Oh shit," he laughed, "and here I was, lecturing *you* about casinos." Paladin reveled in my story, from the Bali motorcycle crash to the Straits casino boat; from my troubles with Asian Mafiosi to my current unlikely role as co-inventor of the Macau junket business.

"For now, that's all you need to know, Kelley, other than that I am stupidly rich—this junket business is obscenely profitable, a true miracle. My wealth pile grows with each passing day."

"Delighted for you." Was that a small frown hovering over his drink?

I took my shot. "So here's an idea, Kelley—why don't you join us?" He stared at me and pursed his lips. "That seems a logical next step, restarting your former career path. Get back into gaming but now as management. No charity here: you'll be working hard and seriously helping us. And you'll love my partner: a sharp Macanese dude." I could tell him the full Jackson story later.

I opened my palms in the universal gesture of *So-whaddya-think?* "Want to help us write this new chapter in the history of the North Asia gambling business?" I waited for his eyes to sparkle.

My idea could give him his life back, just as others had once done for me—when Little Fatty invited me to Johor, or when Demy took me under wing. I felt good, luxuriating in the warm buzz of magnanimity. Things were coming full circle.

But he shook his head.

"Don't get me wrong, Dash. I am grateful. Quite an offer." He gulped more whiskey. "But no."

How can he refuse? It was my turn to be confused and hurt.

"Dash, simply put, I am *done.* I need, really need to get back to the States. Go home, right now. Maybe stay with my parents a while and do nothing. It's been ten years since I've seen them! After that, only then, maybe I'll restart my life and deal a little blackjack in Reno or Vegas."

I was speechless.

"Your offer is incredible but if you really *are* rolling in the dough now, pal, I only need a small favor. Just for old times' sake, you know?"

"Of course, anything! Just name it."

He rewarded me with a one hundred percent classic *Paladin smile*. "Maybe stake me cheap airfare, a one-way ticket to the States?"

"Absolutely. But cheap? No way. First class all the way. And this is no loan, it's on me."

The fierce grin elongating his mustache seemed to stretch from ear to ear. Wrinkles radiated outward from both eyes and his cheeks rose atop dimples. Now *there* was my old cowboy buddy!

"But first, Kelley, we hang out and do some catching up. Eat, drink and have fun. We'll get you some new threads at my tailor in Causeway Bay over in Hong Kong. Whatever you need, consider it done."

He smiled. "One other favor, Dash. Since you *do* seem like some kind of gorilla in this casino—"

"Yeah, a fucking silver-back, actually. Why?"

"Fire that baccarat dealer." He grinned. "Slimeball's a total cheat. Not shitting ya."

We dove into a week-long debauchery that lasted until the morning I finally took him to Kai Tak in my chauffeured Bentley. The ride was filled with mutual admonitions.

"Just take it easy, Paladin, and you'll be back on your feet in no time. And whenever you're ready, head back on out to HK/Macau. Your position at Celestial Winnings will be waiting."

Kelley grinned. "Appreciate it, man. And you too. Don't overlook taking care of things in your personal life."

That was mysterious. "Whaddya mean?" I scrunched my eyebrows and chewed on my lower lip.

"I mean like that whole Fiona deal. What a mess! And it's just sitting there, wide open and unresolved. If you've got the cash (and you do) why can't you just head to Taiwan and see her? For closure, if nothing else?"

I really didn't want to get into any of that with him. Kelley as my father confessor? Bad idea, but all that stuff I'd shared with him was now boomeranging back at me.

"Thanks, anything else?"

"Well, sure. About that writer guy, Remy or Demy or something? And you've got some Asian mobster . . ."

"Okay, I get it. I know. Fix up all my life's nagging loose ends, still dangling. But thanks for the sentiment."

Kelley smirked. "Free advice. No charge, amigo."

We pulled up at Kai Tak and he checked-in. At the gate, amid hugs and emotion, we vowed to reconnect but probably both knew that was unlikely. He boarded his flight to San Francisco connecting onward to Reno, and was gone.

    I was happy for him. A dear friend on his way home, returning to his roots for renewal and healing after a wild, decade-long Asian adventure.

CHAPTER THIRTY
The Chase for Taiwan Money

By year three we were ripe to expand beyond HK. Next in line was Taiwan, a Chinese island nation packed with gambling-thirsty millionaires. An ocean of wealth-bloated Taiwanese gamblers were primed and ready for our pipeline to funnel them to Macau's gaming tables.

Jackson had always been fixated right from the start on the Taiwan treasure chest . . . and my partner was usually right.

Under the theory that gamblers everywhere had universal drives and urges we assumed Taipei whales would crave benefits similar to what worked in Hong Kong. Elite status and over-the-top entertainment (like food, women, and booze). Generous credit. Easy, privileged transportation, luxury accommodations and strict confidentiality.

But we lacked true inside knowledge of the Taiwanese gambling psyche. There was no way we would bet the ranch on just our hunches.

"Plus we are both outsiders," Jackson warned. "So that means our make-or-break factor will be in finding a superb local partner. We need a brilliant and well-financed Taiwanese businessman. Someone we can trust who is aggressive and has high energy, with powerful connections, both commercial and political."

"I absolutely agree, Jackson. But don't look at me. I haven't a clue."

Jackson winked. "Lucky then that I *do*. I've asked my father to quietly search the Macau casino records for names of big Taipei gamblers. That produced a promising list of wealthy

Taiwanese familiar with Macau gambling. So if we screen those, maybe we'll find some leads. If we look for the best business minds, we might find our partner."

We aimed to create a new and separate company, *Celestial Winnings Taiwan,* to share with a Taiwan partner. And we intended to hire only the very best to run it, staffing the Taipei management team and ground agents with Stanford and Wharton MBAs or the local equivalent.

A heavy box bulging with files arrived at our HK penthouse corporate headquarters.

Upon opening it we found a treasure trove of personal information on several hundred Taiwanese business elite who regularly visited the Portuguese colony for gambling flings. Using his casino back channels, Jackson's father had really come through.

We needed to winnow this down to select a single winner for our partner. But all the rest, we could solicit as initial clients.

We sifted and massaged stacks of paper for weeks, reviewing candidates' wealth, business acumen, political and casino connections. Eventually one candidate stood out, a Taiwanese billionaire in his early seventies whose name was even propitious. *Ng Chin-Tsai* meant something like *'Mr. Ng who is always making a fortune'*.

Ng built a multi-billion dollar business empire via real estate developments that dotted all major cities of Asia and leveraged this by backward-integration, enriching his related businesses in support of the real estate activity. Ng's business holdings eventually came to include steel mills, glass factories and cement plants, all churning out materials used for his building projects. Ng could boast that every new office tower or residential block built by his construction company sat upon land acquired by his real estate company; consumed raw material and heavy equipment purchased from Ng-owned supply companies; ran on fuel supplied by his oil distribution company; and was financed by banks he owned.

Though Ng possessed an astounding wealth-creation machine, cranking out endless riches, he lusted at nearly a hormonal level for thrills achieved only by challenging and beating the Fates at casino tables. In short, he was a die-hard Asian gambler for whom baccarat wins confirmed his ability to charm and overcome a hostile universe. When winning, he felt able to cause positive outcomes by sheer force of will. And like most inveterate gamblers, he quickly forgot about losing trips.

His file showed that Ng compulsively stole time and flew to Macau several times each month to visit the green baize tables, winning or losing several million dollars each trip over just a few hours of action, with nary a second thought.

We flew to Taipei to meet our man and found a blustering presence, hefty and graying, mentally sharp as a razor. As a businessman, Ng couldn't help but rhapsodize about the magical opportunity we were presenting, a chance in Asia to be "the house." And the gambler lurking inside him doubled that enthusiasm.

We quickly struck our deal as three equal partners owning Celestial Winnings Taiwan, though we vowed to defer to his wiser judgment about matters on his home turf.

Ng moved fast and recruited an impeccable local team to develop the Taiwan market. Prospecting for clients was similar to the HK challenge, but Ng's stellar business contacts made lists of blue-chip prospects much easier to come by (he *owned* Taipei banks and investment houses, for God's sake!) By cross-referencing those names with the Macau casino data provided by Jackson's father, our rich initial 'whale' hunting grounds were well defined.

"But Taiwan is not Hong Kong," Ng warned us, speaking Mandarin Chinese, in which Jackson was fluent and I was conversant. "Must adjust for some differences."

So we customized the amenities package for Taiwan whales. For example, the longer air distance to Macau meant we would lease several mid-sized corporate jets to run on a regular schedule, not quite the 'drop-of-a-hat' travel convenience offered by our "Hong Kong Helicopter Club." But all other sumptuous amenities matched the HK standard. Once our Taiwanese clients reached Macau they were pampered in the same luxury hotel suites with endless food and drink, shining limousines maneuvered by white-gloved chauffeurs, night clubs, women and, of course, those all-important gambling lines of credit for play in our VIP rooms.

Ng was visionary and an astounding partner in many ways. Gruff and humorous and totally down-to-earth, he always remained completely open and honest with us. Our partnership proceeded smoothly. After a while, he revealed he could speak some rudimentary English, too, allowing me to get closer. Many decades older than either of us, our business partner acted like an odd, lusty billionaire Chinese grandfather.

He designed a recruitment methodology specifically for Taiwan. We invited pre-screened groups of prime candidates to sumptuous banquets hosted in elite Taipei restaurants. No one ever turned down the flattering invitation to hear about some mysterious new service for the ultra-rich—the chance to socialize with an elite group of fellow tycoons and local grandees hand-picked by the famed Ng Chin-Tsai.

Breathless word of these dinners flew across the Taipei moneybags grapevine and before very long, unsolicited requests for invitations began to flow in. We ignored these. If you had to ask you weren't elite enough, which only increased CWT's exclusivity and cachet.

Once our business was up and running, Jackson and I flew to Taipei each month for a week packed with client recruitment dinners and partnership meetings at Ng's office, enabling us to keep our hand in and better understand the market.

All was beautiful until the night, at one of these enjoyable dinners, when my entire world threatened to turn upside-down.

Ng rubbed his beefy hands and his broad face shone with perspiration. He beamed a huge grin at us.

"Tonight, gentlemen, we host three big tables! Best place in Taipei, *King Phoenix Restaurant*. And then for the second place, we take group to a private room. Highest prestige night club."

Jackson and I anticipated a night of luxury and pampering. We'd just finished a long day of partnership meetings and Ng was now briefing us on evening activities. That was pure Ng, always productive and displaying amazing stamina, especially for a man in his seventies.

Ng handed us a list of names that I briefly skimmed.

"Our guests tonight are the highest level targets: all with great business success, substantial wealth and premiere credit." These elite prospects had already survived detailed screening and deemed highly desirable as clients. So our mission that night was to close *them* as new VIP accounts.

My personal goal was to briefly chat with as many of them as possible.

About 9 p.m. a police motorcade led us through the capital's dense traffic with sirens blaring, running red lights and leading Ng's long black sedan down Taipei's bustling, neon-lit streets to the restaurant. Guests had already been arriving for an hour so our entrance would be late and lordly (the calculated intention) but not rude. The XO brandy and scotch had been flowing so as we entered we heard ebullient toasts echoing around the rich wood-paneled dining room.

Our prospects were all in high spirits so the three of us split up, each hosting a separate table.

There were nearly twenty men seated around my large circular table: bankers, oil investors, military brass, wealthy real estate developers, and even famous Taiwanese entertainers. The group also included several characters whom I understood had piled up fortunes in the nation's vice trade. But Celestial was an equal opportunity purveyor of VIP gambling services so their money was more than welcome.

Despite expectations of highest glitz and sumptuous cuisine, the restaurant surpassed even its own stellar reputation. Attractive waitresses in slinky violet silk dresses, slit thigh-high and trimmed in gold brocade, moved quietly among the tables while a crew of waiters in sharp suits kept brandy glasses full. A succession of exotic and intricately-staged dishes arrived on polished silver platters.

After the main courses were finished, the men at my table began playing a drinking game.

A thick glass tumbler was filled to the brim with brandy plus maybe just a molecule of water—a real killer of a drink—and placed on the table's center rotating glass serving tray. This was then spun for essentially a game of *booze roulette.* The unlucky diner where the tumbler stopped had to chug down the alcoholic bomb.

Though dangerous, my luck was good. I only had to drink once and assumed the game seemed fair enough.

But one of our prospects bucked the odds. The old man was wealthy and highly-regarded, famed as a king in Taiwan's night club business. To his dismay he lost several times in a row and after draining three of the poisonous tumblers began to show ill effects. His head bobbed, bounced and slowly dropped toward the table. When his nose touched the dinner plate, it jarred him awake and he sat upright again, to the table's noisy delight. His pupils dilated and his speech thick, he swayed side to side and looked primed for a dash to the toilet at any moment (if he didn't pass out first).

Then, incredibly, the deadly glass stopped in front of him a fourth time. The entire table erupted in a split second of anxious mirth before then falling deadly silent. Several diners insisted he drink no more, but the stubborn old night club owner considered it a matter of honor and refused to back down. He reached for the glass with an unsteady arm.

"Stop!" An angry voice boomed across the room, from Jackson's table. "Wait!"

A prematurely balding young man rose and briskly strode over to our table. He grabbed the tumbler of brandy and bolted it down, as a proxy for the old man. All three tables roared their approval.

"Dad, please stop now. No more. You can't." He looked with concern at the nearly unconscious elder who cradled his head in his arms on the table top. "And besides," he sniffed, looking around the table with disdain, "this game looks rigged."

His gaze carefully circled the table, slowly searching until he found something. He walked over and pointed to a chopstick, levered off a small soya bowl and wedged under the rotating tray. A brake.

The men sitting near it just shrugged and shook their heads, looking shocked at the discovery.

Just as the bald young man appeared ready to level an accusation, his eyes locked with mine. And only at that moment did I recognize him since he had changed so much.

It was *Harry Lo!*

Brother of Fiona, my lost love.

So that drunken, nearly unconscious old man was Fiona's father. By reputation, a man powerful and dangerous who, I once feared, had wanted me dead.

Looking momentarily shaken, Harry abruptly returned to his seat and the dinner resumed. But for the balance of the evening I caught him staring my way and concluded, uncomfortably, that he'd also recognized me.

Later that night all sixty men regrouped at Taipei's wildest and most posh nightclub. Hidden in a concrete tower, the place was a spectacle of loud music, flashing color and female flesh, all undulating through thick clouds of tobacco smoke and laughter. Ng booked three connecting VIP rooms where a bevy of curvaceous beauties, hand-picked for their charm and looks, would provide his guests with imperial pampering.

I sat in the dark at the end of a leather sofa, sinking deep into the cushion and a warm, brandy-induced buzz, when a hand clapped down on my shoulder and a body sat heavily onto the sofa, beside me.

"Harry!" I feigned nonchalance.

He shook his head with a wry smile. "Ah, Dash Bonaventure. Been a while, no?"

"What a surprise—"

"Not for me." He lit a cigarette. "When I saw your name in the brochure, as part of the Celestial Winnings Taiwan ownership group, I decided to give this dinner a flutter. Unlikely, I thought, but it might be you."

"Well Harry, I certainly had no idea *you* were on the list."

"Course not. Sixty Chinese names and to *gweilo* ears, one rich Taiwanese businessman-gambler sounds just like the next, right? That's what your partner, Mr. Ng, is for."

Harry pushed a slim, jewel-encrusted gold case toward me, flicked it open and offered me a Japanese cigarette. I recalled all his anger and threats at our last meeting in the Denpasar hospital. There seemed little sense in avoiding our shared obsession.

"So about Fiona—"

He grimaced and let out a loud sigh. "Going there so quickly? Uncool and so direct ... so *gweilo*."

"Is she okay?"

"Depends on how you define *okay*. My poor sister has suffered thought a decade of surgery, skin grafts and physical therapy. Would you believe she still often wears a half-face mask when out in public? Like a Chinese female version of the Phantom. It's more out of habit than necessity. Thanks to the surgeons' skill and my Father's checkbook, she actually doesn't look too bad anymore."

I hoped time had blunted any lingering enmity toward me: by Harry, his father, even Fiona.

"I wouldn't blame you, Harry, if you still wished me dead."

"Dead?" He laughed.

I hoped that was a good sign.

"Dash, it's been over ten years. As deserving as you might be, it's hard to keep violent emotions alive that long. Bitterness is hard to sustain." He stubbed out his cigarette in a glass ashtray. "Besides, Fiona herself has overcome most of it. Her limp, the disfigurement, much of that is nearly gone. She's getting active in the family business now. And it's said one even forgets pain, eventually."

Was this benevolence or had they just grown tired of hating me?

Whatever, I was pleasantly surprised and even emboldened. "So then, about Fiona . . . is she here in Taipei? Wish I could see her." Harry took a swig of whiskey and shook his head.

"Let's not go there, just yet."

The guy was hard to figure out.

"Okay. But despite our past, are you two actually serious about joining the Celestial junkets?"

"They might provide some enjoyment."

Practical fellow!

"But while you and I can never be friends, Dash, there are other possibilities."

I wondered what that was all about. Harry leaned in, conspiratorially.

"Frankly, we are interested in taking an equity position in your Taiwan company. It's a natural fit with our nightclub business. But no rush. I'm sure this might come as a surprise. But do consider our interest and please discuss this with Mr. Ng, okay?"

"Sure," I smiled, controlling my demeanor and trying to project neutrality. But Harry and his father, as buying in as partners? No way!

"But back to Fiona," Harry said, recapturing my full attention. "Total honesty. Let's talk man to man." Sincerity shone from his eyes so I listened with an open mind. "For her sake you *must* stay away. She no longer has any relationship or interest in *any* man, after a decade of pain and self-doubt, hidden behind a mask and all of that. Hard on anyone, but particularly a woman in Asia. And you, Dash, were the direct (if unintentional) cause of all that grief. So no, she shouldn't ever speak with you again, much less resume a romance."

"Got it. Thanks." It hurt but sounded like the truth.

"Listen, Dash." Harry's tone suddenly sounded ironic and almost brotherly. "This entire world is full of women. So why worry about just one?" Harry waved his hand and summoned a comely, wasp-waisted Taiwanese woman to the sofa. Her breasts bulged against the silk of her skimpy outfit as she refilled our glasses. She leaned down and kissed Harry on the cheek. "See what I mean? Whole world full." He chuckled and wiped away the bright red lipstick print with a napkin.

I stayed quiet and didn't let on I actually felt heartened and undeterred. Had a possible path materialized toward reconciling with Fiona? One thing was sure: I wasn't about to start taking lessons in practical morality from the likes of Harry Lo.

We looked over at his father, passed out on another sofa. I felt a sudden inexplicable warmth for him and his son. Probably just the booze. "Know what, Harry? It's *really* good of you (your dad, too) to forgive me. Bygones and so forth."

Harry chuckled through a sour smile. "Forgive you? Ha! Not my dad. Never. Why, he'd slice your nuts off, right here in this nightclub, if he knew who you were."

My neck tingled. "You mean—"

"Correct. He's got no idea. When I spotted your name I didn't share my suspicions. Lucky for you, eh?" He read my concern. "Don't worry, I can manage this. You're no longer top of mind. I doubt he even still remembers your name. And I'm pretty sure that after all these years, dad would prefer a piece of the enormous Macau casino VIP business over revenge for some *gweilo's* ancient offenses."

Around 2 a.m. the entire group was fully soused and ready for sleep. Guests began drifting toward the front of the building where a parade of expensive chauffeured cars queued up. I helped

Harry hoist his father, still passed out, and stuff him into a cashmere overcoat. He maneuvered the old man toward the foyer where a chauffeur and bodyguards took over, tucking the geriatric tycoon into a massive customized Rolls Royce.

As we were shaking hands, Harry's attention abruptly shifted to a man standing in the queue, waiting for his car.

"Dash," he said with a note of urgency, "something I need to take care of, right away. Will be in touch."

"Sure, but—"

"Gotta go."

Then I understood. Harry made eye contact with several bruising men who shadowed him. His bodyguards, no doubt. They all cruised up and stood at the queue, behind the "brakeman" who had been sabotaging his father during the drinking game. Harry began chatting up the man and smiling.

"Dash!" Jackson stood at the open door of Ng's Bentley, ready to shuttle us back to the hotel. He looked impatient and waved me over. "Let's go!"

I was unable to watch Harry any further, but something told me that brakeman's evening soon took an adverse turn. I joined Jackson for our ride back to the hotel, filling him in.

CHAPTER THIRTY-ONE
Snakehead & Little Fatty, Redux

Our heady rush to success felt almost impossible as we piled up mega riches. Believe it or not, after the first twenty or thirty million, even wealth begins to pale. You can only spend *so* much. But on the other hand, every day's challenges and successes felt like a narcotic hitting your bloodstream. It left us always needing more.

Eight years after I'd fled Johor, our junket operation had become immense. Celestial Winnings hosted four or five VIP rooms in *every* casino in Macau, each customized to cater to specific, unique client profiles, with different decoration schemes, games on offer, table limits and staff language capabilities. We had rooms specifically aimed at Taiwanese, others for Koreans, some for Indonesians but most of all, for Hong Kongers. We had several rooms with staff who were entirely European or North American. And in a select few rooms, geared to absolute *super*-VIPs, our baccarat table minimum bets averaged $50,000 (that's U.S., not HK dollars) to attract the ultra-wealthy and powerful, like Indonesian timber tycoons or Brunei royalty.

Success had made a bigger man of me. Financially but also physically. Life in luxury hotels and all those whale recruitment dinners packed about twenty-five pounds onto me, with their rich food and all those XO brandy shots. I hardly ever exercised, other than my fingers on the keys of my pocket calculator.

This version of Dash would have been unrecognizable to my backpacking self of the past. I was continuously outfitted in thousand-dollar bespoke silk suits to meet expectations of our super-wealthy clients. And I even finally succumbed and started smoking. After always carrying a gold cigarette case in my suit breast pocket, always ready to offer a smoke to a client, that proximity was deadly. As with most smokers, the habit started with just one or two a week but relentlessly progressed until it was one or two packs a day.

Now, many Chinese believe the number eight is lucky, so perhaps it was no accident that eight years into Celestial Winnings, a miraculous event occurred.

I was cutting across a casino main floor and heading toward one of our super-VIP rooms for Southeast Asian clients. Moving fast, my head was down as I pored over a cheat sheet on players I'd soon encounter.

Suddenly from off to my side, a gruff voice intruded and its familiarity jarred me. A laugh I recognized. In my peripheral vision I spied a flash of thick, silver hair. Almost unconsciously I felt myself wheel around and found myself staring straight at Snakehead Goh.

Was I hallucinating?

No, it was him all right, all six V-shaped feet of him, wide shoulders and slim hips. With his platinum wire-rimmed glasses glistening he appeared as handsome and charismatic as ever as he chain-smoked and drank from a personal bottle of blue label scotch, tended by a solicitous cocktail waitress who hovered nearby.

A small audience had assembled behind him at the baccarat table, drawn by his charisma to watch him play, being charmed and entertained along with fellow gamblers and casino staff alike.

And perched right next to him, copying Snakehead's every bet with a smaller one of his own, was my dear friend, Little Fatty.

My heart soared!

Neither noticed me as I quietly walked up from behind, praying neither the croupier nor other casino staff would spoil my surprise. Usually upon my approach the fawning respect began since I was well known on the casino main floors and feared as a powerful man.

Snakehead slammed down an aggressive bet on *Banker,* a tall stack of $1000 chips, and Little Fatty followed with his own $300 wager. Banker had won three consecutive hands and appeared off on a run. I glanced at a player's scorecard and saw the shoe had been streaky, with long winning runs. Every gambler at the table followed Snakehead's lead, hoping to slip-stream on his luck. The entire group was giddy with the shared high of a joint winning streak and instant best friends.

I spoke loud and in an exaggerated drawl.

"Hey y'all don't think the Banker hand can keep on winnin' like that, do ya? Reckon must be time to bet Player, bound to win." All ten heads at the table swiveled to shoot scowls at this unwelcome advice from some naïve foreign fool, blind to the reality of lucky streaks. Every gambler in the East knew that betting against streaks in progress (a classic mistake championed by neophytes from the West) was a sure road to deep losses.

Just before the table was ready to rise en masse and expel the nuisance spectator, Snakehead and Little Fatty recognized me.

"Aiee-yah! My *gweilo* brother!" Little Fatty hollered in joy. "And look, you're fatter now, too. Just like me!"

"Hey, watch it," I fake snarled.

Snakehead walked over smiling, his arms outstretched. "Our Al Capone friend, isn't it?"

Little Fatty scampered in to join our group hug.

"But how can this be? You left for America." Little Fatty shook his head side to side in delighted confusion. The two scooped up their winning chips and left in mid-winning-streak, with apologies to the muttered disappointment that rose from the table.

I steered them to the fine Cantonese restaurant on the casino hotel rooftop and we feasted on chewy stuffed dumplings, shark's fin soup and steamed fish. As usual, the cooked fish came out intact (head, tail and all) and a server then deftly removed the flesh without disturbing the skeletal structure or flipping it over (bad luck, like a fishing boat capsizing).

With so much catching up to do, we went at it for hours. I went first and stunned them with the improbable story of how their young friend became a North Asia gambling chieftain.

"Yes, I'd heard that David Toh's son was cornering the junket business up here, working the sweet spot between the casinos and the VIP gamblers," Snakehead said. "And that he had some *gweilo* partner, unnamed. But we had no clue it might be *you*." He squashed out a cigarette. "How long does this gravy train roll, Dash?"

I could see the gears already moving. Snakehead was already developing an idea, but what?

"For now, Snakehead, we are hitting this as hard as we can, while we still can." I skewered a dumpling with my chopstick. "Who knows? Portugal gives Macau back to the Chinese in just a few years so everything may change. The CCP may even ban casinos. The risk is immense. Nobody knows." I let that sink in. "Or it might go the other way entirely. After 1999, with the Portuguese out, maybe Macau becomes more open and morphs into a booming, modern market-driven casino industry."

My friends smiled and shook their heads.

"Well," I challenged them, "why not?"

Fatty chuckled. "Dash, you misunderstood. We were shaking our heads in amazement, not disagreement. All this is just so . . . unlikely? You. Macau. Your business!"

Snakehead poked Fatty. "Look! Our little baby brother, all grown up." They grinned at me like proud parents.

"But your turn now, guys. Tell me, whatever happened with *The Floating Diamond*? Is CBC still pissed at me? Tell me everything—a lot can happen in eight years."

Snakehead sighed and finger-combed his silver hair, rubbing and pulling it back from his brow. He massaged his temples and appeared deep in thought. Why was he stalling like that? Fatty just sat there quietly.

"It's a long, long story, my *gweilo* brother," he said with a friendly grunt, "but I'll tell it short." Little Fatty nodded. "First, our *Diamond Floating Palace* is kaput. Famous casino boat is all finished."

That was totally unexpected. "But why? How?"

"It died two, almost three years after you left."

"But—"

I had a thousand questions to ask but Snakehead raised his hand and cut off all interruption.

"Back while you were still with us, Little Fatty and I already knew it would not survive much longer."

What? I couldn't believe that. "It sure looked fantastic and healthy to me."

"Problems were all hidden behind the scenes," Little Fatty said. "Not visible to you."

"Typical, I guess. They say we *gweilos* in Asia never really see much below the surface."

"But Dash, just by knowing that, you are already ahead of 99 per cent of the Westerners here." Little Fatty smiled.

"But our venture was too volatile a mix to survive very long," Snakehead said. "Think of the partnership between so many powerful businessmen, gangsters and politicians? Too many rivals, all greedy for power, tended to blow the venture apart. To be honest, it was a miracle it lasted as long as it did."

Snakehead placed a hand on my shoulder. "Now stay calm while I tell you this next part." Fatty nodded at him. "That's why at the beginning of the Diamond's collapse, you got caught up as a *fall-guy*. That's the correct English expression, right? After your magazine story, it was certain you'd become CBC's prime suspect."

"*Fall guy*, what?" I shuddered and stared at them, not understanding. Were my friends confessing they'd betrayed me? A million hairs stood on end, running from the back of my neck down the length of my spine. As my anger started to rise, my cheeks warmed and I was probably flushing red as a tomato. My hands gripped the table edge tightly. I drank some water to try and cool down, but couldn't swallow.

"Okay," I finally muttered, "start explaining. And this better be good."

Snakehead lit a smoke and smiled, trying to charm me; I scowled back.

"Ah, yes, there he is now. I remember: my *angry gweilo* friend." He playfully patted my hand. "Okay, for you no 'long story, short'. You deserve 'long story, long.'"

I just stared back, waiting.

"Dash, was I not the mastermind behind our floating casino? The brains and drive. True or not?"

"True." That was just the facts, not bragging. "I give you that."

"All completely mine: the idea, the plan and partners . . . *everything*."

"Okay already."

"Well in order to succeed, this venture required a difficult partner mix. People who otherwise would never meet and certainly not work together. For Malaysian land and political influence, I found *The Sheikh*. For shipping know-how and Singapore insider power? Madame Tan of *Eastern Ferry & Bus*."

"And for mafia muscle, CBC. I get it."

"CBC was a critical cog. With his wide connections across the underworld and influence in business and government, he brought huge gravitas to the enterprise. Word went out, far and wide: *Don't anybody try and fuck with this venture.*"

Snakehead's story was disappointing me, going nowhere so far. "Heartiest congrats, Snakehead, but don't wait for any applause. None of that justified screwing me, your good friend, and maneuvering me right into CBC's gun-sights."

"It's rather complicated, please, so be patient." The silver-haired man took another drag and exhaled a smoky cloud. Little Fatty sat there quiet and watching.

And what was Fatty's role in all this? I tried to keep an open mind.

"So Dash," Snakehead continued, "just before you left JB, remember that rumor about an upcoming news expose against our casino? One that, if published, would have forced authorities to seize the vessel and our bank accounts and arrest us? Jail time for all of us, including you."

"Yes but that rumor was false. The story actually turned out to be about CBC's crime network." Snakehead and Little Fatty exchanged winks. "Glad that entertains you, but it's not so funny for me. Remember, I had to flee?"

"See, you don't understand yet," Little Fatty said. "Actually, the casino story rumor was true. But it changed because Snakehead *made it* change."

Snakehead nodded. "I had to act fast."

It felt like viewing an optical illusion, when suddenly a picture's dimensions invert or colors reverse. "Wait. You're saying I was about to go to jail, if you did nothing?"

"All of us."

"But instead, because of your plan, I was able to safely flee?"

"Correct!" Snakehead smiled. "Listen, by the time you left *The Diamond* was already doomed. Another year or two, at most. The partnership was already fracturing and the authorities seemed poised to move in, before much longer, despite our substantial bribes. So I optimized everything, achieving a temporary stay of execution and set up our exit plan."

"Exit plan?"

Fatty nodded. "Dash, Snakehead arranged the expose story about *The Diamond* to be delayed."

"Ah. Got to Branch?"

"Yes. A fairly heavy-handed affair, I'll admit. But effective." Snakehead shrugged. "A few of my men intercepted him one night and offered him two choices. One, run his scoop on *The Diamond* and not live to see the next sunrise. Or two, delay it. We offered a very juicy alternate story, that big exclusive on CBC's criminal empire. Plus to seal the deal, a fat brown envelope with about five years' salary for him."

"How could he resist?"

Snakehead nodded. "We also promised, when the time was right (in a few years) we'd pass to him the *full* inside story on *The Diamond.* Everything. Way more than what his team had uncovered on their own. He would exclusively break that scoop, too. Just later."

Journalism ethics aside, I could see how Snakehead's offer was irresistible to Branch: *two* exclusive stories, plus a shitload of money.

"That arrangement then allowed us time to make a clean exit and cash out," said Little Fatty, grinning. "After the CBC expose ran, we huffed and complained that as legitimate businessmen, we could not be publicly linked with a criminal mastermind. That we felt *forced* to leave the venture. The other partners all rubbed their hands with glee, thrilled to absorb our shares."

"So you sold your—"

"Aggressive, impatient young Gary Tan bought us out. He'd lacked his own ownership stake in *The Diamond* and had been lusting for a piece of the action." Snakehead grinned. "We were delighted to accommodate."

Little Fatty shrugged. "So you see, we were out of the casino business not long after you, Dash. And remember, Snakehead compensated you from his own pocket, knowing he'd soon also be cashing in. And Snakehead was very generous." True. That massive check and the gold bars funded my stake in the junket business.

"What's funny," Fatty continued, "is that the others still don't realize what actually happened."

"So other than putting my life in danger—"

"Never really," snapped Snakehead.

"—it worked out okay for all three of us, huh?"

"Now Dash, don't go fishing for an apology," Little Fatty scolded. "It's a bad look. The part about CBC suspecting you was unavoidable. But we got you out so fast, you were never in any real danger. And your disappearance seemed to support your guilt and drew CBC's focus, which bought us cover and time to maneuver.

"After we sold out, the casino continued to operate only eighteen more months," Snakehead said. "And nobody ever suspected our role in its demise, when we delivered the promised second story to Branch, along with a go-ahead."

Little Fatty's eyes grew wide. "And what a press sensation it triggered! Screaming headlines about an illegal casino boat just offshore, right under authorities' noses. Editorials demanded prosecution of the operators *and* the negligent authorities. A joint, three-nation assault force swooped in: maritime police, customs and tax authorities from Malaysia, Singapore and Indonesia. "Strange but when they arrived the vessel was empty. No staff, no customers, no gaming tables and no documents."

"And what about all our former partners?"

"Funny, but none of their names ever came out. None were ever supplied to Branch."

"Why not?"

"Fatty and I are by no means suicidal."

"So you double-crossed Branch?"

"Maybe just a little, but the story was still fantastic, a journalist's dream."

Snakehead went on to explain how (perhaps no surprise) a *new* floating casino emerged a half year later to fill the gap. None of the former partners were involved. This *Son-of-the-Diamond* was said to involve different government partners, perhaps more powerful. "It was even the same vessel which, after seizure, had been impounded at an Indonesian naval yard."

Snakehead shook his head. "We hear (not too surprisingly) that business is again booming."

"So now we are concentrating on our other legitimate businesses, Dash." Fatty laughed. "In fact, we are here in Macau because we were on a Hong Kong stopover en route to Myanmar, to renegotiate rice shipments."

Once I understood the entire convoluted story, I was chagrined and felt a little guilty to have harbored even momentary suspicion against my friends. Snakehead had thread the needle and saved us all. Feeling grateful and even a bit sentimental, I wanted to make amends. I had an idea, how we could strengthen our relationship for the long run.

"Snakehead, you said all the information and files from *The Diamond* vanished?"

"No. I said was *the authorities* never found any of them. That's quite different." He bounced a shoulder at Fatty. "Before destroying all the files and abandoning the vessel, Fatty and I copied all the critical documents. It's like insurance, you know? All those stacks of paper are safely stored away at my estate outside JB. Just in case."

"Any customer information?"

"Well of course," he chuckled. "That's the most important stuff. Never know when that might come in handy."

"Well, boys, maybe that time is now."

While we noshed on Macanese dessert delicacies, I briefed them on the Macau junket business. "And our next move, gents, is coincidentally to target Southeast Asia. We'll be going after super high-rollers like Malaysian tin and rubber tycoons, the Indonesian timber lords, Brunei royals and Singaporean business titans."

Fatty bounced in his chair, he was so excited. "Why, Dash . . . *that's* the same as our best VIP customers at The Diamond! We have them all—"

"Relax, Fatty." Snakehead glowed with quiet confidence. "I think we're already way ahead of you."

"Yes," I concurred, "that stash of customer information at Snakehead's mansion is about to transform into an endless gusher of cash."

We finished at the restaurant and I brought them to our Macau offices, knowing Jackson would be there and working late, as always.

He came out of his office to the reception area, his shirt sleeves rolled up.

"What's this, Dash? Whom do I have the pleasure of meeting?" Jackson was always courteous nearly to a fault. *You never know,* he always said, *when you might be meeting your next super-blue chip customer.*

"Jackson, these are two of my dearest friends. Remember that Singapore floating casino venture?"

Jackson beamed. "Get out, really? Is this, um, *Little Fat Boy* and *Mr. Snake*?"

We all laughed. "Close. Meet Little Fatty Lee and Mr. Snakehead Goh."

"Same-same," Fatty said with a smile. "Close enough!"

Over the next twenty-four hours we hammered out the details for our next partnership affiliate, this time for Southeast Asia and modeled on the structure used for our Taiwan venture.

The only real hurdle for Snakehead and Fatty would be funding their share as new partners. A huge equity deposit would be needed to underpin new dead chip loans from the casinos, as well as to set up the business and travel infrastructure.

The duo returned home to Johor, aiming to cash in markers and leverage themselves to the hilt.

Celestial Winnings Southeast Asia blasted off to a lightning-fast start, thanks to the mountain of rich detail The

Diamond's files had on regional VIP gamblers. After moving first at Singapore elite, Indonesian tycoons and Malaysian whales, they then cast their eyes northward toward Thailand.

As for me, I was riding a streak of good fortune that seemed unstoppable, reunited with two of my closest friends and owner of a business that was relentlessly expanding.

CHAPTER THIRTY-TWO
Clash of Opinions

By the middle 1990s our young company had risen to undisputed potentate over Asian gaming, controlling the majority of prime casino players from HK, Taiwan and Southeast Asia. Every day, Celestial clients put millions of dollars into play, making our company nearly as lucrative as the Macau casino duopoly itself.

This success even began to trigger some government scrutiny as it was possible to view Celestial as an unregulated financial institution. That was understandable: after all, we regularly accepted massive deposits from investors and whale gamblers, received dead chip loans from casinos and granted cross-border credit to our high rollers within Macau. We were like the *Asia Central Bank of Gambling* and measurably impacted regional money supply.

Jackson's early bullish estimates of $20 million a year each had seemed like a dream but in just a few years we both amassed hundreds of millions in personal wealth. Our timing was golden since money was sloshing around everywhere, driven by a dynamic regional economy fed by China's economic opening to the West, picking up steam.

Desperate foreign companies raced to Asia in a feeding frenzy and set up beachheads in Hong Kong, thirsting to find local Chinese partners for joint ventures inside China. No multinational could afford to miss out. Slick executives and bankers in tailored suits prowled the Pearl River Delta, their gold Rolexes flashing. The Delta itself, just inside China, was a miraculous vision of slap-dash economic growth on steroids: noisy, non-stop construction as far as the eye could see, with cranes perched atop every edifice and girders rising everywhere. Flimsy-looking bamboo scaffolding everywhere resembled cheap caging trying in vain to contain this monster of growth.

A further sprinkle of spice was added to this heady decade by the countdown underway for the return of two European colonies to China, Hong Kong in 1997 and Macau in 1999. How this would all play out remained a mystery, but with enormous impact. Our casino junket business might be crushed and disappear altogether. But it seemed equally possible Celestial Winnings could ride a new boom and see its activity increase a hundredfold.

But on the overall issue of China, my partner staunchly remained a true *China super-bull.*

"If we don't move forward into China, Dash, aggressively and right now," Jackson would argue, "we'll lose our lead and everything, eventually."

For him, nothing mattered anymore other than China. All the rest had just been a prelude, an extended rehearsal. Jackson's strategy was to parlay our past success in Hong Kong, Taiwan and Southeast Asia into a mammoth China play.

"The China market is just staggering in size. Imagine, Dash, China has fifteen or twenty cities the size of Hong Kong, each with more than six million people! And Shanghai is already *four times* larger than HK. And Beijing, *three times*." Jackson's voice always rose when he started talking about China.

"Settle down, buddy."

"This is where we've always been pointing, Dash, all along. Right? Hundreds of thousands (perhaps millions) of potential high rollers waiting for us in the newly-prosperous, more capitalistic China? Entrepreneurs with piles of fresh wealth! Politicians with control over vast amounts of money. All are thirsting to gamble and are prime target customers for us!"

I knew how the rest of his pitch always went. "And whoever wins China—"

Jackson slammed his fist on the desktop. "Right. Wins everything! China plus all the rest of the Asian VIP market."

I couldn't fault his argument. The logic was impeccable. Having invented the VIP junket business, our Celestial Winnings was the proud leader and all our many competitors lagged far behind, trying to play catch-up. But the China opportunity could act like a super-reset button for all of Asia. A 'miss' on China (by being late to enter) would be fatal and crash our existing business. Jackson always argued that loyalty did not exist among our existing super-VIPs, who would migrate to the winner of China. Besides being able to offer superior amenities due to its economic might, the new top dog could also leverage its political influence to choke others out.

Jackson and I had long mastered this dance and now it was my turn to cha-cha. "You know I accept all of that, Jackson. But right now the downside risk is even greater, if we move too soon."

Why was it so dangerous to enter China prematurely?

Consider this: our business model there was still absolutely *illegal*! China's supremely restrictive system imposed a maze of rules, complications and contradictions that kept the place effectively closed off. The more we worked on developing a China strategy, the more barriers seemed to emerge, making entry near-impossible.

But Jackson burned white-hot with China fever and demanded we push ahead. Immediately.

He was so fixated that he seemed to lose perspective. I didn't know if this was due to ambition, greed or an unsatisfied drive for recognition as a world-class businessman. Perhaps he felt the world still viewed him mainly as merely the son of David Toh. But achieving dominion over China's blue chip gambling population would change all that.

According to Jackson, it was time to start going after Mainland whales. "Nobody else is in there yet, Dash."

"Because all the risk and uncertainty is keeping our competitors out, too, Jackson. They aren't suicidal."

I hated my recent role as the prudent one, always applying the brake. This ongoing disagreement began to dominate our relationship and leaked out to stain other areas. We began to argue day after day like an old married couple unable to get past the same disagreement.

My most optimistic view was that we *might* be able to design and execute a prudent China launch in another year or two, if we saw real evidence of changes developing in China law.

But Jackson was tired of waiting and studying and thinking. He was ready to bet the company.

"The concerns that paralyze you, Dash, will also stop our competitors from following us. We can seize an unassailable head start in China."

I shrugged. "So you say."

"And the fight will be over," he said, "before it even begins."

Maybe so. But I was in no rush to see the entire past decade of work crumble and Celestial Winnings bankrupted. Nor to find ourselves imprisoned in China.

Nope, no hurry for any of that.

Our strategic differences reached the breaking point during a contentious dinner in Macau. All day long Jackson and I had reviewed consultant reports commissioned on the China opening and its impact upon our business. But we found it all vague and noncommittal.

"Still too many roadblocks, man," I said as I chop-sticked a chewy, crab-stuffed dumpling. "Can't just put everything on red and spin the wheel."

"Hmm." Jackson just grunted, frowning.

"Listen, there's a good chance we might lose *everything*."

"Dash." He shook his head. "All business involves risk. We just have to find ways to mitigate it." He sipped his tea.

"Mitigate, sure, but not eliminate. Huge risks will persist."

He frowned. "Such as?"

"Well, for one, until China changes its laws our services there are not even legal! Enticing PRC citizens to send their money outside China to gamble is a capital offense. Capital as in executions."

Jackson sighed. "Don't be naïve and melodramatic. We won't set up offices across China with big signs publicizing Celestial and gambling junkets. Gotta be smarter than that inside the Middle Kingdom. We can stay very low-key. Maybe open up tourism companies and travel agencies offering luxury trips . . . including to Macau, with *special amenities*."

"Hmm." My turn to grunt.

"Just the tip of an iceberg pokes out of the water, Dash, but the other ninety percent stays submerged. That'll be us: most of what we provide will be hidden and unsaid, but be well understood by prospective customers."

"Seems like a real stretch."

"Not really. For centuries, we Chinese have been renowned for being oblique. Masters of vague implication and operating around the rules."

I hit him with another barrier. "Okay. But China's money doesn't even convert into dollars. That's a monster issue, no? A super no-go."

"Yes, that one's big."

"Enormous. We don't want to be paid in money worthless outside China. And if our Chinese whales can't change their yuan or renminbi into dollars, they can't legally get their money outside China, or take their winnings back home. No way around it."

He nodded. "Tricky for sure but just another business challenge to solve. Probably unlimited ways to get money out of the PRC and convert it into dollars."

"Legally?"

"Well, *almost*?" Jackson snorted out a contagious laugh and I joined him. At least for a moment we were both smiling again. "Consider whales with family living outside the Mainland, like in

HK? Maybe we can work through relatives outside China, to fund the guy inside?"

"Might work in some cases, but it's a very limited solution."

Jackson rolled up his sleeves. "Come on, Dash, even you'd admit that having money piling up inside China is largely a good thing—"

"Ha! Sure, other than the fact that it's stuck in there and in the wrong currency? Perfect, otherwise."

Jackson grinned and dunked a dumpling in soya sauce and chilies. "We could always *buy things* inside China—wonderful, valuable, movable things like gold, art, gems, whatever. Easily transportable."

"*Transportable*? As in secretly exportable? Great, so now we're going to be smugglers too?" I couldn't suppress a sour look.

"Just gotta keep spit-balling ideas, Dash. But you need to grow up a little, okay? Forget smuggling if you're too good for that. Another option might be to buy *immobile*, super-high value assets inside China, which we can sell to buyers outside the country, for dollars. You know, assets like land and buildings."

He kept going. "Or try this idea: multinationals are setting up JVs in China, right and left, and are injecting dollars for their equity shares. If we could become middlemen and front-run some of those deals, we'd be set. Buy a portion of the JV company with our renminbi and sell it to the foreigners for dollars."

This was getting too complicated.

"We'd of course have to pay a *commission* to insiders on the Chinese side of these ventures; why else would they steer such deals our way? But this method would allow us to move hundreds of millions of dollars out of China, *almost* legally."

"Holy hell, Jackson, are you kidding me? Do you stay up nights thinking up this crazy stuff?"

"Yes," he smiled. "Yes I do, in fact." His imagination was fertile and he tossed out more ideas. "Consider all the wealthy Honkies who'd like a mansion in Shanghai or just some property in the PRC, for future development. Some anticipate a great opening to China after 1997. We could land-bank properties bought with our renminbi and sell them later for enormous profits."

"But we can't buy real estate on the Mainland. We're not citizens."

"Hah! Just another detail, Dash. Naturally we'll have to establish a legal presence of some type in the PRC, a vehicle like *Celestial Winnings China.* And since one can only completely trust *blood*, we'd make use of my extended family, the Tohs. They are in Shanghai, Guiling and Guangdong." He smiled. "See? No worries."

We were viewing the same complications and deriving completely opposite implications.

"Jackson, your energy, intellect and business ingenuity amaze me. You're brilliant. And all that is only matched by the depth of your passion. Always said you were a freakin' brainiac."

He grinned, almost swelling with pride.

"But—"

"Shit, there's Dash, always with the *but.*"

"But I gotta go with my gut. This whole enterprise you're describing sounds illegal and probably violates all sorts of laws, even money laundering. I can't see us running a business whose primary activity is essentially providing a route for mainlanders to smuggle cash out of China."

Jackson was boiling and his face turned crimson.

"My friend, they say that in China these days there are only two real problems. The first is getting rich. And the second is getting your wealth out of China." He stared at me and chuckled derisively. "Honestly, the issues you've raised? *None* of them matter."

"Yet to me, Jackson, nothing else does."

He shook his head, a rueful look on his face. "I hope you're not going to keep fighting me on this, our greatest opportunity, at the optimum time."

"Sorry, amigo, but I am protecting us *both* so yes, I will keep fighting. Because I remain your truest and closest friend, regardless of how it may feel to you."

At that moment we both understood the depth of this breach.

Jackson muttered something and threw down his white serviette, rose and stormed out of the restaurant, followed by his bodyguards. I'd never seen him so incensed and was more worried about our friendship than the business or the partnership. I phoned an hour later from my Macau apartment but he didn't pick up.

So I rang Violet Kwan, his stunning assistant who always *did* pick up, twenty-four hours a day.

"Mr. Toh has just flown back to Hong Kong, sir," she purred. "He was in a hurry and seemed upset. Is there a problem?"

I ignored that. "Violet, be a dear and arrange a mid-morning *dim sum* breakfast for Jackson and me at that Kowloon restaurant. You know the one, his favorite. And please invite him for me." If he didn't show up, all would be clear. "And lastly please alert the heliport. I'm also leaving for HK right now."

Book Six

The General's Mistress
SE Asia (in transit), 1995

CHAPTER THIRTY-THREE
Nostradamus of The East

Rooftop private heliport
Celestial Winnings HQ, Macau - 1995

It was already 2:30 a.m. when the stainless steel elevator doors silently parted and my bodyguards escorted me across the roof and onto the bird. After its sole passenger boarded, the craft rose above the gambling fantasy-land, leaned forward and began to glide over the Pearl River Delta for the fifteen-minute run back to Hong Kong.

As we approached HK its monumental skyline was outlined in twinkling fluorescence and the running lights for a constellation of vessels dotted the magnificent harbor.

The sleek chopper banked and eased down onto the rooftop landing pad at our HK corporate headquarters, a glass tower in Central.

My chauffeured sedan and HK security contingent would be standing by as usual, waiting at the private elevator door in the basement car park. I climbed out and yawned as I trudged toward the private elevator. Half awake at best, all I wanted was to snatch a few hours' sleep before the breakfast meeting with Jackson. Somehow, I needed to find a way to appease him.

After a pleasant ding, the stainless steel doors opened with a soft metallic swish to reveal our elevator operator, poor old Mr. Wong, leaning against an inner wall. There he was as always, despite the ungodly hour, waiting. And always smiling. Wong was a chain-smoking, wheezing bag of bones pushing eighty if a day. His wide grin revealed shocking purple gums and a pair of jaws only half populated with teeth.

He gave me a vigorous welcoming nod, his eyes all but disappearing into deep fleshy pockets. Poor sod. It was the middle of the night and I had to wonder when he ever slept.

Wong beamed so earnestly he was nearly vibrating. He zapped me with the usual *Mr. Wong question*. Every time I saw him he uttered, without fail, the same words. Probably his only English.

"Going down, Mr. Dash?" As if I had some other option. I always just nodded or politely smiled.

But just this once, Wong via his question played a veritable Nostradamus of The East for indeed, I *was* going down.

The last I could recall was a crushing thump to the back of my head along with a simultaneous blinding flash. The tiled elevator floor rushed up at me while, in utter silence, my vision pixelated like glitter and faded to black.

When I later slowly came to my senses, everything was dark and the back of my head throbbed. My mouth was full of the sweet metallic taste of blood and I realized I was hooded. My hands were cinched behind my back and my ankles were bound together.

What was going on? I was trussed up like a pig, ready for a Chinese cook's chopper.

I tried to kick and my foot hit a restraint. Fabric? I seemed to be inside a sack.

My mind raced. Who did this to me? I couldn't imagine *anyone* hating me that much, it just seemed over the top, way too much effort. Almost flattering in a twisted sort of way.

I told myself to stay calm and think logically.

This was probably about money, that's all. A ransom attempt. As the wealthiest *gweilo* in Asia, I made for an inviting kidnapping target, hence my multiple security details.

Oddly, that hypothesis began to brighten my outlook. Yes, money . . . we can deal with that. Cash, after all, was *nothing*.

Jackson could easily peel off a couple mil and buy back my freedom, *bang,* just like that.

I lay there, thinking. What about sweet old Mr. Wong? Could he have been in on this? He knew about the gap in my security, that uncovered minute after each rooftop landing, while my HK bodyguards were waiting at the car.

And he didn't call out a warning when the assailant swooped in from behind me. But maybe he just couldn't see anything, out in the dark.

I found myself perversely hoping the old coot *had* turned traitor because only then, as an accomplice, he might have survived.

But after hundreds of elevator rides, I knew that sweet old fellow hadn't a treacherous bone in his withered body. So as an eminently disposable witness, Wong was probably already dead.

A throbbing pain enveloped me while my fingers and toes tingled. I was probably still in shock but started trying to consider other possible assailants. The suspect list was long but not very convincing.

The CBC grudge was from long ago, ancient history. And besides, Snakehead already confirmed it was over. Same went for Harry and his father. Fiona? It was impossible to picture her bitter enough to do something like this, even after her disfigurement and decade of pain.

That left Jackson.

Nah, no way. Sure, he was tremendously frustrated with me, but that was just a business disagreement. He remained my blood bro.

The exercise was useless.

But it was only then that I became aware, for the first time, of motion. I'd been too far gone to notice anything, up until then, but indeed I was bouncing along in a vehicle of some sort and being moved.

My cinched hands touched a hard, lumpy surface under me that gave off a vague, vegetable odor. Familiar but just beyond recognition.

My best guess is I was in the back of some truck, maybe one hauling turnips or potatoes.

Great.

"Please! Can someone help me?" I was yelling at the top of my lungs but out came only soft, breathy wheezes no louder than whispers. I tried to arrest growing panic by distracting myself from other, fearful thoughts trying to ricochet around my consciousness.

How long had I been out? A few hours?

I pictured the familiar map of South China and I knew that would be long enough to drive beyond tiny Hong Kong and cross over into Guangdong, China.

Right about then, the harrowing realization shook me that I was not alone.

Despite my blindfold and body bag I could sense an ominous presence right beside me. I realized my captor had never hidden himself, I'd just been too loopy to notice. The man continually farted, burped and hocked up loogies. His harsh body odor and halitosis filled the air with a stench born of strong local cigarettes, garlic-laced food and *baijiu*, the cheap local whiskey.

When the mysterious captor started to fiddle with the rope on my body sack, my heart began to thump. False alarm. He only lifted my hood slightly and placed the mouth of a plastic water bottle between my lips. While greedily chugging, coughing and choking, I tried to catch a peek but could only see him from the waist down. A thick black weighted truncheon branded *Royal Hong Kong Police Force* dangled from his belt. Probably the very baton used to knock me out at the elevator.

Good Lord, were HK authorities involved in my abduction? That idea was just too chilling. No, it was more likely someone was just using one of their billy clubs. Weighted, balanced and deadly, those beauties were prized weapons.

He cinched up my hood and body sack and then roughly grabbed a handful of my upper arm flesh through the fabric.

"Ow!" I tried to yell. Only another whisper.

"*Aiee-yah!*" He slapped the back of my head and growled something in Cantonese.

A moment later, I felt the sharp bite of a needle and finally understood it all: I'd been anesthetized for transport. So as far as I knew, I might already be days away from Hong Kong.

That stunning realization started to crack my composure but a fresh wave of the narcotic was already speeding through my bloodstream and dampened that. Numbing chills radiated across my skin and thousands of follicles squeezed tight.

In those waning moments of lucidity, as the entire world receded into darkness, I feared I might indeed be lost.

CHAPTER THIRTY-FOUR
Southbound Fishing Boat

Hours later (or was it days?) I emerged from the void, hung over from whatever they were injecting. My stomach clenched and nausea gripped me as I held onto the floor and tried to order the room to stop spinning. But I blinked my eyes open to a thrilling discovery: though it was dark, I could see and was no longer hooded or blindfolded.

And as my head cleared, I realized my hands and feet were free. I was naked but for a loincloth, no longer bagged like a couple hundred pounds of potatoes. And speaking of potatoes, the support under me had changed to smaller lumps now. But with odd little sharp points here and there, poking up through some kind of tarp, it was even more uncomfortable. The air smelled sour and fishy.

Then came the biggest hint of all as an arrhythmic sway tilted me from one side to the other, then up and down.

I was in the cargo hold of a fishing boat, out to sea. The vessel's warped wooden joints regularly creaked as an engine thumped away in a low cadence.

I felt around to discover I was covered with scales and slime. "Hey, please! Anybody there?" When I hollered, my words now burst out at full power.

As I reached out in the darkness, I found the tarp edge an arm's length away and out beyond that came erratic, flip-flopping sounds. Yechh, I was surrounded by fish and some were still alive and protesting. I shivered to picture razor-toothed barracudas and sharks. Probably not them, I thought, but that didn't matter. I didn't like *any* kind of fish.

"Hey!" I started yelling with more passion now. "Come on, damn it! Get me the fuck outta here."

A sudden burst of laughter came from above, followed by footsteps. Then an overhead hatch squeaked open sending a blinding stream of light pouring down on me. It knocked me back like I'd been physically slapped. I lost my bearings and fell. More voices sounded, amused and chattering in a clearly Asian but unfamiliar language. None of the vernaculars I'd picked up like Indonesian/Malay, Thai or some of the Chinese dialects.

A thick rope tumbled down and whacked me on the head, triggering a fresh chorus of guffaws. My vision was adjusting to the light so I made out the fist-sized knots that studded the rope every few feet. They wanted me to shinny up to the top deck.

Rope-climbing was never a strength but being very motivated, I scampered right up like a Hindu circus performer. As I neared the top a flock of hands alighted on me and grabbed at my arms and head, pulling me up the rest of the way.

Hauled out onto the main deck, I stood there nearly naked and blinking under a blinding tropical sun ablaze in a cloudless blue sky. As I stood there, woozy, someone secured a rope to my left hand and foot and tied it to a thick wooden mast.

I studied my captors, who looked like fishermen, about twenty of them and smaller than typical South Chinese. Also not Indians nor dark enough to be Cambodian. Possibly Vietnamese? That made no sense as I had *zero* Vietnamese enemies. I decided these fisher-folk were probably just hired hands, having taken a hand-off from the South China potato truck people to deliver me somewhere.

I was still mystified but began to grudgingly admire the level of planning and coordination my abduction entailed. Who had staged this? And why?

The fresh sea air and sunshine started to revive me and my senses were sharpening. I deduced from the sun that we were sailing southward. It was already significantly warmer than back in HK, so we must on the move a good while already. Far off to the right, I saw a verdant green land mass slipping by. Vietnam?

Just as I was getting onto a good deductive roll, the sudden chill from a bucket of saltwater shocked me. Harsh (but bracing and refreshing) and not a bad thing at all, what with me all sticky and stinky.

My fisherman-jailers started to pantomime an insult at me. They smiled and pointed at their rumps and penises. That may pass for big-time humor back home in Hanoi but, damn it, it just stoked my anger.

But just as I was about to explode, I realized they weren't teasing: they wanted me to take a piss and a dump. An excellent idea! With my single free hand I loosened the loincloth (it fell to my feet) and aimed an impressive stream of disturbingly dark, yellowish-orange urine over the side and into the rolling, foamy, blue waves.

The crew responded with applause and amused gabbling. I suspected they were also commenting on my imported Western equipment.

Just as I was wondering how to defecate with *any* dignity whatsoever under such public display, the crew obligingly turned their backs to resume seafaring duties. None seemed all that interested in watching an American evacuate.

Once I finished, a stout well-muscled man approached with two buckets of seawater. He started pouring the first after motioning that I clean my privates with my left hand. I followed orders. The seawater burned my crack, which was understandable since I was developing the mother of all diaper rashes. I hoped that the sun and open-air drying would fix that.

Then he showered me with the second bucket.

After that, I was left tied to the mast and the crew mainly ignored me, knowing my escape was impossible.

My head was now fairly clear, probably many hours since my last sedative injection.

The biggest problem on deck was the lack of shade, only a small patch from an overhanging tangle of rope and sailcloth. I scrambled to that tiny spot and tried to avoid being cooked by the blazing sun, a problem that would only worsen as we steamed toward the equator.

The vessel was a wooden rattletrap, painted a cheery pastel blue, that creaked and groaned as it putt-putted down the South China Sea. But to where?

An unanswerable question.

So for now, I sat back in my little patch of shade and basked in a Zen moment, almost enjoying the salty sea breeze and watching the verdant shoreline hypnotically unfold along the far horizon.

The boat moved along at a steady pace. Whenever it momentarily slowed, the stench of ripening fish from below would rise up to attack.

All day long we followed the attractive green coast and glided through fine weather under a relentless sun. It seemed to grow warmer by the hour. Any cooling breezes were a godsend. I tried to stay within the moment and fight off useless anxiety. I was almost (but not quite) able to enjoy this.

A trio of crew members were assigned to keep watch over me, still anchored to that mast by thick rope. Their names sounded something like Born, Vorn and Orn. But the security wasn't necessary. There was no way could I survive a jump overboard or the long swim to shore. But nobody was taking any chances.

The distant shore kept rolling by (surely *South* Vietnam by now) and waves rhythmically slapped the sides of the boat in a music that lulled us all into somnolence. By mid-afternoon, Born, Vorn and Orn were all dozing atop a folded sail up near the bow.

Despite the shade my pasty, Illinois boy complexion was turning crimson under the heartless sun.

The crew members, wiry and dark, remained indifferent to it. I was convinced these small, hard-looking men, muscular and lightweight, were legitimate fishermen. Perhaps they were delivering a fresh catch to port when an irresistibly lucrative offer floated by: *Sail south and deliver a package.* Me. They probably had no idea who I am and didn't care.

Some unidentified enemy had gone to a lot of trouble on my account and was throwing around a lot of money: hiring abductors, renting trucks, paying off an entire fishing boat and crew. I marveled at the backhanded compliment and wondered what was next?

By nightfall, I'd been broiled to a painful crisp by the intense tropical glare and my skin blistered and split, seemingly everywhere. So despite the evening's cool, I couldn't sleep.

The crew by now was being pleasant enough, courteous if not actually friendly.

At the next dawn, one of my minders (was it Vorn?) wrapped a rag around my head for solar protection, like an Asian fisherman, drawing an amused reaction from the crew. But the headgear immediately reduced my discomfort level from impossible to merely awful.

After Born (or was it Orn?) pointed out dorsal fins slicing the water's surface in our wake, I couldn't *stop* seeing them. All those sharks constantly trailing our boat, dozens. I shivered to think what an imported delicacy I'd be: juicy pink, sun-dried American shark food.

The crew scrambled about in occasional (seemingly at random) thirty-minute bursts of energy. They gunned the motor, righted the rigging, lubricated this and swabbed that, fishing out clogs of seaweed tangled into the propeller blades.

But for the vast majority of the day, they generally sat around and swapped stories, sang songs or ate fish from the smelly hold down below. Although I don't speak Vietnamese, I *am* expert in universal *man talk,* and judging from their gestures and occasional employment of falsetto voices, it seemed clear they were usually talking about women. As men do.

Having seen my share of comely Vietnamese women slinking around Saigon, I could easily second their choice of bull session material.

Oh, and they slept . . . a lot.

Every day about noon, one of them pointed a gun-like device at the sun to read the latitude. Then would look at me, shake his head and laugh. And resume his nap.

But finally on the third or fourth day (not sure which), his sextant clocked in the desired result and he cried out an alert. After so many relaxing days at sea, a sudden electric tension gripped the entire crew, as tangible a change as the abrupt drop in temperature when a weather front moves in.

The crew exploded into pre-assigned tasks, scrambling all over the deck. The boat, after paralleling the distant coast for so long, now veered toward the right and bore directly toward the distant shoreline, many miles away. Over time, palm trees, sandy beaches and other coastal features began to come into view.

Born stood atop the main cabin roof and searched for landmarks, chattering excitedly.

He finally pointed at a white rocky cliff that cantilevered out from the shore, surrounded by green hills. Crew members nodded and, chuckling, patted me on the back.

I pointed at the formation, too, and raised my eyebrows in question. The crew smiled back and nodded. I guessed we'd arrived somewhere . . . but where?

Just as things were getting interesting, a rough hand yanked off my headgear and replaced it with the smelly hood. Before I could fully panic, hollering out my complaints, they made soothing, clicking noises with their tongues, urging me to just relax and go with the flow.

They zip-tied my wrists and then four or five pairs of hands lifted me up. I knew where I was headed and dreaded going back with the catch.

But I also knew that for the crew this made sense. To coastal authorities, they were just a boatload of Vietnamese fishermen way off course with a cargo of fish going bad. They could say they'd been pursuing a rich school, lost track of time and location and wound up way down here. No law against that.

They lowered me with care. I took that as a positive: respect, if not affection.

Just a bunch of regular guys, hired to do a job. Nothing personal.

But when they dropped me the last few feet (unavoidable) a few rigid upright dorsal fins penetrated my skin like needles and I yowled. The crew growled at me to be quiet and one dropped down into the hold to pull out the spiny fins.

We were probably off the coast of southern Thailand, but why? I was sure I hadn't a single enemy in The Kingdom. Assuming it would take at least an hour to chug to shore, I closed my eyes and, exhausted, dozed right off.

CHAPTER THIRTY-FIVE
Prisoner Transfer

I woke when the fishing boat bounced off something and sent me sliding across the top of the fish pile and into a wall. Footsteps on the deck above me pattered back and forth and voices rang out with excitement.

Others answered, floating in from farther away. I made out some Malay words but also the rising and falling tones of spoken Thai. That mix all but confirmed we were somewhere on the isthmus, near the Malaysia/Thailand border.

My Vietnamese captors probably couldn't converse nearly at all with the shore folk. But I listened carefully, hoping to pick up clues.

The crew trundled me up to the top. I was still hooded but could tell from the symphony of tropical evening sounds that the hand-off was taking place under cover of night. Quiet, careful voices filled the air with Thai and Malay. The tone was stifled but urgent and no helpful information leaked out.

They walked me down a rough, squeaking wooden plank and onto a shaky dock where a flurry of hands seized and hustled me to shore, tripping over gaps. We stopped as negotiations broke out among my captors. Yet another tongue was now heard and frustration was evident from the language barrier.

Once things were settled, they lifted me into what I sensed was another cargo truck. A rough shove sent me tumbling against a pile of heavy sacks full of bulk rice, maybe. At least no fish.

I sat down as doors slammed, gears ground and the vehicle lurched forward. I tried my best to hang onto my perch with bound hands as the truck began to bounce through deep ruts and potholes and labor over an unmaintained road. It reminded me of our private dirt lane in Johor, overgrown with weeds. Probably a secluded path used by smugglers. But today, kidnappers.

I pushed some bags with my feet and maneuvered them into a more comfortable sitting arrangement, your basic rice sack lounge chair. I settled in and tried to relax.

After a long day's drive, I was marched up a gangplank and onto another vessel.

Somebody briefly removed my hood and I caught an eyeful. The ship was a hulking metal monster, massive and powerful. With just that glimpse I also noticed a lot of uniforms.

Probably a naval or coast guard vessel, but for what country? I saw a flag I couldn't recognize. And although the crew hardly spoke, snippets heard were from no language I knew.

My hood cinched tight again, I was taken below deck and locked in the brig.

The engines roared to life and the pen began to fill with heat, vibration, fumes and a deafening noise. The ship's acceleration pinned me against a back wall and the loud, bassy roar from powerful engines drowned out all else.

Compared to before, this was the relative luxury phase of my journey as a captive, in a modern military cruiser moving at high speed, skipping over and cutting through waves.

I again tried (and failed) to sort out the mystery.

I suspected the last truck had driven me across the Thai isthmus and we'd boarded a vessel on the other side, the Indian Ocean. So where were we racing to? Down south toward Sumatra? Maybe across to India or Bangladesh? Sri Lanka? At the risk of being repetitive, none of those places made any sense. I had no enemies there. I dozed off.

When they later awakened me, I realized the engine noise had stopped.

We'd arrived, but where?

Though I'd been asleep, the trip didn't seem long enough to have crossed over to the subcontinent, so where were we?

My captors roughly bundled me into a military truck and we then bumped along for an entire day, burrowing through heat and clouds of dust.

CHAPTER THIRTY-SIX
Jungle Cell

This all felt like something out of Kafka. They (whoever *they* were) hosed me down and tossed me into a cell along with a packet of loose-fitting pajamas sewn from rough cloth, like hippie flour-sack garments. The pants had a long drawstring so either they trusted me to be rational and non-suicidal or didn't care if I hung myself. Save them the trouble?

Thank goodness, though: they removed the hood and no longer restrained my wrists or ankles.

The place had the feel of a rural military outpost, somewhere upcountry. I peered out through a small air vent cut through the thick concrete wall and saw lush green tropical landscape. A slim man ambled by, on the other side of a chain-link fence and I studied him, hard. He looked petite and wore a Western-style button-down shirt but with a *sarong*, not long pants.

Maybe that was significant. Though sarongs were common in many parts of Asia, in others they were less so. And this combination with a dress shirt eliminated many locations, too. The fellow's slender bone structure and fair complexion ruled out more. I was certain he wasn't Indian, Bengali or Indonesian. My subconscious mind whirred like a computer, processing so much data about my captivity, trying to reach a working hypothesis.

Was this Burma? No, but nearly correct. For that was when I spotted a tiny tag on the jail's pajama-style pants that revealed all.

Product of Azkaria, it said.

Azkaria? This revelation absolutely confounded me. That tin pot dictatorship sandwiched between Myanmar and Thailand?

Literally the last place (other than the moon) where any vengeance-seeking enemy of mine might lurk.

Infamous as a hermit kingdom cut off from the rest of the world, tiny Azkaria made the infamous brutal dictatorships of North Korea and Burma look downright democratic and open-minded in comparison. I couldn't even recall my last (or first, for that matter) interaction with an Azkarian. The past days as I non-stop sifted through memories in the hunt for enemy mastermind candidates, the place never once came up.

In an odd way, this new Azkaria angle lifted my spirits. The plain fact was that nobody in Azkaria hated (or even knew) me. That meant the only abduction rationale that made sense was a ransom plot.

Considering the mountain of cash we'd made together, Jackson should be the very model of cooperation and would happily write checks for whatever amount was required, well before we got anywhere near the finger-cutting stage.

Time had become something of a blur since my abduction at the rooftop heliport. It felt long ago but thinking hard, I reconstructed the journey and realized it had probably been only a matter of days. A week at max.

So it was possible my absence was only now starting to draw any attention back home. It wasn't unusual for one of us to disappear for weeks at a time on a whale hunt, sometimes with little prior notice to the other. We were both big boys and trusted each other to do what our business required. I shuddered.

Jackson still probably didn't know I was missing.

Days passed and my cement cell followed a pattern, heating up by the hour until reaching an oven-like temperature by mid-afternoon that lingered deep into the night. The high constant humidity only made things worse. It was like living in a sauna.

Sleep was only possible for a few hours before dawn, once the overnight chill penetrated the jail to cool things down. But then an hour after the next sunrise, the heat would start to return, the whole miserable cycle repeating.

I marked time's passage by just four benchmarks: sunrise, sunset and the twice-daily arrival of low-nutrition food on a plastic platter. With my entire existence revolving around eating dirty gray rice and trying to get some sleep, I was constantly dazed, headachy and drowsy most of the time as I wrestled with distressing thoughts and unanswerable questions.

What was taking Jackson so long to write the ransom check? Just pay them already.

I tied and untied the long drawstring on my pajama pants but avoided considering the most morbid option of all. I vowed to deny them that, whoever *they* were.

One afternoon, I heard the familiar jingle of keys as a guard approached and prepared for the twice-daily race versus prison rats for the plate of food to be slid in through a slot at the bottom of my cell door. But I was then mesmerized instead by the metallic sounds of a lock being keyed open, a screeching bolt being thrown and rusty hinges creaking. The door was thrown open and banged against the gray cinder-block wall.

Blinding light flooded into the usually-darkened cell.

At first I could only make out black silhouettes against the light streaming in but once my eyes adjusted, I saw uniforms of soldiers. They were decorated in requisite badges of their rank: purple and green shoulder epaulets, golden brocade ribbons, snappy military caps. Four of them spilled into the cell and barked out orders in harsh voices and their unfamiliar language.

All four trained weapons at my head and my hands immediately flew into the air in a reflex survival action. My head involuntarily hunched down between my shoulders, as if that might help protect me. I just wanted them to understand I was totally compliant. I would cooperate and do what they wanted.

Just as I was thinking *please don't hurt me,* they pushed me up against the far wall and secured my hands to a ceiling hook I hadn't noticed before.

CHAPTER THIRTY-SEVEN
Square Cell, Full Circle

They turned me to face the door with my hands cinched high. One soldier stayed close and laughed while shoving the muzzle of his automatic up against my neck, then between my legs. But after at least a week of harsh treatment, I was just too fatigued and dazed to provide the response he desired.

Another young soldier was frozen at attention outside the cell door, with fear in his eyes. He saluted two officers who entered my dingy cell, leading a petite woman who clicked loudly atop stiletto high heels.

A cloud of floral, citrus-tinged perfume swept in and invaded the cell with a sickly sweet odor I inhaled against my will. Her features came into focus. She was highly painted-up and bejeweled with long dark hair and bulged against a shimmering, tight dress. She strode up and imperiously glared at me, staring into my eyes from just inches away with a barely-restrained fury. She hovered so close I could see the pores under her makeup.

This mystery woman might even be attractive to the male eye, under different circumstances. But today her inner rot overwhelmed any external beauty as she muttered and hissed at the soldiers, impatient and demanding. She broadcast a foul aura of moral decay.

And there was one certainty: I had never, *ever* in my life seen this devil bitch before. (Some things, one never forgets.) I guessed she was in her late twenties to early thirties and though still young in calendar terms, something was horribly wrong. There was a disconnection between her physical age and her underlying psyche, which seemed world-weary and decrepit. She was emotionally worn-out and no amount of cosmetics could hide that.

I found her equally repulsive yet fascinating. She just seemed so bitter, but why? As if she'd already exhausted her life's full ration of delight and knew it, with everything downhill from there. Bitterness leaked from every fiber of her being, tainted all in her presence.

Anyway, after a whole ten seconds with her, that was my amateur psychologist's profile. And who the hell was she? Nothing to do with me. There had been some mistake, I was sure.

"You filthy pig!" she shrieked as she wound up and slapped me, full force. "You are lower than shit!" She hit me again. Her English while oddly accented was pretty good. "You miserable son of a whore . . ." she growled as she rubbed her hand and winced.

Good, I thought, it hurt her, too.

A surprisingly bassy, guttural noise started rising up from deep within her, a sound that would have made even the most grizzled old Chinese street cleaner proud. She hocked up a generous gob and spat squarely into my face. Mucus dripped down my cheek as this devil witch began to kick at me with the sharp toes on her high heels.

I thanked God when she lost her balance and toppled over (served her right) just as she was about to take a shot at my privates.

"So, you bastard, I am sure you remember me. Right?" She was nearly howling as she climbed back onto her feet, her eyes hot and her breath heavy.

But I hadn't a clue. Who was this delusional monster and why had she hallucinated that I'd harmed her? But impossible as it seemed, she appeared behind my kidnapping. My ransom theory was dissolving and none of this was adding up.

"Miss, I have no idea—"

She slapped me again. "Think back!" Another slap. "Remember now?"

I wished I could. All I knew was that if this scary, self-important little perfumed monster had triggered my abduction and all my recent misery, she was a seriously powerful person.

"I will never forgive your disrespect nor the obnoxious way you treated us!"

This had to all be a mistake. I remembered nothing.

"You personally insulted me and made *all of us* lose face."

All of us?

"And for such a grave offense, you will pay."

It seemed impossible I could have unwittingly done anything serious enough to trigger all this. I was starting to lose it.

"Miss, perhaps there's been a mistake?" I tried to smile humbly and speak slowly, in a low tone. No eye contact. But it was a mistake to even talk.

She reached out to seize a guard's rifle as he cowered. My eyes involuntarily closed and I braced, with a single thought running through my mind: How can this be the end? I don't even know what I did.

It was already dark when I revived, sprawled across the cement floor and free from that ceiling hook.

I deduced it was just before dawn, judging from the cell's coolness, and a monstrous goose egg bump bulged from my forehead, throbbing with pain. Despite being groggy and floppy-woozy I put it all together: the angry bitch had knocked me dead unconscious with the rifle butt.

What on earth was going on? Well, for one thing, it appeared certain none of this was about ransom money.

The woman claimed to recognize me, one hundred percent, and threatened mortal retribution for some alleged offense. I could only cling to a waning hope that, as a dreadful mistake, this might still be fixable.

I pressed my goose bump against the cool cement floor, hoping the pain would recede. As my senses gathered, I searched memories for anything (*anything*, however minor!) relating to that furious woman.

Had I met her decades ago, while hitchhiking through Indonesia? Or perhaps she'd been an exchange student, way back at university, whom I'd given a hard time while Demy's assistant? Nah, ridiculous —those were ancient history.

And what about her comment about how I'd insulted *them all?* Her group?

Over the past decade we'd imported thousands of VIP gamblers on our junkets into Macau, but I prided myself on knowing most all of them. And I hadn't even a glimmer of recall on this dragon lady.

What's more, Celestial didn't even fish in the miniscule Azkaria market. We wanted whales, not minnows. Might Celestial's new Southeast Asia unit have branched out there in a limited opportunistic foray? Possible. But then why would I be the bad guy? Little Fatty or Snakehead should be the targets chilling in this cell, not me.

Apprehension gripped me as keys jingled on a metal ring one was inserted into the door lock.

Now what?

The rusty hinges squeaked the door open and two soldiers entered amid the usual stunning wash of light flooding the room, their decorative shoulder brocades swinging. As they roughly hustled me to my feet, I noticed dried blood encrusting my still-chained wrists and rivulets tracing curving lines along my forearms to the elbow.

The first soldier led me out and the second trailed, occasionally prodding me in the kidneys with his muzzle. We emerged into brilliant light and as my eyes adjusted they shuffled me down a dusty hallway toward a room at the end.

I tried to steal sidelong glances at my surroundings but that only provoked the trailing guard. He yelled and poked me hard with his rifle. I understood: head down, eyes forward.

But I'd already seen enough. This was definitely not a prison, but rather your typical modest Third World army barracks, upcountry style. I heard the angry voice of a drill sergeant in the courtyard pushed his troops and caught a brief glimpse of them marching in formation under the unfamiliar flag of Azkaria, purple with a golden eagle crest.

They herded me into an office and sat me roughly down, chaining my legs to the flimsy metal chair and cinching my arms behind my back. The office furnishings were spare but betrayed indications of some rank. This sad place belonged to an officer, maybe this picayune rural base's commander.

"So, whose office—"

"Silence!" roared the young soldier no more than an early teen. "Shut up!" His few but ferocious words in English surprised me.

"Sorry, brother," I tried. "But there's been a mistake—"

The youth poked his rifle into my sternum. It hurt.

"You! Only to shut up. Big man coming."

Big man?

"You mean the base commander?"

Must have been a bad guess because both soldiers laughed and gabbled in the local language, obviously deriding me.

"No, stupid man. Not the CO." It was now the older soldier's turn to surprise me with fairly serviceable English. "This is *the* Big Man. And coming just for little turd like you. Amazing! He is number two in all Azkaria, second only to *The General!*"

The mystery was deepening by the second.

I'd long heard about Azkaria and its military despot, the type of seamy feature story that popped up annually in all the bigger international news. Sunday morning reading over coffee and pastries. One shook his head and thanked providence for not living in such a crazy place.

But now, there I was.

"And Big Man won't be happy. Long trip from the capital, too much traveling just to dispose of your miserable case." He seemed to enjoy my predicament and shook his head with a cruel smile. "You must have made an enormous mistake, if Big Man himself is personally handling your case."

My case? What was all that about?

A rush of confusion and fear flooded over me. A national figure in this two-bit country was journeying to take care of *me?* Why? But perhaps he'd be someone I could speak with, intelligently, and finally get some answers. Sort things out.

"But sirs," I kept my voice low and humble, "what do people *think* I did?"

The older soldier smiled, showing off gums stained red by a betel nut habit. "Remember that pretty lady who sang you a lullaby with my rifle?" He held it an inch from my nose.

"Hard to forget. I mean, look at my souvenir." I motioned with my eyes toward the bump bulging from my forehead. The knob must have looked ridiculous because it just made the soldiers guffaw. And equally amusing, I suppose, how a woman so petite had manhandled me.

"Her name *May Myat Win.* And this very bad for you: she hate you."

"So I gathered."

The older soldier sighed. "In Azkaria, she is famous. Everyone call her MMW. She is The General's *other* wife."

"Your dictator's wife?"

"No, stupid man. Not official one—his *other wife.* But MMW is partner he loves most. His best girlfriend for a long time. Already one year, nearly two."

Great. So I'd somehow royally pissed off the romantic interest of a tin-pot Southeast Asian military dictator? That didn't sound good.

The older soldier wiped sweat from his brow but seemed to enjoy ratcheting up my dread. "And don't say *dictator*. Very rude. Our leader, The General, will do almost anything for MMW."

Oh boy.

The door swung open behind me and the soldiers suddenly bolted upright into rigid stances of fearful attention.

Slow, heavy footsteps shuffled into the room and a sweating, rotund man waddled into view. He sauntered around the desk and dropped into the chair which creaked in protest to his enormous weight. He shot a disgusted look at me and glared at the two soldiers.

"You all go! I'll be quite safe here with this worm. Clown is all tied up." He placed a loaded pistol on the desktop. "But keep a rifle trained on his head, through the open door." He smiled in my direction and shrugged. "If I signal, just shoot him."

This unnamed Big Man came across as completely cruel and lacking in any mercy whatsoever. Also bored and totally irritated by his assignment, my 'case'.

He frowned at me in silence a long time, breathing heavily, until finally speaking. "God it's pathetic, no? A man of *my* stature being forced to travel to this little shit-hole army camp, far upcountry, near the Thai border? Let me tell you, it's a horrendous, bone-jarring ride to this God-forsaken place. As you, no doubt, also learned."

Despite all my worries, it still struck me that his English was superb.

Big Man shook his head, as if ruing his bad luck, and grunted a sad laugh. "And all my time and toil for what? Insignificant you. So unfortunate. But when The General wants something done right, and he knows whom to trust."

"They called you Big Man, sir—"

He chuckled.

"But what is your real name?" I don't know what possessed me to speak and was stunned to even be hearing my voice. But my question just hung out there and drifted in the air with his cigarette smoke.

He lit up another imported Japanese cigarette and stretched out his arms to yawn, simulating delicious, luxurious idleness.

"*Big Man* is good enough. You don't need my actual name. How on earth could that ever help the likes of you? Look at me! And goodness, just look at miserable you." He shook his head. "What you should wonder about is not my name, but my role. My position, you might say. And as a favor to a condemned man I can share that. I have time, at least a cigarette's worth." He smiled. "And none of what I say will ever leave this room."

As the blood rushed from my head I began to swoon and fought to maintain consciousness and a speck of dignity. It seemed certain that if I blacked out, it would be forever.

The fat man wore a tailored dark business suit draped with medals, badges and decorative ribbons. But he was clearly no soldier.

"I am," Big Man declared, "the trusted confidant of our nation's leader, *The General.* Father of our nation and our savior. And as his second in command, my power and authority are second only to his. Naturally." He looked at a slip of paper from his pocket. "Let's get this over with. You are Bonaventure, yes?"

"Correct, but—"

"Good. We have the right man."

"But what have I *supposedly* done?"

The obese man chortled, splattering droplets of saliva on the green metal desktop. "You're rather cheeky for someone facing your fate . . . but I like that."

"Sir, I just don't understand. Why would May Myat Win push her lover, The General, to have me kidnapped? Why are you here to punish me?" A brave, unfamiliar force seemed in control of my voice and issued questions as frank as they were dangerous.

Big Man grinned brightly. "Punish you? Oh, no, Bonaventure, you're mistaken. I am not here to punish you. My job is to execute."

He sat behind the rusty desk like an enormous, suited bullfrog draped in medals and ribbons. He bridged his fingers and smiled, as if amused.

"Our leader's woman has identified you, Bonaventure, one hundred percent. Absolutely certain. So have some dignity and drop the sham already. Surely you recall your run-in with her."

"But I don't."

He sighed. "Do you realize what an enormous headache it was to bring you here? So many moving parts to coordinate. I had to call in favors from friends in Hong Kong, Vietnam and Thailand, arrange hired muscle, trucks and ships. All of that! But now that we've met, I must admit you disappoint me! Hardly seem worth all the effort and distraction from more important matters."

"Please hear me out, sir. A big mistake has been made." I had nothing to lose so why not try? "I'm just a casino executive from Macau. And I wouldn't know that lady if she fellated me."

"Haha" He chortled and slapped the desktop in mirth. "Very good one! But it's rather dangerous to talk like that around here." He shrugged. "But for a man soon to die, why not?"

"But I'm absolutely the wrong man. Our casino business has no connection to Azkaria."

"Oh no, this poor fellow lectures me about injustice! Believe me, friend, I know it all too well. Far better than most." Big Man seemed to retreat for the moment to someplace deep inside, where he was silently surrounded by memories, guilt or whatever. Then he looked up. "But Bonaventure, Miss MMW insists that indeed it *was* you who humiliated her. Your fatal mistake! Don't you recall publicly making her look like a fool, in front of the elite delegation she hosted to Macau? Some of the most wealthy and powerful elites of Azkaria."

The tiniest of mental bells suddenly tinkled, from far off in an infinite distance. The microscopic sound of fleeting recognition, lasting but an instant but then gone.

"You treated the supreme level of our society like scum," Big Man scolded. "Like low-level. Degenerate gamblers."

That miserable, nausea-inducing little chime again began to jingle, a little louder this time, as a fuzzy memory fought to clarify itself and come back to me.

And then there it was, yes, two months ago. At the time nothing at all exceptional. No big deal, an everyday business decision.

It started when Celestial refused to fly in a group, or admit them into the VIP junket program, until normal background checks could be completed. Were they from Azkaria? I couldn't remember.

But then the group just pitched up in Macau one day, anyway, all huffing arrogance and entitlement, demanding entrance at one of Celestial's VIP rooms. Our guards were well trained to deal with that sort of thing so they barred the group and summoned reinforcements. Me.

The group insisted they were super-VIPs, all rich and powerful personages, generals and politicians, and *demanded* our VIP pampering. Fine, but they still needed to provide the usual detailed financial information and deposits we required to establish new accounts.

Now I remembered the ringleader, a small shrill woman who seemed to direct things and led their harangue at the entrance to the VIP room.

She just rattled on:

Where are our free hotel suites? VIP limos? We want, we want, we want!

I listened while maintaining a chilly but dignified demeanor and hoped they'd just talk themselves out. That usually worked when we dealt with this kind of thing, all too often.

After she had her say I apologized and explained that nothing could be done. "Next time," I said, "you should apply to Celestial Winnings well in advance of your Macau visit."

I thought it was over but to our surprise the same group showed up an hour later at Celestial's downtown Macau office and a second yelling match broke out. Jackson and I privately agreed their gall and persistence were outstanding but eventually flipped a coin.

I lost so I had to keep handling this.

I tabled an offer that would perhaps help *all* parties to save face. "If you can arrange for funds to be immediately wired-in (a deposit sufficient to cover our financial exposure) we'll immediately grant temporary membership in the program, with full access to complementary lodging, meals and amenities, transportation and our VIP rooms. And you can gamble for now, but on a cash basis only."

They agreed.

But a full business day passed and no funds were received from Azkaria, Singapore or elsewhere. When I confronted the ringleader it became clear she'd taken no action to raise funds. So amid their curses and threats, we evicted them from our courtesy hotel lodging and barred them from our casino VIP rooms.

And now, it seemed certain that ringleader was The General's whore.

I smiled humbly at Big Man, seated behind the metal desk. "Sir, a fuzzy memory is starting to come back. Maybe there *was* a very unfortunate error due to a misunderstanding."

"Ha! An *unfortunate* error? No, more like a mortal one." He waved at a fly buzzing around his head and lit another cigarette, exhaling a thick cloud. "You see, no one humiliates the likes of MMW and lives. Especially when such an insult is delivered before an audience of our society's highest elites."

"But it was just a huge mistake—and mainly her fault, to be honest. They all just pitched up in Macau and gave us no warning. Expecting *(no, demanding!)* that we take care of them. They assumed we'd automatically know how important they were."

"Haha, yes, I see! So very arrogant, no? I agree." The gigantic man chuckled, tapping his fingertips. "And that's because here in Azkaria she is like a goddess. Her sweet little vagina absolutely controls The General and all his power. Imagine! And he of course is our living god." He shook his head and sighed. "She has already lasted more than a year. For his women, that's already the record. Too bad you can't just wait this out. But your time is up."

At that moment, the entire right side of the man's broad, flabby face suddenly imploded in an alarming and ugly contraction that persisted for several pulsating seconds. I watched in stunned awe, this disturbing combination of a wink and a grimace.

What the fuck was that? The tremor or convulsion absolutely shocked me and an electric chill reverberated deep through my bones. I fought to stifle an involuntary shudder.

At the same time, I realized my revulsion was tinged with something else I couldn't explain . . . some kind of recognition? Surely not, but I didn't know.

"Hey, what are you staring at?" The gross political operative's voice was low and threatening. "Rude to stare like that."

"Sorry, sir. But it's just that your severe facial tic really caught me by surprise. That's all."

"Facial tic?" He seemed genuinely confused, along with irritated, nearly malevolent. "I don't know what on earth you're talking about, Bonaventure."

Was it possible for a man to become so powerful that, within his small world, even his most horrible and blatant flaws were ignored? Did no one ever dare to acknowledge his convulsions? Were they deemed to no longer exist?

Did all who encountered the Big Man's bizarre, face-crumpling contortions pretend to not see? It appeared his immense power had expunged this most disturbing aspect from Azkarian reality.

I knew be wary. "My error, sir, never mind. I was mistaken."

But in the back of my mind, another pesky little bell of recognition began to chime, trying to bridge the foggy distance of long-lost, far-off memories.

The hulking man inhaled deeply and sighed.

"Don't take this personally, Bonaventure. I don't know you nor do I want to. And ordering a bullet to the back of your head gives me no pleasure. But no pain either. It's just a job." He tapped his cigarette and ashes fluttered to the floor. "That's no comfort to you, of course."

His hideous facial tic surged yet again, contorting half his face in a quivering ripple that was unsettling and abrupt, nearly monstrous in how all the muscles around his right eye, cheek and mouth contracted. The distortion temporarily made his face nearly inhuman, the kind of sight that was all but unforgettable.

Yet, something that mysterious and hidden something kept tickling at me from my past. Though I still couldn't remember, perhaps on some unconscious level I already knew.

The boldness of my next words surprised even me.

"You know, sir, they have some amazing doctors these days. Close to here, like in Hong Kong, for instance."

It was risky but I'd already plunged in, so no retreating now. The way I figured, as long as we continued talking I would stay alive. But why had I raised the idea of Hong Kong?

"Hong Kong?" His face clouded with anger.

"I'm sorry, just trying to be helpful. You know, to help with that nervous tic of yours."

"Nervous what? I don't even—"

"Perhaps there's a surgical solution, they sever a few nerve endings or maybe just inject some deadening agents." I knew nothing about any of this but rattled on, making it all up. "And if the cause is just psychological, then perhaps a psychiatrist could help. I know some top doctors back home in HK." I didn't, of course.

His face darkened like an impending thunderstorm. "I don't need any help," he scoffed. "Besides, Bonaventure, I haven't a clue what you're talking about." He grunted and scratched himself. "But as for Hong Kong, I will never return there, ever. Personal reasons."

And at that precise moment, the previously tiny, tinkling bell began to clang and gong like a cathedral bell. Its power was deafening as I looked deep into his quivering face, again furiously aboil.

I felt absolute certainty as I gazed back across decades and saw again in his face that poor, persecuted child, The Slug. Now so powerful but still embittered. And clearly, he had not yet recognized me.

"I work in Macau these days, sir, but live in Hong Kong. Superb place, sorry to hear you don't like it. Actually I only returned home to the colony after decades away."

I drew in a deep breath and took careful aim with my best shot. "Would you believe I actually attended the international high school, right there at Repulse Bay?"

It was all pretty heavy-handed but I was ready to follow with even blunter hints, should he prove too dense on the uptake. I expectantly waited, searching his eyes for the slightest glimmer of recognition.

Like a balloon popping, a loud involuntary gasp suddenly burst forth from him. It was almost violent, like the explosive hiss of escaping air. He abruptly waved at the soldiers outside the office to close the door and leave us alone. As he moved closer I peered deep into his face and watched his eyes go liquid, brimming with tears as years peeled away and suppressed memories came flooding back to pummel him.

His eyes were desperate and he stared at me in disbelief. "Oh, my God . . ."

He sobbed and collapsed into his chair while I quietly sat, watching the bubbling vat of emotion. I was afraid to even move. For a full minute (which seemed an eternity) a shocking yet fascinating transformation took place. All his adult bravado dropped away to finally reveal the inner remnants of that persecuted boy, reliving all the confusion and pain of long-blocked childhood experiences. I could see it, too, along with him: the relentless taunting, the cruelty of it all, culminating with Chickie's amateur bomb that detonated, knocking down trees and blowing off his bodyguard's hand.

I could only pray The Slug's memory would be accurate and depict me as one who, at the end, had *saved* his life, not just another oppressor.

When he finally spoke his voice was as soft as the child he had once been. "We . . . we were children. Is that really you?" He appeared stunned and overcome. "You were the boy that saved me. Yes, *Bonaventure*. That . . . that was your name. Dash Bonaventure."

"Wow." It was all I could say, feeling hope for the first time since I'd been abducted.

We just looked at each other for a full minute until a smile crept across my lips. "So, buddy, we meet again. Just can't make up this kind of crazy bullshit, can you?"

The Slug just sighed and remained silent.

"So what happens now?"

He shrugged and shook his head. "No idea, my friend."

CHAPTER THIRTY-EIGHT
Payback

I prayed the grown-up Slug would see no other alternative. That beholden to me, big time, he'd *have to* save me. Nothing less than cosmic justice demanded he accept his obligation for payback. But people don't always follow the script. And so far, all I could read in his face was that I'd presented him with a monumental problem.

"This is far more complicated than you think, Dash."

"Come on, man."

"No, really. Common sense would be that I just go ahead with The General's orders. As my patron and essentially God-on-earth, his orders here are the law. And our personal history (you and I) doesn't change any of that. Maybe had we been closer . . ." His voice drifted off.

Was I hearing him right – he was still going to have me killed?

"Now wait a minute, man! Listen, I was awfully sorry all that bad shit happened to you back then, and tried to help . . . Maybe I could have done more, I don't know. But remember, we *were* all just kids."

The Slug nodded. "Indeed. But with a friend, someone helping, it could have gone a lot better for me. And now it turns out I had a friend all along. Just didn't know it." I burned anew with guilt for failing to do more, to act, decades ago.

The Slug smiled wistfully and shook his head. His cigarette smoke rippled and drifted through the air.

"So anyway, Dash, relax. You *are* a friend and I am very aware I *do* owe you a debt. My life. So how in good conscience could I ever have you killed, even if ordered by a living god?"

Okay, now that was better.

He lit a cigarette and slipped it into my mouth. My first smoke since being captured. It tasted fantastic. We chatted a little more about the past and I think this brief conversation helped us both find more closure. But then his face became sour and deadly serious.

"But about that nasty kid—"

"You mean Chickie?"

"Yes. Your pal, the bomber boy."

"What about him?"

"You don't know?" He grunted a chuckle. "His bad karma caught up with him, maybe ten years ago." The Slug gave a matter-of-fact shrug, looking satisfied.

"What do you mean?"

But I only met with a wall of silence until the Big Man moved on to the next order of business, hatching my liberation plan.

"This is critical, Dash. For my sake, after you are freed you must lie low for quite a while. My life is at stake."

"I understand,"

"Truth can be cruel. Here in Azkaria *your* personal value is pitiful. Zero! The General doesn't really care about you or how you die. All left to me. You're *that* unimportant. Sorry if that bursts your bubble."

"Feel free to burst away, if it makes my escape easier."

"Quite so. So after your *execution* you must disappear for a while."

"Months?"

"Many, perhaps. Let The General and his bitch assume you're dead. With time they'll forget, as long as you're not prancing around, throwing it in their faces."

"Got it. And I'm pretty good at vanishing." Jackson could run Celestial without me. After our little piss-up over China, maybe he'd prefer me absent for a while anyway.

"You may even get lucky, Dash. The General is already way past due to change out his woman. Tough role to play, *girlfriend-to-the-dictator*. They usually don't last as long as her."

Was he convincing me or himself?

"And once she *is* cast aside, you can miraculously rise from the dead, bulletproof. Even now the General really has no personal interest in your death. He even seemed weary, giving me the order. A nuisance." The fat man thought for a moment and smiled. "Hmm, yes. Perhaps I can speed up things and push The General toward a new love interest? Place compelling temptation in his path. I know his particular tastes. We've been together a long time."

He explained how I would supposedly die, having over the years disposed of many enemies for The General. He always adhered to time-tested methods and used reliable troops, familiar with the task.

"We drive to a remote isolated area near the border. There we shoot and dispose of the body in a dense thicket of woods. Heat, humidity and scavenging animals quickly take care of the remains." He continued with enough details so I'd know what to expect. Wrapping up, he stubbed out his cigarette butt and leaned closer across the steel desk. "But be very clear about one last detail, Dash. This little drama creates enormous risk—for me!—so if anything goes awry, your actual execution *must* proceed. No other choice."

I gulped my understanding back at him.

Our conference finished, he began to bark out abrupt, angry-sounding orders. The door exploded open and soldiers burst in.

At his curt instruction they bundled me into the back of a military transport truck and locked it down. The Slug climbed into the front seat beside the driver and the engine roared to life. We sped off after the metallic sound of grinding gears.

The squad of soldiers exhibited the confidence and calm that flowed from experience. No doubt all had pulled this duty before. After hours of travel along rough-paved and winding blacktop roads, the truck clambered off the small highway and onto a small rutted gravel that wound through a heavily forested area.

As the vehicle struggled through axle-deep potholes, clouds of insects surrounded the vehicle and feasted on us.

After several hours of travel we at last pulled over and parked amid thick vegetation. The entire world went silent other than for jungle sounds of insects and birds.

"You!" roared a young soldier. "Out!"

The Slug and four soldiers marched me, hands still bound, deep into the woods. We stopped next to a boulder the size of a Volkswagen, above a bend in a creek, where they ordered me to strip. The teen soldiers collected my white prison pajamas, grinning at my pasty nakedness. They ordered me to lay down on the ground and be still.

The Slug ordered them to all return to the truck. After only a few shrugs of disappointment they marched off around the boulder in silence and back toward the truck, apparently having seen this move before—The Slug wanting to personally dispatch a prisoner. Before long the two of us were alone, deep in the jungle.

"What do we—?"

"Silence!" breathed The Slug, hushing me with an outstretched hand.

After several minutes he looked at me.

"They are a half kilometer away by now." Then he fired three rifle shots into the ground, waited a moment and fired a fourth.

"That last one was a kill-shot. For your head. Make sure you were dead." He winked. Perspiring heavily, the obese man used his knife and sliced the ropes binding my wrists. He reached into his small shoulder satchel and, with a friendly nod tossed something at my feet. "You will need this," he said in a low voice.

It was my passport (confiscated at my abduction's beginning) and a small wad of Thai baht, plus a tight white bundle that would unroll into a fresh set of white prison pajamas.

"Now lay still here, Dash and count slowly to, oh, three thousand. Only then, get up and get away."

My odd savior, Big Man or Slug, turned away and without another word slowly trudged off through the woods. I watched his lumbering shape go round the boulder and then grow smaller in the distance until he disappeared behind the trees, bushes and thickets of fern branches.

I lay there patient and motionless, as instructed, and tried to ignore the bugs, stones, itchy dirt and weeds. I listened carefully but mainly only heard my elevated pulse throbbing in my ears.

After a while I thought I maybe heard the far-off sound of a metal door slamming and a diesel engine coughing to life, followed by a grinding transmission. If not my imagination, that meant the truck had turned around and was heading away.

I lay frozen still there and almost naked. I began to count.

Breathing deeply and counting slowly I drifted into a state of total relaxation, like meditation. The pulse I'd heard pounding in my ears now diminished and slowed to a crawl as I listened instead to a symphony of soothing forest sounds. After several minutes passed I realized this crisis was over.

I was safe.

But I kept to my promise and kept counting. At three thousand, I stood and slipped into the pajamas. I slid the wad of currency into my passport and jammed that precious document under the waist drawstring.

As I began to hike back toward the main road, beads of perspiration quickly dotted my forehead. A cooling, light breeze delighted me as I pushed through walls of lush greenery. The jungle chirped and clicked, seeming to celebrate my freedom.

Once I reached the asphalt road, I turned in the opposite direction from which we'd come, guessing that would take me north or east. Before long, I came upon a road sign: *Thailand border - 10 km.* I continued to walk along at a steady pace, drinking in the sheer beauty of existence and found myself at a small border outpost in less than an hour.

The immigration formalities were virtually nonexistent. Perhaps the authorities see frazzled *farang* folk like me every day, popping out of the jungle in cheap white prison-style pajamas. Quite a bona fide hippie look, actually.

Whatever the case, nobody at the quiet border post showed a speck of interest in yet another vagabond crossing over from Azkaria to Thailand. The sleepy Thai agent briefly glanced at my Western face and U.S. passport and thwacked down a purple entry stamp, as if by reflex.

I padded into the dusty border town on painful bare feet but a heady rush of freedom sweeping over me.

Up ahead I spotted a string of long-distance taxis queued up and awaiting passengers at the small town's main crossroads.

I'd promised to disappear for months and found myself surprised by the flood of options. Life always, until now, always just seemed to *happen* to me. I didn't make big decisions. So it was unsurprising that now, faced with choices, I felt paralyzed by choice.

There was the dream of relaunching my writing career, heading to my fantasy cabin in the mountains. Lord knew, after the crazy past decades, I had plenty to write about. And I could also see myself reconnecting, somehow, with Prof. Demy. I liked that entire vision. But another thought interrupted this.

What about Fiona?

I felt I should apologize in person for the horror caused by that collision. Yes it had been an accident, nothing intentional, but did that really matter? If Fiona hadn't met me her life would have been radically better, avoiding a decade of pain, mutilation and therapy.

And I recalled the potent magic we'd brewed. I had to wonder: What if she was, for me, *The One*? My soul mate. What if, despite all that transpired, it was still fated for us to be together? Emotions tossed me about like a flimsy vessel on violent seas.

I drew in a deep breath and told myself to try and be rational. About that mountain shack, for all I knew I'd probably turn out to be just a shitty writer.

I probably should return to my life in Macau, as soon as possible. After all, I was one helluva talented casino business executive, even if it was dumb luck that first thrust me into that profession. I really enjoyed it, too. Granted, it wasn't some idealistic, hosanna-chanting, world-saving pursuit . . . but it brought out my most genuine self and probably promised my most authentic future. I'd enjoy myself and be happy, committed within a satisfying partnership with Jackson, my all-time best friend. To be sure, we had our differences, but those only made us better as a team.

And I feared that Jackson, amazingly, needed me—to help and protect him from his one blind spot. He was heading straight into mortal danger, due to his lust to enter China too early. I could keep him focused and out of trouble. Oh, and in this version of my future, there was also that *immense wealth* thing. An honest consideration.

But also by staying with Celestial, I'd remain in closer contact with Little Fatty and Snakehead. Some of my happiest days had been spent with them. Occasional trips would return me to Singapore and South Malaysia, and they would regularly visit HK and Macau.

As I shuffled toward the taxi stand, such thoughts kept zinging me, nearly at random. There was no stopping them. And I found I tended to favor whichever idea I'd last mulled over. And yet, still more came.

So much for my attempt at pure rationality.

I remembered other friends. I'd come full circle with The Slug and we'd had closure. But what about other old friends, like Chickie—what did The Slug mean about his *karma*?

Given my financial resources, it wouldn't be that hard to track Chickie down if he was still alive. Strange how our youth spent together and relationship all so abruptly vanished—poof! – and under such strange circumstances. So much left undone.

I tried to slow my thoughts, reminding myself I had a lifetime ahead to process all this stuff, but they kept racing. Instead, another image jolted me from a decade back. I saw good old Paladin Kelley, on his hands and knees on a Bali beach and vomiting up a river of black gooey tar onto the sand, growling out horrible noises. He'd tried a local stomach remedy and chewed up an entire bottle of charcoal tablets.

Balinese locals and European tourists watched in silent horror as he puked up carbon black. The beautiful Angelique stood there beside him, transfixed but perhaps just a touch amused. It was astounding.

What about Kelley's future? Could I help, now that he'd been financially and emotionally wiped out? I was really riffing on ideas now. What if I found Kelley and proposed we return to Bali? That's plenty far away from Azkaria and The General. We could build a classy hotel at Kuta or Ubud, take that business upmarket. And once we'd mastered one, we could replicate that and open a hundred more. Create a worldwide chain.

Why not?

It would be fun and energizing for us both, and would certainly get Kelley back onto his feet.

I had more than enough cash.

Ah, yes, and there was also *that*. The inflow from Celestial was nearly obscene, there was so much. I really *could* do anything I could think of. So much freedom stared me in the face that it was almost intimidating.

This storm of thoughts raged on, my options and obligations bouncing off each other. Unable to sort them in some logical relative ranking, I was shocked that I couldn't tell the best choice from the worst.

I smiled. There was no single way forward. I wanted to do them all.

"Boss!" the taxi driver barked, impatient. *Bahs*. "Boss go where?"

I snapped out of my daydream and found myself standing at the head of the long-distance taxi queue. The lead driver had grown impatient with me, apparently yet another drugged-out, low-funded hippie traveler fresh from Azkaria. He stared at me in disgust and barked out possible destinations.

"Boss go where? Chiang Mai? Boss want Phitsanulok? Chiang Rai? Boss want airport?"

I laughed, opened his cab door and dropped onto the sticky vinyl back seat. I absently toed the striations of the rubber floor mat and slammed the door shut. He revved his motor and cranked the air conditioner to high. Despite all its noisy fury, the contraption blew a stream of lukewarm air that, after weeks of captivity, still felt to me like the height of luxury.

"Boss!" The driver turned around from the front seat, vexed but now almost smiling. "Boss go where, *khap*?"

Where indeed? That *was* my existential question.

But at that moment, an inexplicable confidence began to suddenly engulf me and a strange optimism bloomed. If life had always *just happened* to me before, why should it change now? Luck, fate or karma didn't matter. I would always just enjoy the ride.

That dusty Thai road ahead of me led everywhere and to everyone I would ever need. That entire flood of ideas and plans. Crazy bullshit, no?

I told the driver what I could, in my rusty Thai. "*Pai, trong trong!*" Go straight ahead.

I smiled and pointed at the blacktop up ahead, through the car's windshield.

He shook his head *(another nutty farang),* ground the gears and stepped on the accelerator. The rattletrap taxi spit blue exhaust and lurched forward.

<<<>>>

A Note to the Reader:

Thank you for reading this novel. I do hope you enjoyed riding along on Dash's adventures exploring Asia as well as life itself.

My only goal in writing this work was to create a pleasurable reading experience for you. So, if you liked PACIFIC DASH, please consider writing a review (Amazon, Goodreads, etc.) to recommend it and guide other readers to my work.

Thank you!

Best regards,

Chet Nairene

New from Chet Nairene and Banana Leaf Books!

~~~~~~~~~~

If you enjoy this book, then don't miss

PACIFIC ODYSSEY: The Curious Journey of Lew 2.0

'Like Poltergeist meets Wall Street in tropical Asia'
— James Roby, UrbanKnights Series

An exotic, dark comedy about a young American tech star's impossible cultural <u>collisions</u> in Asia.

On sale now in paperback and eBook from Amazon.

Printed in Great Britain
by Amazon